THE SEASONS WILL PASS

Also by Audrey Howard

THE SEASONS WILL PASS

Audrey Howard

Hodder & Stoughton

First published in Great Britain in 2000 by Hodder and Stoughton
Published simultaneously in paperback in Great Britain in 2000 by Hodder and Stoughton
A division of Hodder Headline

10 9 8 7 6 5 4 3 2 1

A CIP catalogue record for this title is available from the British Library

ISBN 0 340 71813 7 Hardback
ISBN 0 340 79349 X Paperback

Typeset by Palimpsest Book Production Limited,
Polmont, Stirlingshire
Printed and bound in Great Britain by
Mackays of Chatham plc, Chatham, Kent

Hodder and Stoughton
A division of Hodder Headline
338 Euston Road
London NW1 3BH

Chapter One

The girl moved slowly down the gangplank placing one foot carefully in front of the other as though she were walking on water coated with a thin sheet of ice through which she might plummet. She was followed by a straggle of others proceeding just as slowly, feeling their way blindly from the ship to the shore. They made no sound. One might have expected the excitement, the anticipation of the traveller. "Look at that . . ." "Did you see . . ." but they could have been blind, dumb, deaf for all the notice they took of the hectic activity that went on around them.

The girl was painfully thin, but then they all were. Skeletons on the move, if you could describe the slow, limping pace they each adopted as being on the move. Men and women alike in the tattered garments which could hardly be called clothing, fluttering like empty shrouds in the stiff breeze that came off the river. There were no children. When they reached firm ground they hovered at the bottom of the gangplank, uncertain which direction to take, blocking the path of those who wavered behind them but not one complained.

"Come on, then, look lively," a burly seaman who stood at the foot of the gangway exhorted them. "We've not gorr all day."

The girl was the first to move off. She was tall, her height emphasised by her extreme slenderness. She had a pair of patched black boots several sizes too large on her feet and from them her candle-thin white ankles protruded from the hem of her skirt which barely covered her calves. She carried a small, knotted bundle. About her head and shoulders was a threadbare shawl. Little could be seen of her hair or face which didn't matter since no one was looking at her anyway. In Liverpool they had become used to such sights in this the spring of 1847. The two winters just gone were referred to by the Irish themselves as the Great Hunger, the bad life, the bad times, by those in Galway and Limerick, in Mayo and Donegal, in the county of Clare from where the girl had come. Those who could find the money for the fare, or who had been given the money for the fare to get rid of them, were crossing the Irish Sea in a great swelling multitude, some of them on their way to the golden land called New York, others only to Liverpool since that was as far as the few shillings they had would take them. They were looking for work, hoping for life, willing to labour at anything in order to be paid what was becoming known as "Irish wages", to put food in their mouths.

The girl lifted her head and painfully straightened her back then turned to look pensively at the river, and further north to its entrance where the North Battery could be seen and, on the opposite shore of the Wirral Peninsula, the Black Rock Lighthouse. The cargo boat on which she had travelled from Dublin had sailed between these two landmarks but scant interest had been shown, by her, or by the men and women with whom she had shared the horrors of the past two years.

There was a wooden box close by and the girl sat down on it, pulling her shawl more closely about her. She placed her bundle on her lap, leaning her elbows on it as she studied the tumult about her. She could not, despite her deep and crippling sorrow, her exhaustion and dread, help feeling a pinprick of animation at the sight of the lively scene. A flicker of interest passed across her pale, sad face hidden beneath the edge of her shawl.

She had come, by a devious and life-shattering route, from

a remote village in County Clare, no more than a handful of tiny cottages thrown up in a huddle beside a narrow tributary of the River Shannon. It was a community whose population had for generations been no further than five miles from where they had been born and until she got to Dublin, a journey she could barely remember, she had never in her life seen more than three or four dozen people in one place at a time, and that in the parish church. They, like herself, had been born, weaned, grown from childhood to adulthood, digging peat, tending their potato plots, their pigs and chickens and vegetable patches – if they were lucky enough to have such luxuries. They grew old in its daily peace and died in the same cottage that had seen their birth, but it was gone now. They were all gone except her, and this, where Father Seamus and the nuns had sent her, was to be her new world.

And what a lively world it was! It was a cool, bright day in March and the River Mersey rippled like a moving sheet of pewter as a vagrant shaft of sunlight slid from behind a cloud and shone for a moment on the water. She stared out across it to the other side where the views were clear and sharp. There were woods, a lacy silhouette of newly greening foliage to the south, surely a message of hope with their promise of spring to come? To the north was the dancing, shimmering highway of the Irish Channel along which she had journeyed and in between the two banks was what seemed to be a seething mass of ships of all shapes and sizes and going in every direction with a fair chance of colliding. A brigantine was making haste across the water, dipping and diving like a swallow on the wind and dozens of pilot boats buffeted through the swell as they guided ships to and from their berths. There were small, strongly built sloops, smartly painted, with a mark on a flag at their mastheads and she wondered what the mark was for. Their sails were full and cracking as they skimmed lightly across the water. There were four masted barques and swift sailing brigs, frigates, schooners and a clipper ship so beautiful, so graceful it caught her breath in her throat. Moving among these elegant, bird-like creatures, butting their blunt prows into the heaving waters, were the ferry boats, heading out amongst the mêlée towards Woodside, Birkenhead and New Brighton.

Of course the girl had not the faintest notion of what sort of craft she was studying, or where they were going, but she found she was watching the scene with more interest than she had shown in anything for many months. It was so . . . so *alive* it seemed to her there had not been a moment's quiet nor a cessation of movement since she had sat down on the box. As far as the eye could travel, stretching north and south, the busy docks of the great port of Liverpool were crammed with a forest of swaying masts, so densely packed she could barely see the sky above them. They dwarfed the men, the horses and waggons on the quayside, those that had come to take away the thousands of tons of cargo which had been brought here from every corner of the world. Men shouted and cursed, hammered and whistled and sang and she felt a small lifting of her spirits, for surely here in this land, a land she had heard described as a land of plenty, she could make a fresh and decent life for herself.

But she wouldn't find it sitting here gazing about her like the grand ladies she had heard tell of who had nothing to do with their time but watch the passing parade. She needed work. She needed a roof over her head, money in her pocket if she was to survive. She noticed without a great deal of concern that one or two of the seamen who were coming from ships recently berthed were eyeing her shawled figure with a certain amount of interest, hesitating in front of her, but when she showed no response, or perhaps catching a glimpse of her gaunt face, her hollow eyes, they moved on. She supposed they were not used to seeing a lone woman hanging about the dock area, not if she appeared to have no purpose there. There would be certain women, women whose trade it was, who would be – what was the expression she had heard in Dublin? – looking for company. She was not one of them. She might have been, given the chance. She would have done anything, despite the sin, to save her family, but by the time she and they had got to that stage she had nothing to offer but a bag of skin and bones with a hank of dusty hair on its head and was of no interest to any man.

She stood up and shook out her meagre skirt. She pulled her shawl more closely about her, for she felt the cold dreadfully, then moved off, almost falling over the boots on her feet, for, until a week ago, when passage had been arranged for her, she had gone barefoot all her life.

"You all right, queen?" a gruff voice asked her and a hand took her elbow.

"Thank you, I am," she answered him, the soft lilt of County Clare in her voice.

"Jus' gorr off boat, 'ave yer?" the voice asked kindly and she chanced a quick peep from under her shawl. The face that was bent towards her was weathered from working out of doors, just like her daddy's had been, not a young man and with nothing in it but concern.

"That I have, thank you kindly." Her voice was polite but cool as she gently withdrew her elbow from his grasp. "So I'll be on me way."

"An' where's that to, queen?"

"Oh, I've grand lodgings in the town, so I have," which was a lie. "I've it written down," and she patted her pocket. The big man, though he appeared kind and harmless, was still a man and therefore a possible danger to a defenceless woman like herself.

The man, evidently a dock labourer, was broad-shouldered and tall. She was as tall as he was but as scrawny as a plucked chicken, he could see that now she was standing. But then weren't they all, those who stumbled from what were beginning to be called "coffin ships". He craned his neck further to get a better look under the drab shawl and was unprepared for the full impact of her eyes as she finally and steadily looked into his. Her face was almost grey, every bone in it standing out in sharp relief but her eyes were an incredible green, framed in a thick, spiked fan of dark lashes. They tilted at the outer corner, wide-spaced and luminous, the pupils as black as sable. They were quite devastating but they were filled with that wary expression he had seen once in a cornered wild cat. A boy he had been, looking for trouble with other boys and the idea of a bit of fun with the cat had seemed a good way to break up the tedium of a Sunday afternoon. The cat, before it had streaked away between their legs, had had such a look as this girl. He felt a great need to pat her shoulder, to comfort her in some way for whatever had been done to her, since he had daughters of his own. But how could he do that? There were so many of them crowding into Liverpool and how could he help even this girl, let alone the tragedy of Ireland?

"Well then, yer'd berrer gerrof, queen. Best be indoors soon fer it'll rain or go dark before nightfall."

With this small witticism and a friendly wink he moved off and so did she. She didn't know where to, just away from the dock area, from the stinking crowded boat which had brought her here and from the life she had known for fifteen of her seventeen years.

Crossing the road from George's Dock looked as dangerous as moving through old man Ryan's field when the bull had got in among the cows. Vehicles of all sorts came from every direction: horse-drawn cabs, all in a desperate hurry; loaded waggons with enormous horses the size of Ryan's barn between the shafts; smaller carts carrying smaller loads; men on horseback; barefoot, filthy-faced urchins racing between the dangerous legs of the horses; confusion as one waggon driver took exception to another; the shrill blast of a police constable's whistle; shouts and curses; even the baaing of sheep which were being herded up from the dock.

There were men with wheelbarrows and brushes sweeping vigorously, since horses, and there were many, created a great deal of muck. The street cleaners wore a uniform like that of a soldier with a flat, round-brimmed hat, and the vagrant thought slipped through her tired mind on how fascinating, two years ago, she and her brothers and sisters would have found all this.

Crossing her fingers and clutching her rosary which the nuns had given her, she took off towards the other side of the road, darting as the ragged lads did, dodging and diving and when she got there she felt a faint flutter of satisfaction. It was a small thing that she had just done and it had taken all her small reserve of strength, and her breath, but she'd done it: the first step on her journey away from the boat safely negotiated.

Holding her bundle tightly against her – it contained nothing but a clean pair of drawers which she'd never worn in her life before and a garment that was known as a chemise to be worn under her bodice, the nuns had told her – she began to trudge up what was called Water Street, though she was not aware of it since she couldn't read. It was not what she was looking for really, whatever that might be, since it seemed to be thronged with businessmen going in and out of doorways, three- or four-storey buildings with flat windows through which she could see men at high tables scribbling in big books. There was an enormously tall building on her left, its walls grimy and running with water, a monster of a place with a board across its front proclaiming it to be "Messrs Bailey's Iron Warehouse" though again she did not understand the words. She kept close to the wall, not because she was afraid of the men who jostled her and each other as they hurried on some urgent business of their own – would she ever know fear again after what she had been through? – but to steady herself should she waver.

She walked for an hour. She didn't know what direction to take and wondered whether she should be turning so many corners or whether she should keep to the same street. They were all heaving with people, more even than Dublin which had almost taken her breath away. She was quite bewildered by the sheer noise and vitality. There were street musicians, fiddlers around whom children shuffled, an organ grinder with a small grimacing monkey and even a dancing bear. It had the saddest face and seemed to moan under its breath but the owner merely jerked on its chain to encourage it into a pathetic jig.

Nobody took any notice of her and she had begun to think she was invisible, which wouldn't have surprised her; that is until she sank down on to a handy step and was immediately pounced on by a splendidly dressed police constable. The weak sun shone on the polished metal buttons of his dark-blue swallow-tail coat and scarlet waistcoat, and his white duck trousers were like unsullied snow, so immaculately were they laundered.

"'Ere, yer can't sit there, me girl. In fact, yer shouldn't be loiterin' 'ere at all. This is Bold Street where ladies shop an' they don't want ter see the likes o' you 'angin' about, so yer'd best be on yer way."

His stern face softened as he put out a hand to lift her to her feet and hurry her on her way, for she was like a bit of a shadow in his hands, nothing of her but enormous eyes and arms like pipe cleaners. Her face was drawn with something more than exhaustion. She swayed against him and all about her the fashionably dressed ladies were frowning and drawing their skirts aside, for really it shouldn't be allowed, the way the lower classes imbibed gin!

"Where yer from, lass?" the constable asked as he led her away down a side street, though he knew, of course, for weren't they pouring in their thousands into Liverpool.

"County Clare, sir."

"Is that in Ireland?"

"It is that, sir."

"Well, yer'd best get yerself off ter't Female Night Asylum before it gets dark. They'll tekk yer in. Give yer a birra grub."

"Where . . . ?" she asked faintly, since she felt as insubstantial as a handful of mist; that her bones were made of the same mist and would not support her for much longer.

"Freemasons Row. It's not far. It's warm and t'ladies are kind."

Over the door of the Night Asylum was written: "*Knock and it shall be opened to you*" and it was.

She spent three nights there which was the maximum allowed, sharing a thin palliasse and a worn blanket with a twelve-year-old prostitute whose customer had not only refused to pay her but had given her a good hiding for asking.

Each day she went out to look for work and because of the night's sleep and the plain but nourishing food, a small amount of which she managed to digest, she grew a little stronger.

"Try Duke Street, my dear," the superintendent at the asylum told her. "There's decent houses up there and they might take you on scrubbing," though how this poor creature was to walk to Duke Street and then at the end of it scrub floors, she couldn't imagine.

"We don't tekk no Irish," she was told by a haughty housemaid at the first, and more or less the same at each one as she made her slow way along the respectable Georgian crescents which were laid out in a semicircle from the river.

At one house, just as she was beginning to despair, the cook, kinder than the rest, told her she could scrub the scullery floor, not for money since she'd none to spare but for as much as she could eat of the appetising stew which was bubbling on the stove and was meant for her and the kitchen-maid's dinner. The trouble was, her stomach had become accustomed to being empty and had shrunk and though the woman kept exhorting her to "eat up", she couldn't, only managing what wouldn't keep a sparrow alive, the cook protested.

"Eeh, an' after all that 'ard work an' all. That there floor's never bin ser clean. Tell yer wha', I'll wrap summat up fer yer ter tekk wi' yer. That'll see yer on yer way. I'd keep yer on 'ere if I could but the missis wouldn't 'ave it. Me and Flora 'as ter do't lot, don't we, Flora?" The thin skivvy nodded miserably. "Cookin' an' cleanin' an't rest. Anyway, where yer off?"

"Anywhere there's work."

"Lass, there's thousands like you an' work fer only a few. Wharr else can yer do?"

"Farm work . . . digging . . ."

"You! Diggin'! Likely yer'll dig yer own grave, looks o' yer."

"I'll manage somehow."

"I reckon yer'd best head up towards Old Swan then. There's farms up that way. Childwall an' Knotty Ash. They might tekk yer on," she added dubiously. "'Appen yer could gerra ride wi' some carter which'd save yer legs."

She realised later that she would never have made it had it not been for the kind-hearted woman who was cook to a skinflint of a housewife in Duke Street, and who had put her on the route she was to take. The bundle of food wrapped in a clean napkin and tucked into a neat wicker basket – with her spare drawers and chemise – kept her fed for three days until she was well clear of the city. She found it necessary to go at a slow pace due to her bone-deep weariness, the result of two years of starvation and illness. Cheese and bread, a wedge of cold bacon with no more than a slice gone, half a pork pie and some cold potatoes. A feast to the girl who had once dug up a putrefying potato in her father's patch, boiled it, sieved it and fed it to her family. A girl who had gathered seaweed from the shore and hunted seabirds' eggs, who had chewed on roasted rat and even the pencil-thick worms from the bottom of the stream. It had done no good, for they had all died except her.

She was lucky enough to be offered several rides, first on a milk float, then with a carter who was taking a piano to a lady in Knotty Ash but who dropped her off at Roby, and then on the back of a farm cart among crates of squawking chickens. Each night the early falling darkness helped to hide her when she crept into a handy barn, a stable or byre where she slept, unconcerned by the company of heavy-breathing cows, the snorting of horses, softly clucking hens and even pigs.

It was October when she reached the outskirts of Oldham where she had been told there was work to be had in the cotton mills which seemed to her, with winter coming on, might be an improvement on farm work, even if there was farm work to be had! Through the warm summer months, for which she thanked the blessed Virgin on her knees every night, since she was well aware a cold, wet summer would have finished her off, she had worked her way from farm to farm where she had been shown rough kindness by some farmers' wives, and the door by others who, like the maid in Liverpool, "wanted no Irish here". Where one brusque soul during the fortnight she worked for her had tutted irritably but neverthless had insisted on pouring pints of milk down her, saying she had never seen such a "skinnymalink" in all her born days, which the girl took to be a Lancashire saying. There had been others who fed the itinerant workers, men, women and often children, on what looked and tasted like pig swill, and she had eaten that before! She had performed casual labour planting, then weeding potatoes, carrots, onions, swedes and turnips, and, in season, helped to harvest them.

In September, stronger now, though still as thin as a rake, her skin tinted to a warm honey by the sun, she had worked from dawn to dusk helping with the harvest, putting away a farthing here and a farthing there in readiness for the day which would undoubtedly come when there was no more work to be had. She kept herself apart from the other casual labourers, nodding pleasantly as she worked beside them but at the end of the day stealing away from the barn where the farmer housed them, finding some dry and private spot where she could mourn in peace for those she had lost.

The names of the farms where she worked during those months were like a string of beads in her mind: Roby Farm,

Oake Farm, Windy Bank Farm, Park Farm, milestones in her trek to even she didn't know where. She wanted to settle, get decent, permanent work which surely must be available somewhere and which was surely imperative before winter set in. A room of her own! A life!

The farmland, arable farmland which was a feature of the Lancashire lowland, had slowly given way to moorland as she strode out. She had passed through sun-filtered woods, up mossy banks and down into sheltered valleys, lifting her shawl-covered head to sniff the cool, scented air on which the fragrance of autumn was already strong. When it began to rain she felt her heart drop. It became a steady downpour which soaked through her shawl as effectively as though it were made of tissue paper, through her skimpy skirt and bodice, patched half a dozen times in the last few months when she could beg a needle and thread from a farmer's wife, and the water dripped into her boots which were lined with old newspapers. She stopped to take them off, hanging them round her neck by the laces. She trudged on, her head down, squelching barefoot through fallen leaves and rain-soaked mud which squeezed up between her toes.

Feeling it gave her more respectability than her tattered bundle, she had hung on to the basket the kindly cook in Liverpool had given her. In it, except for her change of undergarments, was no more than a heel of a loaf and a sliver of cheese which she ate curled up in an increasingly wet hollow beneath a sweet-smelling hedgerow. She tried to sleep, her teeth chattering in her head which she had laid carefully on a pillow of clover and she must have dozed. When she awoke the next morning her bones ached and the chill rattled through her, wearying her so that she felt disinclined to stand up.

She didn't know how far she walked that day but as she lay down when darkness fell in what appeared to be a bed of wet heather she knew she could not manage it again. Years ago, before the bad time, she and her family, though living from one year's potato crop to the next, had been strong and wiry and capable of working, or walking from dawn to dusk with no ill-effect. But it looked as though she, the last of them, was to perish here in this foreign land without a hand, family or otherwise, to comfort or ease her going. It didn't matter really, for if Father Seamus was right she would surely be in heaven with Mammy and Daddy and her brothers and sisters very soon.

She drifted in what seemed an unusual silence with not even the dripping of the rain from the heather to the wet earth to disturb her. She knew she should fight her way back to reality through the denseness that was swamping her thoughts, but on that second morning and without even a morsel of cheese to stir her into action she thought she might as well stay here.

She got up. She swayed like Paddy O'Hara just come from the shebeen on a Saturday night and, putting one foot in front of the other, she moved on, pushing her way through the heather and bracken. She had expected to come to the thriving cotton town of Oldham, which, she had been told, was the cotton spinning capital of the world, but all she had encountered for two days were long sweeping folds of moorland, deep, wooded valleys and hills she didn't think she had the strength to climb. She felt so *cold* and her head ached.

There was a sudden thundering roar which startled her until she almost blundered into the mountain stream that caused it. She knew she would have to find shelter soon if she was not to collapse altogether, shelter from the needles of rain that pierced her. She needed to discard her clothing which was so heavy with rain it was dragging her down.

She saw the straggle of cottages drifting towards her through the downpour, not unduly concerned that cottages could actually drift. After the many strange and appalling things she had seen in the past, nothing surprised her any more.

She *was* disconcerted but eternally grateful when strong arms lifted her, when a man's voice, with the broad vowels she had come to recognise as a northerner's, spoke into her ear. When she was carried as though she weighed no more than a feather, which, to the man, she didn't, into somewhere warm and dry.

She distinctly heard him shout for someone called Nelly but, knowing she was safe, she couldn't have said why, she let herself drift away, ceasing to struggle on, allowing the strong arms and the gentle voice of the man to take her wherever he pleased.

Chapter Two

She awoke to the mouth-watering smell of frying bacon and was instantly aware that for the first time since she couldn't remember when, she was hungry. She could hear the sizzle of it in the pan and the chink of a metal object against another. She could hear the splutter of a coal fire as the flames leaped merrily up the chimney and the sound of a cat purring, a fat, contented sound. Her family had never owned a cat, since food put into a cat's mouth could more easily and sensibly be put in a child's, but Jinny O'Neill who owned the shebeen had harboured one, saying it kept the rats down, and this one sounded just like it. The memory stabbed her and she hastily let it go.

From further away came the rich trilling song of a golden plover, a melody she had known all her life but which she hadn't heard since she left home. Though her eyes were still closed she was conscious of a shaft of light coming from somewhere, glowing red through her eyelids. Sunlight, she thought. It seemed to indicate warmth and cheerfulness, something she had not encountered for a long time.

She sensed that there was someone else in the room but was strangely aware that whoever it was posed no threat to her. She stretched and yawned, warm, rested and ready to contemplate the returning strength of her body, her growing sense of wellbeing, the feeling of being able to go on to wherever she was going from wherever it was she had fetched up.

She opened her eyes and turned her head and the movement attracted the attention of a man bending over the fire, and at once he straightened up. He had a frying pan in one hand and a fork in the other. He laid them both down on the oven top to the side of the fire and walked slowly towards her. She could not recall ever having seen him before. He was smiling, an open, easy smile that tugged at the corners of her own mouth. He was tall, lean and straight as an arrow. Not an ounce of bulk about him but a whipcord strength which seemed to promise toughness. He had an amiable air but his mouth hinted at a stubbornness which could, she thought, prove dangerous, making him a difficult opponent if pushed too far. There was a humorous curl to it nevertheless. His hair was brown, uncut, untidy, inclined to curl over his forehead and his eyes shone a clear and steady grey. Not a handsome face but pleasant and with the kindest smile she had ever seen. He was a working man, she could tell that by the heavy boots on his feet, by his corduroy trousers and collarless shirt, over which he wore a sleeveless leather jerkin.

All this she observed in the time it took him to walk from the stove to the bed into which she was warmly tucked. She appeared to be in some sort of an alcove set back in the wall, lying on a shelf which was covered by a palliasse which was not quite long enough to contain her tall body. Obviously she was in a kitchen, for there was an oven and all kinds of things hanging on the wall which were unfamiliar to her. Things used in the kitchens of the English, she supposed, not the plain forks, wooden spoons and the odd pan or two her mammy had cooked in.

The sunlight shone, warm and bright, falling on what looked like golden pans, a dresser crammed with cups and plates and dishes, all with a pleasing pattern in blue and white, and on a row of scarlet geraniums placed in the window bottom. The purring cat was not on the rug before the fire as she had thought but curled up against her on the bed. She found she enjoyed the sensation.

"Well, lass, feelin' better, are tha'?" the man asked, his voice soft-spoken, hunkering down beside her and bending his head to search her face. "Tha' gave us a rare fright, I can tell thi', comin' out of nowhere like that. Like a wraith, tha' were, driftin' in't rain, looking like Cat here when she fell inter't water butt."

He put out a hand and fondled the cat's ears and immediately the purring went up a level.

"To be sure an' I'm sorry to have troubled you, sir," she began in a low voice but at once he rounded on her.

"Nay, my lass, don't say that. Tha' were no trouble and it wasn't your fault tha' were so poorly. We could see, me and Nelly, when we got them wet clothes off, tha'd known hard times. Well, tha' weighed no more than Marie Bretherton's Maidie an' she's but a babe of twelve months. Tha' were like some half-drowned rabbit, all draggled an' ready to measure tha' length on't cobbles. Tha' woulda done an' all if I hadn't been at gate."

"My clothes?"

He bent his head lower to catch the thready sound of her voice.

"Aye, lass, we had to get 'em off thi', me an' Nelly. Tha' were shakin' and rattlin' yer teeth so bad . . . well, we thought we'd lost thi' but Nelly's handy with potions and such and she got fever down and here tha' are, right as rain, I'm glad to say." His smiling face became stern. "But tha've not to think o' gettin' out o' that there bed, not yet awhile. Not until Nelly says you can an' what Nelly says, goes round here. A right bossy beggar she is. She manages everyone an' woe betide them if they don't obey orders."

"Nelly is . . . your wife?"

He laughed out loud at that, almost falling backwards on to the well-scrubbed flagged floor. His teeth gleamed white and even in the amber-tinted smoothness of his freshly shaven face. His chin was strong and firm but his eyes had the softest expression in them. Like her daddy's when he was nursing a sick piglet or holding their Declan on his lap before the peat fire.

For a second an expression of devastation crossed her face and the man beside her saw it. At once he was serious. Reaching out, he took her hand which had escaped the coverlet, but sensing that words could not heal what she suffered he said nothing, merely folding its extreme slenderness in his own strong brown fingers.

"Nelly's my next-door neighbour," he went on. "She an' her Will an' their three children live there an' she rules them an' all of us wi' a rod of iron. A tigress if ever there was one but wi't biggest heart this side of Oldham though if she heard me say it she'd box me ears. Anyroad, she took tha' things an' knowing her she'll have them washed an' ironed and fit for't queen up in London to wear. She'll fetch them in when she's ready. I reckon she's frit tha'll jump outa bed an' go striding off up lane if tha'd owt ter wear."

"Frit?"

His smile broadened. "Frightened. It's a Lancashire saying."

"How long since . . . ?" His hand was warm, as steady as a rock and for the first time in many, many months she felt safe and at peace without the need to struggle on and on, looking for she didn't know what.

"Tha's been here three nights, lass."

"Did Nelly . . . ?"

"Did Nelly what?" He leaned nearer to her so that she could see the lights in his eyes; like stars, they were, shining with the goodness she knew was in him.

"Who . . . was it yourself an' Nelly . . ."

"What, lass?"

". . . who undressed me?" She could feel that she wore some garment which covered her from neck to knee but underneath that was only bare skin.

"Aye, like I said, me an' Nelly."

She felt her whole body flush with embarrassment. The very thought of this strong, masculine person, whose name she didn't even know, studying her naked, emaciated body was too much for her and she tried to withdraw her hand from his. He wouldn't let her though and she felt too weak to struggle.

His face was perfectly straight.

"But I promise I didn't look," he told her, then grinned boyishly. "I'm teasing yer, lass . . . eeh, that's a grand smile," he added, though the smile had actually accentuated the sunken pallor of the face on the pillow.

"Now, I'd best fetch Nelly or she'll give me what for. She made me promise I'd give her a shout the minute tha' woke up. She's itchin' to get some of her shin beef broth in tha'. An' she's bound ter want me ter fetch some more milk an' eggs." His warm smile deepened and two grooves appeared, one on either side of his mouth. "Lass, she'll have tha' as fat as butter before she's done with thi' an' it's no good arguing. She'll have her own way, choose how."

"Please . . ."

He was rising to his feet but as she spoke he squatted down again.

"Aye, my lass?"

"Will you not be tellin' me your name?" She looked up at him shyly from beneath her lashes.

"It's Lew Earnshaw. An' yours?"

"Clare. Clare Hanrahan."

"Clare. That's right pretty. I'm glad ter meet yer, Clare Hanrahan." He gave her hand a gentle pat as though afraid he might damage her with a more vigorous approach.

It was the first time she had been called by her christian name since she left Ireland, for nobody in the wandering gangs who worked the fields beside her was concerned with a tall, silent, skinny girl who was Irish.

"Hey you, you in the grey skirt," or "Look lively, you,

yes you with the funny hair," had been the only greetings she had been given and to hear the name her mammy and daddy had chosen for her on this stranger's lips seemed to unlock something inside her, something that had been tightly closed against invasion from outside forces. Something hard, hurtful, well nigh unendurable. She closed her eyes but it did no good. The tears forced themselves from beneath her lids, clinging for a moment to her lashes – the only fragment left to her, apart from the eyes themselves, of the comeliness that had once been hers – before rushing in waves across her face and into the pillow beneath her head.

Lew was appalled, wishing to God Nelly was here, for in her down-to-earth, no-nonsense way she'd have this over and done with in no time at all, the girl mopped up, her nose wiped as though she were one of Nelly's own, shushed and patted back to calmness and probably told to "give over that racket"!

But this was no child's tantrum, this was deep, tearing grief, a sorrow too great to be borne and there was only him here to deal with it.

"Nay, child, there's no need ter skrike. Tha're safe here wi' me ... wi' us. We'll look after thi'. Eeh, lass, don't ... don't."

But her past, whatever it contained, would not let her be and her body began to rock as her grief and despair overcame her. The cat, with one offended look, leaped from the bed and stalked off, her tail straight up in the air.

Lew did the only thing he could. Sliding his arm beneath her shoulders he lifted her against his chest, his fingers combing through her painfully short hair, smoothing her thin neck and shoulders, saying nothing until the storm of weeping began to subside.

"There, lass ... there, yer as safe as a kitten in a basket wi' me," he told her gently. "Now, wipe yer eyes an' blow tha' nose," producing a clean square of linen from his trouser pocket, mopping her up as though she were one of the twenty-odd children who lived, squashed like peas in a pod, in the five cottages adjacent to his own.

"That's better. By 'eck, I'd cop it if Nelly was ter come in an' find tha' skrikin'. She'd be bound ter think it were my fault."

As though his words had conjured her up, a short, wiry little woman, hardly bigger than a ten-year-old child, came bustling across the threshold of the open door, casting a shadow momentarily over the girl in the bed and the man beside it. She stopped dead in her tracks and with an exclamation of exaggerated horror, just as though they were up to no good, clapped her hand to her forehead.

"Fer shame, Lew Earnshaw, what's goin' on 'ere, I'd like tha' ter tell me, that's if tha' can. That girl's not well enough ter be 'andled."

Lew laid Clare carefully back on her pillow, pulling the blankets up about her neck, then turned irritably on the woman who had just come in, his own face colouring up.

"Fer shame tha'self, Nelly Bradbury. She were upset, skriking over whatever's 'appened to her an' I were only tryin' ter give her a bit of comfort. There's nowt wrong with that, is there?"

"Hmmmph . . ." the little woman remarked, skittering across the kitchen and, barely giving Lew time to rise to his feet, pushing him to one side. "We'll see about that."

"See about what, for God's sake?" he asked testily.

"Never you mind. Now, get down ter't farm an' fetch me half a dozen eggs an' a quart o' milk. An' tha're payin' fer it, mind. I've enough feedin' me own wi'out doin' same fer every stray tha' take in." The words were brusque, ungracious even, but the hand that was placed on Clare's brow was not, and neither were the warm blue eyes that gazed down at her. They were brimming with what Clare could only describe as "loving kindness".

"Go on, tha' daft lummox. I've a word or two ter say ter . . . ter . . ."

"Her name's Clare."

"Ter Clare."

"Right then."

Lew peered round Nelly's narrow shoulder to smile at Clare.

"I told thi', didn't I?"

"Told 'er what, Lew Earnshaw?"

"Never you mind, Nelly Bradbury." He winked at Clare and she felt a bubble of optimism awake inside her and begin to smile.

"Right, my lass," Nelly said briskly when Lew had gone. "Let's get thi' changed. I've fetched a clean nightie an' while I'm at it I'll give thi' a sponge down. Now then, do tha' want t'chamber pot?"

"The . . . ?"

"Chamber pot. Ter piss in."

"To . . . ?"

"Eeh, lass, 'aster never seen a chamber pot?"

Clare hadn't. She and her family had relieved themselves at the back of their sod cottage, and in the fever hospital it had been a case of any handy container, or even on the floor. This was a grand affair, creamy white decorated with birds and flowers with a handle to one side. Its beauty was marred by a small chip in its rim.

"It were me mam's," Nelly went on proudly. "She were in service in Oldham. When it got chipped mistress wouldn't use it so 'ousekeeper, knowin' me mam was ter wed, give it 'er as a present. Grand, i'n't it? Now see, 'old on ter me," she commanded, helping the bemused girl on to the pot.

Nelly was to say time and time again, only to the women who were her neighbours, of course, that she would never get over her first sight of that child's body, no, not if she lived to be a hundred. She can't have weighed more than a kitten with not a pick on her, she told them, but if Nelly Bradbury had anything to do with it she'd have her plump as Davy Bretherton's pig which he was fattening for Christmas. How in heaven's name she'd got from Liverpool – which they found out later was where she'd started – and which was ... well, Nelly wasn't a scholar and couldn't really say how far it was but it was a damn sight further than Crossfold which was their nearest town. She was only sorry Lew had been witness to it as well. The child's thinness, she meant. If Betty, Maggie, Annie or Marie had not been on the day shift at the mill, she would, naturally, have sent for one of them, but she couldn't manage, not on her own. The girl, despite her slight frame, was tall, and semi-conscious into the bargain, and she herself was no bigger than two penn'orth of copper. Mind, with a decent chap like Lew it didn't seem too improper. It was not as though the lass was owt to write home about and was certainly not one to stir up lust in a man, not in her condition. Bones ready to break through her fine skin, which had nasty sores on it and was not a colour Nelly had seen on any woman before. A kind of putty yellow and no breasts to speak of.

The women who lived in the five cottages had seen it for themselves later, for they had set to and nursed her between them, scandalised when Lew insisted on taking a turn at sitting with her, saying it was a woman's job to nurse another woman.

"You've all got jobs ter go to, husbands, children an' I've nobody so what's wrong wi' me sitting in me own kitchen an' keepin' an eye on her?"

"An' that's another thing," Nelly began stubbornly.

"What is?"

"She shouldn't be stayin' in your 'ouse. Not wi' thi' a single chap an' 'er no more 'n a young girl."

"So where d'yer suggest she stays?" he asked fiercely. "Out on't moor or happen in Davy Bretherton's shed wi' 'is pig? She needs a bed an' I'm the only one who's got one ter spare."

He squared his chin in Nelly's direction then turned his steady gaze on the sleeping girl. This conversation had taken place on the day after she had fallen into his arms on the track outside his cottage and though Nelly hadn't liked it she had been forced to admit that there really was no alternative at the moment. The girl – whose name they did not then know – needed shelter, good food, a warm bed and the care she and Betty and the rest were only too willing to give. At least until she was recovered and on her way, wherever that was. Perhaps when she had regained full consciousness and the ability to talk coherently and not the babble her high fever had caused they might find out who she was, where she was from and where she was going, and her all alone, too.

Perhaps with a bit of reorganisation among the cottagers' children the lass might be decently squeezed in with one of them, for Nelly was not happy with the present arrangement. But no matter how she brooded over it Nelly didn't see how they were to do it and Betty, who was sitting with her and the girl while Lew was at the mill, agreed with her.

Each cottage had once been what was known as a "laithe-house". There were many such scattered about the valleys and hillsides around Oldham. Half home and half workplace with a loom shop above and stalls on the ground floor for cattle, though it was a long, long time since any of them had sheltered there. There was a kitchen and two tiny bedrooms in each cottage, among which, besides Lew, five couples and some twenty children cheerfully fought for a bit of space and with Marie Bretherton ready to give birth to another any day.

Once upon a time, years ago now, a Manchester merchant had supplied them with the raw yarn which the women would spin on their "jennies", the children carding and cleaning the fibres. When this was done the menfolk would operate a hand-loom, or even two, weaving a "piece" of cloth which was taken once a week to Crossfold and the Cloth Hall there. A good and satisfying way of life, gone now, of course, with the coming of the semi-automatic and then the self-acting spinning-machines which men like Barker Chapman, Oliver

Wingrove and William Hopkinson had introduced into their newly built cotton spinning-mills in the Penfold Valley. They erected enormous combing sheds and weaving sheds so that the whole process was done under their direction and they could call themselves not just spinners or weavers but manufacturers. It did not take long for these gentlemen to finish off the independent spinners and weavers of the Pennines and now they all worked, like it or not, men, women and children, in the mills of Chapman, Wingrove, Hopkinson or one of the dozens of others which had sprung up in the last twenty years in and around Oldham.

When Lew had gone for the eggs and milk, clicking his fingers to a rough-haired terrier which Clare had not noticed and which followed him through the sunshine-filled door into the lane, Nelly turned to the fire, crying out fiercely when she spied the cat delicately helping herself to the bacon in the frying pan on the hob.

"Gerr outer that, yer dratted animal," she shrieked, picking up a broom and brandishing it threateningly in the cat's direction. "Shoo . . . shoo. Outside wi' yer an' yer might as well tekk that bacon wi' yer now since it's not fit fer 'umans after tha's mauled it about. Glory be ter God, I don't know why Lew Earnshaw bothers ter keep such a useless article. What wi' that an't dratted dog it's like a dratted zoo in 'ere, not ter mention muck bein' traipsed in, an' fleas, I shouldn't wonder. If I 'ad my way they'd be outer 'ere before day's end. Now see, get that down yer."

Still grumbling and muttering what sounded like curses under her breath she thrust a steaming mug of something at Clare which she had apparently just poured out at the fire.

"Come on, lass, sit tha' self up." As Clare struggled to do as she was bid Nelly tutted impatiently just as though Clare were being deliberately awkward, but, putting the mug to one side she lifted her to a sitting position, stuffed cushions from the chairs at her back, wrapped her snugly about with a shawl and put the mug between her cupped hands. Her movements were quick, birdlike, curt even, as though she hadn't a moment to spare, but her hands lingered gently about Clare's shoulders and head and her eyes were warm in her grim face. She might pretend impatience, unconcern, an inclination to let this vagrant girl get on her way and stop bothering *her* who had troubles enough of her own, but she could not control her eyes which said the opposite.

"That's good beef broth there, lass, an' there's many a body'd like ter ger their 'ands on't recipe, fer it puts strength back in't weakest. Me mam told it ter me an' when time comes I'll pass it on to my Milly an' Dorcas. A few o' them inside yer an' yer'll be outer that bed in no time an' dancin' down't lane like a two-year-old. Good, in't it?"

Clare had to admit that it was. Even before she took a sip the fragrant aroma brought saliva rushing to her mouth. She nodded at Nelly between sips, knowing she had to get every drop down or Nelly would want to know the reason why.

She drank it all and Nelly nodded her approval. "I'll fetch tha' some more later, an' when Lew gets back I'll do thi' an egg in milk an' 'appen an egg custard."

Clare could feel the weariness creep over her again. The effort of sitting up, and drinking up, had drained her and when Nelly turned to her she saw that she had slipped back into sleep. She tiptoed across the kitchen and put a gentle hand on her forehead. It was cool and so was her pale cheek. This was a natural sleep and would heal the child; that and Nelly's good beef broth!

When Lew returned, clattering in ten minutes later, Nelly hushed him fiercely, at the same time swishing her skirts at the dog who bounced in after him.

"Can thi' not keep that there animal outside?" she hissed but Lew and the dog took no notice, both of them going over to the bed to look compassionately at the sleeping girl. Even the dog, who had put his paws on the coverlet, seemed to sigh.

"Poor lass, poor little lass," Lew murmured, standing for a moment before turning to put the eggs and milk on the table.

"Aye." Nelly shook her head sadly. "It must be bad over there fer a body ter get in such a state."

"It is, Nelly. Famine an' riot an' fever, it says in the newspapers. Two winters an' no potato crop, which they rely on, ter feed them. There was a letter in't *Times* – don't let on but I pinched it outer Gilbey's office yesterday, an' I dare say he got it from old man Hopkinson – any road the letter describes state o' the people, those who still live, poor souls, an' honest ter God, I wouldn't like ter describe it to yer."

"An' yer reckon that's what 'appened ter this lass?" nodding in the direction of the still figure in the bed.

"Aye, I'd say so. She's not said more 'n a word or two but she's Irish all right."

"An' what are we ter do wi' 'er, Lew Earnshaw?"

They sat down, one on either side of the fire in two battered rocking-chairs, sipping the mug of tea Nelly had prepared for them. She could always be sure of a decent cup of tea in Lew's house, since he was better paid than any of them and had nobody but himself to spend it on. The cat jumped up on Lew's knee and began to purr loudly and rhythmically as Lew's hand smoothed her fur. Both Lew and Nelly stared into the glowing coals of the fire, busy with their own thoughts which, though neither was aware of it, did not run on the same lines.

The afternoon was drawing in and beyond the window the valley was filling with shadows. Higher up where the cottages stood on the track to Crossfold, the sky retained some light, and over Besom Hill, which was the last to feel the sun's touch, a fine line of apricot turned the dying bracken to a lovely shade of gold.

"We can't do owt with her, Nelly," Lew said at last, "except see she recovers. Build her up best way we can. Give her a chance ter rest. She must've come by way o' Liverpool an' that's a bloody long walk."

"Language, Lew Earnshaw," Nelly corrected him absent-mindedly, for Nelly could not abide what she called a *mucky* mouth, or a mucky *anything* come to that whether it be verbal or in her own home. In fact in anyone's home. "So, what do tha' suggest, lad? Me an' Will 'ave a hard time feedin' ourselves an' the young 'uns, an' if our Arthur, Milly an' Dorcas weren't fetchin' in a bit of wage, though it grieves me ter send 'em ter't mill, we'd not manage. An' t'others up along are't same."

"Aye, I know, but don't tha' fret. I'll see to it. If I can't spend a few bob ter't feed lass . . ."

"Tha' do enough as it is, lad, ter 'elp us all out."

"Aye, well, if I can't manage summat it's a poor do."

"What about that there cause o' yourn? Yer give 'alf yer wages away as it is."

"I'll manage, Nelly."

"I 'ope yer will, lad. You bein' overlooker at mill'll help, I suppose."

Those in the row of cottages beside Lew's couldn't help but marvel and be proud of Lew Earnshaw who, though born in the same circumstances as themselves, had "got on". When lads of his age were out rabbiting, or playing the games lads like to play, Lew, encouraged by his widowed mother, had tramped off regularly to Sunday school where he had learned to read and write, skills none of them had. Later he'd spent his evenings at the Mechanics Institute and when his abilities had come to the notice of Mr William Hopkinson in whose mill Lew worked, he had been promoted to overlooker. Of course Mr Hopkinson was not aware of Lew's interest in the People's Charter and his belief that without it nothing would save the Irish peasant from starvation or the English labourer from exploitation at the mill or the mine. They must all be free of the "ruling class" that governed them and the only way to obtain that freedom was through education and the vote for all men. Only through the ballot box would come salvation and Lew tramped miles every week to put his radical views to his fellow labourers, gathering them about him on the windswept moors. William Hopkinson would have had Lew over the doorstep of his mill if he caught a whiff of it.

"But she can't stay 'ere wi' thi', lad. It's not decent."

"Oh, give over, Nelly. She can't even stand up, let alone make advances ter me an' I'm not likely ter pay attention to a child like 'er. Give me some credit, Nelly."

"I know that, Lew, but it's just not . . ."

For half an hour they wrangled, but in the end Nelly stood up and left, saying baldly that Lew hadn't heard the end of this and if the lass needed owt in the night he'd only to clatter on her wall.

He stood up and moved slowly towards the bed. The dog who dozed at his feet lifted his head and watched him, his head half cocked. Lew gazed down at Clare, an expression of sad musing on his clever face, wondering what her return to full consciousness would divulge. By God, but she was scrawny, plain. Her long, dark lashes were very clear on the pallor of her thin cheek. They fluttered and she turned her head, mumbling something, but when he put a hand to her cheek she quietened. A great wave of something he could only describe as tenderness washed over him and later he was to admit to himself that it was at that precise moment he gave her his heart.

Chapter Three

By the end of two weeks she could get out of bed. Word had got about that Mrs Bradbury said she could and no one wanted to miss it, especially the children.

Whenever Nelly or Lew were looking the other way during those first two weeks, even for no more than a minute, several of the children from the row of cottages would creep shyly over the threshold to stand, one bare foot on top of the other, staring in fascination at the scarecrow in the bed. At first it had disturbed Clare, then seeing the big-eyed innocence of a toddler with its thumb in its mouth who peeped out from behind an older girl's shabby skirt she remembered Declan and with a frail gesture she held out her hand. The toddler shrank back behind the protective skirt but the others, all under the age of five or six, she thought, encouraged by her smile and show of friendship, moved two or three steps nearer to her. No one spoke, not her and not them, for even talking tired her out and they were too overcome with shyness to start a conversation, but when she smiled, they smiled, continuing to watch her as though she were some strange creature from another world which she supposed she was. Then Nelly had come blustering in from next door, scattering them like a flock of starlings disturbed by a cat.

It seemed from the exchanges that took place between Nelly and the other women who came in to sit with her, to sponge her down, to spoon-feed her the nourishing little dishes Nelly made for her; who changed her bed and her nightgown and who performed the awkward task of sitting her on the splendid chamber pot, that all four of them worked as spinners at one or other of the cotton spinning-mills in Crossfold which was two or three miles down the track from Edgeclough. Betty had four children, two of whom worked as "little piecers". Maggie had five but only her Charlie, twelve years old, was employed as yet in the mill, the others still too young. Annie, with seven children, was accompanied by three of them to the spinning-rooms and weaving sheds of Crossfold and the remainder, including one-year-old Maidie Bretherton, were in the charge of Nelly Bradbury. If anyone thought eleven children ranging from one year to seven seemed a handful for one woman past her prime then they weren't acquainted with Nelly Bradbury who, or so Lew declared, would have no trouble keeping a battalion of soldiers on their toes. The women, desperate to keep their children out of the mills for as long as possible, paid Nelly a few coppers a week to keep her eye on them, but sadly three of them, Midge Marsden, Emma Cartwright and Mary Bickerstaffe, all three just turned seven, would soon be taking their places beneath the singing, but nevertheless potentially lethal spinning-frames their mothers and older sisters "minded". Little piecers whose job it would be to mend a thread should it break, or employed as cleaners, gathering the enormous amount of cotton waste that collected under the machines each day.

Betty and Annie and Maggie, being good mothers who loved their children, kept them at home as long as they could but times were hard and every penny counted. All the women were skilled at the task of making twopence do the work of a shilling but even so the few pence the children brought in often made the difference between a decent meal with a bit of scrag end in a pan brimming with vegetables, which their menfolk grew in their little plots of land behind their cottages, or just a bowl of oatmeal and hot water. They had plenty of the latter. They ate potato cakes baked in the oven, again with vegetables, bread of their own making, perhaps a bit of cheese or bacon, boiled sheep's head which was cheap and tasty, pig's feet and, as a special treat, savoury ducks made from the scrapings of offal the butcher in Crossfold gave away and which was mixed with oatmeal and onions and baked in the oven. They drank weak tea, using the same tea leaves several times, the men weak ale, and, like many Lancashire communities and the tradition of neighbourliness that prevailed, shared what they had with one another if hard times should hit. Let a wage-earner be struck down and the inhabitants from the whole of the row of cottages would rally round in support, the Lancashire habit of humour, of seeing the funny side of things, emerging as a sort of defence against what life threw at them.

But on this day Mrs Bradbury and Mr Earnshaw wrapped her up in a quilt which had been passed on, like the chamber pot, from Nelly's mam to her daughter. A pair of Mr Earnshaw's warm, woollen socks were put on her feet, and, done up like a parcel, or so it felt, Clare was carried outside and placed tenderly in the chair. Mr Earnshaw fussed about her, pulling the quilt up to her chin, demanding if she was warm enough, was she comfortable, arranging her feet on a stool, shooing away Cat who had taken a fancy to her and wanted to sit on her lap, and those who watched, especially the men, nudged one another and exchanged glances.

She felt a great shyness. More than that, a certain reluctance to be treated as though she were a spectacle set out for them to wonder at, but after a moment or two of inspection she realised she was wrong. In appearance they all tended to be undersized with pale complexions and one or two of them coughed as if they were prone to chest complaints. They seemed good-humoured though, with a look of stoicism about them that reminded her somewhat of her own people before the bad time.

"Mornin' ter thi', lass," one of the men said, the tone of his voice flat, the vowel sounds long.

She nodded her head and smiled and they all agreed that she looked better. No colour in her face to speak of but with a hint of the clear buttermilk and honey which they felt might be her normal hue. Still as thin as a thread but Nelly had washed her hair and it stood about her head in a dark cloud. Nelly had also gathered agrimony which grew beneath the hedgerows further down the valley, brewing an infusion from the plant with which she had bathed the sores on Clare's body.

"Tha' needs some greens inside tha', lass," Nelly had said. "Me granny, 'oo passed it on ter me mam an' me mam ter me, reckoned there were nowt like green stuff, watercress, cabbage an' 't like, which my Will grows, ter set tha' right. Sadie Shaw what worked aside me at Hopkinson's told me that 'er brother what were a sailor an' at sea fer months on end were fed wi' nowt but salt meat an' 'ard biscuits an' 'e 'ad sores like yourn, so get that cabbage soup down tha' while I do thi' some egg in milk. Lew fetched some more up an' ses tha' mun sup it or 'e'll box tha' ears. I dunno, tha'd think 'e 'ad a long sock way 'e spends money but then I reckon we all know't reason why, don't we?" And though Clare hadn't any idea what she meant she obediently ate or drank everything Nelly thrust into her hands.

Nelly's voice, which rarely stopped, washed over her for most of the day in a pleasant ripple, like little wavelets on the seashore at home. Making barely a cat's-paw on the surface of her mind, it soothed and comforted, requiring little or no response. From it she learned the names and relationships of the families in and around the hamlet of Edgeclough, their ages and dispositions, their family histories and their hopes for their children which were, basically, to keep them above starvation level which Clare fully understood and sympathised with. She fell asleep with the monotone in her ears and when she awoke it was still there and she was to wonder if Nelly stopped talking while she, Clare, was asleep.

Though it was October the sun still had warmth in it. There

wasn't a cloud in the sky except for a group on the far side of the valley which resembled several fat woolly lambs following nose to tail across its blue width. The thick pall of smoke which usually hung like a sour blanket over the town was missing today since it was Sunday and the mill chimneys were clear. It was nothing but moorland up here, wild and fit for no living creature but sheep, wide sloping stretches folding in on one another as far as the eye could see, outcroppings of grey pitted rocks, rough tracks of tiny, scattered stones, tufted spiky grass on which only sheep could find sustenance, bracken and gorse and heather, fading away as winter crept closer. On the mild air was a smell of honeysuckle and thyme and from one of the cottages drifted the scent of fresh baked bread.

Further down towards the valley bottom where the river lay there were still pockets of farmland with neatly walled fields, lanes leading to small, sturdy farmhouses, swathes of uncleared woodland stretching beside the river, rough tracks bordered with hedgerows beneath which wild flowers flourished. Plumes of smoke rose straight into the air since there was no wind, a pale grey against the pale-blue sky. The farms were a legacy of the days before the factory and the mill; before the machine age which was to take away the independence of the hand-loom weaver. Generations ago clearings had been cut in the forests which had once covered the area and scattered farming communities had grown there, living out their peaceful lives with no presentiment of what was to come. But agriculture alone was unable to sustain the growing population, and hand-loom weaving, which had been carried out since the Middle Ages, had flourished with the help of the damp climate which was so suitable for the brittle cotton fibre. Until the age of the machine there was little change, but it was all swept away with the coming of men like Kay, Hargreaves, Crompton and Arkwright and their brilliant mechanical inventiveness.

Far below, Clare could see a ploughman, no bigger than the size of a thumbnail, turning a field from a tattered brown jungle into incredibly straight furrows, an orderly series of small valleys stretching far into the distance. There were trees on the edge of the fields, their leaves already thinning, sheltering the wild flowers in the ditches.

Behind the row of cottages the moor rose up dramatically to the top of the South Pennine heartland and on into Yorkshire. Clare could hear the roar of a mountain stream tumbling over rock and stone to the more placid waters in the valley below. Again there was moor heather and bracken spreading up to the skyline and though she had known nothing but the flat fields and shoreline where she had been born and had lived out her young life, she could feel the rugged beauty all around her move into her heart and take a special place there.

The mellow day seemed to act softly on the group of people who had come, not to gape, Clare soon found out, but to ask after her health, to wish her well. The men were quiet-spoken and courteous, not soft or lacking in masculinity, but gentle and sympathetic. They longed to know her story, of course, they all did, but she had divulged it to no one, not even to Nelly or Lew, but with the inherent reticence and good manners of their kind, they merely nodded their goodwill.

The men moved off first. It was Sunday and they had their vegetable plots to turn over and weed ready for planting. Arthur Bradbury and Charlie Cartwright, both twelve years old, thin as sticks, for no child who lived and worked in the mills of Lancashire ever put on weight, but wiry and tough like their fathers, were off rabbiting since a rabbit was always welcome in their mams' meatless pots. Several of the younger girls began a complicated skipping game with a bit of rope which was played to a chanted rhythm of:

Owd Brown's Cow
'Ad a wooden leg
An' every time 'e milked 'er
'E 'ung it on a peg.

The little ones, barely more than infants, gathered round Clare and with eyes like baby owls gazed at her, waiting for her to speak, to say some amazing thing, which they had been led to believe she would, for she had come from "over the water" wherever that was. A magpie chattered on a gate to be joined by another. The older girls stopped for a moment to see if a third would join them and when it did began the jingle;

One fer sorrow
Two fer joy
Three fer a weddin' ...

At the last word they turned as one to stare at Clare and Mr Earnshaw, trying hard not to giggle, then resumed their game.

Rooks swirled overhead and Clare, in their company and the company of these undemanding children, felt at peace. Lew, who sat on the step beside her, was smiling. He had his knees drawn up and apart and he rested his forearms on them, his chin resting on his forearms. His eyes were a smoky grey beneath the shadow of his narrowed lids and dark eyelashes and not until one of the older girls sidled up and with a shy smile, a bob of the head and a tiny bunch of scarlet and white campion did anyone break the silence.

"I fetched yer these," she said, placing the flowers on Clare's lap, since her hands were wrapped up along with the rest of her beneath the quilt. She had bright blue eyes and a steady gaze which said she would not look away even if rebuffed.

Clare struggled to get her hand free and when she did she touched the flowers as though they might have been stars fallen from the sky. She picked them up carefully and held them to her face, breathing in the fresh scent of lingering summer, then turned to the girl.

"Thank you."

Encouraged, the girl smiled back. "Me name's Lavender."

Clare, knowing something more was expected of her, cleared

her throat and clutched at the flowers as though in self-defence but Lavender waited patiently, having been told by her mam that the stranger had been right poorly

"Now ... isn't that ... a pretty name?" Clare managed at last. She was badly out of practice in the art of conversing with another human being. Her daddy had often said, his eyes, as green as her own, twinkling with his love for her, that she was the biggest chatterbox this side of Ballynacally, though the very idea of it seemed hard to believe for now she could barely string one word after another. Lew was another who talked to her at the end of his working day, but again, like Nelly, he seemed to expect no answer.

"Them's me sisters," Lavender went on, turning to point at three of the chanting girls. "Poppy, Daisy an' Primrose. Me mam likes flowers," she added unnecessarily. "Clare?" she continued. It was a tentative question rather than a greeting.

Clare nodded. Lavender was, like the rest of them, thin as a bootlace and pale. She had small budding breasts and a fresh prettiness about her which comes to young girls but which, in her station in life, quickly fades. Lavender was fifteen.

"I know wheer there's some wild blackberries. Mixed wi' oatmeal they mekk a gradely puddin'. When tha're better I'll show thi'," she said abruptly, then darted off as though amazed and afraid of her own boldness.

Lew's face had a smile on it when she turned to look at him. "Tha'll be wantin' ter know what gradely means, I reckon." She nodded. "It's Lancashire fer 'grand' though if tha' were talkin' about a man or woman tha'd mean 'straightforward'. It's a compliment. Dost know what I mean, lass?"

She didn't, as she had been brought up in ignorance of the outside world, of clever words, of books, living the simple peasant's life that her family had known for generations, but she nodded and sighed, for the day was quite lovely and she wished it could go on for ever. She didn't know how long she was to stay here, or even where she was to go when she left, but these few days with these good people had strengthened her and she knew now, perhaps for the first time, that she would survive.

The weather continued warm, an Indian summer, Iggy Marsden said to her in passing a week later. Day after day she was able to sit in the sunshine, helped at first by whoever was in charge of her but more and more able to get about on her own. She began to take short walks along the track in front of the cottages, nodding and smiling at all those who greeted her, dressed in the freshly washed, ironed and mended tatters she had arrived in, her black boots polished to a mirror-like shine by Lew. None of them had ever worn a pair of boots, or "shoon" Nelly called them, since clogs were standard footwear in these parts and they were greatly admired.

Whenever she went for a walk she was accompanied by Cat who was called by that name because Lew said he couldn't think of anything else. The animal strolled along behind her, tail in the air, back end swaying, looking for all the world as though she were unaware that Clare even existed, let alone that she was following her, turning to hiss now and again at the dog who liked a walk too, his manner said. His name was Fred. Lew told her it was after his pa who had been called Fred and had been a good man. Since the dog had proved to be a good, kind, loyal and gentle companion he had given him his father's name, and why not. Fred Earnshaw had been a legend in these parts. He had taken part in marches and protests in support of the exploited working man. He believed in justice and freedom for every man and he had said so wherever a crowd gathered, to the fury of mill owners, manufacturers and indeed every man who employed another. A radical then, like his son, who had tramped over the moors here, there and everywhere with him, drinking in his father's words as he had once drunk his mother's milk and had been nourished by both.

And then there were the children, sometimes as many as eleven of them, becoming bolder as they grew used to her. They even began to squabble as to who should hold her hand, one on either side of her, until she made them understand that they must take it in turns. She found that she had lost none of her skills in keeping children in order, for she had been the eldest of twelve, six having died at birth or in infancy, and she had been a second mother to her five remaining brothers and sisters, minding them while her mammy was in the fields, then when she herself began to work keeping the younger ones busy in the belief that they were helping her. She remembered songs and games and stories and it was not an uncommon sight for her to be found sitting on the warm grass on the far side of the track, a group of children about her as she told them tales of Irish fairies, of leprechauns and pixies and all the legends that her own daddy had told her. Of Irish kings and queens and all the colourful history of the land Daddy had loved.

She felt herself to be in a state of waiting, in a kind of dream world where nothing was real. It was very comfortable. She felt better, more or less recovered, at least physically. The wound inside her was still raw, making her wince at times, but she was rested. She didn't have to think, for Lew and Nelly did that for her. She had no decisions to make, no plans to consider, though she knew that would come. She drifted, feeling nothing much, the people about her like kindly shadows, the only time she peeped from behind the screen she had erected about herself when she was with the children who accepted her just as she was, were not sorry for her since they didn't know there was anything to be sorry about. At night she climbed into her little alcove bed, warm and safe with Cat curled up beside her and Fred on the floor by the bed, falling asleep with the ease of a tired child, not even waking when Lew crept down from his tiny bedroom, made himself a cup of tea and gulped down a couple of potato cakes made the day before by Nelly, then slipped from the cottage to be at the mill for the five o'clock whistle.

The long-running arguments of what was right and proper and the way "things looked" began in earnest that evening. Nelly had been muttering for over a week that there was absolutely no reason, now that Clare was mobile, why she shouldn't move to either her place or Marie Bretherton's who, having only the one child, was willing to put up a truckle bed in her kitchen for Clare to sleep on. She was not fit to go out looking for work yet, Nelly went on, glaring about her as though expecting an argument, but until she was things must be done decent.

It had been evident that Nelly had something on her mind all evening, for she had spent an hour fiddling unnecessarily with this and that, wiping over every surface, eyeing the animals as though they might be in for it, until even Lew noticed and set down the newspaper he was reading with a flourish.

"Leave it, Nelly, for God's sake. Tha're not goin' ter get it any cleaner. It's like a new pin as it is."

"'Appen it is an' 'appen it's not, Lew Earnshaw."

Though Nelly loved to utter these cryptic little remarks and he was well used to them, the man in the chair looked amazed. "An' what's that supposed ter mean, fer God's sake?"

"Never you mind." Nelly clattered a pan on the stove with such force Fred leaped to his feet and Cat lifted her head and stared resentfully.

"Never mind! Right, Nelly Bradbury, tha's evidently got summat on tha' mind so out wi' it and then we can all get to our beds."

"Aye, that's what I'm on about. That lass 'as no right bein' 'ere an' it's time we talked about it. Proper, I mean, with no arguments. It's not seemly fer a lass an' a lad ter be—"

"Are tha' sayin' me an' Clare are up ter no good, Nelly Bradbury?" Lew's face took on a dangerous, narrow-eyed look and Clare sat up slowly in her chair as the raised voices, the sharp, offended tones in Nelly's voice, scattered all thoughts of drifting off to sleep from her mind. She remembered the first time she had seen Lew. He had smiled so kindly, his face conveying nothing but goodwill, but round his mouth she had noted a stubborn line which said he might be dangerous if provoked and it seemed Nelly was provoking him.

"'Appen tha' think that now Clare's stronger she might take it into her head to climb the stairs and—"

"Watch tha' tongue, Lew Earnshaw," Mrs Bradbury said to him sharply, her face screwed up in tight disapproval. "Tha' know it's not right an' that's why tha's tekkin' this road. I'll not be put off, lad. Clare's a decent girl an' don't deserve what folk'll say about 'er."

"What folk? Nobody's said owt ter me."

"Not ter tha' face, no, but they'll be sayin' enough be'ind tha' back, so think on. Now termorrer me an' Marie'll get that bed ready so don't gie me any more lip."

She reached for her shawl and though she had only to slip next door wrapped it warmly about her. It had turned colder that day and Clare had given the children the slip and climbed slowly up the well-defined track at the back of the cottages which led on to the moorland itself. There was a scatter of rocks, pitted and covered with lichen and sitting down on one to rest for the journey home she had absorbed the crisper, colder air into her lungs and the splendour of the panoramic view spread out before her. Her ears were filled with the singing of the streams as they fell from a dozen places, leaping from rock to rock to disappear below. She had sat for an hour, for the climb had tired her, thinking on how *settled* she had become in this wild and lovely place and now, because of her, Lew and Nelly, who were devoted to one another, were quarrelling bitterly.

Now she got to her feet and so unused were they to her voice, when she spoke both their mouths fell open in surprise.

"I'll go tomorrow,' she told them. "Sure an' haven't you been kindness itself an' me not knowing what I'd have done without you but I'm well now, so I am, and it's time I moved on."

Nelly recovered first. Her mouth thinned to a grim line and her eyes, such a lovely warm blue in their kindness, turned flinty. "Don't talk daft, girl," she said tartly. "Tha're goin' nowhere. Tha'd not get ter't top o't lane wi'out fallin' on tha' face."

"That's not true, Nelly. I'm really quite well. I knew I couldn't stay here for ever so . . ."

"Why not?" Lew said abruptly, so abruptly both Nelly and Clare turned to stare at him. "Tha've nowhere ter go, 'ave thi'? No one's expecting yer, are they? What's ter stop yer . . . well, we could sort summat out, couldn't we, Nelly?"

Lew Earnshaw got to his feet and, brushing past the open-mouthed Nelly, took both of Clare's hands in his. His jaw was clenched with his effort to appear nonchalant, casual, a friend offering a way out of some dilemma, but if Clare was deceived, Nelly Bradbury wasn't. She knew exactly what was in Lew's heart. She had known him from the day she had helped his mam give birth to him, had watched him grow from a cheeky lad to a decent young man and not once in that time had he looked twice at any girl. He was a well-set-up chap and there'd be many a lass more than willing to take him on but he had remained heart-whole and fancy free. But there was something in this gawky, stork-like lass that had called out to something in him; not her looks, that was certain, for as yet she could claim none. He'd always been one for bringing home wounded creatures, a bird with a broken wing, that blasted cat which he'd found almost drowned in a ditch, various small birds or animals, driving his poor mam to distraction and perhaps this with Clare was the same. She hoped so but she didn't think so, not really.

"Listen, why don't tha' tekk my bed," he was saying, but at once Clare pulled her hands from his, an expression of distress crumpling her face and yet, was that hope Nelly could see there? She didn't want to go, that was certain, so happen she felt the same way about Lew as it seemed he felt about her.

"No. Oh no, Lew, I couldn't. You've done enough for me, so you have. Saved my life, you and Nelly," turning her long green eyes on the woman who stood, unusually for her, silently by the table.

"Rubbish, we'd a' done the same fer anyone, wouldn't we,

Nelly?" Which Clare knew was true but it didn't make any difference. She had to go sometime and this seemed as good a time as any. She could probably walk down to Crossfold, find a job at one of the mills, rent a room and begin to make a life for herself. She could still see them all, Betty and Annie, Lavender and Archie, who reminded her of Declan, and ... Lew. On a Sunday she would walk up here and sit with Nelly and ... and ...

Watching the play of emotions across her face, which ranged from determination, hope, dread and what seemed to Lew to be despair, he did his best to speak rationally, reasonably, sensibly. She was not ready to be sent out into the world on her own but if she thought she was causing trouble she would be off, her expression said. He put his hands on her shoulders, handling her as gently as a child. He wanted to shout and bluster and forbid her to go, recognising what was in himself, but leading her to a chair he sat her down in it, scarcely noticing Nelly who stood, grim-faced, by the table.

"Clare, tha're not strong enough to go striding off across the moor and certainly not capable of working at a spinning-frame which is the only work open to thi' in Crossfold. It's hard work, lass, fourteen or sixteen hours minding perhaps four machines. The 'fly' gets on tha' chest an' mekks tha' sick. An' then there's no tellin' tha'd get work since tha've no experience."

"I could clean ... scrubbing ..."

Nelly snorted and looked around her as though to ask an invisible company had they ever heard such nonsense?

Lew ignored her. "Scrubbin' is it. Well, if tha' wants ter scrub why don't tha' work fer me? This floor's always needin' a good scrub."

Nelly gasped in resentment. "Now listen 'ere, Lew Earnshaw ..."

"An' Nelly'd be glad of a hand wi't children, wouldn't yer, Nelly?"

"Well, I dunno about—"

"An' as for't bed I've bin thinking on it fer a while now" – which was a lie – "an' I reckon me an' 't lads could fix up the stalls below ter make me a decent little place ter lay me 'ead. Snug as a bug I'd be, and you'd 'ave cottage ter thissen which ought ter satisfy all these folk Nelly keeps goin' on about."

Nelly was scandalised. "If yer mean me, Lew Earnshaw, I'll thank you to—"

"Leave it, Nelly, there's a good lass. It's settled. Until Clare's properly recovered she's to 'ave this cottage, startin' tomorrow. If she wants ter move on in't spring, when weather's better, I'll not stop 'er. Is that a bargain, lass? Eeh, lass, there's no need ter skrike . . ."

His arms came round her and her head drooped to his broad shoulder and he held her carefully to him.

Nelly shook her head in disbelief but had the last word as she usually did.

"Well, don't say I didn't warn thi'," she said grimly as she let herself out of the cottage.

Chapter Four

She first saw the man at the top of Friars Mere. The tops, Lew called it and it had become a favourite retreat for Clare when she wanted to get away, not only from the children who were partially in her care now, but from Nelly who thought she knew what was best for Clare every minute of every day. Nelly had been overruled on the matter of the truckle bed and what she thought of as the senseless idea of Lew setting up sleeping quarters in the cow stalls but that hadn't stopped her from vouchsafing her opinion on every aspect of Clare's recovery and the best way to go about it, which she did morning, noon and night. And on the whole her advice was sensible, and it worked, for she was a level-headed woman with a great deal of experience in the care of her fellow human beings. They all went to her: when a child had a stubborn cough; a woman a painful "monthly": or the absence of a "monthly" which might spell disaster in the teetering balance of a family's financial affairs; a man with a bashed thumb or a gash that would not heal. Her old granny and her granny's granny had been healers, women who had learned the efficacy of plants in the restoration to health of their harassed and poverty-stricken neighbours who could seldom find the fee a doctor demanded. The knowledge had been passed down from mother to daughter through the generations and Nelly's care and kindness to Clare could not be denied, but no matter how she tried Nelly could not prevent herself from believing that *her* way was best. She did not try very hard, naturally, for she sincerely believed her way *was* best. She could not resign herself to the arrangement with the cow stalls, nor to Clare becoming what was virtually Lew's housekeeper, though she did admit grudgingly that Clare was in a fair way to turning into what was, to her, the highest compliment she could pay, and that was a proper *Lancashire* housewife, though of course she wasn't a wife. Nelly liked to "throw her weight about" as Lew put it, bestowing advice and opinions whether they were asked for or not. She was self-willed and severe with those who did not heed her but she was the kindest woman Clare had ever known.

It was quite a stiff climb, scrambling up and down banks overgrown with briars, clambering over dry-stone walls, which she noted were in good repair, across narrow timbered valleys or cloughs, as she had been told they were called hereabouts, all the time going upwards. She crossed old pack-horse tracks on which nothing moved these days except rabbit and stoat and the occasional band of itinerants looking for work, and when she reached the top she was out of breath but it was worth it, for the view was quite magnificent. It was all so empty which, to a girl who lived in the combined company of over thirty people from morning until night for seven days a weeks, was a blessing.

It was January, three months since that day she had fallen into Lew's arms. It was cold, though her own brisk movements had kept her warm, with a blue sky that only a frosty day in winter could produce, and the ground was iron hard. Spikes of stiff, frosted grass, sentinels of last year's bracken and heather, withered and brown, stood all around her, lying in a haze that went no higher than her knees.

She had Fred with her.

"We'll rest for a bit, Fred, shall we, though 'tis not the day to be sitting about. Come here an' lean against me knee and we'll warm each other."

She was dressed in the clothes in which she had left Ireland but beneath the skirt and bodice she wore a pair of Will Bradbury's old combinations tucked into a pair of woollen stockings Nelly had knitted for her. The combinations were much darned and far too short but snug and hidden beneath her skirt, and over her dress she had wrapped herself in a woollen shawl which covered her head and crossed her breast to tie at her back. A pair of woollen mittens completed her outfit. She wore clogs now, keeping her boots for some special occasion, she didn't know what and the clogs certainly kept her feet warm and dry.

"To be sure it's a fine sight, Fred," she murmured to the animal who leaned closer to her knee. She fondled his ears and his eyes became unfocused with rapture. "I never thought I'd be liking anything as well as the fields an' rivers of Clare but this takes a bit o' beating. That stretch of meadow where the Fergus ran into the Shannon was grand, so it was, an' I don't suppose there's a place on earth that will be quite like it, wherever I tramp, but there's something to be said for this bit of England. Daddy would've loved this, you know, Fred. He once told me he'd never seen a mountain, for he never went north in his life but I could tell he'd have liked to. And wouldn't Patrick have loved splashin' about in all them grand streams?" She sighed and leaned her back against the grey-veined rock that formed the seat on which she rested and fell silent. Her breath smoked round her head and on her cheeks was a touch of what could almost be called colour which returning good health and the cold air had painted there.

"And these folk are grand as well. Nelly treats me like a baby, so she does, a baby without any sense, but then she wouldn't be knowing that in some ways I'm older than she is so can I be blaming her? And Lew, well, I know how Lew feels, so I do, for haven't I seen it in his face, but there's nothing much left in me, you see, Fred. It's empty I am and it might be a long time before what was once there comes back. I loved them all and it was ripped away from me, leaving me without a feeling for very much at all. Lew's a good man, Fred, a kind man, you know that, don't you, and he'd be easy to get on with but would it be right to . . . ?" She stopped speaking and shook her head. "Jesus, Joseph an' Mary, folk'd think I was mad, so they would, talking to a dog like this but I can't talk to anyone else, not yet, at least. But can I go on like this, Fred? Hanging about fillin' in me time doin' jobs for Nelly and Lew and depending on charity. I must find a job soon no matter what Lew says. I'm meself again now an' strong enough to work at something."

The dog licked the end of her bare fingers and she bent her head to smile at him. "Bejasus, Fred, 'tis gradely here, as they say, an' I'll be sorry to leave, so I will, but it's got to come."

She returned her gaze to the slope of land before her, to the fold of hills that went on into the misted distance and to the deep wooded valley far below her. She was quiet, deep in her own thoughts, distracted by the splendour of what lay before her. For perhaps five minutes she sat and was just about to stand up and turn towards Edgeclough when she heard the chink of a horse's hooves on the stony path behind her. Fred stood up and began to bark. Her heart jumped, for it was not often a horseman rode these moors and in all the time she had been coming up here she had met no one.

The head of the horseman was first to come into view as he crested the track, followed by the horse's head and then the rest of them both. He was obviously deep in thought, his eyes gazing at some spot between his horse's ears and he was visibly startled when he caught sight of her and Fred, pulling back on the reins so that the animal's head was drawn sharply to one side.

"God almighty!" he snorted, seeming to be particularly put out about something, beginning to frown as he brought the horse to a stop. "You gave me a shock there, lass. What the devil are you doing up here on your own, for Christ's sake? Don't you know that there are all sorts of ruffians crossing these moors all ready to . . . well, I'll not go into detail but if I were you I'd get myself home. It'll be dark soon. Besides which the weather up here can be treacherous. In fact I have a feeling it might snow."

Clare stood up and smoothed her ragged skirt. During her stay on the rock she had pushed back the shawl from her head and the loose curls, which had grown and regained their dark gloss with her health, were lit by the sunshine with russet lights. She did not smile, nor speak, but her startling eyes, a dark and mysterious green, tilted to look up at him.

The horse, evidently wanting to get home to its stable, rattled impatiently on the stony path and for a moment the man wrestled with it, then, with a muttered oath, threw his leg over its back and jumped to the ground. It was an extremely handsome animal, even Clare, who knew nothing about thoroughbreds, could see that. A coal-black mare with a coat like satin, rippling as she fidgeted under her master's hand, her head tossing, her eyes rolling. The man held the reins, speaking to her in a soothing voice until she quietened, then he turned again to Clare.

She felt she should be nervous, up here all alone with a perfect stranger but she wasn't, she couldn't have said why. He appeared to offer no threat to her, big and arrogant-looking as he was. He was lean of waist and belly and hip with strong, muscled shoulders beneath the sleeved cloak he wore. His hair was thick and a rich, dark brown, curling vigorously in the nape of his neck. He wore no hat. He was amber-skinned and clean-shaven and his eyebrows were inclined to dip in a frown of perplexity over eyes that were watchful. They were a vivid blue and framed by long, black lashes. He was undoubtedly an attractive man but his face was too strong, his mouth too stubborn and his chin too arrogant to be called classically handsome. But there was a hint of humour in the curl of his lips which told Clare he was a man who did not take life too seriously.

He saw a tall, exceedingly slender girl with a dark tumble of hair which was cut unfashionably short. Her eyes were a curious colour being a dark green but in them there were golden flecks of light, reminding him of a leopard he had once seen in a zoo. Her skin was pale, unblemished, as fine as bone china, but her mouth was as rosy and full as a young child's. She had a fragility about her, a look so ethereal she brought to mind the saintly pictures he had seen in the books read by his mother, who had been of a pious nature. She was very poorly dressed and wore the clogs and shawl of the working woman. But no working woman would be found hanging about at the top of Friars Mere. Working women didn't have time for it!

"Are you lost?" he asked her, amazed at his own concern, for what did he care about a woman wandering like a fool over this rough moorland? Perhaps it was because of her frail appearance, or was it her total lack of concern over her own safety? Whatever it was it annoyed him slightly, since he didn't really have the time or patience to be fretting himself over a woman he did not know.

He secured his animal's bridle to a protuberance in the rock face before turning back to her. "Where are you headed?" he questioned, for perhaps she was on her way somewhere to look for work though where in hell's name that would be up here he couldn't imagine. Again he was astonished at his own unease for her safety but whatever it was he could not ignore it or her.

"Oh, no, thank you. I'm just out for a walk." She regarded him steadily, not the slightest bit alarmed at his large, male presence.

"A walk, and where to, if I might ask, and on a cold day like this? You'd be better off indoors, lass." Indeed she looked as though a puff of wind would have her over.

"Sure an' that's kind of ye but I'm to be off home now."

"And where's home?" He was intrigued and he wondered why, for this slip of a lass was not the sort to appeal to Martin Heywood. He liked his women to be robust, full-breasted, perhaps with a touch of the unusual, the exotic, even the coarse about them and the description could not be applied to this one. He liked his women to be obliging and cheerful, teasing with a touch of impudence, but this girl was what he could only call self-contained, distant in a polite sort of way and not at all interested in Martin Heywood. It was almost like meeting a child who had wandered far from home and who had to be set on the path to safety but where home was he couldn't decide, for she had a lilt to her voice which said she wasn't from around here.

"I'm stopping in . . . Edgeclough."

"But you're from further away than Edgeclough, I'd say?" Intrigued despite himself.

"Yes, I'm . . . I've come over the water from Ireland." Her voice was low and somewhat strained.

"To find work?" He bent his head to look into her face, for though she was tall he topped her by six inches.

"Aye."

"And did you find it?"

"No, not yet."

"What are you looking for? Something in the mills, happen?"

Dear God, what was wrong with him standing here wasting his time on some Irish migrant when he should be getting home to his warm fireside, which was still a couple of miles away, to the well-cooked meal Mrs Case would have prepared for him and an evening spent studying his farm accounts, the profits which had increased again during the last year. It was bloody cold up here on the moor at this time of the year with a biting wind which came down like a whirling dervish straight from the wastelands of Siberia. He should know. He'd lived here all his life on the prosperous farm that had been in his family for generations, passed down from father to son, each generation building on the success of the previous one. His land stretched over many hundreds of acres, employing a dozen men, six of them shepherds, for he was a sheep farmer, mainly Lonks which did very well in this inhospitable part of the country. They were to be found in the mountains and moorlands of south-west and west Yorkshire, east Lancashire and north-west Derbyshire but Martin Heywood prided himself that his were the best in the country. Their fleece was fine but denser and heavier than that of other breeds and was much sought after over the border in Yorkshire where most of his business was done, and the quality of their mutton was excellent.

For some reason he sat down on the flat rock from which the girl had risen at his approach and for some reason the girl re-seated herself next to him. The dog settled between them and the girl's hand went to his ears which she pulled and smoothed, to the dog's evident delight.

"You'll spoil that animal," he found himself saying. "I have dogs, working dogs, collies. They make the best sheepdogs in the world. We've bred what are known as 'merles' for generations. Most collies have brown eyes but these of ours have bright blue."

He waited for her to speak, to answer him in some way, even if it was only to say, "Well, fancy that," but she didn't. She merely stared out, her chin in her hand, over the sweeping expanse of hills and moorland below them as though she were alone, or he were no more important than the dog at her feet. Less so, for the dog at her feet evidently meant a great deal to her the way she was fussing over it. Martin Heywood felt a strange sensation come over him and he could hardly believe it himself when he realised it was pique. He was affronted because the effect he usually had on women, any women, was not happening with this one. It seemed that she was unconcerned whether he went or stayed and his efforts at conversation – why was he making them, for God's sake? – meant nothing to her. Martin knew himself to be attractive to women and not just because he was the richest farmer in the south Pennine foothills but because, let's make no bones about it, he had a handsome face, a certain way with the ladies which was audacious but at the same time gentlemanlike.

He tried again.

"How long have you been at Edgeclough?" he asked, doing his best to be patient though it was not really his nature.

"Since October."

"And you're staying with . . . ?" He left the question hanging delicately. Like most of the inhabitants of this wild bit of moorland north of Crossfold, he was well acquainted with those who were his neighbours. Just as he and his family had lived and worked hereabouts for generations, so had most of those not as fortunately placed as himself. The cottages in Edgeclough, which he owned since they were on his land, had been occupied by the same families through the heyday of the hand-loom weaving and spinning, through its decline and the rise of industrialisation in the textile trade. Though they were not and never had been in the same class as himself he knew most of them well enough to bid them a gruff good-morning or enquire after their health.

The girl seemed to come to with a start as though her daydreams, whatever they were, had been interrupted.

"Oh, I'm with Mr Earnshaw."

"I beg your pardon? You're stopping with Lew Earnshaw," he heard himself say in a manner that implied he was seriously offended and she heard it, flushing slightly at the wealth of meaning in his voice.

Two years ago Clare Hanrahan had been a high-spirited, good-natured young girl with nothing malign in her life beyond the constant grind of all those in her village to get through the year from one potato crop to the next. Her family had known sadness when Mammy had lost children to one of the many childhood illnesses that afflict the desperately poor but on the whole her life, and theirs, had been a contented one. They were an impoverished but deeply loving family devoted to one another's welfare and Clare, or so her daddy was fond of telling her, smiling indulgently, would be lucky to find a chap willing to take on a girl who was as stubborn and determined on her own way as Clare was. A bright, hopeful girl had been Clare Hanrahan, with a lively sense of humour and able to hold her own with anybody, even the local landowner's son who had made it plain he would like more from her than a polite good-day. That was two years ago, but now, suddenly, the girl she had once been was back.

"I beg your pardon, but I'd be glad if you'd be telling me what business it is of yours? I don't know you and though you seem to believe you've the right to meddle in everybody's business an' ask any questions you fancy, let me be telling you that you haven't."

If the dog had turned to him and told him to bugger off he could not have been more amazed.

"Well, I beg *your* pardon if I offended you, lass, but it all seems so out of character with what I know about Nelly Bradbury and Lew Earnshaw," he heard himself babbling, but at the same time he felt annoyance run through him, for what the hell did he care what the bloody girl said, or did, or even what had happened to her? If she was staying with Lew Earnshaw, as his guest, or as his mistress, what the devil did it matter to Martin Heywood?

But it seemed the temper had run out of this strange and complex girl and she drooped in on herself, just as he had found her earlier.

"I . . . Mrs Bradbury looked after me. I . . . I wasn't well when I came."

"I can see that," he told her roughly. "What was—"

She didn't seem to notice. "I'd been ill, so I had . . . and then the journey . . . Mrs Bradbury and Mr Earnshaw, didn't they take me in, good souls that they are and then . . . I stayed on, so."

He wouldn't give up though. "You're staying with Lew Earnshaw and you're telling me that Nelly Bradbury has had nothing to say on the subject. One of the most *proper* women I've ever known, is Nelly Bradbury and I just cannot imagine her . . ." He leaned forward and peered with what looked like suspicion and disapproval into her face. "Unless you and Lew are married. Is that it?"

Again she turned to him, her face showing her amazement. "Oh, no, we're not married, me and Lew."

"Then . . . ?"

"Then what?"

"What's going on? Why is it that you and Lew are living together and you not married without Nelly Bradbury poking her nose in as you have just accused me of doing?"

He had her attention again and he could see he was stirring up what might be more resentment in her placid, passive demeanour and, what's more, it was doing her the world of good. Her head rose and so did her chin and if Lew or Nelly, or indeed any of those who were now familiar with her at Edgeclough had seen her they wouldn't have believed it. For the past three months they had become used to her shy, quiet presence, the bending of her head on her slender neck, her hesitant speech, her avoidance of their company, except that of the children.

"Begorra, but you're a one for the questions, aren't you, Mr . . ."

"Martin Heywood, I'm—"

". . . Mr Heywood, and I'm not sure I want to answer them but I suppose, to clear Lew's good name, which is important to me, I'll tell you this. Hasn't he given me his cottage for the time being. I cook for him and clean and wash his clothes and doesn't himself sleep in the cow stalls under the cottage. The men, Mr Bradbury, Mr Marsden and the rest helped him to make it cosy and he says I'm to stay upstairs as long as I please but I – Sweet Mary, I don't know why I'm tellin' you this, for it's no concern of yours – but, well, it won't do an' I must move on an' so I will when I can find a job. Sure an' didn't I want to go in the mill but Lew says—"

"Dear God, child—"

"I'm no child, Mr Heywood."

"No, I suppose you're not but it makes no difference how old you are, you'd not survive a day at a frame. Have you ever been inside a mill? No. Then you haven't the faintest idea what it's like."

"Maggie an' Betty an' the other women work there."

"Aye, ever since they were children and are used to it."

"And don't their children go in at about seven?"

"Aye, and in the mill where Lew's an overlooker he makes sure they aren't overstretched. Others aren't so merciful. Those children you see at Edgeclough are lucky. Their parents are responsible, caring and make sure that if they starve themselves their children are fed. They grow a lot of their own food."

"Yes, I know."

"And they seem to have devised a system where if one family is in a poor way the others help out, but down in Crossfold where there are more houses, if you can call them that, hovels, no more, to the square mile, and more families living in them, ten or twelve persons to a room, it's not so healthy nor so salubrious."

Clare wasn't sure what this strange man meant by the last word but she could guess. She had lived most of her life in a sod cottage but it had been situated in Ireland's good green land beside the beautiful River Shannon. Where wild flowers had grown in the hedgerows and ditches and the air was clean and sweet and pure. Where the rushing gurgle of the stream passing their door on its way to the river was the music to which they fell asleep at night. They might not have had shoes to their feet and were more often than not only just on the right side of starvation but they had been blessed with what they had, for did it not cradle them all in the goodness and sweetness and peace of a loving family. Sharing, supporting one another in whatever sadness came their way and all done in the sight of what Daddy had said was the most beautiful land in the world. They had not questioned him, though Daddy had never been further than Ballynacally in his life and had certainly seen none of the world that lay beyond it but if Daddy said it was so, then it was.

"So what will you do?" Mr Heywood asked after a moment

or two of gazing outward over the valley. "Could you perhaps do housework, or . . . ?"

"Nelly says I've a knack for polishing, but then, she taught me." She smiled and he was amazed and delighted with her small joke.

"Nelly Bradbury always speaks the truth," he said gravely, "and she always speaks her mind. She used to do a bit of scrubbing for my mother years ago."

"Did she now?"

"Aye, and never were there two women with stronger wills than Nelly and my mother. Why they got on so well I'll never know."

"She's been kind to me."

"Aye, she's kind enough."

They were silent for another few minutes, sitting in what seemed to be a harmonious silence, absorbing the crisp air into their lungs while the singing of the streams which fell from a dozen hidden places into the river below sang in their ears and the pale winter sunshine picked out diamonds from the hoar frost that had come in the night. A curlew began its song with long, sweet notes which increased in speed and ended with a magnificent bubbling trill and Clare tipped her head back to listen.

"What's your name?" Mr Heywood said abruptly.

"Clare Hanrahan."

"Well, Clare Hanrahan, if you fancy it I might be able to arrange employment for you at my farm. My housekeeper is always grumbling about the lack of a decent, hardworking maidservant. If you knock at my door tomorrow I'll tell her you're coming. Moorhouse Farm just over that hill. Now I must be on my way so I'll bid you good-day."

His voice was gruff, almost angry-sounding as though he didn't know what the devil was the matter with him, getting involved in the hiring of a maid, for God's sake! Lord, he barely knew the names or status of any of his house-servants. They were there merely to keep Martin Heywood well fed, clean and warm and how they achieved this was not his concern.

It was a mystery that was to plague him for a long time but as he swung into his saddle and put his horse to what seemed a dangerous gallop to Clare, none of this was visible in his expressionless face.

Chapter Five

She lifted the heavy brass knocker then let it drop slowly and quietly. It was a handsome knocker in the shape of a ram's head and was highly polished. In fact the whole building, a manor farmhouse of two hundred years old or more, looked as though it were highly polished, the well-painted door, the many small windows and the immaculate front step that led to the door. It was built of stone, long and low as though squatting out of the way of the winds that scoured the land most of the year. The door had an arched, decorated frame and the door itself was made of stout timbers and looked as though it might need a decent battering ram to get through.

Nobody answered her knock so she lifted the ram's head again and this time let it fall more loudly. There was no sound from within but finally the door opened and a woman in a grey woollen dress covered by a snowy apron stood with her hand on the latch. Her hair was completely covered by a large, white mobcap, frilled about its edge. She might have been handsome but her hair hidden under the cap had been strained back so severely it dragged at her fine skin and gave her eyebrows an arched and surprised look.

"Yes?" she asked shortly, eyeing Clare up and down as though she were some urchin who had been caught stealing, taking in her well-mended clothes, her boots and shawl until her eyes reached her hair. It had been blown every which way by the tramp across the moors and stood about her head like a dark and glossy chrysanthemum bloom and you could see the woman seriously disapproved of it.

"Sure an' I'm to see the ... the housekeeper," Clare stammered, her vow to herself that she would let no one intimidate her flying away with the playful wind.

"Oh yes, an' who ses so?" the maid said haughtily. "I haven't had any *h*instructions about it. Any road, tha' should be at back door, not fetchin' folk to't front as if tha' were gentry. Only Mr Heywood's friends come to't front door so tha'd best be off afore I call one o't grooms."

"Mr Heywood told me to come." Clare's voice shook slightly but she lifted her chin a little higher and stayed where she was.

"Give over," the girl answered, her haughty stare saying she'd never heard such nonsense in her life.

Very much as Nelly and Lew had received the news that she was to walk over to Moorhouse Farm the next day in search of work: with total disbelief and increasing indignation. Inclined to laughter really, for what would Clare Hanrahan know about being a dairy-maid or a laundry-maid, for heaven's sake and what the dickens would Martin Heywood be doing inviting a girl he didn't know to apply for such a post?

"An' where did tha' meet Martin Heywood, lass, that's what I'd like ter know," Nelly said suspiciously, "fer I 'aven't noticed 'im 'angin' about Edgeclough lately, nor is 'e likely to be offerin' jobs ter the likes of us if 'e were."

"Didn't I meet him on the tops when I was up there with Fred? I told him I was looking—"

"Dost tha' mean ter tell me Martin Heywood stopped ter chat wi' thi'?" Lew said dangerously, just as though Clare had invited the man to dally with her. "An' what the hell were tha' doin' up on the tops all on yer own? Tha' knows there's all sorts o' riff-raff hangin' about up there."

"Yes, Mr Heywood said so but—"

"Oh, he did, did he, an' what's it got ter do wi' Martin Heywood where tha' go? He's nowt but a womaniser an'—"

"Sure an' what has that to do with me, Lew Earnshaw? If I'm taken on I'll not be sittin' down to dinner with him."

If he was surprised by her sharp tone where there had only been softness and quietness, he made no show of it. "I'm just warnin' yer. Tha'd best be careful round him. Steer clear of 'im if he crosses tha' path again, d'you hear?"

Both Clare and Nelly stared at him in consternation as jealousy sank its poisonous fangs into his heart and made him say more than he should. Nelly had known almost from the start that Lew Earnshaw loved Clare Hanrahan and was waiting patiently, or as patiently as her nature allowed, for him to declare himself, since it would solve two problems at once. Nelly had become fond of the strange Irish girl who had drifted into their lives and apart from the upheaval it had caused in Lew's living arrangements believed that they would suit each other admirably. It would keep Clare here, safe and sound where Nelly wanted her to be, and it would be good for Lew to have a woman in his bed, one whom Nelly approved of, naturally, to keep him warm and satisfied of a bitter winter's night, and a wife at his hearth to see to his creature comforts as Nelly was training Clare up to be. She was showing a great deal of promise and if only Lew would stir his stumps – she'd dropped enough hints and what more could she do? – they could have a spring wedding and everything settled entirely to Nelly's satisfaction.

And Clare was also aware of the fact that Lew thought of her as more than a friend or some lost and injured waif he had taken in and put together again. He had never spoken of his feelings but they were implicit in the warm smile which, though he smiled often, was totally different to the ones he bestowed on others. In the way his eyes followed her and the sudden tension in him when she came unexpectedly into a room.

"Well, I don't know what ter say," said Nelly, who had never before been stuck for a word, but it seemed the statement was not true and was only the opening remark of many. "Except I'm not 'appy about it, dost tha' 'ear me? What's wrong wi' stayin' wi' us, tha' friends? When tha's stronger Lew'd get thi' inter't mill, wouldn't thi', lad, where 'e could keep an eye on thi' an' then ..." She didn't finish her sentence, for it involved the future when, if she had anything to do with it, Lew and Clare would be married and if Lew, who was bringing in a decent wage as an overlooker, had a mind for it, Clare would not need to work at all. If Nelly knew Lew, who was a manly man, virile and lusty, there'd be a baby before the year was out which would mean that Clare would be firmly anchored where she, Nelly, could keep an eye on things. Nelly had two daughters, Mildred and Dorcas, but she could not remember ever being as fond of them as she was of Clare. They were independent, as she had made them, sturdy lasses, self-sufficient, like her, undemonstrative, good little workers at William Hopkinson's Townecliff Mill where Lew worked too, which was a comfort to her. They brought in a few bob a week, which with her Will and son Arthur's wage, and the few pence Annie and Maggie and Betty paid her to keep an eye on their younger children, meant that all in all the Bradburys managed with what might seem comfort to those crammed into the hovels that housed the hundreds of mill workers in Crossfold. She didn't want Clare to go into the mill, strange as it might seem since both her daughters were there, for Clare had a delicacy about her, a kind of ladylike frailty, a fragile loveliness which awoke the protective side of Nelly's nature. But at least as a spinner she would come home every night and Nelly would still have her in her sights.

"Tha' know tha'll live in at Moorhouse, don't tha'," she snapped. "They'll not 'ave thi' traipsin' across moor every mornin' an' night. An' t'work'll be 'eavy, scrubbin' all day long, fer they'll not set thi' on as a parlour-maid. No, it'll be a sackin' apron an' a mobcap, a bucket an' brush, up ter tha' elbows in 'ot water ..."

"I don't mind that, Nelly. I'm used to hard work, so I am. From the age of five I dug potatoes and peat from dawn till dusk when ... when ..." She faltered for a moment, since she had told no one of her past and wasn't about to do so now. She had put that section of her life firmly into a secret part of her heart where no one could look, except herself when she could stand the pain, and the loveliness of the memory of it. "So I'll soon get into the way o' things. Nelly, I must work, I must. Don't you understand? I can't go on living here on your charity."

"Give over, charity indeed." Lew, who had sat quietly during this exchange, exploded into anger and like men who are quiet and reasonable for the most part, his anger was all the more terrible. "Tha' work fer me an' by rights I should be payin' tha' wages. In fact, I'll start right away. Tha' cleans an' cooks an' ... an' tha've ..." He turned in anguish to Nelly. "Tell 'er, Nelly. Tell 'er she's not ter go. Tell 'er as 'ow we'll not 'ave it."

"Tha' tell 'er, Lew Earnshaw. Go on, lad, tell 'er what's in tha'." But Lew, who was a self-contained man and had no wish to pour out what was in his heart in front of Nelly, merely turned away and reached for his pipe. He was a self-educated man who still attended lectures at the Mechanics Institute on history and music and such things and every Thursday night met with others of like mind to discuss works of literature and philosophy and was an ardent member of the Chartist movement of which there was a secret group in Crossfold. There had been threats of uprisings in Nottingham, Leeds, York, Newcastle and Manchester over the years in which Lew had been involved, threats of strikes which Lew had encouraged, for how else was the working man to get what he was entitled to, which was equality. Unless he was careful and made sure his employer did not hear of it, which Nelly constantly begged him to do, he could be in trouble, for mill owners and manufacturers alike could not abide Chartism, nor their members who would have the People's Charter or die in the attempt. He drank a pint of ale once a week in the Packhorse and read the tavern's copy of the *Northern Star,* talked to others who were of the Chartist persuasion like himself and in Nelly's opinion marriage to Clare would settle him down and get rid of all this political nonsense once and for all.

She had gone when Lew asked Clare to marry him and when she refused, quietly and gently, for she had been expecting it, he had turned away, his face bleak. She tried to explain to him that it was not fair or right of her to take advantage of his fondness for her just to find a safe harbour. He was honest and warm-hearted and would make no demands on her she could not satisfy but he deserved a wife who would return his affection. She had no emotion in her heart, which was still broken, beyond that of friendship, but as she had done her best to express her reasons he had turned away from her, his face grim, and simply walked out of the house. When she left the next morning to face the tramp across the moor to Moorhouse Farm, he was not there.

"Tha're set on goin' then," Nelly said grimly from her doorstep, bitterly disappointed that Lew had been unable to persuade Clare to stay.

"Yes, Nelly, I am."

"Then watch thassen, lass. Tha'll cop it if tha' cross Clarice Case."

"Who's she, Nelly?"

"She's 'ousekeeper ter Martin Heywood."

"I haven't got the job yet, Nelly."

"Lass, it's yourn if Martin Heywood ses it's yourn."

"If I'm not back by bedtime . . ."

"I'll know tha're not comin' but tha'll not ferget us, will tha'?"

With a swift movement of what might have been despair Clare hurled herself at Nelly and enfolded her in her arms, crushing her to her, pressing Nelly's face into her shoulder. Nelly did not resist and she did not respond, for such things were not her way. Her hands rose at Clare's back, floating in mid-air but not touching her, then she pulled herself away.

"Give over, lass, tha'd think tha' were off ter Lundun instead of over th'ill ter't next valley."

"Nelly . . . acushla," calling Nelly by the endearment her own mother had used.

"Gerron wi' tha', lass."

"Ye'll not be lettin' Fred follow me, Nelly?"

"It'll not be Fred as follers thi', lass." Then Nelly turned and went indoors. Clare walked away quickly before she changed her mind.

And here she was treading carefully along a hallway on brightly polished flagstones which were shaded from deep ox red to the warm pink of a carnation with a touch here and there of grey or blue. There was an enormous hallstand made from some solid wood that looked as though it had grown there, set in the centre with an oval mirror. There were capes and cloaks and caps hanging on pegs and in an umbrella stand beneath the mirror were walking-sticks of every shape and size along with several umbrellas.

There were stone steps, wide and shallow, leading to some upper reaches of the house, well worn and well scrubbed, with a handsome and elaborately carved wooden balustrade. Clare peered upwards but the maid called out to her to keep up and at the end of a long, quite narrow passage they came out into the largest room Clare had ever seen in her life. Again the floor was of stone flags, spotlessly clean, and at one end, just about to finish her scrubbing, was a little creature who looked as though she'd never have the strength to wring out her cloth never mind lift the bucket to empty it. On her head was a cap similar to the one worn by the maid who had let Clare in. The rest of her was shrouded in sacking.

"Wait here," the first maid said and Clare did as she was told, standing just inside the kitchen door and glad of it, for it gave her a chance to look about her at this splendid room whose every surface was so highly polished it reflected the light and hurt the eyes. There were two enormous tables bearing copper pans, bowls filled with fruit, a pair of scales on each, glazed crocks which seemed to contain flour, or sugar, or was it salt, large, well-scoured chopping boards, and on the end of one table half a dozen pies straight from the oven. There were stools to the sides of the tables and by the fire a rocking-chair. The walls were tiled in white, and along one, covering the whole wall, was a splendid dresser with what seemed to be hundreds of pieces of crockery of every sort, along with copper utensils, silver covered dishes and much more, the use for which was a mystery to a girl who had thought Lew Earnshaw's bits and pieces were a miracle. Two massive ranges stood side by side on a second wall, the fire between glowing with coals and holding a gently steaming kettle. Above the ovens was a contraption made of slatted wood which was drawn up almost to the ceiling and hanging over it were several freshly ironed white aprons and overalls.

The girl at the bucket got to her feet wearily and turned a shy smile on Clare who smiled back. She was not the room's only occupant. A second girl was busy at a bowl, whisking and stirring as though her life depended on it and though she cast a curious glance at Clare she did not smile or speak.

The first maid came hurrying back from wherever it was she had been, coming into the kitchen as though she hadn't a moment to spare and would never catch up after this interruption, beckoning to Clare imperiously.

"Mrs Case'll see you now." And with a nod in the direction of a door along another narrow passage, left her to find her own way.

She tapped at the door and when a voice within told her to enter – just that: "Enter" – she moved hesitantly inside. Again she was overwhelmed by the size and what she saw as the splendour of the room. It was no more than a housekeeper's parlour but to the girl who had lived in a sod cottage for the first fifteen years of her life it might have been the queen's drawing-room in her palace. There was a good fire in the blackleaded grate, and standing on the hearth was a pair of copper fire tongs, plus a coal bucket of a handsome polished wood. There was a deep armchair with many cushions, a footstool in front of it, and beside it a round table, small and low enough to be immediately to hand, on which stood a white china teapot with cups and saucers to match. The carpet was red and blue and very cheerful and there were pictures on the walls of animals and poultry and birds flying against a stormy sky. The curtains at the window were heavy and long and Clare could imagine how cosy the room would be when they were drawn.

There was a massive table, leather-covered, and behind it sat a woman, well bosomed, her face empty of all expression and her iron-grey hair drawn back in exactly the same way as the maid's.

Neither of them spoke, Clare because she hadn't the slightest notion of what to say since she had never before applied for work, at least of this sort, and the housekeeper because it was a habit of hers to let her underlings droop and dither and wonder why they had been summoned to Mrs Case's private parlour.

Since somebody had to speak Mrs Case did so.

"Your name?" she asked abruptly.

"Clare Hanrahan, missis."

"Irish?" as though Clare had professed herself to be some heathen savage from a land beyond the reach of civilisation.

"I am." Clare felt a small surge of what might have been anger at the woman's contemptuous dismissal of the Irish race but she kept it under control, for she wanted this job.

"Mr Heywood didn't tell me you were Irish."

"Sure an' I'm sorry about that, missis, but he did know."

"So you say, and before another word is spoken I'd be obliged if you would address me either as Mrs Case, or ma'am. I am the housekeeper at Moorhouse, and also the cook. I run the house for Mr Heywood and it is not customary, at least in *this* country, to address someone as *missis!*"

"I'm sorry, ma'am."

Mrs Case sniffed as though to say and so she should be,

again falling into silence as she studied Clare from head to foot. She even stood up the better to see her, walking round her as though she were an exhibit at a waxwork show. What she saw evidently satisfied her. Clare had bathed that morning in the tin tub before the fire, after locking the door when Lew had gone. She had washed her hair which lay about her head in a bright swathe of glossy curls. Her underwear was clean and so were her boots which she had polished the night before, glad that she had saved them for this special occasion. Everything about her was immaculate, even the shawl which had once been Nelly's and the bundle she had in her hand containing her change of underwear. Anticipating that the job was hers and that she would begin at once, she had brought everything she owned, even her clogs which were wrapped up in the bundle.

Mrs Case sat down again and, instead of studying Clare, gave her own hands a close look, twisting them in one another as though she were washing them, then she looked up, her face inscrutable.

"I'm not happy about this, you know. It is not customary for the master of the house to engage a servant, and I'm not happy about it but it seems there is nothing to be done. I shall give you a month's trial, I told the master that, and if you don't suit me, and let me say I'm hard to please, then you shall go. Is that understood?" It was clear she thought her master mad and Clare up to something, perhaps with him, but she had been given her instructions and could do nothing about it. She had tried, arguing with Martin Heywood who was no more than a slip of a lad to her who had worked at Moorhouse since he was born but it had done no good. He had the Heywood obstinacy and for reasons best known to himself he had asked her, commanded her, to take on this Irish biddy who didn't look as though she had a good day's work in her. Thin and pale, with a look about her of . . . well, Clarice Case could only call it great sadness. But at least she was clean and quiet. Mrs Case had a dislike of talkative servants.

She stood up without warning and walked round the table to the door, indicating with a twitch of her head that Clare was to follow her.

"You'll start in the kitchen, of course. Scullery-maid. Do you know what that is?"

And Clare, who was almost running to keep up with her, had to admit that she didn't.

Mrs Case sighed dramatically. "Gracie, who should have finished the kitchen floor by now, will show you where to put your things and where you will sleep and then you can help her. The passages to the back door need doing, the scullery, the pantries, the stillroom and the steps. When you have done that report back to me. I am to cook the master's lunch – he is at home today – and when I have finished the kitchen will need doing again. Is that clear or shall I repeat it?" Just as though Clare were a particularly obtuse child who had to be told twice, or even three times how to go about things.

"No, ma'am. I'm to be scrubbing the passages to the back door, so I am, the scullery, the pantries, the stillroom and the steps and then, when yourself's finished the cooking, the kitchen floor."

If Mrs Case was surprised she did not show it, merely turning, as they entered the kitchen and saying with irritation, "And do try not to speak in that Irish way, please."

That night she fell like a log into the narrow, painfully clean bed which Gracie had indicated was to be hers. She removed her boots, her skirt and bodice, ignoring the voluminous nightgown Gracie held out to her and Gracie's words that Mrs Case'd not like it if she slept in her clothes. She was asleep almost before her head touched the hard pillow, so that Gracie, who was a lonely little scrap of a girl who had left her mam and pa and a dozen smaller brothers and sisters at the age of twelve, and who had been looking forward to a bit of prattle with the new girl, fell into her own bed in great disappointment. It had made a wonderful difference to her own drudgery having Clare work beside her, for Clare seemed to find a great deal of satisfaction in going like a mad thing from one end of the place to the other, and then when she had finished approaching Mrs Case and asking her if there was anything else she wanted doing. Gracie could see that even Mrs Case was a bit confounded.

"Well, there's a pile of pans need scouring and Belle's busy with those vegetables so you could make a start on them. Have you ever cleaned pans?" she asked with that little curl to her lip which she used when she was feeling nasty, just as though there were anybody in the world who hadn't at one time or another cleaned a pan, Gracie had thought. She made out that the new girl, who was Irish, probably ate with her fingers off a bit of newspaper and coming from where she did had never seen a pan in her life.

"Very well, ma'am. In the scullery, is it?" Clare had scrubbed the scullery floor and so knew just where that was.

"Yes, and I want to see my face in them when you've finished," says Mrs Case.

"Yes, ma'am, and so you shall," said the new girl and Mrs Case didn't like that. She thought the new girl was being what Mrs Case called "impudent" and for the next five minutes she was treated to Mrs Case's carping reminder that she was here on trial and to watch her manners, while the new girl, who had a flush on her cheeks by now that you could warm your hands on, remained absolutely still, her face blank, her eyes ... well, if Gracie had known the word she would have said "inscrutable".

She had enjoyed her food, though, Gracie could tell that, for she tucked in with the rest of them round the kitchen table and ate every scrap of what was put before her. Mind you, it was good food, the best that Gracie herself had ever tasted, for Mrs Case, whatever else she was, was a good cook. They all came in to eat, the men from the yard and the fields about the farmhouse, the grooms and some of the shepherds and though they eyed the new girl curiously none of them spoke to her or indeed to anyone else, for while Mrs Case was about you kept your trap shut.

Clare awoke in the night and for a heartcatching moment didn't know where she was or what had awoken her. Gracie's gentle snoring reminded her. It was January and the room in the attic space, which it seemed she was to share with Gracie, was as cold as death. The window was tightly closed but she thought the sound that had woken her came from outside. The room had a dormer window which overlooked the stable yard and though she was loth to leave the warmth of her bed which, she had to admit, had plenty of soft blankets on it, she crept to the window and peeped out. She had no idea what the time was but there was a bright, silvery crescent of moon in the blue-black sky and stars by the million which helped to light the yard as though lanterns were hung at every corner.

Martin Heywood was just dismounting from his beautiful black mare, calling out in a voice which said he didn't give a damn who he woke, telling a man who ran towards him to give Sable a good rub down and a handful of oats.

He stood for a moment as the groom led the animal away, stretching and yawning and then, as though he knew where she would be, he looked directly up at the window. She was certain he couldn't see her, for there was a sketch of a curtain across the glass but still he continued to stare upwards and she continued to stare down.

Then, turning on his heel, he strode towards the kitchen door. She got back into her warm bed, feeling a quite unusual sense of reassurance, though why she didn't know, then at once fell into a deep and dreamless sleep.

Chapter Six

She thought she would never get used to the vista which was hers from morning until night, the endless vista of the warmly coloured flags of the scullery, the kitchen, the many passages which led here and there in the old farmhouse, the pantry, and the steps that led out from the kitchen to the yard. Nothing else, no change in her routine which was to fill her bucket at six o'clock each morning with the hot water that was for ever bubbling on the stove. Into the hot water a certain amount of caustic soda had to be tipped, for it was this, Mrs Case insisted, that brought off the grease, the deposits dropped by careless kitchen-maids, not *her* naturally, and which must not be left on the flags to become fixed. It played havoc with the skin of her hands and she and Gracie both suffered with raw chilblains, Gracie's worse than hers since she had been at it all winter. Mrs Case was a fanatic about cleanliness and the floors were done at least twice a day and Clare was often to wonder how Gracie had managed before she came. Their last wearying effort was usually about seven thirty in the evening when the men had eaten and gone, the master's meal was on the dinner table and Mrs Case allowed her staff to relax before they were sent off to their beds. Mrs Case directed them all, except for the activities of the outside men, of course, dictating what they should do and when they should do it every minute of the day from when they got out of their beds at a time she decided on, until they got back into them, again at her dictate.

Though Clarice Case wouldn't dream of telling her so she was pleased with the way the new girl shaped. She had watched her like a hawk in those first weeks for any sign that she and the master might be more to each other than was desirable, since her suspicions had been fiercely aroused by the master's request, or rather his order for her to employ the Irish girl. But the girl rarely left the kitchen, let alone the house and as far as Clarice Case was aware, and she would have known if they had, she and Martin Heywood had never met since she had arrived, let alone exchanged a word. On the day she started work in the kitchen he had sent for Mrs Case and asked if she had turned up but after that he had shown not a scrap of interest in her so what she was to make of that Clarice Case didn't know. The girl was extremely hardworking, despite her seeming frailty. She was willing and conscientious and once she had been shown a task she did it with a minimum of fuss without having to be told again, as Gracie did. She never got what Mrs Case called "flummoxed" though now and again the housekeeper saw a gleam of defiance in her eye when she, Mrs Case, gave Gracie the rounds of the kitchen. She would often make Gracie cry but never the new girl, no matter how she goaded her and so, realising the girl would never be provoked, she stopped doing it.

Let it be said that the housekeeper was not a cruel woman as many are who have others in their domain. The browbeating she inflicted on her staff was merely a test of their stamina, for she demanded a servant be strong and steadfast and capable of bearing the hardships that went hand in glove with domestic service. From six in the morning until sometimes ten or eleven at night they laboured and she wanted no weaklings. Once they had proved themselves, as Thirza, who was head housemaid, as Belle who was kitchen-maid had proved themselves, she treated them fairly and even with a certain degree of kindness. Gracie was about halfway there!

She began to watch the new girl even more closely, not just for signs of intimacy with the master, but in the way she went about things to do with her work. She rarely spoke to anyone, and certainly none of the men. She was polite and pleasant with the other maidservants and would give a helping hand if asked and she got on with her work if not cheerfully, then without complaint. She was fastidiously clean, her growing hair, which had been a source of much comment at first, always tucked tidily into her cap. When questioned on why it was cut so short the new girl had answered curtly that she had been ill. No more than that, her expression defying them to quiz her further. They had accepted it and no more was said.

She had begun to look better. She had put on a bit of weight, since if there was one thing Mrs Case insisted upon, which was rare in domestic service, it was that those under her, and that included the men outside, ate good, nourishing, appetising food, and plenty of it, and thus she kept them strong and capable of doing a good day's work for which Mr Heywood paid decent wages. Mr Starling the gardener, who had, it was said, green fingers, handed so much stuff over the kitchen step each day Clare often wondered how it was all going to be eaten. Cabbages and sprouts, carrots, onions, leeks and marrows, potatoes by the bushel, or so it seemed, much of which went into Mrs Case's stockpot from which she made the most delicious soup which they were encouraged to eat several times a day. There was fruit, grown at this time of the year in Mr Starling's greenhouses, oranges and tangerines, apricots and grapes, apples and pears stored from last summer and not just for Mr Heywood and his guests to consume, but the servants as well. Clare had never tasted half of them, nor indeed the delicious cakes and tarts, the biscuits and puddings Mrs Case seemed to turn out in an endless stream. She was training Belle and between them they fed the Moorhouse servants as well as the nobility up in London, probably better, for Mrs Case was one of those enlightened women who believed that good food produced good bones and teeth and healthy flesh.

Clare thrived on it, despite the hard work she did, gaining a little colour in her cheeks, growing strong and supple, due no doubt to her endeavours with the scrubbing brush, and when Mrs Case told her casually that she was to give the front steps, the wide hallway that led to the front door, the staircase up to the bedrooms and the stone passages that led to the bedrooms a going over, in fact the *front* of the house, she was not to know that she had been given a promotion. This was not, of course, until she had been at Moorhouse Farm for three months. Thirza, who was the only maid Mrs Case trusted with this important task, though it wasn't strictly speaking in Thirza's duties, was so pleased she began to make little overtures of friendship towards the Irish girl of whom she had been so contemptuous on that first day.

On the fourth Sunday after her arrival, just after dinner which they ate at noon, she was flustered when Mrs Case, from her rocking-chair by the kitchen fire where she liked to drink tea and oversee the work of her handmaidens, asked her what she thought she was doing with that bucket.

Clare stood still, her mouth agape and the expression in her eyes bewildered, for she could think of nothing she had done wrong. She was so surprised she began to stammer, as she had her every move planned down to the last detail and Mrs Case seemed to approve of it so why was she to be reprimanded?

"Why . . . I'm after fillin' it, ma'am. To be sure there's the pantry . . ."

Mrs Case had got over her aversion to what she called the new girl's Irish way of talking, mainly because she liked the new girl's way of working.

"I take it you don't want to have your half day off then?" Mrs Case sipped her tea and though she had said it without malice she was evidently enjoying her maid's confusion.

"My . . . ?"

"This is not a prison, Clare, where the inmates are forced to spend their time every minute of every day until their release."

"I didn't think ..."

"That's the trouble with you young girls, you never think." Which was unfair and she knew it, for the new girl, as she was still called, had a good brain and if she stayed on, which it seemed she would, Mrs Case had plans for her.

"Yes, Mrs Case, but ..."

"Don't you want to have an afternoon off, girl? Would you rather stay here and scrub out the pantry because if you would I don't mind."

Mrs Case usually allowed Sunday to be a more relaxed day than weekdays since Mr Heywood was often off visiting here and there in the area, perhaps hunting over the hills with the small, local hunt, shooting across his own private grouse moor, fishing, or any of the other gentlemanly pursuits the gentry got up to at different seasons of the year. Of course, Martin Heywood was not gentry. He was a hardworking sheep farmer who spent his time raising his flock and selling his wool to the mill owners across the Pennines. He had half a dozen shepherds to keep an eye on things but today the reason for the leisured atmosphere was because it was lambing time and all the men were out on the hills checking for the new arrivals. Martin Heywood's rams had been introduced to his flock and had remained there for about six weeks to make sure that every ewe conceived. This took place in September when the ewes came into season and now, five months later, their offspring were making an appearance. It was a busy time so that even the master was called in to help. In his and the men's absence the day was as good as a day off, the maidservants told one another.

There had been snow in the new year but on the whole, apart from the odd day of hard frost, it had been a relatively mild winter and the maidservants drifted about the kitchen, doing their work certainly but at a slower pace. They smiled dutifully at Mrs Case's witticism.

"I didn't know ..."

"Didn't you notice when Thirza was absent last Sunday, or Belle the Sunday before?"

"Well, yes, but I thought . . ."

"Oh, go on, lass, get your bonnet on and go and do . . . well, whatever you want to do providing it's decent and make sure you're back before dark."

She hadn't a bonnet but whirling her shawl about her and shouting goodbye to Gracie who was at the back kitchen steps, her nose to the worn stone, she ran across the yard and out of the gate into the lane. She had barely been out of the farmhouse since she arrived, apart from a brief venture into the stable yard at Mrs Case's instigation to tell the men to look lively, for their dinner was on the table. She had approached the building from the front on that first day but she had been aware of nothing except its size. She supposed that one day she would be allowed, if she kept in Mrs Case's good books, to have a look about the house beyond the wide flagged hallway and upstairs passages, at what she knew to be many rooms, on both floors, and which Gracie had told her, though Gracie herself had never seen them, were quite splendid. She knew there was a garden, a flower garden at the front and to the side and vast kitchen gardens at the back but she had yet to see them.

The lane along which the hawthorn hedge was beginning to show signs of spring led directly on to the moor and before she knew it, climbing steadily and easily, she was on the top of Friars Mere. It was still cold but as it had done the last time she was here the sun shone and in the newly sprouting grass violet roots were sending up little green trumpets of new leaves. The gorse was well on its way to golden glory and down in the valley bottom the elm trees were just breaking out into blossom and along the river bank she could make out the willows which were showing dainty white catkins. A lark sounded its heartbreaking song but though she tipped her head back until she thought her neck might break, peering up into the blue arch of the sky, she could not spot it.

Archie was the first one to see her as she strode down the rutted track to Edgeclough. He had his bottom on his mam's step and in his arms was Cat who seemed not to mind being tightly clasped about her belly. Archie's baby face was disconsolate, since he had been refused permission to accompany his brothers, Frankie and Nipper, up on to the open moor where they were off to find and, hopefully, trap a rabbit or two. When he saw Clare his face lit up, he dropped Cat who slunk off thankfully, and, pointing and babbling, not one word intelligible except her name, scampered on his thin little legs towards her.

Because it was fine most of them were outdoors, the younger girls playing their interminable games, the women gossiping at their doors, the men, pipe smoke drifting about their heads, hammering, digging, or merely pretending to do so in case their wives should find some task for them in the house.

Lavender was banging her mam's rag rug against the wall of the house, the dust from it rising about her truculent face, for she and Poppy, who had been roped in to help her, would much rather be out on the moor as the lads were. But Sunday was the day for scrubbing and scouring, for donkey-stoning the front step and polishing windows and as young girls who would one day be wives and mothers they were being trained to be true Lancashire housewives.

When she saw Clare she let out a screech which lifted every head in the vicinity so that those who had not been alerted by Archie stopped what they were doing to stare at the girl they had not been awfully sure they would ever see again. She had come unexpectedly into their lives and just as unexpectedly gone out of it again, without a word of goodbye, and though Nelly had explained what had happened and where she had gone they had not been quite sure what to make of it, or her. Now she was back among them looking blooming, they all agreed, a smile on her face which they remembered as shy and serious, ready to split it into two.

Bending down, she lifted Archie in her arms, swinging him round and round until he squealed, then, as he put his arms about her neck, nuzzling into the soft spot under his baby chin as she had once done with Declan.

"It's Clare," Lavender shouted as though none of them had recognised her, only herself. Suddenly shy, she skidded to a halt before Clare and the giggling boy but Clare reached out an arm and dragged her to her, saying nothing, and neither did Lavender, for they were both somewhat overwhelmed by the strength of their feelings.

The women smiled a welcome, stepping over their front steps which they had just donkey-stoned, like Lavender pleased to see her but, somewhat more restrained than the young girl, in the way of their kind not making any great show of it.

The children did though. She might have been the queen come up for a visit from London the fuss they made of her, swirling about her, dragging on her hands, all talking at once, drawing her forward until she stood in front of Nelly's cottage where Nelly herself was leaning her shoulder on the door frame.

From her casual manner she might have seen Clare yesterday, but when Clare moved nearer she could see the moistness of her eyes and the glow on her cheek and, with a soft sound and whether Nelly liked it or not, she put her arms about her and held her for a second or two. But Nelly, being Nelly, soon began to struggle and push her away, telling her not to be such a daft "apporth" though every last one of them who knew Nelly Bradbury was as soft as clarts could see she was secretly pleased.

"Where's Lew?" Clare asked.

"He's 'ere," a quiet voice said behind her and when she spun round there he was, a spade still in his hand, the soles of his clogs thick with the good rich soil in which he had been digging. His hair was tumbled about his forehead and already his face was brown with sunshine.

Though their parting had been difficult and Clare had been prepared for a cold welcome she should have realised, she told herself later, that it was not Lew's way to bear a grudge. She had refused his offer of marriage and in many men this would have been a signal to end their friendship, but he was the same as he had always been. He was evidently much moved at the sight of her, despite their unhappy parting, though he did his best not to show it. A smile hovered at the corners of his lips and his eyes crinkled and in them was the strength of his love for her for all to see. She had refused him the last time and he had taken it hard but he was a stubborn man, and there is nothing stronger than a stubborn man who is in love, his expression told her. Nevertheless he seemed unsteady, not at all sure how to greet her or how she would receive him. He was tall, lean and strong and yet he was vulnerable, she could see that, and when Iggy Marsden shouted out, "Go on, lad, aren't tha' gonner give 'er a kiss", his face took on the hue of a tomato. Nelly tutted at Iggy's lack of diplomacy and his wife gave him a sharp nudge in the ribs at which he looked surprised, for they all knew how Lew felt about this bonny Irish lass, and she was bonny now.

"I don't think he is, Iggy" – Clare laughed to ease the situation – "so I'll be givin' him one instead." And leaning close to him, smelling the male sweat on him, the aroma of the soil in which he had been digging and a pleasant fragrance which came from some bush he had tangled with, she kissed him heartily on the cheek. At once he threw down the spade and putting his arms about her drew her to him, placing his cheek on hers and holding her quietly in the safe harbour of his arms.

"Clare ..." he murmured in her ear, then, laughing, he let her go. "There, Iggy Marsden, are't satisfied," he roared and what might have been an awkward moment was defused.

She had to spend a moment or two in each of the five cottages of the neighbours, admiring Marie Bretherton's new baby who was a week old, answering the children's eager questions. They all seemed genuinely pleased to see her as though she were a member of each family who had been gone for a while. The women, in the privacy of their homes, hugged her, for had they not been instrumental in returning her to the health she now possessed? The men were vastly embarrassed when she pretended she was going to hug them too, for they were north countrymen, dour and uneasy with emotion, but smiling nevertheless, and something inside Clare Hanrahan began to loosen its iron grip on her heart, something warm and soothing, like a balm on a wound that has ached and ached for a long time.

At last it was Nelly's turn.

"Now turn thi' round an' let's get a good look at thi'," she ordered when at last Clare was inside her own door and they were alone. Lew, as though he knew they needed time to be on their own, had returned to his vegetable patch and could be seen, pipe smoke wreathing about his dark head, patiently turning the hard ground in readiness for spring planting.

Clare obediently spun round. She was wearing the decent grey woollen dress which Mrs Case had pressed on her, saying she'd have no girl of hers walking about for all the world to see in that dreadful attire Clare had come in and Clare was to put it into the furnace at the back of the house at once. Mrs Case said it rebounded on her if her girls went about looking as though they'd been dressed from a rag-bag and she'd not have it and Clare, having the measure of Mrs Case by now, had not argued. The dress was plain but had a snowy white collar and cuffs and she looked well in it and a far cry from the waif who had been carried over Lew's doorstep four months ago. She even had a touch of colour in her cheeks and her eyes shone with health and what Nelly knew was delight in her warm welcome. She wore her much-polished boots and the shawl Nelly had given her and looked like a servant girl from a decent household, which she was, but the loveliness that had been hers before the Troubles was returning to her. Her hair was growing and soon would be long enough to tie up with a ribbon, one of which, in scarlet satin, Nelly happened to have in a drawer. Even her breasts had developed, softly filling the front of the bodice of the gown. The lovely Irish looks of her were slowly emerging and though Nelly seemed satisfied by what she saw she also felt a measure of unease, for what man, and there were many in Martin Heywood's household, including Martin himself, could ignore her delicate beauty. She wished to God she and Lew could be wed, or at least the promise of it, for then Nelly would be able to let go her vague worries.

When she had sat Clare in the chair before the fire and put a cup of tea in her hand Nelly said, "Now then, lass, tell me all about it. Dost tha' get on wi' Clarice Case? I tell thi', when I worked there, that were in days o' old Mrs Heywood, she were head maid and she did 'er best ter 'ave 'er way ower everythin' as went on in't kitchen. Mrs Ball, 'oo were 'ousekeeper then, were gettin' old an' Clarice were determined ter 'ave 'er job. She did an' all."

"Sure an' she's not so bad, Nelly, as long as you're willin' to work hard. Aren't I scrubbin' from morning till night but I don't seem to suffer from it. I sleep well and you've never seen such food."

"Aye, I can see that. Tha've put on a bit o' weight an' it suits thi'. So everything's all right then?"

"Except the chilblains, Nelly. Me an' Gracie'd be glad of something to put on them, if you've such a thing."

"Aye, lass, that I 'ave." And, standing up, Nelly moved to the cupboard where she rummaged for a moment before producing a pot of something. "'Ere, put that on at night an' they'll be right as rain by't weekend. Now, what about this Gracie an't'other girls. Dost treat tha' right? Friendly, I mean."

"Oh yes, they're comin' round. Tell me, Nelly, why is it everyone's against the Irish?"

"Because tha're tekkin' work from men an' women as were born 'ere, lass. Tha' work fer starvation wages an' 'oo can blame yer fer where there's babbies ter be fed a mother'll work fer owt."

They talked for an hour or so but the afternoon was drawing in and mindful of Mrs Case's warning and the four-mile walk she had ahead of her, Clare began to look round her for her shawl.

"I'd best be off, Nelly, but won't I be back in four weeks' time? Would you believe it," she exulted, "I'm to have a Sunday afternoon off every month so look out for me."

"That I will, lass, now tha'd best be sayin' goodbye ter Lew. I'm surprised 'e's not bin in ter see tha'."

But it seemed Lew had his plans made, for when Clare appeared at the door of Nelly's cottage he was there waiting for her.

"I'll walk thi' back," he said shortly, his manner saying he'd have no arguments.

"Really, Lew, sure an' won't I be fine? There's no need."

"I'll walk thi' back," he said stubbornly, moving on a few steps where he turned to look back at her. She sighed, then, bending down to the children who clustered about her skirt, she hugged them one by one, holding Archie to her as though her arms, bereft of Declan, needed it.

"I'll see you all in four weeks, so I will," she told them, looking especially at Lavender who would have walked with her if Lew had not been there. She and Lavender, if chance was kind, might become good friends, she thought, despite the two-year gap in their ages.

They walked side by side in silence, striding out easily, the crisp air striking them sharp blows which brought colour to their cheeks and made them gasp. Clare's shawl, which she had tied loosely about her shoulders, whipped back and out, like the wings of a bird, and Lew made her stop while he tied it securely about her, his hands lingering for a moment longer than was necessary at her shoulders and his eyes looked steadily into hers. There was kindness and courage in them and she wished desperately that she could return the feelings he had for her. He must have read her mind.

"I'll never stop asking tha', Clare. I know tha' don't feel what I feel but I know tha' feel summat an' one day it'll be enough."

"Lew . . ." Though she made no attempt to withdraw from him he let her go and stepped back.

"I know, my lass, an' I'll not rush thi' but think on. When tha're ready I'll be waitin'. Now, 'ave thi' a minute ter sit. There's summat else I want ter say."

"Of course," sitting obediently on a rock. He sat down beside her and for a moment they were quiet as they watched the flight of a bird, a smudged charcoal sketch of wings against the pink winter sky; then he turned and took her hand.

"What would tha' say if I was ter teach tha' ter read. Would tha' like that?"

The breath left her body and she turned to him with a gasp, her eyes brilliant with excitement, her hand gripping his with a force that made him wince.

"Lew . . . oh, Lew . . ."

He smiled, his white teeth gleaming in the growing darkness. "I tekk it tha' would?"

"Oh yes, but when?"

"Can'st get out of an evening? After they've gone ter bed, happen."

She thought of Gracie and she thought of Mrs Case and her heart quailed, but, surely, with the coming of the lighter evenings something could be arranged. She didn't speak, she couldn't but Lew knew what was in her mind. He could see it in her blazing eyes as he continued.

"Next time tha' come over I'll 'ave summat worked out. Books an' pencils an' things I want tha' ter do when tha's alone. Tha'll 'ave ter work bloody 'ard, lass, but us'll manage it fer it's summat we both want. Now, I'll say no more. We'd best get on." He stood up ready to continue and no matter what she said or how she protested he insisted on walking her to the end of the lane that led to the stable yard gate.

"Well, that's done you good, I must say," Mrs Case remarked somewhat suspiciously as Clare walked into the kitchen. "I hope you've not been with some lad, young lady," for Clare's eyes were shining and her cheeks were rosy which, in Mrs Case's mind, could mean only one thing.

"No, I haven't, Mrs Case. I'm not bothered with lads and they're not bothered with me."

She felt she was telling no lies, for who in their right mind could call Lew Earnshaw, who was going to teach her to read, a lad!

Chapter Seven

She did not see Martin Heywood, despite the fact that they lived under the same roof, until she had been at Moorhouse Farm for five months.

It was about nine o'clock and dusk was settling in the highest folds of the moor and the scent of honeysuckle and thyme drifted across to her mixed with the pungent whiff of grass cuttings, since Mr Starling had been mowing the front lawn that day. Despite Moorhouse being a working farm a Mrs Heywood of a previous generation had been extremely fond of flowers and her husband, newly wed and indulgent, had parted with a plot of land at the front and to the side of the farmhouse so that she might have a garden. Roses, the young Mrs Heywood had loved, sweetbriar, cabbage rose, moss rose, old White Damask and Maiden's Blush, all carefully tended now by the green-fingered Mr Starling and their scent was heady in the dying warmth of the day. But besides the roses there was the brilliant colour palette of sweet william, iris, peonies pinks, wallflowers and canterbury bells, for Mr Starling liked a bit of variety and for many years now he had been the sole authority on what grew in *his* gardens.

The farm was perched halfway up a slope of the Penfold Valley, set on a wide shelf that was sheltered at its back from the bitter north wind that scoured the moor. It looked down at the silver sliver of the river that wound through the rounded hills and moorland, a splendid vista to the valley bottom where Martin Heywood's cattle grazed on the lush green grass which was a feature of the valley. There were still strips of broadleaf woodland, oak and elm, hazel, alder and birch, and flitting from tree to tree, under the branches of which Clare and Lew often spent their Sunday afternoon, were starlings, great tits and blue tits. Some woodland had been retained about the farmstead, further protecting it from the prevailing winds, but beyond the wooded areas the moor stretched into infinity, heather moors, managed for grouse by rotation burning, scarred with dry rocky outcrops and damp flushes of cross-leaved heath and bog-asphodel. Golden plovers nested beside dunlin, their nests hidden in clumps of rush or cotton grass. The heather attracted bees and large heath butterflies and Clare delighted in the frantic dancing of the butterflies and the equally frantic droning of the bees. Higher up, the sheep-grazing country was not so rich in wildlife, for here sheep reigned supreme, Martin Heywood's prize flock as thick on the ground as the stars in the sky at the dead of night.

Clare was doing what Lew called her "homework" but somehow the peace and beauty, the fragrance that floated about her, not just of the flowers in the long dead Mrs Heywood's garden, but the homely smell of the farmyard, seemed to capture her senses and guide them away from her books. The double-storeyed barn was silhouetted against a tangerine sky where the sun was sliding down behind it. There was no sound bar that made by the sheep and their half-grown lambs up on the tops and a faint sleepy twitter of the birds in the heavily leafed trees at the back of the farm as they settled for the night.

She was curled up in the angle where the barn joined one of the tack-rooms, a corner where she would catch the last rays of the sun and its evening warmth, and though she had left Gracie moaning that she wouldn't know what to say if Mrs Case should come upon her and ask her where Clare was, as she did whenever Clare felt the need to slip out of the little-used side door, Clare knew, or was pretty sure, there was no chance of that. Once she had seen her girls up the stairs to their bedrooms, Belle and Maddie in one, Gracie and Clare in another and Thirza, being head maid, on her own, it was extremely unlikely that the housekeeper would poke her nose upstairs. So sure was she that not one of her girls would dare disobey her orders, or defy her in any way, that it did not occur to her to check and at this precise moment she would be sitting in her little parlour having what she termed her "nightcap" – a tot of Martin Heywood's best malt whisky – prior to making her own way to bed. They would all be up at the crack of dawn tomorrow, particularly Clare and Gracie, for it was their job to clear out and relight the kitchen fire before the others came down. It was because of this, even though it was still light, she insisted they should be abed as dusk fell. Those who worked with livestock and looked after the men who worked the livestock lived the hours the livestock lived, and you wouldn't find a sheep, a cow, a horse, a pig or any of the hens which pecked in the yard, staying cosily in their beds until the sun was halfway across the sky, would you?

Clare had her book open on her lap, the one that Lew prepared during the four weeks in between her Sunday visits to Edgeclough. Though he was not consciously aware of it, Lew had the attributes, if not the qualifications, to be a teacher. He was patient and, more importantly, innovative, so that he was able to put together what amounted to lessons which would not have gone amiss in a good English school. They were aimed at the youngest child, of course, which was what Clare was in the area of education, work that could be done on her own. It wasn't teaching her to read as yet, but it taught her to recognise the letters of the alphabet and their sound.

He had begun with the word "cat" believing, correctly, that an object that was familiar would be easier for Clare to understand. From one of his Chartist companions who, like

Lew, believed that a child's only hope for a better way of life was through education, he had borrowed a book called *A Child's Best Instructor,* not enquiring where the chap had obtained it! In it were pictures of everyday objects, such as *cat, dog, bed, rug, jug, sun,* nothing with more than three letters, and underneath the name of whatever it was. The letters were large, simple and though it had taken many weeks of patience on Lew's part on the way each letter sounded and how they linked together, after five months she was progressing to words of four letters, the first being *Fred.* She copied these words diligently and repetitively on to a sheaf of cheap paper Lew had knotted together with string and which he called her homework book, repeating over and over again the sounds the letters made and the words the letters formulated. For an hour or more after she and Gracie were tucked up in bed, working by the light of the ends of candles that she and Gracie managed to filch, she laboured over her work, understanding not a word at first, driving poor Gracie, who wanted to go to sleep, quite mad, which was why, now that the light nights allowed it, she often stole out to her hiding place by the barn.

She and Nelly had been worried about Lew, both of them concerned with the way he had taken the failure of Feargus O'Connor, who was a leader in the Chartist movement, to get their latest national petition to parliament. Lew had travelled up to London last month on a railway train, which no one in Edgeclough had ever seen, let alone sat in, accompanying O'Connor and as many as could afford the train fare, to present the petition, but it was decreed by government that not more than ten persons should be involved in a demonstration at any one time. The police warned the procession that had been got up that they would not be allowed to cross the bridges north of the river and so the petition, on which Lew had placed such hopes, was taken in three cabs to the House while the demonstrators made their way as best they could, some from as far as Lancashire and Yorkshire, back to their homes. The movement seemed in imminent danger of collapse and Lew had taken it hard. He had believed in and worked for the People's Charter for the best part of his life and its collapse would be a bitter blow to him. He had been silent, morose even, ever since, quoting the great Duke of Wellington when he said that the English were a very quiet people, respectful of authority and obedient to the law, which, Lew said, had worked against them in their fight for equality. It was as though, for the time being, the purpose had been taken from his life and Clare thought that perhaps his interest in and concern with her attempts to learn to read might help to disperse his melancholy.

She heard the footsteps first, his boots ringing on the cobbles. She was ready to panic and at the same time she wondered what the devil whoever it was was doing round here outside a tack-room that was rarely used. She cringed back among the weeds and wild flowers which grew thickly in this corner and would have escaped his notice if it had not been for the dogs with him. The dogs slept in a corner of the stable by night but at first light they were brought out, walking obediently at the shepherd's heel up on to the tops where the sheep were. They were handsome dogs, of the true blue merle colour, well looked after, for they were valuable animals, trained to answer every whistle and command the shepherd made and it was well known that these two were considered to be the master's dogs since it was he who had trained them.

They did not bark, as they had been trained to make no unnecessary noise. They merely nosed into the corner and then stood there, front paws splayed, "guarding" her until their master came to investigate, as they would with a sheep that was down or a lamb that was lost and found.

"Now what's the matter?" she heard Mr Heywood say, just as though he had suffered a long day filled with troublesome pinpricks and was not pleased to be presented with what might be another.

The dogs continued to guard her, their blue merle eyes watchful but not alarming. She was tempted to put up a hand to them as she would with Fred but these were not domesticated animals like Fred but working dogs who were not used to petting.

She sighed, because she had liked this job and had felt that she was getting on well and what would Mrs Case have to say when the master, for it was he who stood before her, his face a picture of amazement, told her the kitchen skivvy was not only where she shouldn't be, but was learning to read into the bargain.

She scrambled to her feet, her book, her pencil, her sheaf of papers clutched to her protectively and lifted her head to stare defiantly into her master's incredible blue eyes. And they were incredible. They were the colour of the carpet of bluebells among which she and Lew had sprawled a month or two ago, or the speedwell which grew in the grassy verges of the lane, set about with long dark lashes and above which his eyebrows dipped in menace. The last of the evening's light placed the brilliance of a sapphire in them, not that she had ever seen one, and hidden in them was amusement, watchful and mocking as though so far he had found the world an entertaining place. She remembered him as tall and lean but had forgotten, or had not noticed, his strong muscled shoulders, his vigorously curling dark hair. He was clean-shaven but with a shadow about his chin which suggested he was a man who might need to shave twice a day. He was amused at the moment, and intrigued, but his chin was thrustingly arrogant and his mouth firm, hard even, yet sensual with a lift at its corner which spoke of humour.

"Who the hell are you and what the devil are you doing in my yard?" he demanded, clicking his fingers at the two dogs who dropped back to stand one on either side of his feet.

"Clare, sir," she answered somewhat despairingly.

"Clare, sir, and what am I supposed to make of that? This is private property and you are trespassing, did you know that?" And all the time he spoke his eyes were assessing her speculatively with that look that the male assumes when presented with a good-looking female.

"I'm not trespassing, sir. Sure an' I know I'm not supposed to be here but . . . well, 'tis a lovely night, too nice to be indoors an' besides I'm driving poor Gracie mad with my . . . so didn't I slip out of the side door and come here where 'tis quiet."

His face was still a picture of irritated bewilderment but suddenly his expression cleared as though a candle had been lit in his mind revealing the answer to the puzzle.

"Bloody hell, it's the Irish girl. I wouldn't have known you until you spoke. I must admit you've improved beyond recognition since I last saw you up on Friars Mere. What the devil have you been doing with yourself to . . . well . . . you've put a bit of weight on and by God if it doesn't suit you."

It was very evident that Martin Heywood could not believe what he was seeing. The last time he had clapped eyes on this girl – when was it? months ago – at the top of Friars Mere, she had been like a skinned rabbit, frail and without colour in her cheeks, gawky somehow, like a growing child. Tall she had been when she stood up which had seemed to add to her air of instability and he remembered wondering at the time why the devil he was taking any interest in her. But for her eyes, which were a vivid green with specks of gold in them, there had been nothing much about her to draw a man's glance.

But would you look at her now, which was what he did and with great appreciation. In the few months since he had seen her she had grown, if not exactly plump, she would never be that, but shapely. A slender waist above which her breasts were high and rounded. A long white neck, like a swan, he found himself thinking, the flesh at her throat fine and unblemished, only her hands and forearms rough with the work she did for Mrs Case, he supposed. Her hair had grown and was tumbled somewhat wildly about her head and shoulders. It was thick and silken, shot through with tones of russet and chestnut, dark with the gloss of good health. His expression said he was astonished and not only that but he liked what he saw: it was in his own eyes and the curling expression of his well-cut lips which were ready to smile with pleasure, in the slight drooping of his eyelashes in admiration.

If she felt a small stirring of resentment at being looked up and down as though she were a mare who had caught his fancy and which he might purchase she did not show it. Mr Heywood had a reputation, so it had been whispered to her in the kitchen, for dallying with the ladies, sometimes other gentlemen's ladies, and more besides and, in Mrs Case's opinion, though she did not voice it, the sooner he took himself a wife the better it would be all round. His charm, a kind of boyish charm of which he pretended he was not aware, wreaked havoc in many a female breast, and he knew it, but he seemed incapable of settling on one pretty face when there were so many to choose from among the daughters of the men with whom he did business, on both sides of the Pennines.

His smile deepened appreciatively. Putting his shoulder to the wall he lounged there with his hands in his corduroy pockets. He had been up on the hills with Eppy, who was head shepherd at Moorhouse, inspecting his flocks ready for the shearing that would begin soon. Martin Heywood was what was known as a gentleman farmer whose mixed farm showed great profit but despite this he was not afraid to get his hands dirty and had even been known to deliver a difficult lamb. He knew his business and often tramped about his estate with his men. He wore stout knee boots and an open-necked shirt which showed off his strong brown throat and the fuzz of chest hair in the vee of its neck.

Clare felt something stir in her breast, making it suddenly difficult to take a breath, the feeling moving down to the pit of her stomach where it lay, warm and very uncomfortable. She looked up into his face and for a long moment could not look away again, held by something she was unable to name but which her female body instantly recognised. His eyes had narrowed in sudden concentration and he looked faintly surprised as though at something *his* body was telling *him*. Somehow she found herself with her back to the wall, unprepared for the sheer force of the feelings that swept through her and she knew, with a sort of panic, that she was in grave danger, not from him but from herself and was aware that she must, absolutely must, get away and back to the safety of the bedroom she shared with Gracie.

But Martin Heywood was her employer and it was in his face, as though he had read what was in hers, that she would leave when he said she could leave and he had not yet done with her.

"I work in your kitchen, sir," she heard herself babbling, anything to fill the gaping void she felt about her and which she seemed in danger of toppling into. "You told me to speak to Mrs Case so I did and didn't she take me on?"

"Of course, I remember now." He grinned, his lips curling over his strong white teeth. "She told me you'd come and she was willing to give you a month's trial. She's like that, old Clarice, thinks I'm still a lad in knee breeches and I'm not." You can see that, can't you, his impudent smile was telling her. I'm a man, a full-grown man with a full-grown man's needs and desires and if I'm not mistaken you're a woman who could satisfy those needs, but of course he did not say so in so many words.

"So what are you doing out here, Clare Hanrahan? See, I even remember your surname. What are you hiding for, or perhaps, from?"

Suddenly suspicious, he glanced around him as though some local yokel might be hanging about ready to sample one of Martin Heywood's kitchen-maids and when none materialised, beginning to smile again.

"What have you in your hand, lass?" he questioned affably, holding out his own hand with the clear intention of having Clare's books put into it.

"Nothing," she said hastily, putting her books behind her back, but his smile deepened.

"Oh, come now, I won't tell old Clarice I found you out here if you'll show me what you have in your hand."

Clare felt a great surge of what she knew to be the temper she had once had, or so her daddy had told her. It filled her chest, and her mouth wanted to curl contemptuously and her tongue to spew forth words like, "An' what the divil has it to do with you?" but she could not afford to get on his wrong side, could she? Besides which she was rather proud of the progress she had made with the work Lew prepared for her. She could already recognise and *say* each letter of the alphabet and could read "cat", "dog" and "Fred" besides several others which were to do with her day-to-day life. Lew said she was doing very well and that though it was taking a long time since they saw each other only once in four weeks when she really got the hang of it he would begin to teach her to read a proper book. He even had one ready for her. It was called *Pride and Prejudice* by a lady who was named Jane Austen and though it was a tattered old thing he had bought at a bookseller's in Oldham, it had been purchased especially for her. It was a carrot to make the donkey run, he said laughingly and she had no need to have that explained for her. It was about a family of sisters who . . . well, he said, he was not going to tell her what it was about but he had read it and he knew she would love it.

Slowly she drew her hand out from behind her back, keeping her gaze on Martin Heywood's face, which had a smile of curiosity on it. It was plain he thought her to be up to some girlish thing, something that maidservants got up to which could not be to do with books since none of them could read.

He took the tattered pieces of paper and the equally tattered book, looking down at them in bewilderment.

"What's this?" he asked her, frowning, turning the *Child's Best Instructor* over and over, then studying her exercise book and the childish squiggles, or so they appeared to him, which covered sheet after sheet. One of the dogs sat down and scratched vigorously at its ear but the other, older, stood firm where his master had put him. A hen which should have been in its coop suddenly strutted round the corner of the building and began to scrabble in a bed of nettles and Martin Heywood continued to stare at what was in his hand.

"What is it? What are you doing?" He was so astonished he seemed unable to marshal his thoughts. Here was his kitchen-maid who several months ago had been a whey-faced walking skeleton on whom, he supposed, he had taken pity – which was unlike him – not only blooming and bonny but with a book in her hand and, he noticed, a defiant look on her face. What the bloody hell was going on, he would like to know, and at once.

She lifted her head with an air that seemed to ask what had she got to lose but her job which, after what she had already lost, was hardly worth considering. She needed it, of course, but now that she was strong there was work to be found in the mills no matter what Lew and Nelly might say.

"I'm learning to read, so I am," she declared, not quite adding, "and make of that what you will."

"Now are you indeed and who, may I ask, is teaching you?" His tone was mild which, if she had known her master rather better, signified nothing. Martin Heywood could shout and roar his displeasure with the best, having been brought up to believe by a doting mother that he had only to ask, demand, state a preference and whatever it was would be delivered to him at the earliest possible moment. But it was when he was quiet that he was at his most dangerous, as many men in the world of business knew only too well to their cost. If he didn't like the idea of his kitchen-maid learning to read, and, more to the point, who was teaching her and where and when, he would put a stop to it.

She lifted her head bravely and stuck out her chin and something in Martin Heywood quivered and his breath became short and hard in his chest. He was a man well used to the charms of women, many women. From an early age he had sampled them. From one side of the Pennines to the other he had roamed, somewhat wild in his youth when his father was alive to see to the demands of their vast estate. He was settled now at the age of twenty-eight, not to domesticity but to the requirements of his business.

He studied the rebellious expression on Clare's face. No anxious humility for her. She lifted her head even higher with an imperiousness that said someone in her Irish past might have worn a crown.

"Lew Earnshaw." No more.

Martin Heywood's face remained bland, giving away nothing.

"Lew Earnshaw from Edgeclough who works for Will Hopkinson?"

"Yes."

"And may one enquire when this takes place, this reading lesson?"

"On my afternoon off."

"Which is?"

"Every fourth Sunday."

"I presume Mrs Case knows nothing of this . . . endeavour? You know she would not approve. You might get ideas above your station, or think yourself better than the others and—"

"If ye're after telling her then there's nothing I can do about it, but I'll not be givin' it up, so," she interrupted him, taking the offensive, letting him see that no matter what he said, or did, or what Mrs Case said or did, she would not be moved from her objective. There was a lovely flush on her cheeks and he noticed that her lips, poppy red to start with, had taken on even more colour. Being a man he knew what that meant and at once he smiled and held up his hands.

"Far be it for me to oppose the gaining of an education, though I must admit I would not like it if the lot of you were at it. But if Mrs Case finds out you know she will have you off the premises as fast as your legs could carry you with probably a clout about your impudent ears into the bargain."

He turned away, his face impassive, for he would not have

liked her to read his thoughts which were somewhat of a jumble even to himself.

"Take care, Clare Hanrahan, and good luck."

Mrs Case was taken aback the next evening when her master, after dismissing Thirza who was helping to serve, asked her how the new girl was getting on.

"The new girl. What new girl?" forgetting to add "sir" in her bewilderment, for by now Clare was as familiar about the kitchen as any of the others.

"The one I asked you to take on, Mrs Case." His tone was autocratic, telling her this was his home, his farm, his land and that she worked for him despite her dominance in the kitchen. He had a perfect right to enquire after anyone, man or woman, whose wages he paid, a fact which Mrs Case was aware of; nevertheless it astounded her.

"D'you mean the Irish girl, sir?" Though of course she knew just who it was he was speaking about, for she remembered her amazement when he had made his request.

"Was she Irish? I didn't realise."

"Yes, sir, come from Ireland on account of the Troubles, I believe."

"She talks about them?"

"Oh no, sir. Not a word, but there are so many of them now, knocking on my back kitchen door looking for work, or a handout. But the girl's not like that. She's proved a good worker and I think it would be no boast to say I have put her back on her feet. She was like a thread of cotton when she came but now . . ."

Mrs Case stopped speaking abruptly as she remembered that first suspicion she had harboured regarding the Irish girl and her master. It had died away over the weeks but suddenly it came back to her, for never, in all the time she had worked for him, had Martin Heywood showed the slightest interest in anyone he employed. At least not in the kitchen. She couldn't ever remember him coming *in* to the kitchen. This would bear watching, this concern the master was showing for a girl who, she realised it now, had grown in beauty and strength since she had come to work at Moorhouse Farm and if she had seen it so had Martin Heywood!

"So you're satisfied with her then, Mrs Case."

"Yes, sir. So far," she added primly, folding her arms under her plump breast. "Will that be all, sir?" And when he said it would she returned to her kitchen, giving "the new girl" a wary look as though to say she would keep her eye on her in future.

Chapter Eight

"Now, read the whole sentence. There's words in there tha've done a hundred times, that tha've read separately one by one but I want thi' ter put 'em all together an' mekk a sentence. See, what's that word, the first 'un?"

"The . . ."

"That's it, now the next."

"B . . . o . . . y . . . boy."

"An' the next."

"Sat . . ."

"Just keep goin', lass. Tha' can do it an' tha' know tha' can so why—"

"Lew, will you not shut yer gob, as Archie says, and let me get on with it. The trouble is—"

"Trouble is, my girl, tha're not doin' tha' homework. Tha' read this last time word-perfect an' now . . ."

Clare frowned, sighing deeply as she peered at the book on the table.

"An' there's no need fer that. Dost tha' want ter read or not?"

"The . . . boy . . . sat . . . on . . . the . . . mat . . ."

"And . . . ?"

"And . . . ate . . . his . . . p . . . p . . . pie."

"There, I said tha' could do it an' I were right. Now say it again wi'out stoppin'."

"The boy sat on the mat and ate his pie."

"Good lass." Lew turned in triumph, grinning at Nelly who was sitting in his rocking-chair beside his fire darning his socks, a task he had given over trying to stop her doing. He could darn his own socks, he told her but, being Nelly, she took no notice. Nelly was in a bit of a tizzy, as her old mam used to say, for she was torn between leaving Lew and Clare to get on with it by themselves, meaning the time they spent together in his cosy kitchen, where, hopefully, Clare would succumb to Lew's persistence and agree to marry him, or playing chaperone in order to ensure they didn't get up to no good. Mind you, if they did get up to no good and a babby was the result her wish would be granted, hence the tizzy she was in. The trouble was Nelly had standards of what was and was not proper, which made Lew smile, for after all they were not gentry who guarded their daughters as a valuable commodity in the marriage market. He often said, privately, of course, that he wouldn't mind betting that half the couples in the row were not legally married, for often finding the parson's fee was impossible to a man and woman starting out in life together. They needed every penny they could lay their hands on just to get going. They might have a child already on the way so they would just move in together and get on with raising a family. They were faithful to one another without being prayed over and having nothing to pass on to their children in the way of worldly goods, since they had none, did it matter if their offspring were illegitimate?

But that was not Nelly's way, nor was this daft idea that the lass should be taught to read and write. "The boy sat on the mat and ate his pie!" It made no sense, did it? And what good was it to a scullery-maid, tell her that, or indeed to anyone in their social position, which was no position at all when all was said and done? She had never learned the skill and neither had anyone she knew and they'd managed well enough, hadn't they? She wanted to add, but did not, that, if Clare was to marry Lew, which Nelly was determined on, Lew could do all the reading and writing that was necessary, which, in her opinion was very little!

"There, what dost think ter that, Nelly?" Lew grinned. "She'll be on *Pride and Prejudice* before th' end o't year at this rate. As long as she practises. That's the secret, my lass, practice. Trouble is tha' need summat interesting, summat to mekk thi' *want* ter read ter get thi' really goin'. This children's readin' book's all very well ter start with but tha' could do wi' summat ter whet tha' appetite. The old carrot an't donkey. I tell thi' what. Can tha' not slip inter Martin Heywood's study, or whatever the man 'as up at that place, an' pinch a newspaper, fer there's nowt more likely ter encourage thi' than to read about what's 'appenin' in't country. Nay, in't world. I know the words'd be 'ard at first but tha' know tha've only ter run the letters tergether."

"Eeh, Lew Earnshaw, will tha' listen ter thassen," Nelly declared hotly. "*Pinch* a newspaper, if tha' please. Dost tha' want ter lose the lass 'er job?"

"Well, borrow, then. I bet he gets *Times* an' there's all sorts in there that'll interest Clare so that—"

"That's all very well fer them as likes such things but our Clare is no more'n a working lass 'oo . . ."

The use of the possessive pronoun was noticed by none of them and if it had would have caused no comment since Clare belonged to them now as surely as if she had been born here. Which she had in a way, Nelly often thought, for she'd been more dead than alive when she was carried across the threshold at back-end and it was her and Lew and the other women who had brought her back to life.

"Give over, Nelly. Clare's got summat rare in 'er an' if she wants ter better 'ersenn—"

Clare thumped both fists hard on the table so that Cat and Fred, both dozing companionably together on the hearth-rug, lifted their heads in alarm.

"For the love of God will both of you stop talkin' about me as if I wasn't here, or as if I was a child of six."

"Now then, my lass, don't tha' go speakin' ter our Lew like that," Nelly snorted, shifting sides with the ease of long practice. She had found that it confused folk, set them off on the wrong foot if they found she had changed horses in midstream, so to speak.

Lew looked amazed. "I thought tha' were against . . ."

"So I am, lad, but that doesn't give lass right ter say—"

"See, you're doing it again. Talking to one another as though I wasn't here, or couldn't speak for myself. I can and I will, so. Sure an' it's hard at times even to get the time to 'practise' as Lew says. I work hard, so I do, an' at the end of the day all I want is me bed but I never give in to it. Gracie thinks I'm mad. Isn't she afraid that if I'm caught she'll get the sack as well as me."

"Why should tha' get sack?" Lew protested, foolishly in Clare's opinion. "Last I 'eard it weren't against law ter read."

"It is where I work."

"No, it's not, lass."

"Mrs Case would say so."

"Oh, bugger Mrs Case."

"Lew Earnshaw, if tha's goin' ter talk mucky, I'm off." In a great huff Nelly stood up, gathering her shawl about her, for the summer day had turned cold and wet. It had been the weather that had brought her in here in the first place since she wanted to make sure that the lass, who was wet through after her walk over from Moorhouse Farm, got herself properly "aired". She would never forget the state of her when she had first staggered into Edgeclough and nothing Clare said would convince her that she was not to go into a decline with that chest of hers if Nelly was not there to see to her!

Nobody tried to stop her as she opened the door, which disconcerted her for a moment since she had expected Lew to protest but Lew Earnshaw had other ideas and they did not include spending the few precious hours he had with Clare in her company.

Nelly waited a moment, sniffing, her arms akimbo. "Right,

I'll be off then," she repeated, as she stepped over the doorstep.

"I'll be in ter see you before I go, Nelly," Clare told her.

"Aye, see tha' do or else."

There was silence for a moment or two after Nelly had strenuously banged the door to behind her. The two animals stretched and yawned and fitted themselves into a more comfortable pattern of sleep on the hearth-rug.

Lew leaned forward and took Clare's hand, holding it between his own which were big, brown and work-scarred.

"How are thi', lass?" he said gently, just as though they had not already spent a couple of hours in one another's company. "I mean over there at farm? Dost think tha'll settle?"

"What else is there for me to do, Lew?" Then realised that she had fallen neatly into the trap he had set for her.

"Nay, tha' knows answer ter that," he said mildly.

She studied his sun-browned face, the thatch of brown hair which fell untidily across his broad, intelligent forehead, the steady light in his clear grey eyes which shone with good humour and the slow burning of his love for her. His tall, lean frame was bent over the table. His expression was one of kindness, no humility there, rather pride, for he had only himself to thank for what he was and what he had done with his life, but there was a spark of something she had not seen before and she wondered what it was.

Lew stood up abruptly as though the time for action had come. He had waited patiently for months now, sitting beside her as they pored over her books and, being a man after all, he wanted to move on for that's what men and women did.

Without giving her a chance to protest he drew her to her feet and put his arms strongly about her, pinioning her own to her side. Narrowing his eyes he studied her surprised face for a second or two then deliberately placed his lips on hers. Softly, gently, his lips pressed down, barely more than the touch of a butterfly on a petal, then, as she made no resistance, more urgently, caressingly, folding her lips into his own, taking courage as hers opened beneath his. One of his hands moved to the nape of her neck under her hair, holding her firmly as though afraid she might break away, while the other smoothed the length of her back and the small of her back down to her buttocks. Encouraged by her lack of opposition he pressed her closer to him and though this was the first time she had ever been held by a man, kissed by a man except her daddy, she would not have been a woman if she had not known what it was that was thrusting manfully against her.

"Clare . . . my heart," his voice moaned as his lips slid down the length of her throat to where the neck of her modest bodice was unbuttoned. "My love, let me . . ."

He was looking round for somewhere to lay her, not the walled bed for it was not long enough and he dare not chance taking her upstairs in case, on the way, she might take fright. The rug then, where the animals lay, but they were hard to shift for they were warm and comfortable and as his foot stirred them urgently she came to her senses, not because of anything Lew might or might not have done but because of the vivid blue eyes, set in a strong brown face which became indelibly etched against the inside of her eyelids.

She had not seen Martin Heywood for two weeks now, though she had heard his voice shouting for hot water, a pot of coffee, a clean shirt or complaining that his boots were not cleaned to his exacting standards and what did that lad, meaning the odd-job boy think he was doing. He was a man used to efficient, unobtrusive service and if it was not immediately available, which did not happen often, he soon let his displeasure be known. She had heard the clatter of his horse in the yard and the slamming of doors which meant he was home, but though she had slipped out a couple of times on a warm, still night, not even reasoning why, since she could just as well read in the bedroom she shared with Gracie, he had not been in evidence. Sometimes he spent the night away, over in Leeds or Bradford, so Mrs Case told them, on business, she supposed, not caring to wonder why she found his movements of concern to her.

She began to struggle but Lew Earnshaw was a man roused, a man in love who had, for a few moments, thought he was about to have his longings fulfilled and his male body was outraged by the interruption.

"No. No, Lew," she managed to gasp, pushing against his chest so that they almost toppled into the fire.

"Yes. Yes, my love . . . yes . . . let me. I love you, you know I love you. Let me . . ."

"No, don't make me . . . please."

"Clare . . . Clare . . ." He groaned as though in severe pain but he had begun to loosen his hold on her, for he was a decent man who would force no woman.

She moved away from him and, as women do, put her hands to her hair and the neck of her bodice, tidying herself as though she had been in a fierce struggle, then she turned to stare out of the window at the rain which still drifted across the valley and he did the same though he looked into the fire, leaning on one arm, his hand on the mantelshelf.

"I'm sorry, lass," he said at last, "but tell me this. Did tha' find it not much to tha' likin'? Me wi' me arms about thi'." His voice trembled and she whirled about in horror, for though she couldn't say how it was, she loved this man and would not hurt him for the world.

"Oh no, Lew, no!" She moved across the room to stand at his back, her hand lifting as though to touch him but then she lowered it again, for she knew she did not love him as he wanted to be loved and would it not be kinder to let him know it right from the start.

"Then, will tha' not marry me? Us'll manage wi'out tha' wage. I'll work hard, lass, tha' knows that. We've a snug cottage 'ere an' tha'll not go short. Of owt."

Her heart was breaking, the heart that she had thought to

be stone-cold dead and incapable of ever being warm and loving again. It would be wonderful to let this strong and patient man take her into his arms, his life, his bed. It would be so easy to take up the career all women were destined for which was wife and mother and for the life of her she couldn't think why she couldn't bring herself to do it. She had felt herself respond to the hard demands of his body a moment ago. His kisses had been pleasing and his hands on her body had awakened some warm and sweet thing that had been very satisfying. But not enough. *Not enough!* Why she should think that when she had no yardstick by which to measure it was a mystery to her.

"Well?" he said, not turning towards her and she had no answer. If he had asked her if she loved him she would have answered that she did and that would have led to catastrophe. He would not understand, being a man, that . . . that . . . what? What was she trying to reason in her own confused mind? And why, sweet and holy Mother of God, did the face of the man in whose kitchen she worked keep coming between her and this man who loved her? Would she marry Lew if Martin Heywood had not come into her life? The question itself appalled her, for Martin Heywood could never be anything to her, nor she to him. He had been astounded to find her reading behind his barn, curious, she supposed, that a maid in his service was doing such a thing but he had obviously not complained of it to Mrs Case, for nothing had been said. He had not given it, or her, another thought and she must do the same about him. Perhaps – who knows? – later, when she had been given more time, seen what was to become of her, she might consider Lew's offer of marriage, for what could be more suitable? They were, in a way, alike. He had learned to read and, she had been told, offered to teach any of the children in the row who were interested to do the same, but only one, and that was Lavender Bickerstaffe, had shown any interest. But she, Clare Hanrahan, had jumped at the chance so perhaps she and Lew had more in common than just the circumstances of their birth and social class. He was a good man. She would have a decent life with him so why did she dither about doing her best to erase Martin Heywood's impudently smiling face and amazing blue eyes from her mind?

Lew sighed and straightened up, not looking at her, for her answer was in her silence. "I'll walk you home," he said quietly and he looked so beaten she almost gave in.

"There's no need."

"I'll walk you home," he repeated stubbornly and later the man who had heard them coming up the track to Friars Mere stepped back behind a sprawling outcropping of rock, watching them go by. It was still raining and his cloak was dark and sodden, testifying to the length of time he had been up there. When they had gone, the sound of their footsteps dying way into the distance as they descended towards the distant sprawl of buildings which was Moorhouse Farm, he climbed on his mare and with a fierce gesture put her to the gallop away to the east, up and up to the top of the undulating moorland from where he could see Diggle Edge and Millstone Edge to the east and on into the mists of Yorkshire; across to Broadhead Noddle in the west, to Castle Hill and below it his own farm where two tiny figures, barely discernible in the drifting rain, stood for a moment and then parted, one to vanish into the huddle of buildings, the other turning south and the track back to Edgeclough.

He sat for fifteen minutes, leaning his forearms on the pommel of his saddle, the rain cascading down his cloak and into his boots, from the brim of his hat, and though he kept his head bent as he brooded over something that was evidently distasteful to him, down his face into his collar. The mare, disheartened by the rain and the blackness of her rider's thoughts, which she sensed, stood abjectly, head hanging, rider and animal seeming to share their mood. Then, with a swift cry which startled the mare, the man on her back set off at a harebrained gallop down the treacherous track that led to home.

* * *

She did not dare light a candle even though she had never before been in this part of the house except to scrub the shining tiles in the hallway. She and Gracie shared a room at the top of the house so she had two flights of stairs to negotiate, one down to the family's quarters where only the master slept now and then down again to the wide hallway. The rain had stopped at last and a little light filtered through the windows of the rooms on either side of the hall, leading her terrified steps down the stairs and into the front hall where, somewhere, was the master's study. And how was she to recognise it? she anguished, wishing to God that she had not listened to Lew's crackbrained scheme. And even if she found and recognised the room as his study, which she had heard Mrs Case mention, there might be no newspaper to be found and if there was . . . Oh, holy Mother and all her angels, would she have the nerve to remove it and then, Jesus, Mary and Joseph, wouldn't she have to return it before morning when it would be discovered that it was missing? Not that any of the other maids would want to read it since they hadn't the skill but Mrs Case had, though she usually only flicked through a *Ladies Journal* or a recipe book. The newspapers were saved to make firelighters, each page rolled up and twisted about, then placed under the slivers of wood and coal in the kitchen fireplace.

The next to bottom step scraped harshly as she put her foot on it and she froze, then withdrew her foot as though the movement would undo the sound. She waited, barely breathing for what seemed to be an hour, then, when neither Mrs Case nor the master came shrieking down the stairs demanding to know what the devil she thought she was up to, she moved forward, avoiding the creaking step.

She found the study and wondered why she had been so anxious, for it was easily recognisable as a room where reading and writing took place. It was filled with books on every wall from floor to ceiling. There was an enormous desk piled high with papers of some kind and several large leather volumes. There was a chair at the desk with its back to the wide window and to the left of the desk a deep leather chair with a footstool in which, she supposed, her master liked to relax. But where was today's newspaper, or even yesterday's since the date was irrelevant? She wanted it merely to see if she could pick out any words, not to find out what Lew had casually called "current affairs", whatever that meant.

A clock whose face she could just make out ticked sonorously from the other side of the room. There must have been a window open somewhere, for she could smell the fragrance of the roses, made more potent by the rain that had fallen all day. One of the dogs gave a short bark and again she froze but after several minutes when nothing happened, she relaxed again, or as close to relaxing as she could get in these trying circumstances.

Moving slowly round the room, lit by the night sky which had cleared of the tattered clouds to reveal a star or two, holding her hands out before her as though she had lost her vision, she blundered into a small table on which were a pile of papers. Of what sort she didn't know but by this time her heart was hammering in her throat and she knew if she didn't get back to her room, where Gracie was no doubt gibbering in her bed, she would faint, or scream or yank open the front door of the house and run away into the night.

Grabbing the paper at the top of the pile she fled silently across the room, along the hall, up the stairs, past the bedrooms in one of which her master was sleeping, up the second flight of stairs and into the safety of her room. Gracie was still awake but incapable of doing more than squeak her terror and for several long minutes they clung together like two frightened children who had been deserted in the night by their mother, until at last, beginning to breathe properly, they became disentangled.

"I got it, Gracie, I got it," Clare whispered triumphantly.

"Oh God . . . Oh God," moaned Gracie.

"Sure an' it'll be all right, I promise you."

"Oh God. Oh God, I never want ter go through that again, never, dost 'ear me, Clare Hanrahan. Me 'eart'll never be't same again. Promise me tha'll not do it again, Clare, promise me."

"Will I not have ter take it back tomorrow night, Gracie, but I mean ter see if I can read a word or two first. No, don't blow the candle out."

"Yer never goin' ter read it now?" Gracie was appalled. Not only was she convinced that Mrs Case would at any moment come thundering in to the bedroom demanding to know what they thought they were up to, but didn't they have to be up at five thirty to get the kitchen started? At this rate it would be a miracle if they managed to drag themselves from their beds at all!

But Clare Hanrahan had already started on the drug to which she was to become addicted, the terrifying, wonderful, life-giving drug of knowing what was happening, not only in other parts of the country but of the world. She was to learn of the increase in violent crime in Ireland and of Her Majesty's visit to her subjects there which was described at great length in *The Times*. She was to read of revolution in Germany and then in Italy, the wars in Afghanistan, all of which was totally incomprehensible to her at first, and later of Disraeli who was to become Prime Minister of England, of the birth of a seventh child, a son, to their queen and her husband up in London. But now, on this night in June 1848, all she could do was to pick out a letter here and there, sometimes a word if it was a short one, while Gracie moaned her terror and begged her to blow out the candle and get into bed.

She did so, reluctantly, hiding the newspaper under her mattress for future reading since it would take her many months of careful practice to read it from cover to cover, praying to the blessed Virgin that Thirza wouldn't miss it in the morning!

Chapter Nine

It was a Sunday but despite this Oldham Station was as crowded as a weekday as the train which had travelled on the branch line on its way from Hudderfield to Manchester drew to a stop at the platform. Doors opened noisily and the engine gave a shriek which made several horses standing in the station yard toss their heads nervously but Martin Heywood, who had been into Yorkshire on business, staying several nights, did not notice as he made his way towards the porter at the gate. He handed in his first-class ticket, striding into the yard where he glanced impatiently about him, his eyebrows dipping into a frown, evidently looking for something, or someone, who had not yet arrived. Martin Heywood did not like to be kept waiting. He took out his pocket watch, a gold hunter which had belonged to his father, flicking open the case to look at the time, his frown deepening. The watch caught and tossed back the reflection of the sun which also lit the diamond in the ring on the little finger of his left hand.

He was dressed immaculately in dove-grey trousers and a fine worsted plum-coloured coat, a fall of white which were the ruffles on his shirt, a dove-grey waistcoat and over his arm he carried a cloak, for the day had turned warm. He had a small overnight carriage bag made from the softest leather with a strong rigid frame and for further security two leather straps across it with brass buckles. Placing the bag on the ground and tapping his foot, he glared about him irritably as he again consulted his watch.

The yard was noisy with the influx of passengers who had just alighted from the train and were pouring hither and thither in search of transport. Boxes and crates and several trunks cluttered the entrance to the platform and a well-dressed but elderly lady and gentleman fluttered about them as though they were unsure which belonged to them. A dog chased a cat across the wide forecourt, almost tripping up a man dressed in the familiar garb of a shepherd before the pair of them disappeared behind a crate of squawking hens. The shepherd carried his smock across his left arm, a crook in his right hand and beside him slunk a small collie dog, the sort used for herding sheep. Martin pondered on where he might be going, not on a train that was for sure, watching as, with a minimal command, no more than a flick of his finger, he held his dog, which showed interest in the canine and feline chase, close to his heel. Another man, evidently a prosperous farmer by his dress, hailed him and with what looked like a sigh of relief as though he had been quite lost in this mêlée, the shepherd moved in his company out of the yard.

The sharp clatter of a carriage horse as its hooves dashed on the cobbles caught Martin's attention and a smart equipage drove full tilt up to the entrance to the platform. Springing from within, a young man shouted to the station-master who was about to blow his whistle to send the train on its way to Manchester, running like the wind to fling open a door and leap into a carriage.

A porter shouted something evidently rude but unintelligible, which was just as well, and a beggar whined at Martin's elbow. A tribe of ragged itinerants, dragging a handcart piled with what looked like rubbish on top of which sat half a dozen children, hung about at the wide gates leading into Manchester Street begging for handouts. The soft lilt of their Irish brogue drifted across to him and at once her face flashed disconcertingly across his vision as it had a habit of doing so often these days. His dark eyebrows dipped alarmingly and his full mouth thinned with what appeared to be anger. Every time it happened he felt a sharp needle of exasperation drive through him, directed at her, or so it seemed, as though, like a witch, she had cast a spell on him which was totally absurd. It was not her fault that he couldn't seem to get her out of his mind. It wasn't as though he saw her very often, for their worlds did not collide, but now and again he had noticed her in the stable yard tipping water from a bucket into a drain as he himself rode in, and only last week he had caught her on her knees at the front steps as he ran down them to his waiting mare.

"What the devil are you doing here?" he had snarled at her as he almost fell over her bent back, amazing himself with his flash of anger and his sudden desire to pick up her bucket and fling it and her brush into the shrubbery and lift her to her feet. She had looked up at him in total amazement. It was barely six thirty, early for him to be off anywhere unless it was up to inspect his scattered flock but she had already been on her knees for an hour in Mrs Case's constant war against dirt. "Fettling", Mrs Case called it, the scrubbing and donkey-stoning of the steps. It was a term used in the cotton mill for cleaning under the frames before going home and though nobody knew of it, at least in her kitchen, Mrs Case's mother had been a spinner, and had brought the word home with her.

"Sure an' don't I work here?" his scullery-maid had answered haughtily, to the consternation of George who was holding his master's horse for him. "I've the steps to clean an' it can't be done unless I'm after gettin' on me knees."

"Well, I'd be obliged if you'd do it elsewhere, on your knees or not," the master had retaliated, his face darkening ominously in a way his men would have recognised.

"Will you be after sackin' me, then?" she had demanded,

putting her hands on her hips, her green eyes flashing dangerously, evidently as put out as he was, and George, as he told the other men later, thought the master was about to clout her one, and for two pins, he was sure, she would have clouted him back, so what were they to make of that? It was agreed they didn't know!

"Don't be ridiculous. Just get on with your work and make sure you don't get under my feet again."

He had leaped on his mare's back and digging his heels into her sides had galloped off down the drive with both George and his scullery-maid staring after him in consternation.

He had made a fool of himself, he knew it, doing his best to get some order into his mind to discover why. Why she would keep creeping into his thoughts when he least expected it. Why he found himself looking out for her whenever he was in the stable yard or at the back of the barn where he had first seen her, if you did not count their meeting up on Friars Mere. He often wondered what it was that had made him offer her work in the first place. But he had and it was no good going over and over it. What difference did it make anyway? She was involved with that radical ranter, Lew Earnshaw, and would no doubt end up marrying him. She would leave Moorhouse and finish up in that poky cottage at Edgeclough with a snarl of children at her skirts and that would be the end of it. But that little voice would keep asking, the end of *what*? There was nothing to start with, so how could there be an end? It was then that he would smack his palm to his forehead, shout for his mare and go off at a clip to the Bulls Head Inn at the crossroads where the lanes led to Crossfold in one direction and Longworth Hall, where the gentry frolicked, in the other. In the company of other farmers he could discuss profit and loss, argue the best way to cure foot rot, maggots and liver flukes, the qualities of the Lonk against the Scottish Blackface, drink brandy and eat oysters then ride home with no thought in his head but getting to his bed.

There was a flurry of action at the entrance to the station

yard as the groom from the stables of the inn on the opposite side of the road led in his mare, both of them struggling, the mare to escape the groom's firm hold, the groom to keep an anchor on the restive mare.

"And about bloody time, too," Martin growled. "I've been waiting at least half an hour."

The groom, who had seen the train come in no more than five minutes ago and had at once saddled up Mr Heywood's well-groomed black mare, said nothing in his own defence, for, like Mr Heywood's men, he knew the futility of arguing with him.

"Sorry, sir," he said meekly, clasping his hands to give Mr Heywood a leg up into the saddle. At the last minute Martin relented, as the groom knew he would, and flipped him a coin which brought a grin of gratitude to his weatherbeaten face.

He kept the horse at a steady trot along Manchester Road, behind and on both sides of which were spread in steep, narrow streets thousands of back-to-back two-room hovels which had been run up by jerry-builders to house the operatives who staggered each day to their long stint at loom or shuttle.

On Manchester Road and used by these very operatives, he passed the rather imposing building of the recently opened Oldham Industrial Society which was, so he had heard, a great success and beginning to prosper. The industrial age, as it was beginning to be called, had caused a great upheaval in the lives of people who had come from villages and small rural communities to work in the factories and cotton mills of the fast-growing towns. Their mass move had the effect of leaving these displaced workers feeling uprooted, abandoned and unprotected, which had led to the formation of co-operatives. Rochdale had been the first, Crompton, Royston and Failsworth soon to follow. It was a simple system. Each member had a "check number" and every time a purchase was made the amount was recorded, these amounts adding up and every quarter a dividend, or "divi" would be paid. It offered a convenient method of being thrifty, which appealed to many of the Lancashire housewives, without apparent sacrifice. For many the payment was manna from heaven. No money had been "saved" and yet because they had bought their groceries at the local Co-op, they received a lump-sum payment.

He was in the shopping area here – where there were twenty-two shops and two inns in one block – until he reached Market Place, crammed with stalls, none of which was doing business since Sunday was not a market day, moving along a winding highway whose name changed every hundred yards or so as he neared open country. Yorkshire Street! Brodes of Oldham Lane! Mumps! Bottom of Moor! Greenacres Moor! The Hill turned left towards Crossfold, which he was soon through and up on to the open moor.

There was a fresh breeze in his face, warm and soaked in the fragrance of heather and gorse. It moved the shadows cast along the track by the shoulder-high bracken and rippled through his dark, uncovered hair. To his right a curlew took flight in alarm, its liquid bubbling song rising into the clear air and his high-stepping, mettlesome mare rolled her eyes and tossed her fine head. The sun shone from a cloudless sky. The track was dry and dusty, for it was weeks since there had been any rain and it drifted up about Sable's hooves. Blackbirds and thrushes were going mad with joy, whirling in what seemed to be ecstasy against the blue of the sky. The air was like wine, a spirit of freshness that seemed to soak into him, from the sunshine, from the vivid colours of gorse and heather and bracken and from something he couldn't name, which he didn't want to name but which, though he didn't know why or even how, he was forced to accept at last. He didn't like it, but he accepted it.

He was riding through Edgeclough when he saw her. She was sitting on the step that led up to the front door of what he knew was Lew Earnshaw's cottage. She was reading. Not just stumbling over a child's primer as he had seen her do behind the barn, but with a bloody newspaper spread out across her knee. She was totally absorbed. A cat sprawled on her knee under the newspaper and a rough little dog lay across her feet, and in a chair beside her, something in her hand to which she plied a needle, was Nelly Bradbury. He didn't know where Lew Earnshaw was and he didn't care to find out.

The older woman looked up and nodded.

"Afternoon," she said. "Grand day." No "sir" for her. He might own the cottage in which she lived, as he owned all the cottages in this row since they were on his land, but she didn't work for him.

"Afternoon," he replied, not checking his mare, his eyes going from her to Clare, who had glanced up, he thought reluctantly as though irritated by the interruption, as he rode by.

They looked at one another, neither of them speaking, their glances locked, speaking words which could not be heard but which both understood and Nelly, who saw it all in a flash that was as brilliant as lightning, almost blinding her and certainly taking her breath away, stopped her darning, laying the sock carefully in her lap. She felt a shiver go through her, though it was not cold and her mouth became dry. Her eyes were flat and, though she was not aware of it, snakelike, deadly with the need to protect her own, which Lew and Clare were.

He was gone and halfway up the track towards Friars Mere before either of the women looked away from his retreating back, and when Lew came round the corner from his vegetable patch at the back of the cottages he was at the top of the rise and Lew didn't notice him.

"Well," he said, "that should do it."

"What?" Clare said vaguely, shuffling the newspaper, covering her own confused state with brisk movement.

"That hen house. What dost tha' think I've bin up to? I told thi' Solly 'ad seen a fox sniffin' about but the bugger'll 'ave a job gettin' in there now, I can tell thi'."

He was amazed when Nelly didn't pick him up on his use

of "language". He turned to wink at Clare but she was absorbed with her newspaper and didn't see it.

"I could do wi' a brew," he said at length, feeling somewhat uneasy, though he didn't know why, looking from one woman to the other for reassurance, sensing something strange in their manner. He leaned his back against the stone wall of the cottage, lifting one foot and placing it on the stone, turning his face up to the warmth of the sun, wondering as he did so what had happened to the day which had started out so well and which suddenly seemed to have become ... cool, by which he meant Clare's attitude of disinterest. He lived for every fourth Sunday when Clare would be home, never giving up hope that one day she would agree to marry him and remain here, give up that skivvy's job she had up on the moor and settle down to be his wife and the mother of his children. From beneath his half-closed eyelids he watched a scatter of magpies scuttling about the tussocky grass down the slope of the track before lifting themselves above the bracken and drifting away on almost motionless wings.

Nelly heaved herself to her feet, knowing that Clare, for reasons Nelly couldn't bear to contemplate, had not even heard Lew's last remark.

"I'll mekk us a brew, lad," she said. She moved to the next set of steps, her own, and as well fettled as the ones at Moorhouse Farm, moving up them and into her own kitchen. There was an air of spartan cleanliness about the room which smelled of carbolic and beeswax. Her hearth, before which her Will sprawled in a light, Sunday afternoon doze, was freshly brushed and the stone floor freshly swept. The table was set for her, Will's and the bairns' dinner and on the fire a pan of something mouthwatering bubbled. There were barrels against the wall and stoneware storage jars on a shelf next to bottles of Nelly's cordial. Nelly and the other women in the community gathered field and hedgerow fruits, cowslip and sloe and elder, and the result, as Nelly said, was a real heartener when the effects of overwork dragged a body down.

Absently she reached for her old brown teapot into which she placed two teaspoons of tea, then poured hot water into it, nudging her old man to let him know that there was a brew going.

They drank it in the sunshine. All about them the children larked. Lavender came to sit shoulder to shoulder with Clare, urging her to "say it to her", meaning the news in the newspaper, and Clare searched for something that might interest the girl. Slowly, for she was still learning, she searched the headlines for something she thought might be of interest not only to Lavender but to Nelly. There were pieces regarding plays and ballets in London but since none of them, including herself, had ever seen a play or a ballet, which she thought was a kind of dance, and could not imagine a theatre, she skipped over them.

"Here's one that says beech leaves can be used instead o' feathers in a bed; so what d'you think to that, Nelly, and what about this? 'The court, which means the queen an' them, will leave Windsor Castle in the course of the next week for Claremont where they will remain for a week, during which period Prince Albert will shoot over the royal preserves where game has been strictly reared and is extremely plentiful, especially hares and pheasants.'"

All this was read haltingly and was, it seemed, of little interest to those who had gathered about her and they began to drift away. When Clare had drunk her tea and shouted a goodbye those who remained waved cheerfully and watched her and Lew stride out up the track to the brow where the moor began.

They did not speak much, for Lew sensed that Clare was distracted about something though he had no idea what it might be. When they reached the farm gate he wanted to linger and talk, to bring up the matter nearest his heart but something, he didn't know what, or why, stopped him and he simply took her hand for a moment then turned, tramping away up the lane away from Moorhouse Farm back the way he had come.

She watched him go, then, when he had vanished and since there were still some hours of daylight left, she slipped round the back of the farm and struck off through the shoulder-high bracken, across the lane known as Booth Dean, up and up along the rough track to what she had been told was a place called Badgers Edge, the name of which had intrigued her. Old pack-horse tracks criss-crossed it and it was said that many years ago, how many none of them was sure, a pedlar, or "badger" as they were known hereabouts, had fallen to his death over the edge in a snowstorm.

She crossed a shallow, slow-moving stream which, when it reached the bottom, would wind along the valley floor. She paused for a moment on the old wooden footbridge, looking back at the view spread far below her, for Badgers Edge was higher even than Friars Mere, then moved on until she reached a rough, uneven surface at its peak. There was mist moving in the valley below her but the sky was a delicate pink shading to a pale-blue vault above her head where the sun still shone.

The sun was low since it was late. The air was sweet and she dragged great mouthfuls into her lungs, leaning back against the great pitted rock which was twice as tall as she was, and when he stepped out from behind it she did not even look round since she had known he would come.

He had changed from what she called his "city" clothes into corduroy breeches, an open-necked shirt with the sleeves rolled up and his knee-high riding boots, though he had not come on horseback. Without a word he moved to lean beside her, crossing his arms over his broad chest and they stared out over the splendour of the wide, wild open moors and though she was not Lancashire born, as he was, the austere beauty, which had entered her heart from the first moment she had seen it, settled there, like a child that nestles on its mother's lap.

"How did ye know?" she said at last.

"What, that you'd be up here?"

"Yes." She did not look at him but continued to stare out blindly into the misted valley bottom.

He laughed. "That's easy. I followed you. I saw you arrive at the gate and then take off up the track. I was waiting in the lee of the wall by my mother's rose garden."

"Why did you follow me? What is it that you want from me?" Her voice was jerky but she did not move away from the shoulder that touched hers.

"I wanted to talk to you. But first tell me why you came up here. You were home early from Edgeclough but instead of going indoors you climbed up here. Why? Did you expect me to follow you since you seemed unsurprised to see me?"

She ignored his question, asking one of her own.

"What do you want to talk about? What have you and I to say to one another?" She pushed her hair back from her forehead and squinted at something that moved in the valley bottom as though his answer didn't really matter since she already knew.

He watched her as he had watched her for weeks, bemused by the loveliness of her. She was tall, willowy, slender, like a dark-headed lily, graceful and swaying even when carrying a bucket filled to overflowing with water and he wanted her. More importantly, he knew, since he was a man of the world, that she wanted him.

"I want to talk about us." His answer was slow in coming but it did not take her by surprise.

"Us, there is no us."

"Then why are you here?"

"Sure an' didn't you follow *me*?"

"True, but you expected me, didn't you?"

She sighed deeply and turned for the first time to look him in the face. "Yes, I suppose so but I don't know why. What have you an' me to do with one another? You're a wealthy farmer, a man of some importance and I'm the skivvy in your kitchen. If

Mrs Case was to see me up here with you she'd have me out of her kitchen."

"Mrs Case isn't your mistress."

"No, an' you're not my master. No one owns me."

"Not even Lew Earnshaw?" His vivid eyes blazed down into hers as though daring her to give an answer he did not care for, since she was wrong when she said nobody owned her. She was his, *his*, or would be as soon as he could find some place where there was peace and privacy, which should not be too difficult to arrange for a man of his means. He would put his special mark on her, make her his woman, before she could change her mind. He thought no further than that. He had wanted her for months now, though even to himself he had denied it. Not, of course, from the first moment he had seen her, he admitted that, for she had been a gawky scarecrow who would appeal to no man. But, having said that, he must have seen something in her when he had told her to go to the kitchen at Moorhouse and ask for employment, for he was not known for his charity!

But her loveliness had grown, flowered, bloomed and he knew his purely masculine desire had changed, from desire to something else. He loved her as a man can love only one special woman, though what the hell he was to do about it he didn't know and at this precise moment he didn't give a damn. She was his, he could tell it by the expression in her eyes, by her lack of surprise when he appeared and by the warmth of her quickened breathing which matched his own.

She hesitated and with a movement she had not anticipated he turned her roughly and pulled her into his arms and though her heart bounded joyfully she struggled nevertheless. It did her no good, for his mouth came down on hers with a fierceness that paralysed her so that she fell back in his arms, almost swooning. This was nothing like the kiss Lew had given her. Lew's kiss had been pleasant, warm, enjoyable; this was overwhelming and she felt the instant unfolding of what she knew to be desire, not just his but hers. His arms drew her closer to him and it seemed to her to be a homecoming, finding the place where she was always meant to be, which was absolutely ridiculous. His lips parted hers and his tongue caressed them and she felt a sound gather in her throat which she knew was one of pleasure. She wanted him but she also feared him. She was well aware that the master of Moorhouse Farm was wealthy, eligible, and sought after by all the young ladies who came, so she was told, to Longworth Hall. Many of them had fathers who did business with Martin Heywood, or so the kitchen gossip went, and he could have his pick. In which case it was not likely that an Irish peasant, which she knew herself still to be at heart, would become the wife of Martin Heywood. She was not sure what being the mistress as opposed to wife of a man like Martin Heywood would mean, since he had not mentioned marriage. What kind of life she would lead, where she would live, for she had not moved in a world where such things were commonplace, but whatever it was she knew her daddy would have disapproved and that was the yardstick by which Clare Hanrahan lived.

"What is it that's worrying you?" he whispered into her hair, his love for her making him sensitive to her mood, drawing her gently against him though his body wanted to throw her to the ground and take her, as the male body often does, despite the mind's doubt.

"Let me go, please. Sure an' me heart an' soul are in a turmoil an' I can't think straight."

"My darling, you don't have to think straight. I'll do that for you. I'll find us a place ..."

"I can't ..."

But without waiting to find out what it was she could not do he began to kiss her again, holding her gently, it's true, but very firmly so that she had to flex her own strong body to be free of him.

"No. I'll be no man's ... plaything."

He hooted with laughter, which was entirely the wrong thing to do.

"Plaything, where the hell did you hear a word like that? That's what comes of learning to read, I suppose, but don't you see . . ."

She did not wait to find out what she must see, but turned fiercely and began to run headlong down the rocky track that led from Badgers Edge.

"Clare . . . for God's sake," he shouted after her, beginning to follow, then he stopped, for he knew that at this moment it would do him no good to argue with her. Let her get used to the idea, to the knowledge that he loved her, that he would make a decent life for them both, that he would take care of her always and that she had nothing to fear. She was his love and he was hers, that was evident and all it needed was time and they had plenty of that.

Chapter Ten

He began to waylay her whenever he could do it without them being seen by the other servants. She wasn't sure she knew why he was being so careful since he had made it pretty clear what his feelings about her were and whether he intended making her his wife – which was no more than a possibility in view of their difference in status – or his mistress, the servants would find out sooner or later. As July moved into August, September, October she seemed to spend her days and nights in a continuing dream world, not real at all, not her every day-to-day life to which, over the months, she had become accustomed, but a misted world where she was separate from the others in her life. As though she existed in the glass dome which stood on a table in the hallway and under which was an arrangement of dried flowers wherein a gaily coloured bird perched. She might speak or they might speak to her but the sound they made was muted, barely distinguishable. Even her reading, which she did her best to keep up, meant little to her. She had started on *Pride and Prejudice,* finding it very hard at first, not only to read some of the words but to put them together to make sense of the story.

"I don't know what's up with you, girl. Have you gone deaf or something? I told you the back steps, not the front, so what the dickens are you doing carrying that bucket of water down the passage?" Mrs Case would scold her. "And where's your sacking apron? You'll ruin that cotton one if you don't pull yourself together."

Sometimes when she was on her knees – which seemed to infuriate him – scouring the dim passage that lay between the main hallway and the side entrance which was the one he used to get to the stables he would come across her and before she knew what he was about would lift her to her feet and wrap his arms wordlessly about her. He would kiss her softly, gently, his lips travelling across her face to the corners of her eyes, smoothing her cheek and under her chin. His eyes would give their message of love and his expression would tell her that this was only the beginning. That soon, when she had agreed to it, and he would not rush her, he would take her away and tuck her safely into a place that would be theirs only, where she would have no need of this squalid employment – in fact she had no need of it now – but he would honour her need to move in her own time.

She was amazed at his patience, for she knew he was not a patient man. They barely knew one another. They had scarcely exchanged more than two dozen words in the past months and yet there was this bond between them which tugged at her heart as though a piece of elastic stretched from her to him.

One afternoon he tiptoed exaggeratedly into what had been his mother's conservatory which had a flagged floor and which it seemed Mrs Case trusted her to clean in the way Mrs Case herself would have cleaned it.

She remembered the first time she had been introduced to what had seemed to her to be a garden brought indoors and, unaware of it at the time though Mr Starling had told her since, housed exotic plants from all over the world which could never be grown in the climate of the north. The floor was the same as that in the hallway, a pattern of polished flags in colours of rose and deep ochre, cherry red and carnation pink, all glowing with the scrubbing and polishing that had taken place ever since the conservatory had been built. The walls were entirely of glass and above them in an arch was an exquisitely moulded roof of fretwork, high-domed and again of glass. There were white-painted wrought-iron tables and wicker chairs heaped with vividly coloured cushions, pots in pleasing shades of terracotta, all erupting with brightly flaunting plants. From the ceiling were hanging baskets, again crammed with flowers and trailing leaves which brushed her head. At the far end were fluted pedestals on which stood statuettes and singing birds in cages that shook the senses with the beauty of their plumage and the sound of their song.

She didn't know how he knew she was there but he had again surprised her early one morning, trying to lift her into his arms and when he failed kneeling down beside her and doing his best to kiss her as she swung her brush in an arc of soapy suds.

"Please, Mr Heywood," she had frantically whispered, but he had been so comical that she could not help but laugh and of course he had been encouraged to turn her to him so that they knelt facing one another, the brush hanging in her hand while he cupped her face and kissed her, his thumbs smoothing her cheeks, her heart soft and smiling with her love for him. Oh, yes, she loved him, she had accepted that and he knew that she accepted it but still he did not press her.

"My heart ... you are my heart," he had whispered against her mouth, amazing her, for she had thought him to be unsentimental, a man who had little time for romance, to be romantic. Still kneeling he had folded her in his arms, removing her badge of servitude, her mobcap, and pressing her head into the curve of his shoulder, his hands in her hair which fell loose.

He cornered her in places that took her by surprise, like the strip of yard at the side of the barn as she went to collect eggs when Belle, whose job it was, ate too many ripe plums and was in bed with a bellyache. Mrs Case, who recognised an efficient, trustworthy maid when she saw one, was slowly beginning to give her tasks that were not strictly in the domain of a skivvy. Anybody could scrub floors but it was not often a girl as bright and quick-thinking as Clare Hanrahan came under her command and she was beginning to think the lass was worth more than spending her days on her knees and her nose in a scrub bucket. Gracie, who was a good worker but without the gumption to wipe her own nose without being given a direct order to do so, would never be anything but what she was, but Clare was often to be found hanging over Mrs Case's shoulder when she was preparing a meal and though Belle, who was Mrs Case's handmaiden, did not like it, Mrs Case began to show the "new girl" how to make a decent scone, the best way to coddle an egg, how to clarify beef dripping which could then be used for meat pies, how to preserve pears which were hanging in abundance on Mr Starling's trees and how to make a rich, strong and economical stock which was the basis for a good cheap soup

"Now when you're making your bread," she would begin, as though this were Clare's kitchen and the bread and the ingredients that went into it were Clare's, "you have to make sure your yeast is good and fresh." It was the same with "your" beef broth, "your" lemon dumplings, "your" lobster patties, exasperating the kitchen-maid beyond measure, since when would an Irish skivvy ever be in a position to eat lobster patties? But Mrs Case was quite flattered by Clare's interest, for what woman can resist showing off what she's best at, which, in Mrs Case's circumstance, was turning out a splendid meal.

She would not have been so complaisant had she seen her scullery-maid, whom she was seriously beginning to consider for promotion, struggling, but laughing while she did it, in the arms of Mrs Case's employer in the conservatory and she would have been even more incensed if she had become aware that every fourth Sunday, when Clare had said goodbye to Lew Earnshaw, she raced up the track to Badgers Edge to fall, rosy-faced and laughing, into Martin Heywood's eager arms.

They would sigh simultaneously, studying one another's

faces as though to detect any change that might have taken place since last they met.

"Dear God ..." he would murmur, his mouth descending on hers, pressing her deeper into his arms. He was a man used to taking what he wanted when it came his way. She was sweet and pliant, her body pressing willingly to his, but though his response was strong, with a great effort he subdued it. He lifted her off her feet and kissed her again and she clung to him, for it seemed to her he was the only solid thing in her rocking world. She was giving a little more of herself every time they met, he knew it and she knew it, but in her heart, deep where no one could see it, or hear it, or even know of its existence, a small wordless whisper was beginning to woo her, saying to her that surely, *surely* this man who loved her, how could she doubt it, could have only marriage in mind. He had not mentioned the word marriage, but neither had he talked of *mistress* which was the only other alternative. They had done no more than cling to one another and kiss hungrily as yet. She was young, inexperienced; sometimes inclined to shyness when he told her how beautiful she was. She followed his lead and so far he had not alarmed her. His male body yearned to go on, to satisfy itself as it had always done in the past, to explore and experiment, but she was not the kind of woman who normally would have attracted him and her innocence and trust held him back, but soon they must move on and in a strange way he was afraid to do so.

They spent time, not just quivering in one another's arms but talking.

"Tell me about Ireland," he commanded her one day towards the end of October and at once he noticed that she seemed to withdraw from him, not physically but as though a part of her mind, usually open and frank, had closed a door on him.

"Sure an' there's nothin' to tell."

"Of course there is. Why did you come to England? Where did you come *from* and—"

"I told you. County Clare. Didn't me mammy an' daddy call me Clare because of it?"

"But what happened to them, to you? I know the famine was really bad over there. I read the papers and the description was pretty graphic, and in the last few years it seems that half the population of Ireland has come from over there to over here."

"Is that so?" she said coldly.

"Aye, lass, it's so but what have I said? Sweetheart, look at me," turning her to face him but she sagged like a ragged doll in his arms, hanging her head as though in shame. "What is it? Was it very bad . . . your family . . . ?"

"Don't . . . please, Mr Heywood." In her distress she called him again by the name a servant would use to her master and he shook her roughly, appalled by the way her head lolled on her graceful, swan-like neck.

"It's not Mr Heywood, my darling, it's Martin and if you don't want to speak of it now then we won't. You know I wouldn't hurt you. I love you."

He held her to him and her arms twined about his neck and as though to shut out whatever devastation was in her soul she leaned against him as though she would dearly like to be inside his skin where she knew she would be safe.

"Darling . . . my love," he mumbled. He sank down to the tufty grass and she went with him until she lay across his lap. For only a second he hesitated, for was it decent to take advantage of her obvious distress, but when his hands moulded her waist and then moved upwards to cup her thrusting breasts and she made no objection his fingers went of their own volition to the buttons of her high-necked bodice. She was moaning deep in her throat as his hands moved inside and delicately held her naked flesh, his fingers rolling first one hard and rosy nipple and then the other, at the same time loosening her clothing so that her breasts were exposed to the bright autumn daylight, white and rich and spilling into his hands.

"Martin . . ." she whispered and he could feel her trembling and he knew that this was the moment for which he had been waiting. Once he had taken her, penetrated her, possessed her, she would be totally his, to do with as he pleased, for women are loyal creatures when they love a man. He was thinking like a man who is intent on seduction, and he supposed he was, but in the back of his mind, which soothed what might be his guilt, was the knowledge that he loved this woman and always would. He would care for her, keep her safe and protected but how much easier it would be to persuade her to allow it if the deed was already done.

His hand slid down her body to the hem of her skirt where it caressed her bare ankle and calf, moving up her leg to the soft skin behind her knee and it was at that precise moment as it smoothed its way higher inside the leg of her drawers to the hot, slippery cleft which was his goal that the ram, in hot pursuit of one of Martin's own ewes, came butting round the corner of the rocks.

It was a tie as to who was the most confounded, the animal or the man. From somewhere above them there came the sound of a whistle, the urgent whistle used by a shepherd to call his dog. It was a sound Martin recognised, for he knew them all and in a moment Eppy's dog would follow the ram, ready to drive it back to the flock, as it was mating time up here on the high moorland where his sheep roamed.

If it had happened to another man he might have laughed, slapping his thigh at the irony of it: two rutting males facing one another in astonishment. Then the ram jumped clear and the dog, though catching the scent of the two humans, and recognising one, did not deviate from his work, herding the ram and the ewe it had followed back to the flock.

At once, knowing the spell was broken and recovering more quickly than Clare, Martin had his love covered modestly from neck to ankle. Her face was bemused, her eyes unfocused, her rosy mouth open on the end of the rapturous sigh which had been torn from her and he kissed her tenderly, doing his best to ignore the aching bulge in his breeches. She was his. She would recognise it next time and then she would really be his.

From his point of view, and had he but known it, it had done his cause no good when he had almost swept Clare off her normally carefully balanced feet at the top of Badgers Edge. But he had not completed the act which both of them wanted so badly and in the meantime Clare had had time to think about it, to dwell on its possible consequences, to come slowly to the realisation that a man who has marriage on his mind will speak of it. Martin Heywood had not and she marvelled at her own naïvety in believing that he would. She flushed hotly from head to foot when she recalled how she had sighed and stretched and moaned in his arms and though she did not deny to herself that she loved him, and always would, she was ashamed that she had allowed him to handle her as he had. Her upbringing, meaning the teaching of that good man, her daddy, had taught her the difference between right and wrong and though there was nothing in the world she wanted more than to belong to Martin Heywood, she would not be his whore, nor even the more permanent mistress.

It was this deliberation that had caused Mrs Case to cast her eyes heavenwards and wonder what the dickens had got into the new girl.

He was bewildered a few days later when, catching her alone on the upstairs landing where Mrs Case had sent her to the linen cupboard to fetch some clean cloths, she aimed a clout at his head which, if he had not hastily ducked, would have made his head ring. He had been just about to run downstairs to where his mare was waiting at the front porch. He was off to Liverpool to do business with a merchant who was in need of fresh beef to take to some corner of the world where they had a need for such things, and he was late. His train left Oldham in three-quarters of an hour and he would need to gallop hard to get there in time to catch it but he could not resist a moment in which to recapture that enchantment they had known last Sunday. He had drawn her into his bedroom and closed the door behind her, pressing her ardently to the wood at her back and holding her there where his lips found hers.

But she wouldn't allow it. Turning her head away she struggled fiercely, though her treacherous female body was ready to arch itself to accommodate his.

"Stop it . . . let me go or I swear I'll . . ." She wasn't sure what the threat was that she offered him, since if she drew attention to herself she would lose her job and that was just what she was doing her best to avoid.

"Darling!" He was smiling, damn well still smiling despite the blow she had aimed at his head which made her seethe with fury, and his belief that this was of no consequence, that she would soon respond to his warm, moist mouth and searching hands, which, now that they had known her wanted to know her again, made her wild and dangerous. It was as though she had been living all these months in a fantasy world, a world where dreams would come to fruition if she was only patient, a world where Martin's love had lulled her into a false belief – how could she have been such a credulous fool? – that one day she would be Mrs Martin Heywood. He loved her, she knew that, but he wouldn't marry her, she knew that as well and the despair and rage consumed her.

She was like a spitting cat, her face contorted, her mouth stretched wide over her snapping teeth, ready to scream at him, he thought, if her caution for her job had not held her back. Her hand came up and she scratched him, four runnels that instantly beaded with blood, from the corner of his eye to the corner of his mouth.

"What the bloody hell was that for?" he roared, and down in the kitchen Mrs Case cocked her head to listen but by this time he was in control of himself, and her, her hands pinioned above her head, and Mrs Case, thinking herself to be mistaken, resumed her baking.

"Don't you dare think you can drag me wherever ye fancy,

ye bastard," she hissed, as conscious as he was of noise. "I'm not some doxy who'll lie down for sixpence, or for nothing as you seem to think I would on the moor. Didn't you trap me last Sunday—"

"*Trap you!* You were as willing as I was and don't deny it."

"I know and the thought makes me want to be sick. How I could have been so . . . so bloody stupid as to believe that . . . that . . ."

Her voice began to rise again in her dementia, for that was how she was, demented that she had allowed such liberties to be taken by a man who thought of her as no more than an hour's pleasure whenever he could get her alone. Certainly he had told her that he would take care of her but it was a bitter pill to know that though he was able to marry her, for nothing stood in his way, he would not. He had decided that that was how their lives would be. She would go wherever he took her, to some luxurious little villa in an anonymous town, not too far away, where he would visit her whenever he had a free moment, which might not be as often as she would like but which would be convenient to him. She would sacrifice her independence which, she realised now, she had fought for and won, even if it was only as a scullery-maid, and little by little would be completely possessed by him, completely absorbed, and it terrified her.

"Let me go, damn you, let me go. I'll lose me job if . . ."

"It doesn't matter if you lose your job, don't you see? It would be the best thing to happen, for then you could come with me to wherever we decide to settle."

"As your wife?" Her voice was like stone, hard and cutting and meant to hurt.

He hesitated, holding his handkerchief to his cheek.

"Well . . ."

"No, I see you are not sure of that, so will you be takin' your hands off me and in the future keep them to yourself. Leave me alone, Martin. If it hadn't been for that . . . that animal last Sunday I'd've let you, so it was a narrow escape I had. Now, if you'll open the door I'll get on with me work. Mrs Case'll wonder where I've got to."

"Bugger Mrs Case," he snarled. "I don't know what in God's name has got into you and I'll have a hard job explaining these bloody scratches but for Christ's sake, calm down. I've to be in Oldham—"

"Go to Oldham then, but before you go let me make sure you understand that I'll not be your mistress, nor anything else you think is appropriate for a bog Irish peasant who scrubs the floors in your kitchen. I'm worth more than that, so I am, and—"

"Clare, you can't do this." He was appalled at her sudden calmness and her obvious sincerity. "Let me get this damn trip to Liverpool out of the way and when I come back we'll talk."

"Sure an' what is there to talk about?"

"Clare ..." He was pleading now, something Martin Heywood was not used to doing, not with anyone, man or woman, and it was a measure of his love for her that he even began to consider the wild and totally preposterous idea of marrying her. She was a necessity in his life, like the water that quenched his thirst and the food that nourished him, but it would be social death to make her his wife. His business depended on the goodwill of other businessmen, and their wives, and not one of them would accept a woman who had been scullery-maid in his kitchen. He entertained and was entertained by wool barons in Bradford, shipping men of Liverpool, men who could do him a good turn and which was essential to his profits. She was lovely, gracious, and in an expensive gown there was not one of them would know her from one of themselves. She was even becoming well read, for he had seen her poring over newspapers, those that he knew she took from his study. She was struggling through *Pride and Prejudice*, though where in hell's name she had got it, he didn't know, and he had told her to help herself to any book she fancied from his study. He was proud of her, proud of her determination to be more than a scullery-maid, proud of her brightness, her intelligence and sheer bloody perseverance in mastering the almost impossible task of learning to read.

But it would not be enough. It would become common knowledge that she had worked in his kitchen, that she had come from Ireland with the other starving thousands and could not possibly be received in "good" society. He needed a wife who could play hostess, mix with the wives of his business associates, further his chances in the world of commerce, and Clare Hanrahan could never be that wife.

She stood for a moment, her heart in shreds as she watched the battle between his common sense and his love for her fight tooth and claw for dominance, knowing the outcome even before he stepped back from her. His face was empty of all expression and though she had brought it about Clare was appalled by the terrible blankness in his eyes. He had lost the healthy amber tint that working out of doors had brought to his face and his blue eyes seemed to be drained of their usual brilliant colour. He was badly hurt, she knew it, as she was but there was nothing else to be done. Patrick Hanrahan's daughter could never be any man's mistress, she knew that, and though it was killing her by inches, as it was the man she loved, she would keep to the creed, the lessons she had learned at her daddy's knee.

She opened the door and slipped through and was down the stairs and into the kitchen, moving like an insubstantial shred of mist that will drift away on a breeze, before she realised that she had not brought Mrs Case's cloths. She must have looked strange, ill, she supposed, for they began to crowd round her, even Belle who sometimes resented her, solicitous, telling her to sit down for God's sake before she fell down.

"What is it, lass?" Mrs Case wanted to know. "Has someone hurt you? By jingo, if they 'ave an' I catch 'em ahle pawse 'em," which in Mrs Case's mam's tongue, Mrs Case's mam having come from Yorkshire, meant they would get a good kicking.

"No . . . no, sure an' I'm fine," Clare managed to blurt out though her tongue felt as though it were too big for her dry mouth and her brain was numbed and unable to think of some reason why she was in this state that would satisfy Mrs Case.

"What's to do, then, an' where's the cloths I sent you for? See, Thirza, give the lass a cup of tea. She looks as though she's seen a ghost." And when it was pressed into her hand Clare drank it gratefully, wishing they would all stand away from her so that she could breathe. Even Gracie, bucket still in her hand, for as Mrs Case said, she hadn't the sense to put it down, hung about anxiously.

"I . . . I fell . . . an' banged me head," which would account for her dazed state, but when Mrs Case took off her cap and examined her head, rummaging in her hair as though searching for lice, saying there was no sign of a bump, she simply folded her arms on the table, put her head on them and began to cry.

They were all open-mouthed with astonishment, even Mrs Case, but she found her voice and it was kind.

"Lass . . . there, there, don't skrike, there's no damage done. See, sit there for five minutes and drink your tea and you'll be right as rain in a minute. Now then, you girls, it isn't a peep-show so get on about your work." But as they scattered Clarice Case gave Clare a sharp look, vowing to herself to keep an eye on her scullery-maid for there was more to this than met the eye.

Chapter Eleven

She did not see him again. Whether it was by chance or of his own choosing she did not know; she only knew that her heart was broken, or if not broken smashed into so many pieces it would take a long time to put together and mend.

The half-promised promotion became a fact when Mrs Case declared she was to take up the duties of housemaid which meant that she was still to clean but not exclusively to scrub floors. Another little skivvy was employed to work alongside Gracie while she and Thirza, who was head housemaid and who was getting on a bit, as Mrs Case told her, though not in Thirza's presence, would be glad of a helping hand which Clare would give as under housemaid. Belle was kitchen-maid and Maddie was in charge of the laundry. There was a lad, Sammy, whose job it was to clean boots and lamps, to run errands here and there about Mr Heywood's farm and generally make himself useful wherever he was needed. The outside staff were Mr Starling who was in charge of the gardens and conservatory with his lad Hammy, George the groom and Job who was *his* lad, and the rest, Eppy, Jackie, Harry, Arty and a couple of other men who looked after Mr Heywood's flock of Lonks. There were other men, labourers, ditchers, hedgers, who maintained Mr Heywood's property, cowmen who were in charge of his mixed herd of cattle, Fresian for their milk and Herefords for their meat, and did not come into the kitchens but lived in cottages that Mr Heywood provided with their families, and a brisk, buxom dairy-maid by the name of Francy who was married to George.

It was strange, she often pondered in those first months of winter, that up to the moment when she had spurned Martin Heywood and what she was now aware would have been his offer to become his mistress, she had not taken a great deal of interest in the men and women who worked for him except those with whom she came into contact in her work. It was as though she had conceived the idea that she had no need to acquaint herself with them, as fellow servants that is, or perhaps it was that in those first months she had not yet eased herself from the harrowing grief that she had brought with her from Ireland. They had merely been ghosts, shadows whose lives brushed hers but were of no consequence to her; but now, with her promotion and the dedication she meant to bring to "getting on", wherever that might lead her – and which had brought about an increase in her wages from £5 a year to £8 – they had become real to her. She had not been able to see past Martin Heywood for many months but now that he was gone, not from the house but from her, they became real, they had faces and names and personalities which she came to know.

At first she had been terrified as she moved about beyond the green baize door into what was known as the front of the house, the parlour, the master's study, the dining-room, the sewing-room and small breakfast-room and all the upstairs bedrooms and cupboards which were now her job to clean, that she would come face to face with him, but it seemed he was as anxious to avoid her as she was to avoid him. She heard him about the place as she had done before they became ... well, whatever it was they had been to one another, shouting for this and that, clattering up to the front steps on his mare, giving George what for over some minor infringement in the stable yard, bellowing to Mrs Case to send Sammy to fetch Eppy or Harry since he wanted a word, but he made no attempt to approach her, for which she was grateful. Though she had meant it when she said there was no future for them she was not sure how she would withstand him if he made further overtures.

She and Thirza divided the work between them, though Thirza was quick to reserve for herself the lighter duties which was her prerogative as head housemaid, dusting the ornaments and furniture, the picture frames and knick-knacks collected by a line of mistresses while directing Clare in other, more onerous tasks. They were about their work long before their master was out of bed, for though it was a few years since they had known a mistress's rule, old Mrs Heywood had been a stickler for not only cleanliness but order and they had been well trained to it.

Clare began by taking up the hearth-rugs, sweeping the dust and the damp tea leaves she had scattered about the room towards the fireplace. When this was done she would lay a cloth over the carpet while she cleaned out the grate, blackleading and polishing until the fireplace gleamed and the brass reflected her own face, then she would lay and light the fire. She had her own housemaid's box of which she was very proud, as Thirza did, and when one reception room was completed they would move on to the next, working, they found, in pleasing harmony. The bedrooms were left until the master had breakfasted and dashed off at what seemed to be a tearing hurry, when the heavy work was started. There were the stairs, front and back, the passages and hallway furniture, mirrors, windows, mattresses to turn, earthenware washbasins and jugs to be washed and Clare was often to marvel that all this, all these servants working steadily through the day, were for the benefit of one man who spent very little time in his home.

Mrs Case remarked on it. "I don't know what's up with the master these days," she ruminated. "He's like a bear with a sore head that wants a bandage on it, snapping and carrying on as though nothing's ever right for him. And he's never still, like a cat on a hot griddle he is, for ever galloping here and there, only at home for his breakfast and that only a few days a week. Where does he get to, d'you think?" addressing no one in particular from her rocking-chair by the kitchen fire. "I know he has to go into Yorkshire and that but he never used to be away from home so much."

Though Mrs Case had her own room, these days she seemed to prefer to direct operations from the cosy area about the kitchen fire, ordering this and that to be brought to the huge table when she was ready to start preparing a meal. Even though the master was from home she still had sometimes as many as a dozen mouths to feed at dinner-time and the men had ferocious appetites, especially now that winter was upon them. They needed heaped plates of her special Lancashire hotpot, her liver and bacon served with onions, her meat and potato pie, her cow-heel broth or her pea soup, all of which stuck to the innards and sent them off with a little fire inside them to see them through the rest of the day.

"'Appen he's courtin'," Belle was rash enough to say in a casual manner and was amazed when Mrs Case turned on her. Mrs Case might be allowed to make comments on the life of their employer but a lowly kitchen-maid certainly was not.

"Now you listen here, my girl, I'll have none of that talk in my kitchen. What the master does in his spare time, which is private and not for the likes of us to wonder at, is his own business and I'll thank you to keep your opinions to yourself."

"I was only sayin' . . ."

"Well, don't. That gob of yours'll get you into serious trouble one of these days. Now get on with them vegetables and don't let me hear you make comments about the master again, d'you hear?"

"Yes, Mrs Case," snivelled Belle. Mrs Case, who they had always though of as an ogre, a slave driver, had in the past year become somewhat softer, not *soft* of course, but more relaxed and they none of them knew why. She sat down a lot more often which in the past you'd never see her do and they supposed she must be getting on a bit, but still, her tongue when she was roused could be just as waspish.

Clare was cleaning the plate, silver cutlery, serving dishes, cake baskets, coffee jugs, salvers and all manner of beautiful pieces which dazzled her and which she found a joy to clean, especially after nearly twelve months of scrubbing floors. There were other beautiful objects scattered about the house, clocks of marble, clocks under glass domes, a grandmother clock which chimed musically in the front hallway, what she learned were called cut-crystal decanters and glasses which had been in the family for generations. There were lovely pieces of furniture, not the heavily carved, dark and solid designs fashionable among the wealthy middle classes in this age of Queen Victoria, but country furniture of elm, oak and yew, sturdy but with a simple elegance that pleased the eye, with chests and settles and footstools, with dining tables and sideboards all polished to a mirror gleam in the past by dozens of hands and with deep and comfortable chairs in which a man who has worked all day in the open air can take his ease of an evening. They had been plain farmers who did not usually bother with fol-de-rols, not until men like Martin Heywood, his father and grandfather before him had become more than farmers but businessmen who, travelling about the country, were made aware that a home could be more than just a place of shelter. Moorhouse Farm, the house part of it, had become a manor-house as it prospered and successive wives, bringing decent dowries on marriage, had added to the comfort, even luxury of their home.

Belle's words cut Clare to the heart. All her thoughts of Friars Mere, of Badgers Edge, of being in Martin's arms and feeling his lips on hers had developed a dream-like quality as if it had never happened, but the thought of some other woman knowing what she had known was too much for her. She felt the blood drain from her face and prayed to the blessed Virgin that no one had noticed it, thanking Her that she was sitting down. She couldn't stand the thought of it and her flesh, which had glowed and quivered under his hand, froze to an ice-cold shaft of agony. Though the kitchen was warm, fire bright and cheerful, there was no warmth in her. No, she couldn't stand it. She really would have to get up and go to the cupboard of a room that was hers alone now that she had been promoted, hide herself there with her head under her covers and simply die with the pain of it. But she couldn't.

"And where do you think you're going?" Mrs Case would ask her, and they would all turn to stare if she drew attention to herself by blundering from the room.

She continued to polish with the soft rags which she washed each time she used them in a mixture of new milk and hartshorn powder, boiling them for five minutes as Thirza had taught her. Despite the chaos that reigned inside her she even found it in her to admire the beautiful deep polish this produced. She was dressed in her new uniform of a plain grey cotton dress with white cuffs and collar, a spotless white apron tied at the back with a bow, the ends of which fell down to the hem of her skirt, and on her head, instead of the capacious and unflattering mobcap, was a neatly frilled maid's cap as befitted a servant who would one day be expected to answer the door and even serve at table.

Clare still showed a great interest in the art of cooking which Mrs Case encouraged. Belle was a good lass, hardworking and willing but, like Gracie, she had to be told exactly what to do in the way of mixing, or kneading, or making pastry which needed a light hand. She did everything she was told to do but not with the interest Clare showed. Over the months Mrs Case had taught Clare how to cook a decent roast, the best way to keep vegetables firm but not hard when cooked, how to put together a decent and tasty stew or casserole, the secret of a light and fluffy Cornish pasty, and a cheese and onion pie. She could bake a nice loaf and her scones were a treat. With the fruit with which Mr Starling's trees were laden Clare was becoming a dab hand, or so Mrs Case said, at a tart which, with the cream Francy supplied from her well-scrubbed dairy, went down a treat with the men, though naturally Mrs Case did all the cooking for the master. She was glad of Clare's help, though not wishing to put Belle's nose out, for she had been feeling what she called, only to herself, mind, but in her Yorkshire mother's speech, "powfagged" and was glad of her bed most nights.

"Well, I think it's time we were in our beds, girls," Mrs Case declared at last to Clare's vast relief, rising from her comfortable position by the fire and turning sternly to her cohorts like a sergeant-major marshalling his foot soldiers. "Have you finished that plate, Clare, or do you mean to polish the pattern off it?"

"Yes, Mrs Case. I mean no, Mrs Case."

"Well, don't sound so downhearted about it, lass. I thought you'd be glad to see the back of it. You can do it again tomorrow if you've a mind." She looked round the circle of maidservants in anticipation of the laughter she expected over this sally and was not disappointed.

They each took a candle and followed one another from the warm kitchen up the icy-cold back stairs to the equally icy top landing where the warren of their attic bedrooms lay. Gracie shared with Adah, the new skivvy, now, for which, though she liked Clare, she was truly thankful, for like her, Adah fell into her bed and was instantly in a state of deathlike sleep. The rest did the same, slithering down between their cold, well-starched sheets, shivering and clutching themselves, anxious not to stretch their feet to the bottom of the bed until the weight of the warm blankets with which they were blessed, which many servants weren't, eased them into sleep.

Clare blew out her candle but did not get into bed. She sat at her silver-frosted window and stared out dumbly into the frozen, star-specked night and moaned slightly, almost inaudibly in the back of her throat, for she felt dazed with the suffering which would not go away.

"Holy Mary, mother of God, help me," she whispered

inside her own head. Martin Heywood had fallen out of her life, ripping a jagged hole in the fabric of it and she was lost and frightened. The world was a cold place without him in it, a physical cold which had nothing to do with the bitter temperature of her bedroom. She felt hollow, not aching or hurting but dragged down with a sadness, a numbness which was almost welcomed.

It was the beginning of January now and she had been over to Edgeclough twice since that day in Martin Heywood's bedroom when she had almost scratched his eye out in fury. Not just fury, she realised that now, but humiliation, hurt pride, shame, and an awareness of her own foolish naïvety in thinking that he loved her enough to marry her. And it was only at Edgeclough that she managed to claw back some of the self-esteem Martin had stolen from her. In the affection of Nelly who, though she found it impossible to put her arms about the grieving girl, let her see nevertheless that she was valued, loved, welcomed. In the jubilant reception she received from Archie and Lavender, from Mildred and Dorcas, who were Nelly's lasses, from Midge and Hetty and all the other young ones who sat spellbound while she read to them in Lew's cosy kitchen.

Before the cataclysmic parting with Martin he had told her she was to help herself from his study if there were any books she found interesting, promising as he kissed her rosy, eager face that he wouldn't tell any of the other servants that she could read. He didn't know why she wanted to keep it a secret, he said, for he was proud of her and she should be too, but Clare knew that it would alter her relationship with those with whom she worked and they would look at her with different eyes. She would be considered to be getting above her station in life, which, after all, was the lowest in the social scale, that of a servant. After she had laboured through *Pride and Prejudice* and finding she liked the author's story, someone called Jane Austen, she had gone on to try another, *Sense and Sensibility*, which, probably because she was now more proficient, and quicker, she had enjoyed even more.

But the biggest find had, at least from the children's point of view, been in the unused nursery which was just beneath her own room and which she had discovered when, in her new position of housemaid, she had been set to clean it.

"Rumpelstiltskin", "The Goose Girl", "Jorinda and Joringel", which were fairy tales by two brothers whose surname was Grimm, captured the imagination of the colour-starved children, most of whom worked in the mill six days out of seven. The tales took them, and her, to heights of marvelling delight. There was also Edward Lear's *Book of Nonsense* and one the boys loved the most because it was filled with magical adventures called *The Last of the Mohicans.* With half a dozen children nestling up to her, wanting to hold her hand or sit or her lap, with Lew watching her, his love for her glowing from his soft grey eyes, his kind face smiling through the firelight telling her she was worthwhile, she felt a slow returning of her self-respect and her confidence, which had taken a terrible blow, and though she was sadly aware that she would never relinquish that part of her in which Martin and her love for him rested, she knew, for had she not done it before, that she would recover.

"That's a right proper tale, lass, fer them as likes such things," Nelly said from her cosy corner by Lew's fire, for though she had one of her own she did like to listen to Clare's storytelling, though she wouldn't admit it, not for a gold sovereign. The children had been shooed off to their own homes, much against their will, repeating again and again that they would see her in four weeks and Lew had gone out to the back of the cottage to fetch another bucket of coal, for the day was bitter cold and Nelly, who saw more than Clare gave her credit for, took the opportunity to speak.

"Don't you, Nelly?" Clare leaned forward and took Nelly's flaccid hand, holding it firmly between her own despite Nelly's struggle to release herself. She had the measure of Nelly now and sometimes, though she knew she would get no sympathy and probably what Lew called a real mouthful, she knew Nelly would never turn away from her, and she was overcome with an urge to empty her heart of all that was in it, all that slashed at her day after day. To tell her that her love for Martin Heywood was a live and burning thing inside her that would not ease, to put her head on Nelly's shoulder and weep, to have Nelly's arms about her as once her own mammy had comforted her childish woes. She wanted to tell her that if it was not for this haven with her and Lew and the children she thought she might have lost her reason these last months, but she couldn't, for she could not bear to display the pain lest it get away from her and distort all their lives.

"Nay, 'tis fer bairns and me an' thi' aren't bairns, are we, lass?" Nelly answered surprisingly.

"What?"

"Nay, my lass, there's summat wrong wi' thi', an' 'as bin fer months now. Tha's lost weight again an' I know it's nowt ter do wi't work tha' does up along. Tha' thrived on it at first, gettin' bonny but look at tha' now. I were sayin' ter Betty—"

"Nelly ..." Clare was appalled. "You don't talk about me behind—"

"Give over, girl." Nelly's head reared up in deep offence. "It were Betty mentioned it, like, askin' if I'd noticed an' when I said I 'ad she asked me what were't cause. I shut 'er up but I'd be glad if tha' could tell me, lass. Tha're not poorly, are thi'?" Her face, tinted with a false rosiness from the firelight, spasmed anxiously but she still did her best to pull her hand away from Clare's. Nelly, a true northerner, was not comfortable with physical contact. "Tha'd tell me if tha' were ... poorly, wouldn't tha'?" And Clare had a feeling that Nelly meant something else entirely when she used the word "poorly".

"Of course I would, Nelly. If there was anything to worry about you'd be the first to know, so you would."

"What about Lew?"

"What about him?"

"'Ow long are thi' ter keep 'im 'angin' about like some lost soul at 'eaven's gate? 'Tis not fair to 'im, lass, not way 'e feels about thi'."

"I can't help that, Nelly. I've been truthful with him. I've never given him any reason to believe—"

"'Appen not but 'e believes it just the same. 'E reckons if 'e's patient enough tha'll come ter ... well ..." It was not in Nelly to say the word "love" but she made it clear what was in her mind, and in Lew's.

Clare felt the weight of it fall about her shoulders, for how could she carry her love for Martin Heywood and Lew's love for her at one and the same time? Lew was the best man in the world, she knew that, and would make a wonderfully kind and loving husband, but how could she give herself to one man while she loved another? Lew was a contradiction in today's times. He was a gentleman, far more than Martin Heywood, or the gentry who pranced about at Longworth Hall, or so she had heard. The contradiction was that he was gentle and he was a man. He could hold an injured bird in his hand and it would lie still as if it trusted him, and yet she knew his strength, not his physical strength, though he had that in abundance, but the strength that kept him fighting for the life he believed his fellow man deserved. He was not a prig, neither pompous nor overbearingly moralistic, he just hated the exploitation of the majority by the few and would say so at any street corner where men gathered to listen to him. And yet he could make them laugh as well as think. He could joke and lark about with them, with the children, his great heart strong and honest in their cause. She loved him. She had loved him from the start but she could not say so to him, for it was not the love he wanted from her.

He came in on a flurry of sleety snow, blowing on his hands and stamping his feet on the floor, carrying the bucket of coal to the fireside.

"By 'eck, it's parky out there, lass. Tha'd better wrap up warm fer't walk back an' we'd best get goin', I reckon. It'll snow soon an' I want tha' safe before it does. Now, Nelly, lass, will I fetch tha' some coal afore I set off along? No, then I'll see thi' to tha' front door."

"Give over, Lew Earnshaw, 'tis only next door. If I can't find me way ter me own front door it's a poor do."

They walked in silence for a while, through the dwindling daylight and into the teeth of a cutting wind and though Clare kept begging him to go back, for didn't she know the way like the back of her hand by now, he would not.

"Stop tha' frettin', lass. Tha' knows very well I'll not let tha' walk it by thissen. I'll mekk sure tha's in't sight o' farm'ouse then I promise I'll turn back. It's not stickin' yet" – meaning the snow which was still more sleet than anything else – "an' I'll be 'ome before tha've got tha' shawl off an' tha' feet up ter't fire. They do let tha' sit wi' tha' feet up ter't fire, don't they?" Laughing, for he was a man of his times and knew that men and women, servants, mill hands, mine workers, factory hands were taken advantage of. Clare seemed to be treated fairly though she, like all the others he fought for, worked long hours which were sometimes overwhelming.

She laughed and without thought took his hand.

"What would I do without you and Nelly?" she asked him.

"Nay, don't ask me, woman, tha'd not last a week," he answered, longing to say more but keeping the mood light as she seemed to be disposed to do.

"You're the only friends I have."

"What about them up at farm, aren't they tha' friends?" he asked her and for some reason there was a catch in his voice as though the question had more to it than was obvious.

"Aye, I suppose so, but if I hadn't these Sundays to look forward to I'd be after going—" She stopped abruptly and he half turned to question her but they were at the farm gate by now and she twisted away, knowing she was about to say too much.

"I'll see you in four weeks, Lew. Now don't hang about.

Get home before the snow comes down any worse." And when he turned away, thinking she had gone round the corner of the house, she watched him go, her face wet with tears for the good and loving man that he was. If only . . . if only she could . . .

Her thoughts were never finished, for as she rounded the corner into the yard she was amazed to see that the back of the house was ablaze with lights and through the closed kitchen door there came a wailing and shouting: was that Martin's voice? Oh, sweet Mary, what was Martin doing in the kitchen and how was she to go in and face him with all the servants looking on? But more to the point, her suddenly clearing mind asked, what the devil was he doing there and who was that weeping and carrying on as though a horde of savages had descended on them and was slaughtering them on the spot. It was not just one voice that screeched out something unintelligible but several and over it all Martin's voice thundered, but, it seemed, to no avail.

She opened the door and stepped inside, and with her came the first enormous flakes of snow, falling to the flags and settling there for a moment before melting. Every person in the room, of whom there seemed to be dozens, turned to look at her, and though she did her best to avoid his eyes, hers hurried to meet those of Martin Heywood. For a second, no more, their love was revealed, each to the other as though it were something that was impossible to hide without some sort of prepared defence, then he whirled away in great relief.

"Thank God, here's somebody who doesn't look as though she's going to pieces. Will you take charge of these women, please . . . er . . ." Despite the drama, whatever it was, it seemed he could not bring himself to speak her name. "They are hysterical, every last one of them, and though I concede they have had a shock, there is surely no need to act as though . . . as though . . ." He pushed his hand distractedly through his hair, turning to George and Mr Starling who, bewilderingly, were hanging about on the periphery of the commotion. Gracie and Adah sobbed inconsolably in one another's arms and Belle, sitting at the table, had her head on her arms. Thirza sat beside her, her face like carved white marble, her eyes wide with shock and beyond her, sprawled in her rocking-chair, was the obviously dead body of Mrs Case.

Chapter Twelve

Mrs Case was respectfully carried from the chair in which she had collapsed to her bed – making sure that her skirt was modestly arranged round her ankles – by George and Mr Starling, supervised by Clare who was the only one among them who seemed to have her wits about her. The body of the housekeeper was decently covered with a clean sheet, fetched from the linen cupboard by herself, the candle blown out and the door shut, and when it was accomplished Clare went down the stairs and into the kitchen. Martin Heywood's last retort had been that he'd better send for the doctor, since the magistrate must be informed of any sudden death, so was she to suppose that they were to wait up until the doctor came? She felt quite stupefied, unable to set her dazed mind into any sort of cohesive, helpful channel, and whether it was the thunderbolt of Mrs Case's death or the sudden shock of Martin's appearance in the kitchen she couldn't tell, not yet at any rate.

She fully expected someone, probably Thirza who was the most senior of the maidservants, to have pulled the others back into some sort of order when she returned to the kitchen but they were still sprawled here and there in various postures of disbelief and uncertainty as though, with Mrs Case not to hand, they were unable to make up their minds what they should be doing next. She was surprised, for Thirza had always seemed to be so efficient, so capable, so much in command, at least of *her*, but still, shock took you in many ways and who was she to judge? She noticed that Francy and Maddie had arrived, anxious not to miss the excitement, and out in the yard she could see one or two of the outside men hanging about in the veil of snow.

"Well," she said briskly, for something had to be done and no one seemed to be doing it. They all looked up at her, waiting for her to continue, all except Thirza who continued to stare at the door that led into the house as though waiting for Mrs Case to come bustling through it.

"Well," Clare said again, "we can't sit about here like dollops of dough" – a phrase she had heard Mrs Case say many a time – "can we, so until Mr Heywood tells us what to do, or the doctor arrives I'm after thinking a nice cup of tea would do us all the world of good so get the teapot out, will you, Belle, and make it good and strong."

"What, Mrs Case's teapot?" Belle asked doubtfully, but beginning to sit up straighter as though a voice of authority, even if it was only Clare's, had put a stiffener in her spine.

"Of course. Mrs Case wouldn't mind, would she? She always liked a decent cup of tea and she wouldn't begrudge us one now. An' sure it does no good to loll about waiting for permission. Oh, you'd best tell those men to come in and have a hot drink as well or they'll freeze out there. Now, would someone like to tell me what happened?" Then wished she hadn't because they all began to talk at once, and Adah, who had known Mrs Case a bare three months and had done nothing but get shouted at by her, began to weep loudly and wetly.

"She were only reachin' fer 'er shawl. She said she felt cold."

"I thought she were goin' ter fall out of t'chair inter't fire."

"It give us all a right turn, didn't it, Gracie?"

"One minnit she were givin' Adah what for an' next she were all of a do-dah."

"Maister come runnin' when Thirza began ter scream."

Only Thirza remained silent, still totally absorbed with what she could see by the door, an image vouchsafed to no one but herself. Gracie and Adah, quite overcome at recounting it and reliving it, fell into one another's arms and began to sob wildly and Belle dropped the tea caddy and spilled tea leaves all over Mrs Case's rocking-chair which sent her off again as though she had defiled poor Mrs Case's last resting place.

"For heaven's sake will you all be quiet. There's no need for this, you know," Clare shouted, again wondering why it was down to her to pull them together. She had to raise her voice to make herself heard above the din, marvelling at the fuss they were making, for none of them had been particularly fond of the woman who had ruled them for so long. "Now, Belle, clear up that mess and make us a pot of tea. You, Gracie, get the cups and saucers down and Adah, fetch the milk from the pantry."

In five minutes they were all sipping their tea and staring reflectively at Mrs Case's rocking-chair, even the outside men who were glad of a brew and a warm before taking themselves back to their beds. What the hell was going to happen now? they were wondering, especially the women, for Mrs Case had ruled them all with a rod of iron.

When the bell jangled it made them all jump and glance automatically at the board to see where it came from, though who would it be but the master? It was from the study and Clare's heart began to race as though she had just run down the steep slope from Badgers Edge to the farm gate.

For some reason they all looked at her, then at Thirza, then back at her.

"Thirza ..." she said gently to the stunned housemaid but Thirza began to shake her head, her mouth opening on what might have been a wail of denial though no sound came out.

The bell rang again, more urgently this time and all the maidservants shrank back as though to answer the master's summons were fraught with danger.

"Well, I suppose somebody's got to answer it," Clare said. She threw up her head in a gesture that seemed to imply she was off to the gallows and meant to go bravely, and the expression of every woman in the room, with the exception of Thirza who had relapsed into a comatose state, seemed to say they agreed with her.

The study door was half open but she knocked steadfastly and marched straight in, moving to stand in front of his desk, behind which he sat, head bent over something he was writing.

"This is a note to the doctor," he said without looking up. "Send George, will you. I've explained that Mrs Case is definitely dead and there is no need for him to come traipsing up here tonight. Tomorrow will do, first thing. Get the women to bed will you, Thirza, and I'll breakfast early. Is there someone who can cook?"

"It's not Thirza, sir, and I can cook." Her voice was perfectly steady and when he looked up in what seemed to be horror she watched as he lurched back in his chair as if she had shot him.

"What the bloody hell are you doing here?" he snarled. "Where is Thirza? She's the one to take over until another housekeeper is employed. Get back to the kitchen and send her to me."

She could feel the anger begin somewhere in her breast, a hard knot just where her heart lay. She knew a dreadful resentment that he should feel he had the right to speak to her as though she were no more than the dirt beneath his feet. As though she were not only presumptuous in believing she had the authority to answer his summons over all the other maidservants but that after all that had happened between them she had the bloody nerve even to face him. But she hung on to her temper which she had found, as the months passed, seemed to be reasserting itself. Her daddy had said she had one and after the bad times she had not believed it, nor even remembered it and though, so far, she had found no reason to show it, she knew it was there simmering beneath her outward calm.

"Thirza is not well, sir, but I can send in Gracie or Adah if you'd rather."

"Who the hell are they?" he growled, leaning forward again over his desk to make some mark on the notepaper that lay before him.

"Both are scullery-maids, sir," she said, her face perfectly straight.

"Don't play the bloody fool with me, woman. Send me someone who is capable of ... of setting things to rights in the kitchen. I would like some coffee for a start."

"Certainly, sir. Shall I send it in with the kitchen-maid, the laundry-maid or the dairy-maid? All are available."

He stood up and for a dreadful moment she thought he was going to stride round the desk and knock her down. He was close to giving way to a total lack of control, ready to shout and bluster and she became quiet inside her where the memory of their love was hidden, the remembrance of that love soothing the anger, understanding at last that it was she who was doing this to him. He could, quite simply, not stand the sight of her, could not deal with it, did not want her here where he was forced to look at her. He was a man accustomed to his own way, to getting what he wanted from an early age, she suspected, and her refusal of him had been a tremendous blow, not only to the love he bore her, for she knew he did love her, but to his male and arrogant pride.

"I don't bloody well care, d'you hear, as long as it's not you. Is that clear? Now send Thirza in. She must take over until ... well, just send her in."

"I'll try, sir."

"What the devil does that mean, you'll try?" His eyes were almost silver, the blue draining away in his rage, and for a moment she felt her hand twitch in its need to lay itself on him, as one might on a terrified child.

"Thirza seems to . . . to have taken Mrs Case's death very badly," she told him quietly, "but I'm sure she will be herself in the morning. In the meanwhile I'll make your coffee and send one of the others in with it."

She watched him struggle to rein in his still smouldering rage, her eyes steady, her face studiedly blank, then he turned his back on her and stared out into what looked like a wall of solid white beyond the window. She hesitated for a moment but he told her curtly, "That will be all," so she left the room. When she gained the privacy and dimness of the hall she leaned against the wall for a moment, then, like him, turned her back on what was unbearable but must be borne and pressed her face to the polished wood. She was shaking, momentarily mindless with sorrow that their love should be brought to this, then, squaring her shoulders, she made her way to the kitchen which, it seemed, she was to take over until Thirza was recovered.

"I can't do it," Thirza said, and kept on saying day after day, for without Mrs Case, who had been the pivot about whom Thirza had revolved for many, many years, Thirza could not function. She, like the others, whom Mrs Case had turned into well-trained, efficient but mindless machines, needed orders, a person of authority above her, someone to whom responsibility came naturally. Mrs Case had been that person and the house had run like a well-oiled clock which is wound regularly every night and ticks happily all day long. Mrs Case had prepared the menus, checked the weekly linen, trained the young servants and had in her charge the replenishment of the household stores. Thirza couldn't do that, she wept. For a start she couldn't cook so how was she to decide what to cook? It was beyond her to decide what Mr Heywood should have set before him on his dining table and as for preparing a meal for a dozen hungry servants, never mind any dinner guests he might wish to entertain, it was totally beyond her. Even if she could cook, which she couldn't and didn't want to learn at her time of life, she could neither read nor write and so Mr Heywood would have to find someone else. Yes, she knew she was the senior servant, that she had worked at Moorhouse longer than anybody, apart from Mrs Case and Mr Starling, but it made no difference. This was a good place and she would hate to leave it. She was prepared to go on as she had done for years under any new housekeeper the master employed, but take Mrs Case's place she couldn't. Even Mr Heywood could not persuade her. They could hear him shouting at her through the green baize door that led from the kitchen to the wide front hallway. She would be housekeeper, would have her own parlour, have a housekeeper's wage which could rise to as much as forty pounds a year but it seemed Thirza didn't want it. She liked being head housemaid with an under housemaid beneath her, she cried, and had no ambition to rise any higher.

When their master thrust open the green baize door and imperiously beckoned to Clare, they turned to gawp at one another in surprise. What now? their bewildered expressions asked.

The day after Mrs Case's death and since no one else seemed prepared to take on the job, even Belle who was kitchen-maid, Clare had begun that first day cooking the simple meals Mrs Case had taught her, giving Martin Heywood eggs and bacon, which was easy enough, at breakfast time, with lashings of hot buttered toast to fill him up, as he had been used to a selection of mushrooms, sausage – made to Mrs Case's own recipe – and fried tomatoes. She did an enormous casserole at noon, which was when the servants expected their dinner, made with shin of beef, putting it in the oven at the crack of dawn as shin needed a long, slow cooking time. There was an abundance of vegetables, cabbage and sliced carrots and mashed potatoes, followed by several of her fruit pies served with whipped cream. They all declared themselves satisfied, though somewhat uneasy with Mrs Case's body still lying just above their heads; but when the undertaker had been and removed it, the funeral service, arranged by the master, to be in two days' time, they began to relax.

There was a nice leg of pork in the pantry. With Belle's help, who appeared to be quite happy to take temporary orders from Clare, she managed an evening meal for Martin Heywood, plain but, she prided herself, well cooked, followed by the fruit pie she and the servants had shared at noon. Thirza served it and there were no complaints, she told Clare, though naturally it was not up to Mrs Case's standards. When a new cook/housekeeper was found Clare would, of course, return to her job of under housemaid but in the meanwhile she seemed to be managing well enough.

Again she stood quietly before his desk where he lounged in a chair with his back to the window and the lovely clean sweep of the snow which had fallen the night Mrs Case had died. There were several sets of footprints where Mr Starling and Hammy had tramped across the garden to get to the gate that led into the lane and had to be cleared, but it still looked quite lovely, the shrubs and trees to the side of the house decorated in the bright sunshine with winter's silver and diamonds on white velvet.

He was fiddling with a pen and pretending this meant no more to him than if she had been any other servant. He did not look at her and because of it she was able to study his face which, she noticed, was thinner, with the grooves on either side of his mouth somehow deeper. It was almost three months since they had parted so bitterly and though both of them were not aware of it in themselves, they had both altered. Martin Heywood had never been what might be called a merry-natured man. His wit had been wry, sharp, mocking at times, but there had been humour in him; now he had a taciturn look about him, a dragging down of the corners of his mouth, an unsmiling severity which told her how badly he had taken her spurning of him. And yet it was not her doing, for if he had been the decent man she had believed him to be, hoped he was, he would have offered her marriage. He had not loved her enough and she could do nothing about that.

"Will you take on the job?" he asked her abruptly. "That bloody woman has hysterics every time I offer her the position – I was not aware that she can neither read nor write – and I can do nothing to move her. You have . . . the food has been . . . edible; and I know you to be a good worker – responsible, conscientious – Mrs Case told me so. The job demands someone who can read and write and, I suppose, add up, and you, it seems, are the only one in the kitchen who can do all these things. You have a . . . a good brain, and could learn how to manage the accounts. I could, of course, engage another woman to take Mrs Case's place but I haven't the time nor the inclination, at least at the moment, to be bothered with it. The others seem to have accepted your direction, at least I assume they have, so I am asking you: can you manage it? I would, of course, pay you housekeeper's wages. I would leave it entirely to you. I don't want you running to me with problems, discussions about domestic trivia, you know the sort of thing. You would be in total charge of the house and would have no need to involve me in the running of it."

He continued to fiddle with the pen while she stood before him in a state of stunned shock which held her so firmly she could not answer. It was beyond belief, beyond anything in her wildest imagining and she could not assimilate it into her numbed brain. It was less than two years since she had stumbled from a ramshackle boat to the hectic scramble of the Liverpool docks, weighed down by a sorrow so great she wanted to die. She had been weak, starving, but somehow she had struggled on, moving inexorably towards this man and this destiny and really . . . really . . . she would have to pull herself together, for though he was not looking at her but was giving his total attention to the pen in his hand, he was waiting for her to speak.

"Well?" he said at last, his voice harsh. "Are you to take it or not? I need to know now, for if not I will have to find—"

"Yes."

He looked up then and their eyes locked. "Is that all you have to say?"

"I shall need more staff."

"Dear God, a minute into the job and already you are demanding—"

"Someone must do my work. Thirza cannot manage on her own. And I shall have to have access to Mrs Case's books, recipe books and such, the household accounts which will need to be studied. You yourself must be prepared to—" She almost said *be patient* but when was this man ever patient, so she bit off the sentence. She would not beg him to be tolerant of her first efforts in the art of cooking, the kind of cooking Mrs Case had done and which she was determined to emulate.

"Yes?" His voice was abrupt.

"The tradesmen will need to be consulted so that I can learn how to—"

"Couldn't Thirza help you with that?" he asked impatiently, eager to be rid of her, his manner saying that he wanted her out of his sight, now and in the future. She was to run his house but she was not to show her face to him. *Ever.* He had not said so in as many words but it was implied, and understood.

"That wouldn't work. Sure an' wouldn't I be wantin' to do things my own way, sir, and Thirza will be wanting to follow Mrs Case's methods." Her inner nervousness caused her to lapse into her Irish idiom.

"Very well. See to it but I repeat, I want nothing to do with it. As long as I have good food set in front of me, a clean shirt every day and the house clean and warm, that's all I ask."

As he had done last time he dismissed her by turning his back on her.

The funeral of Clarice Case was well attended, not for any sense of loss or sorrow on the part of those who came but simply to get a good look at the girl, an Irish peasant come over with a boatload of other Irish peasants, who was to take her place. The chapel in Old Delph was crowded with those who had come on foot for miles from all directions, as they were all working folk, to view this paragon who, it was said, could not even cook and until a few weeks ago had been no more than a scullery-maid in Martin Heywood's kitchen. What were they to make of that? they whispered among themselves. She was a bonny lass, there was no denying, and Martin Heywood was known for a lusty man who, in his youth, had been something of a wild one, chasing the lasses, gambling, riding wild horses with those lads up at Longworth Hall and it was only on his father's death that he had settled down. He was there himself, dressed as gentlemen of his wealth and rank dress, which looked strange among all the caps and clogs and shawls. But he and his new housekeeper did not even exchange a glance, never mind a word.

Nobody quite knew where Mrs Case had come from or even if she had any family, for it seemed to them that she had been at Moorhouse Farm from the beginning of time, at least when the old missus had been alive and her gone these five years or more. How old was she? those who sat round the fire at Moorhouse asked one another, at least when Clare was not in the kitchen. As old as the hills she had seemed to the younger ones but perhaps with Clare, they told one another complacently, things would be a bit easier now. She was one of them and, anyroad, didn't know a brawn-presser from a mackerel saucepan so they'd soon let her see what's what.

When the service and interment were over they were startled when the new housekeeper made a beeline for a group of people who stood by the gate and when she put her arms first about one elderly woman and then a tall, lean, working-class chap who held her closely to him, they were slackjawed with astonishment. They had known, as who had not, that she had been taken in by some woman from Edgeclough when she arrived off the boat from Ireland but who was the man and what was going on between *them*? They did their best to shuffle over in their direction in order to hear what was said but the group moved off with Clare's arms through that of the woman and the man. They were not the only ones to notice Clare's involvement with Lew Earnshaw and Nelly Bradbury.

"Wilta be all right, our Clare? Cans't manage job as 'ousekeeper?" Nelly asked her anxiously, her thin face for once showing astoundment, for Nelly Bradbury had thought there was nothing much to astound her in this world she lived in. "We was fair capt when we 'eard, wasn't we, Lew? Lew wanted ter come over right away ter mekk sure tha' was shipshape, especially when ussen 'eard tha' was ter be 'ousekeeper. It's all over Edgeclough an'—"

"Nelly, you're not to worry, d'you hear? Thirza didn't want it an' so Mr Heywood's put me in complete charge. I can do a bit of cooking, Mrs Case showed me, and besides, aren't I the only one who can read an' write, thanks to you, Lew."

"Eh, lass, who'd've thought it," Lew managed to say, but it was in his face that he was in no doubt that this promotion had put Clare even further from his reach than ever.

"I'm still the same, Lew, and won't I be home to see you all as often as possible. Maybe more often seeing that I'm not under-housemaid any more, which reminds me, I'll be wanting a girl."

She stopped speaking, smiling up into Lew's bemused eyes but looking somewhat embarrassed as though she were throwing her improved status in their faces, and from the railings where he had hitched his mare, Martin Heywood's face darkened and he jerked on the animal's reins more fiercely than was usual.

Lew smiled and his eyes lit up with what might have been glee. "Ay up, she's throwin' 'er weight about already, Nelly. She'll be expectin' me ter touch me cap when next we meet an' you ter bob a curtsey."

"Well, she'll 'ave a long wait, lad." And they all three smiled at one another in perfect harmony, in perfect affection, and with a muffled oath Martin Heywood scrambled on to his mare's back and with a shout to those who stood about ordered them to get out of his way, which they did, wondering what was up with Martin Heywood.

Lavender Bickerstaffe, as Lew had instructed her, knocked on the back door of the farm at Moorhouse the next day at just gone six o'clock.

"I'm to see Miss Hanrahan," she told Belle somewhat nervously, for like Clare before her she had never in her life seen the likes of the room beyond the well-scrubbed doorstep.

"'Ave you indeed?" Belle sniffed. "An' who's she when she's at home?"

A sharp voice behind her made her jump and she whirled about; then, seeing who it was, she relaxed. For a moment she had imagined that Mrs Case was back from the grave which gave her goose bumps but it was only Clare.

She smiled, evidently much amused. "There's a lass 'ere askin' fer Miss Hanrahan."

"That's me, Belle, so ask her in and take her to my room. I shall be in in a minute."

Belle gaped. "*Your* room?"

"Yes, you know where the housekeeper's room is, don't you, Belle?"

"Course I do but . . ."

"Then show Lavender where to go and then make us a pot of tea and bring it."

"Tea?"

"Really, Belle, have you turned deaf since this morning?" Clare turned to smile reassuringly at Lavender who had been watching this exchange with great interest.

"I won't be long, Lavender. Take off your coat and sit by the fire until I come. It's a bitter day again, isn't it?"

"Aye, it is that."

Sitting with their bloody feet up to the fire, they were, Belle was to report back to the others, drinking tea as if they were gentry and if Mrs Case got to hear of it she'd turn over in her bloody grave. Aye, it was enough to make a body swear. They shook their heads, sipping on their own cups of tea, their own feet up to the kitchen fire, unaware of the core of steel that was buried deep within their new mistress and which was to make her unbreakable despite their best efforts.

Chapter Thirteen

She thought the next six months were the hardest she had ever spent in her life. Nothing like the bad time in Ireland, of course, for that had been harrowing, life-destroying, so totally unbearable she had only just survived it and even now didn't know how she had done it. No, this was hard, hard slog, hard fought and, in the end, hard won.

Begin as you mean to go on, she had told herself sternly as she climbed into her bed on the day of Mrs Case's funeral, realising that from tomorrow night she would sleep in the housekeeper's bed in the bedroom on the second floor, and sit in the housekeeper's parlour along the passage from the kitchen, but it would need a delicate touch to deal with the ticklish task of compelling Thirza and Belle, though perhaps not Gracie and Adah, and the others who did not actually work in the kitchen, to take orders from a woman who, up until a few nights ago, had been taking orders from them. Belle had been Mrs Case's handmaiden. Mrs Case had been teaching her in the simpler tasks of cooking, though she had not got much beyond fetching and carrying and perhaps beating eggs ready for omelettes, which is why Mrs Case found Clare's own interest and talent so rewarding. Belle had been learning Mrs Case's simpler recipes, blundering through Mrs Case's recipe books and menus in an attempt to learn their complexities, which was difficult since Belle could not read. It hadn't mattered too much, for Mrs Case was well aware that Belle was no more than a workhorse, strong, reliable, cheerful and willing and would, one day, probably suit some lower-middle-class family who required a plain cook. She would never attain Mrs Case's high standards, and could never, in a month of Sundays, have taken over Mrs Case's mantle as housekeeper, they all knew that; but still she had worked in the kitchen for nearly seven years and so was senior to the scullery-maid, in years served if not in age.

Thirza, despite her refusal to accept the job of housekeeper, would not take kindly to taking orders from someone whom she still, in her own mind, called "the new girl" despite the new girl's twelve months in service and her promotion to Mrs Case's job. She was willing to work in harness with Clare, to be partners, if you like, in the running of the house until a new housekeeper was employed which, naturally, they had all expected. She would do her duty as long as she had no responsibility for its ups and its certainly more frequent "downs".

When she had learned who *was* to have that responsibility she had been staggered, but after she had got over the initial shock she quickly adjusted to the change of plan, for it might, in the long run, suit her better. She had no qualms about getting the better of the new girl. None at all. She saw herself as a kind of superior servant, due to her long service in the house, who might be called on for advice, and with the new under maid, the one with the unlikely name of Lavender, to do all the heavy work in the master's part of the house, to continue much as she had done when Mrs Case was in charge, but with more freedom to suit the day and the work she did in it.

She was to be sadly mistaken!

"I think in view of my new position it would be as well if you learned to call me Miss Hanrahan. It would not do to have the housekeeper known by her christian name, would it." Clare smiled round the astonished circle of faces which she had gathered about her as soon as Lavender had been instructed in her duties. They were in the kitchen, Thirza and Belle, Gracie and Adah, Francy and Maddie and Lavender, all, except Lavender, ready to sit down to a nice cup of tea which, since Mrs Case's death, they had become used to having more or less when it pleased them. In fact, Thirza, having got over the shock of the housekeeper's sudden passing, was actually sitting in her chair waiting for the kettle, which was embosomed in the heart of the fire, to come to the boil. The big clock on the wall ticked away the silent seconds and outside the wind gusted breathlessly across the bleak winter landscape.

Thirza sat up slowly and her face took on a hue that could only be likened to that of a ripe plum. She squared her thin shoulders and straightened her already ramrod-straight back as though preparing for battle, which she was.

"I beg your pardon! Did I hear aright? You've been in this household no more than five minutes and already think you've the right to speak to me, and others, who have been here for years, as though you were Mrs Case and we were no more than skivvies. I'll work with you, I've said that, but as for calling you *Miss Hanrahan*, well, you can forget that for—"

"Thank you, Thirza, I think you have said enough, in fact more than enough. I would like you to remember that though you were given the opportunity to take up *my* post, you turned it down, saying you were perfectly content to remain as you were. And that is what you have done. You are a housemaid and *I* am housekeeper. You did not address Mrs Case as Clarice and you will not address me as Clare. Is that understood? There is something else you don't know. I can read and write and therefore I am more qualified to be housekeeper than any of you. Who among you could do the household accounts? None? I thought so. That is probably why the master chose me for the job. Am I making myself clear?"

Clare, whose heart was hammering fit to break through her ribs, showed none of her terror in this, her first crossing of swords with a fellow servant. Her face was composed and her eyes looked steadily into those of Thirza and the rest of them watched avidly, for it was Thirza who would lead where they were to follow. If she dominated their new housekeeper, if she refused to be browbeaten by her, leaving Clare Hanrahan – *Miss* Hanrahan indeed – routed, then that would be the pattern of their future lives. If on this first set-to Thirza came out best then she, despite her calling as housemaid, would be virtual ruler of the kitchen at Moorhouse Farm. It had never struck them that Clare was anything more than an Irish biddy who had come over with the two hundred thousand other Irish refugees who had flooded Lancashire, most of them crowding the tenements of Manchester and Liverpool, rambling about the streets looking for employment, or so those in their cosy jobs at Moorhouse Farm had heard. But not this one. She had dragged herself across the county and taken on the exhausting job of scrubbing floors for twelve or fourteen hours a day. She hadn't a pick on her when she started, giving the impression a stray breeze would have her over but she had overcome her own weakness and had proved a willing helpmeet when there was extra work to be done. She had been no trouble to anyone, very rarely expressing an opinion on anything, quiet and biddable and taken for granted.

But who on earth would have believed that she could read and write and how on earth had the master known about it? When she was taken on it had not been mentioned, not by Mrs Case and as far as they knew not by the master. But he had known! Again, as it had been in the graveyard, they wondered what to make of it all. Surely there was something odd about it. They weren't quite sure what they meant by *odd* but they had a feeling there was something. Twelve months on from being hired she was housekeeper, and, so the last few days seemed to imply, would be cook as well, and not only that but was demanding that they show her the respect Mrs Case had known.

Their eyes were wide and bright with excitement, for they were in no doubt as to who would win this contest of wills. They had all suffered under Thirza's superior thumb and had been amazed when she had turned down the chance to take up where Mrs Case had left off. Of course, she couldn't cook nor, as Clare had just pointed out, could she read or write which was a disadvantage, so perhaps that was why. She would still not have been in complete charge with another woman, a new cook, at the kitchen stove, but still it was going to be interesting, their mesmerised expressions said as they exchanged wondering glances.

"Making yourself clear! You're telling me that I'm to call you Miss Hanrahan when you're no more than a jumped-up Irish scrubbing woman who, because you smiled nicely at the master—"

"*That's enough.*" Clare's voice was icy. "Sure an' weren't you given the chance for Mrs Case's post but turned it down because you haven't the guts for it. Hard work, a good brain, someone who can successfully manage others in the performance of their work and has the ability to get things done properly, that's what it takes, and you haven't got it. I have. Now then, is there anyone else who's sayin' a word because if there is best get it said now. If Thirza doesn't want to work under my supervision she has only to say so. There's the door. I'm sure Mr Heywood would trust me to find a new housemaid. I've done so already and there are many girls like Lavender who would be glad of the job. I've worked here long enough to know what's needed and could train a decent girl to my own standards. You had better get used to it, all of you, and if that's not possible, pack your bags along with Thirza. I'll give anyone who can't work with me and wants to leave a good reference and a week's pay. Now then, is it to be Miss Hanrahan, or not?"

She was still wearing her housemaid's simple grey dress and white apron but she had removed her cap, the other badge of office as a maidservant. She meant to go into Crossfold at the first opportunity and have a dark-blue dress made, one in a serviceable material but smart and well fitting, over which she would wear a pretty white organdie apron let in with lace and crochetwork. There were a dozen in a drawer in Mrs Case's room. Mrs Case had worn black but Clare intended to look not quite so severe as her predecessor, though she did not pause to wonder why it should matter to her. She had already had a good look round the housekeeper's room and had found the chatelaine which was the housekeeper's badge of office and which had been laid carefully in a drawer, presumably by the undertaker's men. It had hung from Mrs Case's belt, a lovely thing wrought in silver and made up of a pair of scissors in a sheath, a pincushion, a thimble, keys, and all linked to a silver chain with swivel catches. It hung at her belt now, catching the light from the flames of the fire.

"I see it's not taken you long to help yourself to Mrs Case's belongings," Thirza sneered, standing up and sauntering towards Clare with the evident intention of bullying her.

"It belongs to the house and to the woman who is in charge of the house. That is me. Now, are you to go or are you to stay, Thirza? I would imagine at your age it might be tricky finding another position as good as this one."

"How dare you!"

"Oh, for pity's sake, woman. Can you not see you lost your opportunity and it will not come flying back to you. Accept it. If you feel so strongly about it why did you refuse? I know you were upset but surely we can work together as we have done for the past months."

"I'll not call you Miss Hanrahan, not if you put me to the torture."

"And you'll not call me Clare, either. None of you will. Now then, enough time has been wasted and I would be obliged, so I would, if you'd get about the tasks you are supposed to be doing at this moment. And please don't forget that, having worked here for a whole year I know what they should be. Is that clear?"

"Yes, Miss Hanrahan," Gracie and Adah and Lavender said in unison, though Lavender was not awfully sure about hers and was not particularly looking forward to working beside the ogre who was standing up to Clare.

Clare moved about the kitchen, her glance noting that already signs of Mrs Case's passing were revealing themselves. A smeared table top, pan lids set any old how on the pans, which needed a good scouring, and traces of mud on the kitchen floor where one of the men had traipsed it in from the yard. The two scullery-maids were lethargically filling their buckets at the sink in the glassed-in scullery, already going at a slower pace than the one Mrs Case had insisted on. Francy the dairymaid and Maddie, who dealt with the laundry, were drifting towards the back door, their heads together, apparently debating what their line was to be and Clare felt her heart sink in her breast, for it was evident that she was going to have an uphill battle. The influence of Thirza would have a strong effect on these servants who had taken it for granted that she was second-in-command to Mrs Case, but it did no good to dwell on it. She must deal with each crisis, and there would be many, as it developed. She was determined to show Martin Heywood that she might only be an Irish peasant girl, straight from the bogs she had heard herself described as, and not good enough to marry, but she was educated. She knew what was going on in the world from the newspapers she "borrowed" from the study. She knew about books, thanks to Lew, and with the household accounts which she had found locked in Mrs Case's cupboard and which she meant to study, and learn, she would be totally in charge of this house, and these women.

Just as you would have been if Martin had married you, a small voice whispered painfully in her head, moving to her heart where it did further damage. She pulled herself together and lifted her head, for it would not do to let them see her bowed down.

"Right, Belle, will you start with those pans? I want to see my face in them, and that table needs a good scouring. And then you can start on those vegetables Mr Starling has just brought in. I shall do liver and bacon for our dinner and when the provision merchant comes let me know, for there are provisions to be ordered. I will be in Mrs ... in my parlour. Now you, Gracie, will scrub this floor and Adah can make a start in the passageway. Have you got that?"

"Yes, Miss Hanrahan," they said in unison, putting on a small turn of speed. Belle was slower in obeying her orders, her bottom lip stuck out in what Clare knew would be mutiny if it was not nipped in the bud. Nevertheless she fetched her scrubbing brush, a bucket of hot water and the soda which was used on the table and began with the vigour Mrs Case had instilled in her, though it was evident she could not bring herself to address the new housekeeper by her name.

"And what are *my* orders, *Miss Hanrahan*?" Thirza asked mockingly, placing both hands on her hips and tossing her head.

"I shouldn't have to tell you what to do, Thirza," Clare said quietly, "and if I do then it seems to me that you are not capable of being head housemaid. I shall have to keep an eye on you. Now, take Lavender and attend to the front of the house. Mr Heywood's breakfast table needs clearing, as you well know, and I shall be up presently to inspect the linen cupboard. I think that's all for now."

Ignoring their slack jaws and open mouths, she moved gracefully from the kitchen and along the passage to *her* parlour where she shut the door behind her, beginning to shake with the nervous tension she had not allowed the others to see. She put her hand to her mouth which was trembling with the need for what she knew would be a "good cry" but she did not give in to it.

Taking the key to the cupboard, she opened it, removing the household account books and placing them on the desk. She sat down behind it and opened the first one, beginning to study the columns of figures, wondering how Mrs Case had arrived at the same figure at the bottom of each one, doing her best to understand them. She *would* understand them, for if she didn't there was no one to explain them to her since there was one thing she was determined upon and that was that she would not ask Martin Heywood for help. She was soon absorbed, forgetting the scene in the kitchen and the scenes that she knew were to come in the future.

It did not take her long to have Gracie, Adah, Lavender, Francy and Maddie firmly under her control, all of them scarcely remembering the day when Miss Hanrahan had not ruled them. She found that providing she watched them carefully, checking on their work and letting them *see* that she was checking on their work, they performed it scrupulously. They had been trained by a perfectionist and Clarice Case had not only insisted upon perfection, as far as they were able to produce it, but had instilled into them the almost automatic response to her teaching which meant that in a way each one was like a mindless piece of machinery, tuned to perform a certain task. They had been under her command since they had come, raw and ignorant from their family homes at the age of twelve, or even younger in the case of Adah, gradually moving when the time was right from days spent on their knees with their scrubbing brushes and buckets up the ladder of promotion.

Thirza had been the first of those who now worked at Moorhouse Farm, many, many years ago, followed by others who had not come up to scratch and were disposed of to other, less demanding kitchens. Longworth Hall, for instance, where the housekeeper was known to be amiable – slack, in Clarice Case's opinion – was one of them. But Thirza had lived up to Mrs Case's stringent standards, moving on to what she considered to be second only to Mrs Case herself. Mrs Case, knowing she was to be trusted, was inclined to let her arrange her work to suit herself, providing it was done properly, of course, Mrs Case making sure that this was so. Though they had not been friends exactly, for a housekeeper who makes friends with a servant beneath her is asking for trouble, they were close associates, both of them proud of their own efforts and achievements in the running of the household. Thirza was invited into Mrs Case's parlour on occasion to drink tea and discuss the progress of this or that servant. Thirza had admired Mrs Case. She was satisfied with their working relationship and was devastated when she died. She believed that no one, not even herself, could take Mrs Case's place and Clare was made aware of this a dozen times a day.

"Of course in Mrs Case's day we never had roast beef without horseradish sauce . . . We wouldn't dream of putting less than a quarter-pint of linseed oil in the furniture polish . . . I can remember Mrs Case telling me never to use the banister brush for the staircase . . . Cleanliness is next to Godliness, Mrs Case used to say . . ." And she was most upset, in fact she threatened she would go to the master with it, when Clare told her that Mrs Case was dead and that she, Clare Hanrahan, was now in charge and if she wished to speak to the master about it then she was at perfect liberty to do so. That was another thing, the affronted housemaid went on, the way Miss Hanrahan spoke, as though she'd swallowed a book, using words that none of them would use, dividing the household into two parts. Them, meaning the other servants, on one side and Clare, on the other.

When Thirza had recovered somewhat from the shock of the housekeeper's sudden death, Clare began to believe that she regretted her hasty decision not to take the post when it was offered to her, her attitude now being that "if the new girl can do it, anyone could", ignoring the fact that she couldn't cook, read, write or add up a column of figures, which Clare was doing with increasing confidence, nor had she the ability to deal with tradesmen as Clare had learned to do.

Francy and Maddie, employed in the dairy and laundry, did not come so often under Clare's eye, for they worked outside the house in their own province but nevertheless she was responsible for the quality of the milk, the butter, the cream which Francy brought over from the dairy and the immaculacy of the linen Maddie laundered and ironed. The dairy was on the north-facing side of the farmhouse. Its walls were thick, the insides covered with Dutch glazed tiles, as was the floor. There were marble shelves on every wall on which the crocks of fresh milk were placed to deposit cream, or to ripen for churning, and in the middle of the room was a small fountain which kept the atmosphere fresh and cool. It was a delightful work area, kept in pristine condition by Francy who, in addition to making cream and butter, milked the cows brought to the byre by Percy, the cowman married to Maddie.

Maddie was in charge of not only the bed linen, which was changed every week, but the linen worn by the servants and by Mr Heywood. She worked in a washhouse next to the dairy which led into another room used for ironing and drying. In the first room there was a range of tubs, each with its own tapped water, which was a constant marvel to Maddie when it was considered that even up at Longworth Hall water came from a pump in the yard. Mrs Heywood, mother to their master, had been a marvellous woman, far-thinking and efficient, and it had been her efforts that had brought this wonder about. There was a boiler and a furnace to heat the water. The flooring was of York stone laid on brick piers to allow for good drainage. In the second whitewashed room were an ironing board, a strong, white deal table, a clothes-horse for drying and airing and a hotplate to heat the irons.

Maddie was an expert in her field, knowing how to remove ink and grease spots, fruit or wine stains before tackling the washing of the garments. Every article of clothing was sorted into piles, for muslin, woollens, cotton and linen required different treatment and Maddie had been well trained before she was taken on at Moorhouse by a mistress of whom Mrs Case would have approved. It took a full week to get through her duties of washing and getting up the linens, starting at six in the morning and working until six in the evening when she went home to her husband and four children who all worked at various jobs in the fields, stone picking or rook scaring, and were all squashed in a two-bedroom farm labourer's cottage a mile or so from the farmhouse. She was a big, strong, cheerful young woman but her propensity for gossip, especially with Francy who worked so close to her, meant that she needed watching. They became used to Miss Hanrahan's visits to the dairy and the washhouse which never took place at the same time of day or day of the week, not resenting her supervision since Mrs Case had been the same. They did not really know her as she had been when a scullery-maid, or housemaid and so it was easier for them to accept her quite incredible promotion to housekeeper. She seemed to find them, their work and their workplaces quite satisfactory and so there at least Clare found a cheerful willingness to co-operate.

It was the same with Gracie and Adah who were really no more than children who had exchanged the hard life and discipline of their childhood for the routine, just as hard, they knew now. Gracie, who had once shared a bedroom with the new housekeeper when the new housekeeper was no more than a scullery-maid, could not forget that Miss Hanrahan had been different even then. She could recall the hours Miss Hanrahan spent with her bits of paper and pencil, making strange marks which seemed to make sense to her if not to Gracie, and with the books from which she chanted *cat* and *mat* and *bat* far into the night. Adah, who had been brought from an orphanage in Oldham by Mrs Case and who would have taken orders from the kitchen cat, knew no different, of course. Mrs Case or Miss Hanrahan, it was all the same to her.

As for Lavender, she was so relieved to be out of the mill, out of the stench and noise, the danger and hard miles she tramped beside her frame for twelve hours a day – despite the Ten Hour Factory Act – she would have worked her fingers to the bone for "Miss Hanrahan". Mind, she had to be on her guard against carelessly calling "their Clare" by her christian name as she had once done when Clare came to Edgeclough on her day off. She had to watch her p's and q's with Thirza an' all who found fault with everything Lavender did, on account of Clare, naturally, and their former friendship, for Lavender was not daft but she was resigned to that, as her new job was grand and she meant to get on.

The only fly, or two flies to be exact, in the ointment were Belle and Thirza. Belle took her cue from Thirza who was openly insolent though she had never yet disobeyed a direct order, and Belle was the same, doing her work to Mrs Case's and Clare's high standards even if she did dawdle over it.

Neither of them had yet called her Miss Hanrahan except mockingly!

Chapter Fourteen

She was so unnerved by Thirza's laconic but knowing statement that the master wanted to see her in his study she almost dropped the big casserole dish that she had just been edging into the oven. And she almost made the mistake of asking "What for?"

She had not seen him for three months. Sometimes she speculated on the strangeness of working for a man with whom she had no contact, except through Thirza, and she often wondered what Thirza herself thought of it. Not once since the day he had appointed her housekeeper had she come face to face with him. Not once had he sent for her. She heard doors bang as he strode through them, smelled his cigar smoke when, in her capacity as housekeeper, she inspected his bedroom, his shirts, his bed linen, seeking to achieve the perfection she strove for and which she knew he demanded of her. She caught glimpses of him in the stable yard, heard his voice shouting for George, the clatter of his mare's hooves at the front door but these days he appeared to spend much of his time away from the farm. He was a landowner, a farmer, with interests in coal mining and the booming development of the railways which were creeping like a spider's web to every part of the land in this decade of what they were calling "railway mania". She did not for a moment believe he was staying away because of her but she admitted to herself that, for whatever reason, she was glad he did.

She was wearing the gown she had had made for her by a small but undeniably smart woman who had a dressmaker and milliner's shop in Crossfold. Miss Hardacre was young, having set up in business only eighteen months ago with backing from her father who had a thriving ironmonger's shop close to the Cloth Hall. Miss Hardacre was clever and imaginative with a good business head on her or Job Hardacre would not have invested his hard-earned brass in her. She was not – at least not at the moment, she told her father – aiming at the wives and daughters of the wealthy mill owners, or the gentry, who were notorious for their slowness in settling their bills anyway. Her customers were managers' wives, up-and-coming tradesmen, those with a few bob to spend but who could not afford the prices charged by Miss Rawlinson. Miss Rawlinson's clientele had included Mrs Joss Greenwood – lately living in Italy – who had once been Miss Kit Chapman of Barker Chapmans, the biggest manufacturer in Crossfold; her sister-in-law, Mrs Jenny Harrison and Mrs Harrison's young and spirited daughter, Tess; Mrs Oliver Wingrove and Mrs William Hopkinson and *their* daughters, and many of the gentry. The Longworths of Longworth Hall, the Taylors of Hadden Hall in the parish of Middleton, and many others who had made a fortune when they parted with an acre or two of land to accommodate the branching railways.

Miss Hardacre seemed to know exactly what Miss Hanrahan who was the new housekeeper at Moorhouse Farm, she had been told, required and soon had her draped in a rich, dark-blue grenadine which was a mixture of silk and wool. The skirt would be full but not excessively so, the material gathered into the waist by "organ pleating", the hem just touching her toe and held out by several petticoats. She had them for sale in a plain cotton but edged with a very pretty lace if Miss Hanrahan cared to see them. The whole outfit would be perfectly plain, of course, as befitted a . . . a . . . well, Miss Hardacre went on delicately, a working gown. The bodice would be close-fitting and buttoned down the front from neck to waist. The sleeves would be snug to the wrist to allow for modesty but not too tight to impair easy movement, with a slight fullness at the shoulder. A completely suitable garment for Miss Hanrahan's new position in life. And would she require a bonnet? Miss Hardacre had several in stock, designed and made by herself, naturally, the price kept down by her own economical methods. She had one in cream straw which would go beautifully with the dress, with tiny cream silk rosebuds about the brim. It would be simplicity itself to sew on ribbons to match the colour of the dress. Would Miss Hanrahan care to see it? Miss Hanrahan, who, a year or two ago hadn't a shoe to put her foot in, let alone a cream straw hat, said she would.

To purchase these wonders Clare had been forced to borrow from Lew, arguing with herself that she really didn't need a new dress, but on the other hand she could not, as housekeeper, continue to wear the shapeless grey cotton dress of a housemaid. Surely soon Martin Heywood would pay her her first quarter's wages as a housekeeper, which would not be far short of eight pounds, she reckoned and then she could repay Lew the money, all his life's savings, she was was sure, he had lent her. She could not resist the bonnet or the petticoats and though she still wore the black boots which had come with her from Ireland they had been expertly mended and were polished by Sammy, the boot boy as he was called despite the range of the jobs he performed, to a high shine.

The outfit had caused a minor sensation in the kitchen when she appeared in it on her first day off, though Nelly's old shawl, the one that had seen her through two winters, looked slightly incongruous draped about such finery.

"Well, don't you look the fashion plate," Thirza sneered, her mouth dropping open, whether in amazement or disapproval.

"Eeh, Miss Hanrahan, tha' look right cumly." This from Lavender whose face shone with admiration and a longing that said she would dearly have liked to be tramping with Clare over Friars Mere to Edgeclough.

"Thank you, Lavender, and I shall take your remark as a compliment, Thirza."

"Well, you needn't. I can't abide folk who think they're as good as their betters."

"Really!" Clare had found that the word, or perhaps "indeed", left Thirza with nowhere to go in the argument she would dearly love to continue. It took the wind out of her sails, as it were, so that instead of the wrangling she longed to carry on with Clare over every decision, request or proposal voiced by the new housekeeper, there seemed to be no answer to Clare's "really", or sometimes "fancy!".

But this time, jealous and incensed by Clare's elegance which in her opinion was totally out of place, she would not be stopped.

"Yes, really. Mrs Case wore black."

"I know that, Thirza."

"And if it was good enough for Mrs Case it's certainly good enough for the likes of you."

Clare, against her better judgement, allowed herself to be drawn into the conflict.

"I am considerably younger than Mrs Case, Thirza, and might I add that you do not dictate to me what I, or my staff, wear. Is that clear?"

"Oh, perfectly. We all know—"

"That will do, Thirza. You have no idea when to keep your mouth shut, have you, and on issues that don't concern you. Anyway, I'm off now and while I'm away you're in charge."

"In charge! By Gow, that's good of you. Are you sure I can be trusted?" She looked round her audience with a deliberately offensive smile.

"No, I'm not, but that's a chance I'll have to take until other arrangements can be made."

Again Thirza's mouth dropped open.

"An' what's that supposed to mean?"

"Carry on like this and you'll find out." Clare lifted her head haughtily and sailed out through the open kitchen door, her pretty hat, tipped over her forehead, bobbing on her glossy hair which was now long enough to fasten at the back of her head in a fat coil just beneath the brim. She didn't know herself what she meant by that last remark. She only knew that she and Thirza must find a way of working together in some sort of harmony before long or there would be serious trouble which could not help but involve Martin Heywood.

He watched her come from the side of the house and round the corner to the gate that led on to the track to Edgeclough and was quite devastated by her beauty and grace. She had on a new gown, simple and elegant, the colour a blue that showed off the pale creaminess of her skin and the full rosiness of her mouth. But for the old shawl which she trailed low on her back and the heavy black boots which were barely discernible under the wide hem of her skirt she might have been any fashionable lady one saw moving along the best shopping streets in Crossfold or Oldham. Even her hat was entrancing, dipping over her smooth forehead and casting a shadow across her face.

As she began the slight climb that led to the tract of wild, unsettled moorland between the farm and Edgeclough, he stood up and moved to the window. He had not seen her for months, nor spoken to her, though he had been conscious of her presence in his house. There was an atmosphere of wellbeing, of calm and order which came from the centre of her own nature and which he knew she had brought to his home. Even when he had held her in his arms he had been aware that she was like the soothing balm his mother had used to heal his many boyhood wounds, like a gentle hand laid on a fevered brow, the comfort and softness of a cool breeze on a hot day, and yet there was in her a promise of something deep and untouched. He had almost had it on the day up on the tops when Eppy's dog had disturbed them, the rising of a passion that would have matched his own, he was certain, but the bloody dog had come between them and from then on they were lost. The chance had gone and she would not come to him now; she had told him so and he supposed he could not blame her, for she was a decent woman with a decent woman's need for marriage which he was not able to give her. He did not stop to wonder why he was so inflexible, it was just so. Though they were only farmers his family had been *gentlemen* farmers for generations, each one marrying a woman from a good family, usually with money. It would be lunacy even to consider taking his own housekeeper, a woman who until a couple of years ago had never worn shoes, as a wife.

But he could not forget. His mind wandered back to so many memories. Oh, how they hurt, those memories of love. The picture of her shape and colouring as she ran up the hill to meet him, the swing and sway of her body, strong and vibrant. The slightly lopsided smile which now and again moved a dimple in her cheek. He seemed to hear her voice which had fascinated him with its lilt of Irish music and these things came between him and his everyday life, the remembrance of them stirring him in a way he had never known before.

He watched her now, the slight undulation of her back as she climbed, the way she picked her way delicately over the rough stones of the track, holding her skirt from the dirt and he knew he loved her still. Idly he supposed he always would.

As she disappeared over the brow of the hill he turned away sighing, the sadness in him so acute he felt the physical pain of it, but strangely it did not seem to occur to him to wonder why.

She caused the same furore at Edgeclough as she had in the farmhouse kitchen. The children, accustomed to seeing her in her plain servant's dress, her shawl and sturdy clogs, hung back hesitantly from this grand lady who smiled with their Clare's face but who looked as though she'd stepped down from a carriage at the bottom of the track.

The sudden absence of noise drew Lew to his door and with a mighty shout he brought the rest, including Nelly, from the row of cottages.

"Well, I'm fair capt ter see thi', Clare Hanrahan, all dressed up like a dog's dinner an' all. Tha' look champion, lass, champion. I'd best get me cap on so's I can touch peak like I do to't gentry."

"You! Touch your cap to the gentry, Lew Earnshaw. That I'd live to see the day. It'd be a miracle, so it would."

He was down the steps in a bound, striding to meet her with his grey eyes adazzle like the sun on water with his pleasure, his honest feelings shining from them with a warmth that never failed to bring gladness to her heart.

"Never mind t'get up, tha' daft wight, though I suppose it's cumly enough. By 'eck, lass, there isn't a pick on thi'," Nelly fretted from her doorway. "What do thi' feed thi' up there? Sparrers food by't look o' yer an' it's no good pullin' a face at me, Clare Hanrahan, fer I'll not 'ave it. Just thi' get summat substantial inside thi' afore thi' go traipsing off back. I've a nice bacon 'otpot in th'oven ..."

The rest of her words were drowned out as Lew's arms came round her, knocking her hat askew and the children, following Lew's lead, crowded round her. They pulled at her skirt, or her shawl, anywhere they could reach to capture her attention and she felt she was home where she belonged. Where she *really* belonged, where she was needed, where she was loved.

She ate a small helping of Nelly's bacon hotpot just to please her and listened to Lew as he talked about the unrest that still stirred the land despite the death of Chartism. Poor harvests had made prices high and competitive and it was the people, the poorest of the poor who suffered. The shortening of the hours of labour had done little to alleviate the dreadful suffering of women, young people and children, and the trade unions, of which he was a member through the cotton-spinners union, were not happy. There had been revolutionary outbreaks in Europe and though they did not have much effect in England surely it was a sign of the way things might go.

"That's as mebbe, lad, but our Clare didn't tramp all't way up 'ere ter listen ter thi' rantin' on as if tha' were addressin' one o' tha' old Chartist meetin's. Let 'er talk fer a bit. Now, tell us 'ow that there Thirza's gerrin' on. Is she still not framin' 'ersenn? She needs a good cloutin' . . ." and so it went, one or other of them demanding her attention, the children clamouring for a story from one of the many nursery books she brought from Moorhouse until it was time to leave.

Lew accompanied her, of course, and as Martin Heywood watched her return, striding down the track with the overseer from Hopkinson's Mill beside her, he tasted the sour bile of jealousy in his mouth and felt a terrifying need to fling himself out of the house and demand what the hell Lew Earnshaw thought he was doing with Martin Heywood's woman!

A day later, out of the blue and causing as much disturbance as a sudden thunderstorm, was the command that the master wanted to see her. From Mrs Case's recipe book she had cooked for his evening meal what was called vermicelli soup made from a stock with bacon, butter and a small trussed fowl. When the meats were cooked they were removed from the stock, which was then skimmed as clear as possible. She had never seen vermicelli before, since it was not a dish familiar to an Irish family living in a sod hut, but Mrs Case's notes told her it was Italian in origin, which probably explained it, she remembered thinking wryly. It was made in the same way as macaroni with yolks of egg, sugar, saffron and cheese added to the paste. There were detailed instructions in Mrs Case's clear hand on how to make it and on the shelf in the cupboard the purpose of the strange cylindrical vessel pierced with holes through which the mixture was forced became clear. When it was converted into long snake-like strips the vermicelli was partially baked before the fire.

Thirza had sneered disdainfully, declaring that you wouldn't catch her eating such foreign muck and when Clare informed her tartly that it was Mrs Case's recipe Thirza had replied that *she'd* never seen Mrs Case prepare it, as though Clare were making the whole thing up. She seemed quite scandalised that the master had eaten it without complaint!

It had been followed by fillet of veal au béchamel, again a mystery to Clare until Mrs Case's marvellously and meticulously detailed book had explained it to her. Béchamel was a sauce in which parsley, cloves, herbs, mushrooms and cream were mixed, which was then poured over the veal. For dessert she would serve a simple gooseberry tart with whipped cream and chopped almonds.

Again no complaint, nothing but an order for his housekeeper to present herself to him in his study.

He was sitting with his back to her, his feet propped on the windowsill, a brandy glass in one hand, a cigar in the other, gazing out on the garden at the side of the house. He seemed to be studying with an unusual amount of interest a clump of elms, thick with buds which had taken on a dark rose colour. Great clouds sailed the darkening blue of the sky, their shadows moving across the highest slopes of the moors where the sun still shone. It was a fine evening, the wind from the west warm and damp and in a corner of the garden a great sheet of aconites laid a golden carpet, and above them, in the tallest trees, the rooks were noisy as they settled down for the night. She found her own eye drawn to the lovely spring scene, the sight of it calming her somewhat. He drew on the cigar then blew a perfect smoke ring into the air before lowering his legs and swinging round to face her. To face her for the first time in three months. He studied her with the casual interest a man might assume when he meets for the first time a woman he does not consider particularly attractive and therefore hardly worth his masculine attention. Polite, incurious, totally indifferent to her as a female, he would have her believe, but in his eyes was a shadow, a shadow that did not quite hide his innermost thoughts and his secret emotions. His total lack of concern gave him away, for a man who has loved a woman cannot but help retain the memory of that love, even when it is dead. Something remains and the studied blankness of his expression showed how desperately he was trying to hide it. It was still there, that bond between them, pulling at them, torturing them no matter how Martin Heywood tried to hide it

Clare could feel the tide of pain rise in her, a despairing pain which, in her new duties, she had done her best to subdue. She had grieved for him as though he were dead which, to her, he was, and for what might have been had he not been such a proud and arrogant fool. If he had been the man of courage she had believed him to be. If he had been prepared to fly in the face of the prejudice and hypocrisy his social equals would have turned on him. But he had not and the loss to them both was overwhelming.

A wave of anguish broke through her, though like him she would not let him see it. Her face was carved into a pale mask and her green eyes were huge and unblinking but her voice was steady as she spoke.

"You wanted to see me, sir?"

"I did, Miss Hanrahan. It seems to me that you have taken to your new duties quite admirably."

"Thank you, sir."

"Oh, don't thank me. It is you who have . . ." For a second he seemed to falter as though the praise he offered her might imply more than he meant. "You have done it on your own. The meal tonight was excellent and encourages me to suggest that the time has come for you to try your hand at something more challenging. You have . . . er . . . practised on me – I think we can say that, Miss Hannahan – and as a man who appreciates good food, I am pleased with your progress."

He drew again on his cigar then reached out to the ashtray,

tapping the ash into it. He looked totally at his ease, his left hand now deep in his pocket, his jacket unbuttoned, even his hair somewhat disarranged. His cravat was loosened, a man relaxed in the comfort and privacy of his own home with no need to impress the woman who worked for the wages he paid her.

"So," he went on unhurriedly, "a week on Saturday I intend to invite a few of my friends to dine. Nine, or ten counting myself, men of business and their wives. Mr and Mrs Hopkinson, who own Hopkinson Cotton Mill and the Mayhews who are old family friends and who will be accompanied by their daughter, Miss Estelle Mayhew. There will be others, naturally. I will let you know their names nearer the time so that you will be familiar with who is who."

His face was like granite, sunbronzed from his days outdoors as he strode the high moors inspecting his flock, but hard and rigid, the muscles twitching in his effort to appear quite normal as he told her of his intention – there was no other word for it – towards Miss Estelle Mayhew. In an attempt to shut out the torment of his words she found herself watching his mouth, the lips that had kissed hers so gently, so tenderly, set in lines of steel. The words he had spoken were meant to tell her what he had in mind and though she knew exactly what it was she refused to contemplate it because, quite simply, though she knew she must, she could not bear it.

"Can you manage that, Miss Hanrahan," he asked her brusquely, "or shall I hire someone to help you?"

"That won't be necessary, sir," she heard herself saying.

"Good, then you will arrange the menus?"

"I will that, sir."

"I will see to the wines if you will let me know what you intend to prepare."

"Very good, sir."

"And naturally, I will expect you to help with serving the meal."

Her heart surged like a salmon leaping a weir. It had been

skittering and darting about ever since Thirza had announced that the master wanted to see her but now it did its best to escape its cage in its panic. He was being deliberately cruel. Not only was she to know that Martin Heywood was contemplating the courtship of the daughter of one of his business acquaintances, he was ordering her to be there to see the start of that courtship. She would stand at the back of the room with Thirza, as servants did, as much notice taken of them as a piece of furniture. She would be no more than another pair of hands, a silent figure discreetly bending over Miss Estelle Mayhew as she helped her to this or that. It was not the business gentlemen and their wives who terrorised her, though that was bad enough, but the thought of a daughter, pretty no doubt, marriageable, highly suitable for a man like himself, who, having been invited along with her parents, could be expected to understand that it was for one purpose only. And she was to watch it. Watch him turn those extraordinarily blue eyes on some other woman, see him smile his lazy, heavy-lidded smile and address her, politely, of course, since she was a lady, with the engaging charm that he had in abundance.

She couldn't do it. She said so.

"I'm afraid that's not possible, sir," wanting to scream herself into hysterics at the look of astonishment on his face. "I cannot prepare, cook and then serve a dinner for ten people. I cannot be in two places at the same time; even you must admit that . . . sir."

"Now see here . . ."

"I shall be needed in the kitchen if I am to give my full attention to the meal. Unless you would rather leave that to one of the kitchen-maids."

He scowled. "It is physically impossible for Thirza to serve ten people, woman. It cannot be done."

"Then what do you suggest, sir?" She stood passively, on her face an expression that said personally she couldn't give a damn who did what. He had only to tell her his wishes and she would obey them. He didn't like it and the tightening of his face muscles told her so.

Then suddenly a bright, eager young face swam into her vision and for a moment she was no longer conscious of the unendurably sweet but snarling presence of Martin Heywood who had racked her dreams and battered her heart so badly. This was who she was now. Not Martin Heywood's woman whom he had loved so briefly but a woman who had earned her place here. Why not? her own quick brain which had brought her to where she was now, considered. Thirza wouldn't like it, of course, but then did she give a tuppenny damn whether Thirza liked it or not. It didn't matter anyway, for she was the one who ran this house, Martin Heywood had made that plain and what she decided, what she proposed to do was the only thing that mattered.

"I think I have the answer, sir. There is someone, a clever girl, clean and biddable, who might just do."

"In the kitchen?"

"No, in the dining-room. I'll see to it at once." And with that she turned on her heel and left the room, leaving him, she knew, though she didn't look back to see, with his mouth hanging open. Let Miss Estelle Mayhew get an eyeful of that!

Chapter Fifteen

Lavender, with the haunted look of someone about to go to the gallows, was nevertheless, as Clare knew she would be, excited at the thought of being taught the delicate art of not only serving at table, but setting out the cutlery, the fragile crystal glasses, the starched damask napkins and indeed all the confusing and magical decorations that were carefully described in Mrs Case's book. There were to be hothouse roses gathered with ribbons and ferns down the length of the table and swathed at the four corners in trails of ivy. In Clarice Case's book there were descriptions of what were called "finger bowls", apparently used at all upper-crust functions – could this dinner party be described as such? Clare agonised – scented with orange and rose and carrying a scatter of pink rose petals on their surface. There was even a detailed account of how to arrange the napkins into what looked like doves about to take flight and which took a fair amount of practice. There were to be scented candles in silver holders, so Clarice Case said, and it was as though the former housekeeper were speaking to Clare through her books from the other side of the grave. Everything the housekeeper had been taught as a young cook and then running a house occupied by a family who might be considered by some as "gentry", had been meticulously recorded and there were even diagrams of table settings and flower arrangements.

Clare marvelled as she mulled over the books where it could have been that Mrs Case had not only learned all these special skills but where she had practised them. She was not to know that Martin Heywood's mother, who came from a family with a decent social position in Bradford – where Martin still had relatives – had brought her with her when she married John Heywood, Martin's father. Clarice Case had been trained by the best and while Mrs Heywood had been alive she had employed all that she had been taught, for Mrs Heywood had been an avid entertainer.

The expected storm from Thirza exploded over them in a crescendo that Clare was sure could be heard as far away as the stables and beyond. She had deliberately waited until Martin Heywood was out of the house before bringing up the subject of the dinner party and Lavender's part in it, knowing what Thirza's reaction would be, reluctant to involve him in this, her biggest challenge since she became his housekeeper, a tremendous challenge in itself. The kitchen staff had settled down to an uneasy truce which each day seemed a little less tense, providing Thirza was kept on an even keel, which meant allowing her to continue as she had done under Mrs Case. She had Lavender and the kitchen-maids to bully and it seemed to Clare that she had come to the conclusion that she was better off, at her age, to bow to the inevitable, which she had brought on herself anyway. She could still throw her weight around if she felt the need for it and as long as it did not contravene Clare's orders and the standard of her work didn't drop – and she was too well trained for that – she could keep her position as the most senior servant which she might not find if she applied for a new post.

But it seemed this was not to be borne.

"I've just been informed by himself that he is to give a dinner party a week on Saturday," Clare told them in the kitchen, her nervousness bringing out her Irishness but doing her best to sound casual about it as though it were the most natural thing in the world. "There'll be nine guests, ten with him, so I hope you'll all do your best to make it a success." She looked round the circle of surprised faces, for it seemed with Mrs Case gone they had assumed entertaining had come to an end. Only Lavender was unamazed or unworried and her face shone from the circle like a small beacon of hope. Clare smiled at her.

"So who's to do the cooking?" Thirza asked, not even considering that it might be the new housekeeper who, though she had managed well enough with the day-to-day cooking for the servants and even the master, certainly could not be expected to attempt the sort of intricate meal that Mrs Case had once produced.

"I am."

Thirza's jaw dropped. "You are! And what are you to serve, pray? Irish stew an' gooseberry fool?"

"I haven't decided yet but I'll go through Mrs Case's books and make my decision. You, naturally, are to serve."

"I can't serve ten people on me own."

"You won't be expected to. Lavender will help you."

If she had said the cat curled on the rug before the fire was to assist it could not have caused more consternation. Lavender blanched and looked as though she were going to make a dash for the back door. It had taken her weeks to become accustomed to the life she now led, the good food, the strict routine Thirza devised for her, what seemed to her to be the amazing luxury of her warm bed at night in which she slept alone, the loveliness of the many objects she handled every day. She liked her new job, which was a great improvement on the struggle she had known as a mill operative. Just to get to the mill in the freezing cold of winter, the run to arrive at the place before the gates were shut at six in the morning. The hard labour of minding her machine, the worry of watching out for their Daisy and Primrose, who, sadly, were still crawling about under those lethal machines. She still rose early and worked late, barely stopping for a bite to eat, at least if that Thirza had her way, but in what different circumstances and it was all down to Clare. She would never, ever be able to show her true gratitude, she had thought, but now, here was her chance. It terrified the life out of her but if Clare said it was possible, then who was she to deny it.

Thirza did not share her belief.

"What! Let a girl only five minutes away from a spinning frame serve a meal to grand folk, friends of Mr Heywood's. You must've lost your mind. It took me months to learn the correct way of going about things, years, and Margaret, who was here at the beginning with Mrs Case, wouldn't let me so much as pass a plate to the mistress for the first six months. There's a correct way of serving and if you think this . . . this chit can just pick it up by a week next Saturday then you're dafter than I thought. A week on Saturday, why, that's only" —she made a rapid calculation in her head— "that's only twelve days away and it takes twelve *months* to train—"

"Well, we haven't got twelve months, Thirza, and I don't think we need it. Lavender is bright and quick to learn and, quite frankly, is there anyone else? Belle and I will have our work cut out to prepare this meal and neither of us can be spared from the kitchen."

Out of the corner of her eye she saw Belle preen herself and gaze round the circle as though she and Miss Hanrahan were to entertain members of the royal family to a ten-course banquet and Clare knew she had said the right thing. She had Belle on her side just by giving her a bit of praise. Adah and Gracie, who were not awfully sure what all the fuss was about, scratched their heads and shrugged their shoulders since it was evident *they* would not be involved, and Lavender clung to the table's edge lest she be tempted to sit down rather abruptly.

"Well, I reckon it'll work out orlight," Belle said somewhat complacently. "With me an' Miss Hanrahan in the kitchen an' you an' Lavender in the dinin'-room."

"Have you all gone loony?" Thirza shrieked, beginning to

clutch at her snowy apron and wring it with a twisting motion as though it were soaking wet. "You're insane, the whole boilin' lot of you. Take a girl like her into a dining-room and expect her to serve her betters. By Gow, up to a few weeks ago she'd never even used a knife an' fork …"

"'Ere, you mind what yer sayin'," Lavender began indignantly, but Thirza turned on her like a spitting cat, her eyes glittering in her dough-like face. It was clear she longed to slap every silly face in the room and she would too, if there was any more of this nonsense.

"When I think how long it were before Margaret would let me do more than pass her the plates an' that was without food on 'em. Eeh, Mrs Case'd turn in her grave if she knew what was going on in her kitchen."

"This isn't her kitchen, Thirza," Clare told her calmly. "Mrs Case is dead and I'm in charge now, so I am. The master has enough confidence in me to allow me to arrange this dinner party an' if I've anything to do with it it'll be a success. Now if there's nothing else to be said, which I don't think there is, we'd best get about our work. I shall be in my sitting-room if anyone wants me."

She left the servants staring after her, goggle-eyed and speechless.

She spent hours when she should have been in her bed going over menus, having found that at the back of the large cupboard in what had been Mrs Case's room were records of all the meals Mrs Case had prepared, in date order, going back twenty years, for the many dinner parties Mrs Heywood had given, and not only that but who had been present at each occasion. It seemed that Mrs Case was a great compiler of lists, a woman of obsessive punctiliousness, and Clare Hanrahan, from this side of the grave, devoured every small detail. Thanks to Mrs Case the larder shelves were full, the drawers and cupboards were scented with sweet herbs and lavender, as apparently old Mrs Heywood had required. According to the instructions of the former housekeeper, everything that should be polished had been polished, every item of linen starched that should be starched, every inch of carpet and upholstery meticulously brushed. Thanks to Mrs Case and Clare's own strict adherence to Mrs Case's records the house was a shrine to order and efficiency.

She had no one with whom to confer on the menu for Martin Heywood's – and her – first dinner party. She was aware that she would get no help from Thirza who, she knew, was hoping she would fall flat on her presumptuous Irish face and make a complete fool of herself. Whatever Clare prepared she, Thirza, and the half-witted girl from Edgeclough would serve, even if it were pig swill, and if the guests and the master looked at it in horror, as Thirza expected them to do, then she could toss her head and say "I told you so" and feel wonderful doing it.

It was three days before the event and Clare had still not decided on a menu that would not only be suitable but one that she thought she could manage. She and Lavender were practising laying the table and serving, Clare playing the guest while Lavender fumbled with plates and sauce boats and all the many items she would be expected to manoeuvre, serving utensils, which consisted of a spoon and a fork arrangement, and of course the soup ladle, being the worst! There would be soup, of what kind Clare hadn't decided, but it was tricky to serve and it was this, and the big soup ladle that Lavender was making an effort to conquer. Thirza had half-heartedly shown her everything she had to do but it was the practice Lavender needed, so she and Clare sat up after the others had gone to bed, absorbed in what was to be to them both the most challenging evening of their lives.

"You must always serve from the left, Lavender, making sure that the guest's head is well out of the way, then, with Thirza, you move to stand by the serving table until the course is ended. Now practise that. The soup tureen has water in it for the moment so have a try with the ladle ... no, slowly and not a lot of liquid or you might drip it on the ..."

"Oh God," moaned Lavender.

"Lavender, you can do it. Thirza has explained it all. You can lay the table beautifully, you've just proved it so all you have to do now is to practise waiting on. Take Mrs Case's book to bed with you and study the setting of the cutlery. You are to have a new dress, cap and apron in black as befits a parlour-maid and you'll do splendidly. Now, try again with the soup. If you can master that you can master anything. And a word of warning, don't always take Thirza at her word. Use your common sense. You're an attractive girl and will make a good impression. Besides, the guests will be so busy chatting with one another they won't really notice unless you tip sauce in their lap. No, no, lass, I'm only joking. I have every confidence in you, so I have and I know you won't let me down. Just be careful and don't rush. Now then, serve that 'soup' and then we'll try the vegetables."

She chose her menu with great care and with a great deal of heartsearching. This was to be the most important event in her working life. This would be the making or breaking of her, for she was aware that Martin would watch her like a hawk. With what in mind was not clear but he would expect her to give satisfaction. Why she thought this was not clear to her, for all he cared about, surely, was that his guests would be well served and not only that but with a meal that they would expect to be expertly cooked. They were used to great things, the Hopkinsons, the Mayhews – who were in banking, Thirza told her loftily – the Frasers who were in cotton. They all, it was rumoured, had not just a cook but a *chef* which was a different kettle of fish altogether and something to live up to! Somehow, instead of petrifying her as Thirza had hoped, this bit of information put her on her mettle. She made up her mind that she would serve a meal that could be compared with anything Clarice Case had knocked up and if he wasn't satisfied then he could find himself another housekeeper, she told herself defiantly.

She decided she would start with Chantilly soup which was simple and took little expertise, for it contained nothing but young green peas, which Mr Starling had in abundance, parsley, young onions and a good stock. She had tried it on the servants and they had all, with the exception of Thirza, declared it delicious though the men did admit they liked their soup a bit more "hearty".

The next course which Mrs Case's book called salmon à la Genevese turned out to be salmon cooked in Madeira wine with a sauce poured over it, the sauce consisting of shallots, herbs, bay leaves, carrots and mace, thickened with butter and flour and then anchovies, lemon juice, cayenne and salt added. It would be presented hot from the oven on a long, flat dish and served at table. Oh yes, Thirza said complacently, she had served it before and could do again if only "that girl" could be trusted to carry each serving to table. There would be sauté of lamb with béchamel sauce, which she had made before, again a simple thing to prepare. She had begun to think that the upper classes cloaked all their good meats in a sauce but then who was she to disagree. If Mrs Case said she'd to serve it with a sauce made from the hard soap that Gracie and Adah used to scour the floor she would have done it.

There was to be a choice of dessert. Apricot cream, which was very rich, or pears marinated in brandy, both again easy to prepare. There would be cheeses and fruit for those who wanted them, coffee and liqueurs, or so Clarice informed her. In her own head, of course, and now and again out loud to Lavender when they were alone she often asked, "Now what would Clarice do?" and the answer was always to be found in Clarice's books.

* * *

Thirza, quite piqued with the way it went, said nothing, of course, except to tell Lavender not to get hysterical about it, but the young maid was so excited, so overwhelmed with the success of it, she whipped them all up into a rare old state of intoxication, even Adah and Gracie who acted as though they had been at the port, as she exploded into the kitchen when it was all over.

"I never dropped a thing, Clare," forgetting her position in the exhilaration of the moment. "T'soup were no trouble at all and when Thirza carved t'salmon I served it a treat. I could feel t'master watchin' and d'yer know what, once 'e winked at me as if 'e were pleased. Eeh, 'e's lovely, int' 'e. Mind, that Miss Mayhew . . . Estelle they called 'er, were a 'oity-toity young lass. Thought a lot of 'ersenn, yer could tell that. She ate next ter nowt, fiddlin' wi' this an' that whilst master—"

"That's enough, miss," Thirza snapped from the chair by the fire into which she had sunk at the end of the meal. The table had been cleared and the guests, who had taken coffee in the little-used drawing-room, were preparing to leave. "Servants don't talk about their betters nor about what they hear in the dining-room so let's have less of your lip. Miss Mayhew is a right marriageable young lady and you can see which way wind's blowin' but it's not up to us to make comments."

"What d'yer mean, Thirza?" Belle asked curiously. She and Clare were helping the young scullery-maids to clear the kitchen and put everything to rights for the morning. They were all worn out. There had been one or two crises in the kitchen during the preparing of the meal, due mainly to the tension that pervaded the room and which caused Belle to drop a box of eggs and then burst into tears. Gracie burned her hand on the hot oven and had to be anointed with butter, and the kitchen cat was stepped on by Adah, turning on her spitting and with unsheathed claws.

"Well, I'm really pleased with everyone," Clare said quietly, the spear to her heart which Thirza had just launched making her catch her breath a little but she thought it went unnoticed.

"Now we'd best get to our beds, for haven't we still to be up early in the morning, but let me say thank you for the hard work you've all put in." They all looked pleased, even Thirza.

The moon was bright in a navy-blue sky, turning the dizzy space about it to a silvered violet, shining in untroubled serenity across the garden, dark paths created by the shadows of the trees. She needed no candle since it shone into the dining-room and touched the polished wood of the dining table where, so Thirza and Lavender had told her, Martin Heywood had made a great fuss of Miss Estelle Mayhew. She told herself she had come in here to check that all was as it should be but she knew it wasn't true. It was a kind of self-scourging, a deliberate act on her part to try and rid herself of the love she had for Martin Heywood. If she was to make herself believe, to accept, even to be unconcerned about him marrying another woman, she must wallow in the pain of it, for surely that would cure her. Salt in an open wound, agonising but none the less healing.

She moved blindly towards the window and stared out at the garden, not seeing it, the desolate feeling in her heart surging and washing over her in great waves. Why, for God's sake? she asked herself passionately. Why should she feel like this after all that he had made her suffer? He had as good as told her the other day that the girl was a candidate for his advances, the advances a gentleman pays a lady he wishes to marry, so why should Lavender's innocent report that the master was paying attention to a young and beautiful girl devastate her so? He would never belong to her, to Clare Hanrahan, and it was then, at that moment, that the absurdity, the stupidity of what she was doing first entered her heart. This was impossible, this striving to be his housekeeper, to become a second Mrs Case, to make a career of living in this house where soon, if what Lavender and Thirza said was true, there would be a young mistress. She couldn't bear to be in the same house, under the same roof, lying almost above the very bed to which Martin Heywood would bring his bride. She would go. She would hand in her notice in the morning and go and work in the mill beside Lew rather than suffer this agony and the agony that was to come when Martin married. She didn't know why it had not occurred to her that one day he would, but she knew now that when that day came she would not be here.

"Clare."

Jesus, Mary and Joseph, she was beginning to hear things now. In her distress she had imagined his voice whispering at her from the shadows and though she didn't turn round she knew he was not there. She was tired, bone-weary and her senses were overworked, over-stimulated by the feverish activity of the evening and the sooner she got to her bed the better, though not for a moment did she think she'd sleep. She could feel his presence all around her in this part of the house where he lived and it was too much for her battered nerves. She had done well tonight, she knew she had. They all had under her careful supervision and . . .

"Clare." And this time the sound was accompanied by a movement at the back of the room just where the serving table stood. She leaned her forehead against the cool glass of the window and moaned slightly in the back of her throat, for the voice was so soft, so tender, so deep and warm and loving how was she to resist it. How was she even to turn round and look at him, see his eyes in the moonlight shining with what she knew was an expression he had given to no woman but her. She didn't know how she knew, she only knew it was so.

She heard him move round the table, his footsteps almost soundless on the thick carpet and then he was directly behind her, so close she could feel the warmth of him on her back. She sensed the movement of his arms and when his hands gripped her above the elbow she began to shiver. It was not a fierce grip. Had she wanted to she could have twitched away from him but the trouble was, and it crucified her to say it, even to herself, she didn't want to twitch away from him. She wanted to turn and sink against him. Be held to his chest in strong arms which would tell her he still loved her. To sigh and melt and feel that languorous magic drift through her ...

"Clare, my darling, how can I tell you ..." His voice broke and so did her heart at the sadness in it. "What can I say ... you did wonders tonight and I was proud of you. I wanted to tell you so but ... Sweet Jesus, more than anything I wanted this. Do you know ... have you the slightest idea how much I love you, poor wight that I am. You weren't in this room tonight, not in body but by God you were in spirit. I wanted to sweep out into the kitchen and tell you. Sweetheart, I've missed you ... won't you turn round and look at me? If you tell me you don't feel the same then I'll go away and leave you alone but ..."

She turned slowly, swaying a little, for she felt the dizzying, heady aura of his masculinity, his vigour, the strong pull which she knew quite positively was his love for her, wrap itself about her. She lifted her face and when he placed his lips on hers, gently, barely more than the touch of flesh to flesh, she moaned again, this time more loudly, more urgently.

"Martin," her mouth murmured against his. She knew it was wrong, and yet she knew it wasn't. She loved this man and he loved her so how could it be wrong, but it was. Did she care though? Did her starved body care enough about that to tear itself from his? What did it matter when his mouth and his hands and his powerful body were demanding of her what she knew only she could give him. Did it matter that she was his housekeeper, and a damned good one at that, tonight had proved it, that there was talk of him allying himself with some pretty little miss whose father was made of money? Did it matter? She heard the question echoing down the tunnel of her mind, blindly seeking escape and she let it, for all that mattered was this, and this, and this.

Without taking his mouth from hers he lifted her in his arms and carried her from the room, up the wide staircase and into his bedroom. Placing her on his bed which Adah had turned down so carefully, humbled by the privilege since she was only a scullery-maid, he knelt beside her and with slow, dreaming hands he undressed her and with slow, dreaming eyes loved every inch of her naked body. He gathered her up in an act of possession into which she found herself nestling with gratitude and what seemed to be perfect content. She wanted him and it was enough. The firm, flat muscles of his body against hers, the exploration of his hands on her skin, the sweeping caresses that would set her purring and glowing. She was offering herself to him, she had no doubt about that and the wonderful part of it was she didn't care. She could smell the odour of his soap and the brandy he had drunk, the smoke of his cigar and she wanted to be possessed by him.

He shrugged out of his clothes and lay beside her, in no rush, his manner said, for this was their first time and it must be as good as he could make it but when, finally, he entered her she felt the frenzy come upon her, a frenzy which demanded that she be not merely possessed but swallowed whole and alive. It thundered through her and she cried out and so did he but upstairs the servants slept the sleep of the exhausted and the lovers were unheard.

She slept then, her head on his shoulder, his arms possessively about her, his lips in her hair. He did not sleep, for his thoughts were busy with how he was to keep this woman, this beloved woman close to him, in his house and in his life when he married Miss Estelle Mayhew.

Chapter Sixteen

Through Martin Heywood gave a great many dinner parties during the summer and autumn of that year, to which Miss Estelle Mayhew was often invited, there seemed to be no sign of the alliance which, among their friends and acquaintances, had been expected. News passed like wildfire from one house to another, for they were all in the same social bracket and their servants were not averse to a bit of gossip, but somchow the expected engagement did not come about. To be sure nothing specific had been said in the first place but it does not need the actual words, a nod or a wink will do, to convince those who were interested in such things that where there was smoke there was bound to be fire and, let's face it, there had been plenty of smoke! Martin Heywood had paid a considerable amount of attention to Alfred Mayhew's lass over the past few months, partnering her at the Assembly Rooms Ball which was held in aid of the Committee for Anti-Slavery in the British Colonies, a cause dear to the heart of many Christian gentlemen. Martin Heywood had taken Miss Mayhew on to the floor at least four times during the evening, a sure sign that something was brewing and at the dinner tables of the society in which they both moved hostesses were beginning to seat them next to one another.

But still nothing was announced and it was said in the circle that mattered that Alfred Mayhew was ready to take offence. Indeed it was rumoured that had it not been for the size of Martin Heywood's account, which Alfred Mayhew had in his charge as a banker, their relationship would have become decidedly strained. No man likes to see his daughter, and one as pretty, well brought up and well dowered as Estelle, made a fool of, so what were they to make of it. They couldn't understand it, really they couldn't, they whispered among themselves, at least the ladies did, on what had gone wrong.

Martin Heywood himself was the only one who could answer that, had he been asked, which he wasn't, for what man will ask another what his intentions are towards a lady? The truth of it was that Martin was so much in love, so totally bewitched with his housekeeper, with her pliant young body which enslaved his whenever he could entice her to his bed, with her rich, full lips, moist and warm beneath his, with her silken arms which wound themselves about him with the immutable strength of steel chains, that he could not – at the moment, he told himself – bear the idea of a courtship with another woman. He would, one day, he promised himself. Hell's teeth, the Mayhew girl was only nineteen. She would make any man a decent wife, a decent mother for his children and had, he knew, like all girls of her class, been brought up to the duties the wife of a man of substance would expect. Her father was rich and influential, which wasn't a bad thing to have at call. She was young and biddable but, he asked himself in the dead of night when his love was asleep in his arms, would he have from her the trust, the love, the passion he was given so generously by Clare, who, now that she had experienced her first loving with him, was utterly his. Her love for him and his for her was deep in their hearts, fastened securely, clamped tight and immovable, agonisingly so at times and nothing, he firmly believed, would ever cut it from them. It was what he was banking on. That when the time came for him to take a wife she would be so deeply bound to him there would be no question of giving him up. There might even be a child, which was what he was hoping for. With a child to bind her to him, a comfortable home in which to place them both, within easy access, naturally, to his own home, she would be unable to cut herself from him and this wonder, this consuming flame of passionate love that linked them so tightly would continue.

They were not casual lovers, for as the summer advanced and they contrived to slip away up to the tops they became friends, easy companions, telling one another their innermost thoughts which neither had revealed to anyone before. He spoke of his education at the grammar school in Oldham, his boyhood on these moors, his mother who had been a strong but loving woman, his father who had died up here helping a failing ewe deliver a lamb.

"He just dropped dead, Eppy said. 'She'll do,' he told Eppy, standing up and then falling down again, to Eppy's great distress, and never spoke another word. My mother never got over it. She was a great one for the social life, parties and picnics and jaunts to Manchester, but after my father went she seemed inclined to follow him. I think she was worried in case he wasn't well looked after wherever he was and so she went after him to make sure."

"They loved one another so much?"

"Aye, they did, and I think I must have inherited their capacity to love deeply and irrevocably, for that's what I feel for you," he said simply, drawing her close into his arms and kissing her tumbled hair, then leaning back against the grey pitted stone to gaze out over the valley and the slow-moving river that ran through it. "They knew a happy marriage, their one sorrow that I was their only child."

He frowned, then sat up somewhat abruptly as though this talk of happy marriages was causing him confusion, but Clare, her thoughts far away, did not notice.

"Sure an' weren't my mammy an' daddy the same, but they were blessed with many children. Twelve Mammy had though six didn't survive babyhood."

She seemed to draw away from him then, though her arm still touched his, turning herself inwards, her eyes becoming unfocused, unseeing; at least she did not see the sweep of summer moorland stretched out at their feet. They had made love and her mouth was bruised and swollen, for Martin had not been gentle with her. It was over a week since she had slipped from her bed and crept like a shadow to his and the fire and ecstasy of their loving had been fierce, taking them together to some place from which it was difficult to return. It was always so, though at times when she was perhaps drifting off to sleep in her own bed, she would wake with that sharp jerk that happens between waking and sleeping, and consider her exact situation and what she could logically hope for in Martin's life. She did her best to ignore it, to retain that steady joy and hope that Martin's love lit in her. She promised herself fiercely that she would do nothing to imperil this sweetness that had come so unexpectedly and which she had accepted so surprisingly. She would bring to her mind the dark, determined lines of his face which would melt into sweetness and love at the sight of her. She would relive their encounters, repeat their conversations, go over and over in her mind the words of love he spoke to her and tell herself that soon it would be as she longed for it to be. She knew he was reluctant to settle down but he loved her. He loved her and for the moment that was enough. Patience! That was what she would foster and one day he would make it right in the eyes of heaven, she was quite certain of it, for could a love like theirs go nowhere?

He lifted a hand and gently pushed her hair back behind her ear, then cupped her chin and cheek.

"Do you want to speak of it, my love? I know when you look like that you're remembering. I know something distressing happened to you; perhaps that's not enough of a word to describe it. You're here in this country alone so . . ."

"Don't, Martin. I'm not . . . ready." Her voice was low, and roughly, his love swamping him, he pulled her into his arms, cradling her head to his chest and rocking her.

"Sweetheart . . . sweetheart," he murmured into her hair and when the moment of agony had passed, lifted her chin and kissed her tenderly, his love blazing from his eyes which, at times like these, were the most incredible jewel-like blue.

It constantly amazed her, and him if he thought of it, which, being a man and arrogant with it, he didn't very often, that not one person in the house or the yard had discovered their secret. It had been necessary to invent some credible reason that would satisfy the other servants as to why she should need to get out of the house at quite regular intervals and it often brought remembered laughter when she recalled the day it had been announced to the maidservants that, as housekeeper, she meant to go into Crossfold and order the provisions and any other household requirements herself.

It had been Martin's idea. It wasn't enough for him that he could only get his hands on her when she was able to slip down to his bed or on the monthly visits she made to Edgeclough when even that brought him to narrow-eyed resentment. She was his, his woman and should need no one else but him and if she imagined she was going to tag him on to the end of a visit to Lew Earnshaw she was sadly mistaken. Her day off should be reserved exclusively for him, he snarled at her, and even as she was making her way towards him on her walk home from Edgeclough his jealous rage reached out and did its best to hurt her as it hurt him. He could see no reason for her to traipse all that way, he declared coldly, for those people were nothing to her, so was he to believe that they were more important to her than he was? Sweet Jesus, she had one full day off a month, which he as her employer was good enough to allow her and she insisted on wasting it on the likes of Lew Earnshaw and that woman, whatever she was called.

Yes, he admitted, though it irked him to do so, that they had probably saved her life when she was so ill but did that mean she owed them the only time she had free? It was not to be borne and he would not bear it. He wanted more than that, he told her roughly, ready to shake her into submission and it took all her strength and love and passion to soothe him and heal his injured pride. He loved her body, he told her fiercely, the smooth, graceful curve of her back as she knelt before his bedroom fire, the lift of her almond-peaked breasts which had grown full over the last few months, the sweet curve of her slender waist and hip and thigh, the fine bones of her ankle and foot which he sighed over like a boy who is in love for the first time. He loved her but he wanted more than the physical act of loving her. He was not fool enough to think he could take her about with him, but he wanted her to have the freedom to get out of the house without comment so that they could meet secretly and not just on one Sunday in four.

"Don't you ever go shopping?" he asked her abruptly one night after they had regained their breath and were lying at peace before the fire.

She lifted her head from his chest and stared at him wonderingly.

"Shopping?"

"Aye, shopping. You know the kind of thing. You go in a shop and say to the assistant, 'Can I have a look at that hat,' or . . ."

"Faith, don't I know what shopping is, Martin Heywood, but what in heaven's name would I be doing . . ."

"Provisions."

"Provisions?"

"Hell's teeth, woman, for the house, for the kitchen. We have to eat and it's not unknown for a woman – my own mother sometimes did it, for she was a practical housewife – to go and inspect the local provision merchant just to see what is on offer and at what price. There's a market in Crossfold where every kind of fresh produce is sold so what's to stop you going there and ordering stuff to be delivered to the house?" He grinned in triumph. "And after the shopping is done you and I could ... well, the possibilities are endless. I'd like to take you to Oldham" – where he was not as well known as in Crossfold, his sharp brain was whispering – "where the shops are very fine and buy you ... I don't know, whatever takes my fancy: a new dress or a bonnet."

She continued to stare at him in wonder, her lips parted, her eyes wide and shocked. He laughed.

"Close your mouth, sweetheart, it doesn't suit you, and then tell me you don't like the idea. A day out in Oldham, or even Manchester."

"But I'm housekeeper at Moorhouse. I can't be away from the place for a whole day and anyway, how would I get there? 'Tis a long walk to Oldham and ..."

"Oh, leave that to me, my darling," and he winked impudently and before she could speak of other difficulties which were quite insurmountable, he began to kiss her, stifling her attempts to argue with him.

The servants in the kitchen were goggle-eyed when, a day or two later, their master stalked into the whirl of activity which usually took place as luncheon was about to be served and glared about him so that both Adah and Gracie trembled at their buckets. His face was stern and forbidding as though he were in a dangerously explosive mood as he demanded that Miss Hanrahan accompany him into the yard. She was as amazed as they were, for the conversation they had had in his bedroom earlier in the week, if not exactly forgotten, had been pushed to the back of her mind as a piece of nonsense he would come to realise was just that.

Belle, who was at the range basting the chicken which had just come from the closed oven, dripped the spoon's contents on to the stone floor and the cat uncurled itself and moved to sniff the fat. As their master's gaze passed unseeingly over them, Adah and Gracie lifted their heads from their buckets and rested back on their heels to stare in disbelief, for to their knowledge the master had only once before set foot in the kitchen, and Thirza, after bobbing a hasty curtsey, froze beside the kitchen table. Lavender froze with her, clinging to the gravy boat she had just warmed to receive the gravy.

"There's something I want you to see," he told Miss Hanrahan brusquely and the two scullery-maids rose to their feet, for whatever it was they didn't want to miss it. Thirza was so spellbound she drifted with the rest to the window, watching slack-jawed as their master escorted the housekeeper across the yard towards the smartest little gig, pulled by the smartest little pony, they had ever seen. The gig had evidently been cleaned and a lick of paint applied here and there, its brasswork gleaming in the sunshine. The pony was plump and well cared for, brushed to a high shine and holding its head was George who had the daftest look on his face, or so Thirza said later.

The master had left the back kitchen door open and the servants heard every word.

"I thought this might do you, Miss Hanrahan," he growled, sounding as though he were furious with her. "It belonged to my mother and she used it almost every day. It is very safe and the pony, chosen by myself, is very reliable. I'm sure you'll find it of immense value. George here will teach you to drive. I wouldn't advise any steep slopes, George, for its one disadvantage, being a two-wheeled vehicle, is its tendency to tip forward if the pony should fall. This pony won't, of course, I made sure of that by purchasing the best. Now then, Miss Hanrahan" – turning to glare down at her as if she had stolen the silver and he was about to send for the constable – "what d'you think? Will it suit?"

Clare felt the laughter, the peals of laughter she longed to let loose, begin at her midriff and move to her chest and she though she would choke. There was a gleam in his eye and the cleft at the side of his mouth had deepened and she knew he felt the same. It was all so gloriously funny and yet they must be serious, play out this charade for the sake of the servants. But how wonderful, how simply marvellous to be able to order out this smart little equipage and take herself off to wherever she fancied and whenever she fancied it. There would be fireworks in the kitchen, she was aware of that but what did she care? She was loved by this man beside her who was doing his best not to shout with laughter and that was what mattered.

"Now then, Miss Hanrahan, would you care to try it out?"

"Well ..." she began feebly as George made a move to climb into the gig but Martin waved him away. "No, I'll take her, George. There's many a time I drove it for my mother. We'll just go up the track to the top of the first rise and you can get the feel of it, Miss Hanrahan." And as George stepped away in amazement, Martin winked at her.

At the top of the rise where they were out of sight of the house they clung together in helpless laughter and it was only the thought that every one of the servants would be waiting to see them return that prevented them from kissing one another with increasing passion.

"My hair ... sure an' won't it be all over the place."

"I can't help it. I've never laughed so much in years. Their faces ..."

"'Tis not their faces that bother me but what they'll have to say, so it is."

"Tell them the master orders it. Now come here and give me one more kiss and tonight, after dinner, I want you to come to the dining-room and we'll make plans."

"Holy Mary, mother of God."

"Just one more thing ..."

"What, in the name of God, what?"

"I love you, Clare Hanrahan."

He walked back with her through the kitchen to the door that led to the front of the house and as it closed behind him they all turned to gaze at her accusingly. It was, of course, Thirza who spoke.

"Well, if I hadn't seen it with me own eyes I wouldn't have

believed it. It's outrageous. A gig for the damned housekeeper, and what I'd like to know, madam, is where you intend to go in it? To visit those fine friends of yours in Edgeclough, is it, or happen you're to drive into Oldham and take tea with the mayor!" She turned to her fellow servants, quite beside herself with jealous rage, for had she not refused the master's offer to be housekeeper when Mrs Case died all this would have been hers and she couldn't bear it.

"Mrs Case never had no gig," she went on, her voice rising with her tearing rage. "Course, she wasn't one to get above herself like some I could mention—"

"Mrs Case was content to shop at her back door," Clare interrupted quietly, "or at least in her parlour when the merchant came. I am not. I intend to drive to Crossfold and inspect the goods on offer and the prices asked. Fresh fish, pork, beef and such can be bought at the market there but without the gig I would be unable to carry it home."

She wondered even as she spoke at how easily she had accepted Martin's exciting plan, and how glib she was at explaining it. Here she was spelling out her intention to go shopping in Crossfold, or perhaps even Oldham which was no more than four miles away and only an hour ago she hadn't the faintest notion of what Martin had in store for her. She was to learn to drive a gig and travel on her own to wherever she had a fancy to go and the novelty of it, the wonder of it, which should have sent her into breathless palpitations, had brought a calm to her, a sureness that she could do it, and would enjoy doing it. It was clear that Thirza was thunderstruck.

"Mrs Case didn't have no gig. She was happy, as most are, to do her ordering—"

"Sure an' I'll not say this again to you, Thirza, for aren't I tired of it? Mrs Case is dead. She's been in her grave all these months but you still insist on digging her up and trotting out what you would have us believe were her ideas. She had her own way of doing things, the old-fashioned way, I believe, and

I have my way. I'm determined to turn myself into at least as good a cook as she was—"

"Never, never in a million years!"

"And I believe that fresh food will help. Mr Starling grows the best vegetables for miles around. We have our own hens and mutton and milk, butter and cheese so now we will have everything else fresh as well. What I can't carry will be delivered the same day."

"I think it's a right good idea, Miss Hanrahan, an'—" Lavender began but Thirza rounded on her and before Clare could stop her slapped her across her rosy cheek, leaving a red mark that quickly turned into a handprint. Lavender was a bonny girl now. She had put on weight since she had come to Moorhouse Farm, despite the hard work she performed. She slavishly copied Clare in everything she did, keeping herself spotless, her hair washed and shining, her neat appearance, especially when she was helping Thirza at table, an example to the others. She was particularly proud of her abilities in the dining-room and had almost burst with pride when Clare told her that even Mr Heywood had remarked on her quiet efficiency, her impeccable manners, her brightness and willingness to learn.

"You mind your own business," Thirza hissed. "This has got nothing to do with you."

"And nothing to do with you either, Thirza," Clare snapped, "and if I catch you striking one of the servants again I shall fire you. You know I can."

Strangely there was no talk in the local community about the new housekeeper at Moorhouse Farm who had her own little gig and was often to be seen bowling along the road that led down from the moor and into Crossfold, or sometimes passing through the town and on to Oldham. It seemed that many housekeepers, some of them from good houses in the area, liked to order their own provisions from the source, as it were, to study what was on offer at the markets and if some of them pocketed the money they saved their mistresses by doing so, it did not seem to signify.

Clare had proved to have good hands on the reins of the little gig and a stern command of the pony who pulled it and who could be frisky if not checked. She became a familiar figure in the market town and the shopkeepers soon learned that Miss Hanrahan was as sharp as she was good-looking and knew to a farthing what the other merchants were charging.

She did not use the gig when she went on her day off to Edgeclough. Nelly and Lew and the others were separate from her life at Moorhouse and from her relationship with Martin. They were her friends, her family and whatever Martin raged about, ready to strike her, she thought, over what he saw as her stupid obstinacy, she would not give up that one Sunday in four that she spent with Lew and Nelly, with the children and with the women who welcomed her as a friend. She often took fruit for the children, or biscuits she had made herself, nothing too ostentatious, for their parents' northern pride would not have allowed it. She and Lew and Nelly would, on fine days, sit on the steps and gaze out over the valley, joined in turn by Betty or Annie or Marie who was pregnant again, her Maidie a cheerful three-year-old, her Joe only just toddling. The men would tip their caps and smile, their dour north country faces showing their pleasure at seeing the lass.

"So, 'tis a pony an' trap now, is it, madam," Nelly sniffed on that first day, folding her arms beneath her thin bosom. She made out she was not at all pleased but there was light in her eye that told Clare that she was proud of the steady progress this girl who had tumbled on their doorsteps almost two years ago had made. What a difference in the lass she had come to love as her own daughter though she had two of her own. She was even growing plump, sleek, Nelly would have said, and some worm of disquiet moved in her though she didn't know why. The lass ate better than any of them, as did Lavender Bickerstaffe who was also doing gradely thanks to Clare, so why shouldn't the pair of them look as though they ate off the fat of the land.

"Sure an' there's not much gets past you, Nelly, is there?" Clare laughed, leaning forward to take Nelly's hand in hers where it struggled to get free.

"Give ower, tha' daft wight. The news were up 'ere an 'our after tha' passed by on't bottom road drivin' the thing. Sarah Johnson come up like she 'ad 'er tail on fire bletherin' on that tha'd waved to 'er. Give ower, I said to 'er. Where would our Clare get a pony an' trap? Tha' must be daft in't th'ead but she would 'ave it it were thi'. So what next, a carriage an' pair?"

"Nelly Bradbury, what next indeed. It's just that Mr Heywood thought it might be a good idea to shop in Crossfold or Oldham instead of letting the merchants come to the house. I can get to the market and buy fresh fish and so on but I needed transport. The gig apparently belonged to his mother and George taught me to drive it. I didn't come in it today as the lane's too steep and anyway, I needed the walk."

"Is that so an' I suppose—"

"Nelly, let the lass alone, will tha'. Tha'd think tha' were sorry she's done so well the way tha' clap dahn on 'er."

"Don't talk daft, Lew Earnshaw. It's just a wonder ter me the way she's turned out when I think o't road she were not so long since, an.' I just can't 'elp but bother messen . . . Nay, tekk no notice o' me, lass. I just don't want ter see thi' come a cropper. Tha' know what's said. The 'igher the climb the greater the fall."

"Now why should she come a cropper, tell me that? She's done gradely in that there job an' I'm proud of 'er."

Lew sighed as he spoke and though Clare knew he meant it, for he was the kindest, sweetest man she had ever known, he would not have been sorry to see her leave Moorhouse Farm and come back to Edgeclough. How lovingly, how willingly he would welcome her home, for it was in his face and his voice that he still loved her and would never give up hoping that one day, when she was ready for marriage and children, she would turn to him to provide them.

They nearly came to blows, she and Lew, when she stood up and shook out her skirts in readiness for the walk home. As usual he wanted to walk with her to the farmhouse gate and the argument was fierce when she refused. Dear God, Martin would do his best to knock him to the ground if he caught sight of him walking next to her and in the past few months, ever since she and Martin had become lovers, she had been forced to lie, to make the most feeble excuses why Lew shouldn't accompany her as he had once done.

"I promised George's wife I would call on her mother who's poorly. She lives in one of the cottages at Linthwaite . . ."

"Lavender said she'd meet me on the tops to pick blackberries," and other similar and equally weak reasons to save her dear friend, who she was forced to lie to, from getting his face bashed in by her jealous lover.

She kissed them all and hugged Nelly close to her, despite her stiffness, turning to wave as she strode up the path, wondering why it was Nelly's eyes followed her so broodingly, then, forgetting Nelly and quickening her stride, she climbed eagerly to reach the arms of Martin Heywood.

Chapter Seventeen

On the first of November, taking them all by surprise, it began to snow. Big fat flakes at first, drifting lazily past the kitchen window, floating in the thin air as though undecided whether it was worth the effort.

They were sitting round the kitchen table tucking in to Clare's pea soup followed by two enormous meat and potato pies which were accompanied by mashed cabbage sprinkled with pepper and knobs of butter. The men had come in from the stable yard, George and Job, Hammy, who was Mr Starling's lad, Arty, one of the shepherds who happened to be working on the lower slopes of the farm bringing in the sheep to their winter intakes and Sammy the odd-job boy. Mr Starling took his meals, cooked by the plump Mrs Starling, in the cosy cottage allocated to the gardener on the far side of the kitchen garden. Percy, who was the cowman and married to Maddie the laundry-maid and also in one of Mr Heywood's cottages nearby, was in the habit of eating his dinner in the farm kitchen with his wife.

There were the maidservants. Belle was serving with the feverish energy she seemed to put into every task since Miss Hanrahan had praised her on the day of the first dinner party. She was at the range, cutting another huge chunk of pie for Sammy, who was a growing boy and with an appetite to match. The rich gravy ran out of the pie across the plate and the succulent pieces of shoulder steak fell apart they were so tender and Belle had to admit that Miss Hanrahan's pies were as good as Mrs Case's had once been.

"'Ere, get that down yer and that's the last," she told the boy. "If yer still clemmed after that it'll be bread an' jam."

"What about one o' them there custard tarts on't dresser?" Sammy asked, grinning.

"Yer cheeky little beggar. 'Oo said they were fer you? By 'eck, yer could get shut o' one o' them in a bite, way you go on."

Belle glanced round her, smirking, making sure everyone appreciated her wit.

"Leave t'lad alone, Belle," Percy said lazily, wiping his plate with a thick slice of Miss Hanrahan's home-made bread, smacking his lips, patting his stomach, then sitting back on one of the benches that ran on each side of the kitchen table. "'E's worked damned 'ard this morning 'elpin' me muck out cow byre."

"Well, this afternoon 'e's ter clean lamps an' brasses, 'asn't 'e, Miss Hanrahan, an' that's a sittin'–down job so 'e'll not need stokin' up." But nevertheless she made no objection when Miss Hanrahan lifted one of the custard pies which Belle herself had made on to the table and began cutting it into thick wedges. Belle was gratified by the new position she held in the kitchen at Moorhouse though it was, in fact, no different to the one she had held under Mrs Case. The trouble was Mrs Case wouldn't let her *do* anything except hand her this or that, whereas Miss Hanrahan trusted her to make pastry, knead the dough, mix sauces and custards and then praised her when they turned out well, which they did more often than not. Mrs Case had been a fair woman and not unkind but Belle did not regret her passing one little bit and was increasingly grateful to Miss Hanrahan for her trust.

Thirza, as head girl, sat at the head of the long table, her face lugubrious, for she could not come to terms, even now, with the position the once scullery-maid had carved out for herself. She didn't mix with her staff, which was, Thirza conceded, right and proper for if *she* was housekeeper neither would she. She was quite often away from the kitchen on what Thirza scathingly called her "jaunts", just as though the woman she considered had stolen her job was off to Oldham to see the latest play at the theatre, but she had settled in and got on well with the staff. She had not made the mistake of favouring Lavender who she herself had hired, and though it grieved Thirza to admit it the girl was a beggar for work and making a decent fist of serving at table.

Maddie and Francy, big, buxom wenches the pair of them – and who wouldn't be on the good food Miss Hanrahan provided – were further down the table among the female servants, their heads together over some titillating bit of gossip they had probably had passed on to them by the dairy-maid or the laundry-maid at Longworth Hall, for the son of the house was known to be obliging where his mother's serving wenches were concerned. Adah and Gracie were pressed into service as serving girls, for the men could not loiter with so much to do outside and had to get their meal down them and be off within half an hour.

"Well, will tha' look at that," Percy said in a tone of utter and comical astonishment, his face to the window. They all turned obediently to where he looked, for a moment not sure what he meant, then a snowflake as big as a child's fist landed on the window and slid down it, followed by another and another.

"By Gow, 'tis early fer snow," George said, getting hastily to his feet and wiping his hand across his mouth. He had been about to accept another half-pint of ale to wash down the grand meal Miss Hanrahan had provided but this was serious. Snow in bloody November! It was almost unheard of, though he could just remember years ago, when the old man had been alive and himself only a bit of a lad, it had begun just like this before Christmas and lasted until the middle of February. Not the snowstorm, of course, but its aftermath which could be disastrous for a hill farmer.

"Come on, lad," addressing Job who was stable lad and then turning to Sammy. "Tha' can forget them brasses. 'Orses'll 'ave ter be seen to first. Master's got Flyer an' Marcus out wi't curricle," he fretted. "Course it might come ter nowt but best be sure. Us'll need plenty of oats an' such brought inter't stables an' blankets an' straw. Master's mare'll 'ave ter be settled an't gig pony an' . . ." His voice followed him out of the kitchen door, with Job and Sammy hot on his heels. This was better than cleaning brasses or mucking out stables, their excited expressions seemed to say, for like all boys they were captivated by any change in the routine of their day.

"Aye, an' them cows'll need beddin' down an' all. Wi' Lily in calf she'll need watchin'," Percy exclaimed anxiously as he followed George, Job and Sammy. "Blast it, if that lass starts early us'll be in a right pickle. Eight months she be but tha' knows what a . . ."

The maids were not vouchsafed the particular peculiarities of Lily in her breeding cycle as Percy, Arty and Hammy, who as gardener's lad would have no special task in the snow, except perhaps clearing it, made a wild dash for the door. It was no more than half an hour since they had entered it but already a thin film of snow covered the cobbles in the yard.

Clare cleared her throat. "Er . . . did the master say where he was going today, Thirza?" she asked as casually as she could.

"Not that I remember. I do know he took the curricle but he didn't say where he was off."

By mid-afternoon it was almost as dark as night, the slanting blizzard, which had caught them all on the hop, as George gloomily put it, ready to engulf them. He peered out of the lamplit kitchen window for a sight, not of his master but the horses the master drove, endlessly informing the maids that the drifts in the yard were already a foot high against the walls of the stable. Not that you could see the stable walls, for there was a solid, moving, violent curtain of snow lashing outside.

"Well then, you'd best get back to your cottage, George,"

Thirza told him tartly, "unless you want to sleep in the kitchen chair."

"I wouldn't mind. It'd be a damn sight warmer."

"Get on wi' you. Your Ethel" – who was George's eldest—"will have a fire halfway up chimbley an' wi' nowt ter do—"

"Never mind nowt to do," snorted their master's voice from the kitchen door which had opened on a fierce gust of wind and snow. "There's sheep to be brought down and they'll not find their own way. Now, see to the curricle, lads" – for Job clung to George like a shadow lest he miss any of the fun – "and get the horses safe and warm and then come back here. I want all the men, Percy, you George, Job . . . no, not you, lad," as Sammy stepped up excitedly. "Not this year, anyroad," reverting to the rough speech the boot-boy understood. "Tha'll need to put on a few more inches. Snow's going to be deep up on the tops and unless we get going we'll be caught up there."

Martin Heywood looked like a snowman built by children, his clothes so plastered with the stuff it was bearing him down almost to his knees. His hat tipped slightly with the weight of it on the brim and he swayed, unable to move another step. There was little protection in a curricle, even with the hood up and he had driven from the station in Oldham at as smart a clip as he could manage.

"Now don't all stand there like dummies," he roared to the startled womenfolk. "Get something to hit me with; yes, that's what I said, this lot's to be beaten off me because already it's beginning to freeze. I'll need warm, dry clothes, and something hot inside me."

"Are you to go with the men, sir?" Clare heard herself say, her heart lurching with fear for him.

"Of course I am, woman," he roared. "We need every man who can stand up. This lot's caught us unawares with the flock not yet brought down to the lower pastures for the winter. I reckoned we had at least a fortnight before we needed to move them but I was wrong. Bloody weather, and it's no good looking at me like that, girl," to Gracie who was beating him with extreme timidity, for was he not her master and should she be striking him with a broom. She was shocked by his language, for Mrs Case would allow none of the men to swear in her kitchen and the habit had continued with Miss Hanrahan.

"Right, that'll do," he protested irritably as he stepped from the widening circle of melted snow, making for the door into the hallway. "I'll have some of that soup, Miss Hanrahan, before I set off and pack me up something to eat. And send a message to one of the shepherds that I'll need to borrow one of the dogs. I'll be down in five minutes so be quick about it."

He ate the soup standing up by the kitchen range while the maids dithered about him and from the corner where she had been booted the cat stared with great hostility at the usurper. Martin wrapped himself in what seemed to Clare to be a dozen layers of warm clothes, pulled on a pair of stout boots, snatched the shepherd's crook which always stood in the hall cupboard and which had been used by generations of Heywood men, thrust the wrapped parcel of food into his pocket and turned towards the door, hesitating a little. She wanted to go to him as a woman would her man who was going into danger, pat him and draw his scarf more warmly about his neck but of course she couldn't. He wanted to speak to her, she could see that, to reassure her that he would be back before nightfall or some such words of comfort but the maids were still hovering, wringing their hands anxiously, though the excitement had been quite a break in the monotony of their lives. For a second their eyes met over the heads of the women and the message that passed from one to the other, if it had been noticed, would not have been understood.

"Don't worry," it said.

"Take care ..." And then, calling to the dog which waited patiently at the back door he disappeared into the whiteness.

She kept them busy, and herself.

"Right, I think we'll make something hot and nourishing

for those men when they get back," she said briskly, clearing the table with a great sweep in readiness for the chopping and mixing that would be necessary. "A good Lancashire hotpot and what about a pan of Scotch broth? That'll stick to their ribs. And we'd best make a few pies, Belle; what d'you think? What have we in the pantry in the way of fruit?"

"Well, only stuff we bottled last back-end," Belle began doubtfully, quite astonished by Miss Hanrahan's sudden whirlwind of energy.

"That'll do and we'll make some more bread, and some scones and I might bake a few biscuits. And you'd best get this floor scrubbed, Adah, and Gracie start on the passage. The master made a fine old mess with that snow. And you, Maddie, fetch the clothes Mr Heywood took off and see to them will you?"

"Nay, Miss Hanrahan, 'ow'm I ter get through ter't laundry in this?" Maddie protested, peering out into the solid wall of snow beyond the kitchen window. "Yard's a foot thick already an' 'ow I'm ter get 'ome, I can't imagine."

"You're right, Maddie, it's getting worse. D'you think you'd best stay the night? We could put up a bed for you in the—"

"Nay, I've little 'uns at 'ome, Miss Hanrahan, an' wi' my Percy out wi't men I must get to 'em."

"Of course. You'd best go right away. Take the lantern and, here, wrap up well in my shawl. Shall Francy come with you? You'd be better not going alone, so you would. Francy can spend the night with you and you can both come back in the morning."

The women spent the next few hours in a swirl of frantic activity as though they fully expected at least a full battalion of the Lancashire Fusiliers to come marching in at the yard gate demanding to be fed. The kitchen was a haven against the worrying and increasing fury of the storm that lashed at the farmhouse. Sammy, who was fond of animals and often helped out the stable men and the cowman when he could, became increasingly worried about Sabre and Archie, Flyer and Marcus, about Lily and Clover in the cow byre for by now the snow was waist-high in the yard and they had been left to their own devices since mid-afternoon.

"That Lily's near 'er time, Miss Hanrahan," he declared, his anxious, twelve-year-old face creased into lines that would not have looked amiss on a fifty-year-old. "Percy'll 'ave a fit if owt 'appens to 'er. They'll want milkin', an' all. An' th'orses aren't used ter bein' on their own all this time. Oh, I know George left 'em plenty o' grub an' blankets an' such but I'd best get over there an' check."

"That you will not, Sammy. The snow's almost to your shoulders and I don't want to have to send out a search party for you. The animals are warm and dry and have plenty to eat. Percy and George will have made sure of that. The cows were milked this morning and can manage until tomorrow. They'll have to. Here, have another piece of apple pie before you go to bed."

"But where'm I ter sleep, miss?" For if he couldn't get to the stables and the snug room above them where he and Job had a bed apiece, what was to happen to him?

"Gracie'll fetch you some blankets and pillows from the linen cupboard and you can curl up on the mat in front of the fire. And the rest of you had better get to your beds. You'll need all the rest you can manage before those men get back."

Clare went up the stairs with the rest of them, all wondering how long that would be but even as she drew her nightdress over her head she knew she would never sleep. How could she when Martin was out in the raging blizzard which gave no sign of letting up? From her bedroom window she could see nothing but pelting snowflakes, so thick it was like looking into an impenetrable curtain of white. Jesus, Mary and Joseph, how could any man survive in this? Out there were Martin, Eppy, Jacky, Harry and Arty, who were the shepherds, along with George and Percy and the lad, Job, all born and bred locally and knowing the moors, the tops, the outcroppings of rock, the tumbling streams, the vast tracts of wildness over which they had tramped since childhood. But the snow would wipe out all the landmarks with which they were familiar, the rough tracks they had climbed across Martin's land. Martin was strong, sure-footed, knowledgeable in the ways of sheep, which could survive for weeks under several feet of snow, nibbling on the scrap of vegetation on which they lay, or even their own fleece! The dogs would find them and they would be brought down to the pastures where they would spend the winter but at what cost to human life. The land could be cruel to those who were careless with it, to those who wrongly read its warnings and it seemed that was just what Martin and his men had done.

Wrapping herself in her shawl and pushing her feet into a pair of soft slippers she padded downstairs and into the kitchen. The boy, Sammy, breathed deeply like the child he still was and the cat, who had curled herself against Sammy's side, lifted her head for a moment, watching Clare with feline contempt. Clare took the teapot down from the dresser shelf and, putting a teaspoon of tea in it, poured hot water from the kettle which was always kept gently steaming on the fire. She sat down opposite the boy, rocking herself gently and sipping her tea, telling herself she would *not* get up from her chair and peer from the window until the clock on the wall chimed eleven, but every few minutes, despite her resolution, she stood up and moved quietly across the stone floor, her nightdress trailing about her legs, her shawl dipping down her back, to stand and look out blindly at the perilous curtain of terror which shook its fist at the window. And she was terrified. He had been gone for hours now, they all had, and surely they should be back. She knew next to nothing about the farming of sheep. She had taken little interest in the men's talk of the coming winter, of the past spring, of when the ram was to be put among the ewes, of lambing time, of shearing time, only accepting that at certain seasons of the year there would be extra men to feed, men who came to help with the shearing. The lambs and their mothers were taken up to the tops in the spring and summer and the flock was brought down in the winter but it seemed Martin Heywood, and Eppy Waring, who was head shepherd and experienced in such matters, had been caught napping.

The clock had just chimed three o'clock when the first weak tap came to her ears and for a moment she thought it was her imagination. She had dozed a little, waking at regular intervals with her heart leaping in terror, and the sound seemed to her to be part of her dream, a dream in which Martin was pleading with her to lift the lid of what seemed to her to be a coffin and let him out.

She leaped from her chair, calling out to the boy, telling him they were here and the women should be fetched, but when she flung back the door, on her face an expression of huge relief, the only thing that came in was a great wave of snow in which a man's hand could just be seen, the hand which had scratched at the door.

The men went out in pairs, for as Mr Heywood said to them there was no use in them floundering about in a bunch. There was still time to find the flock and with the dogs' help bring them down to the comparative safety of the pastures about the farm. It was bad, they all agreed, but not bad enough to give up. If it should become impossible, he said, impossible to know exactly where they were they must make their way back to the farmhouse. There were over a thousand sheep up here and as many as possible must be found and brought down to safety. They knew approximately where the sheep would be, probably huddled together against a dry-stone wall for shelter, against the tumbled heaps of boulders or even in the crevices between, but they were daft creatures as the sheep farmers were well aware and could be found, or lost, without shelter, on the open hillside. The men were to stay out until dark and no longer, for a sheep's life, even a whole flock of sheep, was not worth that of a man. All this was shouted into the fury of the wind and the driving snow.

The men moved off in different directions, heads down, depending more on the instinct of their dogs to scent out the flock and to find their way through the blizzard than their own power of sight, since it was like walking through fog in which a hand held out at arm's length cannot be seen.

Martin could hear the whistles with which the shepherds directed their dogs for several minutes and then they faded as the group drew apart. He ploughed on alone up the slope that led from the track that wended its way to Edgeclough.

The snow had drifted against walls and the waist-high rocks that grew from the moorland and it was these that guided him, for they were as familiar to him as the furniture in his own study but there were large patches where the snow, blown away by the wind, was no more than inches deep and easy to cross. As long as he could see the outcroppings of rock among which, as a boy, he had played his boy's games he would not get lost, though farmers had been known to disappear in a storm such as this and not be found until the snow thawed. Even on their own land which was well known to them. It could not happen to Martin Heywood, naturally, for he had walked this land, first with his father and then with the men he employed, most of his life. And even if he, God forbid, should lose direction the dog would get him back home. Eppy's dogs were well known for their intelligence, their "lambing smell" which meant that if a newly dropped lamb became separated from its mother, his dogs could scent out to which ewe it belonged. Sheep soon learn to outwit man but they seldom challenge a well-trained collie and Eppy's dogs were the best within a hundred-mile radius. This one, Laddie, had been known to bring a flock of sheep two miles without a single command from the shepherd and Martin knew Eppy would trust the animal with his life.

The dog floundered ahead of him, yipping softly when a

ewe or perhaps more than one was found, then herding the stupid animals down towards the lower pasture. Martin thought he must have found at least fifty, some struggling to get out of drifts, the snow heavy on their fleece, weighing them down so that they could barely stand, but with a helping hand managing to do so and scamper down the slope with Laddie at their heels towards safer ground. Sensing that they were approaching safety, they could be trusted to find their own way down to the winter pastures.

Although it was snowing so thickly and so ferociously it was not until he came to the higher ground, the tops, that the worst of the storm hit him.

"Bloody hell," he said to the dog who was sniffing at a drift which was a sure indication that there was something living beneath the snow. "Bloody hell, lad, I've never been in anything like this and I reckon it's about time we made our way back. Those not found will do well enough for a few days. Let's hope it thaws soon." He realised he was talking merely to hear the sound of a human voice, even if it was his own, in this wilderness which had him in its grip. Now that he was at the summit of the moorland he found he was becoming confused, since he had no way of knowing in which way he was headed. Down was the only way, of course, but was he struggling westward towards his own farmhouse, perhaps north to the undulating sweep of dangerous hills and valleys which, in this maelstrom, could not be seen, or perhaps eastwards to the higher peaks of the Pennine range?

He whistled for Laddie and though he heard him bark some way off, in the turbulence about him, a turbulence that stung his face and drove into his eyes, he could see nothing. He whistled again and again but there was no sign of the sheepdog. He was probably doing what he had been trained to do and without a shepherd to whom he could "fetch" the sheep he had found, he would "drive" them away to where his intelligent mind knew there was safety. Blast the bloody dog, he thought murderously, at the same time knowing he was being unfair, for the animal was only doing what he had been trained to do.

God, he was weary! He had no idea how long he had been on these moorlands, though it must be a while since it was totally dark; or was it the force and weight of the blizzard that made it seem so? He was so hung about with snow it was like trying to walk with an extra hundredweight attached to him and the growing depth of the drifts was making it almost impossible to lift one foot and put it in front of the other. He was forced to grasp his leg at the knee and manhandle it from the snow, throwing it forward and then tackling the other.

He saw her face then, smiling at him in the lamplight, her green eyes narrowed, her dark lashes meshed together, not only with her smile but with the intensity of her desire. The lamp's glow turned her creamy skin to gold and her dark hair, grown long now and curling at the ends, hung down her naked body, her rose-tipped breasts peeping out from the darkness. She was life and warmth, vital and strong and laughing, and when in his cold dream he laid his hands on her she purred like a cat. There were no shades of grey when he loved her, just the simple black and white of their loving which had no question marks about marriage and housekeepers and social prejudice. There was just Martin and Clare and that was all.

He suddenly realised that he was lying down. Well, not exactly lying, for that sounded comfortable and at ease, but kind of half crouched on his side. How in hell's name had he got into this position and what the hell did he think he was doing, for it was known to everyone who lived on these moors and trod their dangerous ways in the winter that the worst thing a man could possibly do was to stop and rest, even for a fraction of a second? It didn't take long for the euphoria of resting – just for a moment – to turn into a long sleep from which there was no waking. The snow would continue to fall and the coverlet it laid was soft and comforting but deadly, for it hid everything it touched.

With a moan – what was wrong with his leg? – he managed to push himself up on to his knees, twisting this way and that to escape something that had him fastened at the ankle, or so it seemed, though he was so numbed with the icily growing cold he could hardly move his brain, never mind his leg. The very marrow of his bones seemed to freeze and it was bloody hard to struggle against the lethargy that had him in its soft, welcoming grip but he must get up. *He must get up!* Clare . . . Clare, get me up. My love . . . *help me* . . .

The last thing he remembered was the cold, wet nose of the dog as it touched his cheek, and smiling to himself as he sank comfortably into a place warm and safe and where Clare held on to him with loving arms.

Chapter Eighteen

"Jesus, Mary and Joseph," Clare whispered, then crossed herself hastily, something she had not done since her daddy had died, the last of her family to do so. She stood at the open doorway, the snow avalanching in to the kitchen and covering her feet, and as it invaded the warmth and safety of the room it brought with it the upper half of the body of a man. She couldn't recognise him. She knew it wasn't Martin, her senses told her so, and she was filled with anguish and then with shame at her own savage disappointment. The men had been gone for almost twelve hours and surely should have been back by now and her heart despaired over what it meant. Could they survive in this devastating cold, this nightmare of blinding whiteness where every step might lead to disaster and was it worth it, a flock of sheep against the life of a man? But it was no good shilly-shallying on the doorstep, heartsick for Martin, since this poor soul looked as though he were already dead and if she didn't act quickly he soon would be.

"Sammy," she screamed, and the cat jumped a foot in the air. She took hold of the man's hand – where were his mittens, the ones the good-hearted Mrs Starling knitted endlessly for the men? – and began to haul him in, and in front of the fire Sammy slept on.

"Sammy," she screeched again, then, when still he didn't

respond, she let the man's hand fall and with an oath scrambled across the kitchen and gave Sammy a hearty kick in the ribs.

"Ay . . . what's up?" he moaned, stirring irritably in his nest of blankets.

"You, and at once. Stand up, Sammy, for the love of God. Stir yourself and give me a hand. Sammy . . . Sammy . . ." And with a hard hand she clouted him across his tousled head.

"Give over," he mumbled, but at last he was properly awake and astonished that Miss Hanrahan, who had once given Thirza what for when she hit Lavender, should be doing the same to him.

"Come on, lad," she said more gently, "give me a hand with this poor chap. I'm after pulling him over the doorstep but he's so loaded down with snow he's too heavy for me, so he is. Hurry up, Sammy," for by now the snow was billowing in great drifts into the kitchen.

Somehow they managed to pull the man over the doorstep, flopping him on to the kitchen floor like a landed salmon and with a combined effort managed to shut the door on the howling curtain of snow which was doing its best to fill the kitchen. They were both panting with the effort and wet through with the thawing snow.

"Now run upstairs," Clare gasped, "and fetch Thirza and the others."

"What! Wake them up . . ."

"Listen to me, lad, sure an' if this man's not thawed out soon he'll die and I can't do it on me own. Now run . . . run."

The kitchen was, within five minutes, in chaos, filled with women jabbering and wringing their hands, agonising on where the other men were, not knowing what to do next for the poor soul who lay stiff as a board on the floor which Adah and Gracie had scrubbed only minutes before they went to bed. When it was discovered that the hand that had scratched so dramatically at the back kitchen door belonged to young Job, Adah fell into a hysterical fit since she and the stable lad had been eyeing one another with interest for the past six months. What with her ear-splitting sobs and begging one another to tell them what they were to do for the poor lad, who seemed as though he were already frozen to death, the women were in a state of turmoil and Clare knew that unless she took charge of them, and at once, they would stumble about the kitchen like frightened children, useless to anyone and certainly poor Job. He was stiff and white with patches of what appeared to be frostbite on his blank face, his clothes clotted with snow and clinging like a suit of frosted armour to his body.

"Get him as close to the fire as you can and strip him off, and be quick about it." The young lad was quite still, not even his teeth chattering, which Clare thought might be a bad sign, for did not the body shiver and the teeth chatter to keep the circulation going. She didn't know where she'd heard that, probably read it in a book, but even Job's eyeballs seemed to be frozen in their sockets. A thick shelf of frozen snow clung to his eyebrows and his hair looked as though a cap of solid snow had been shaped to fit it. The rest of him was the same, a shapeless bundle which had to be thawed out and quickly.

"You're not going to strip this lad in front of these young lasses. It's not decent," Thirza began, quite horrified as Clare knelt down beside him and fumbled with his clothing. The snow crusted to him was beginning to thaw, forming a widening pool about him and with a quick command Clare had Gracie and Belle mopping it up as she tore at the lad's clothing. It was like trying to remove solid material with no elasticity in it and even as she struggled the end of her fingers began to bleed, cut by the icicles.

"*Will someone help me with this lad*," she shrieked, "or must I do everything myself? Adah, if you don't shut your racket I swear I'll hit you so hard you'll have a shiner that would do justice to a prize fighter. Thirza, for God's sake stop blabbering nonsense and give me hand; you too, Belle. Yes, yes, I know neither of you have seen a naked man before but unless your modesty is so strong you'd rather see him die then get down here and help me. Gracie, run upstairs and fetch blankets and several of those rough towels Mr Heywood likes and Sammy, stoke up that fire and make sure there's plenty of coal in the bucket. Now then, get to it and for the love of God, let's save this lad's life."

The embarrassment that the unmarried women might feel at the sight of Job's thin, lifeless body, even the flaccid mass of his genitalia which hid between his legs, was ignored as they took it in turns to rub him briskly from top to toe, turning his body over with little regard for their own roughness on the big towel Clare had spread out beneath him. They needed to get his blood flowing and the ice from his veins, to turn his white and frozen body to a healthy pink, to try and rid him of the white patches which were mainly confined to his feet, hands and face. He was still alive, thank the holy Mother, Clare kept telling them, which again shocked them, since they had had no idea she was of the Catholic faith, but at last the lad began to stir and at once, to save *his* embarrassment, Clare wrapped him in the blankets that were warming at the range. On his feet were two pairs of Martin Heywood's warmed woollen socks and when, between them, they lifted him into the rocking-chair he looked like a little old man, dazed and nearing the end of his days. Adah was feeding him sips of warm broth with a teaspoon, her broken heart mended, her plain face soft and almost pretty as his mouth opened obediently to the spoon and his brown eyes gazed up at her with shy gratitude.

"Well, I think we did real well there though I say it meself," Thirza told them in a self-congratulatory tone, looking round the circle of doting faces just as though it had been all her doing. They watched Job as if they couldn't get over the miracle of returning the stable lad to some semblance of his usual robust good health and though he was still dazed and unable to speak his eyes looked at them wonderingly, for he'd never had so much attention in his life.

"He'll do now, I think," Clare told them quietly. "And yes,

you all did well, Thirza, but what I'd like to know is where are the others?"

They came in pairs, their dogs beside them in much the same condition as Job and were treated in exactly the same way as Job so that the maids, not one of them married, became quite accustomed to the sight of naked men littering up the kitchen. Though the men protested feebly, those that were able, it made no difference to Miss Hanrahan who, having had such success with young Job, treated them in the same forceful manner and they had no option but to submit, since they hadn't the strength to do otherwise. As there wasn't the faintest chance that any of them could get to their quarters across the yard, not unless they wanted to return themselves to the same condition they had arrived in, beds were aired and men tumbled in to them, two to a bed for extra warmth. With their stomachs full of Miss Hanrahan's hot Scotch broth and their bodies tingling painfully from the ungentle treatment they had received at the hands of the maidservants – would they ever be able to face them again? went through every male mind – they fell into the deep sleep of the exhausted.

The only one still not returned home was their master.

Clare sent the maidservants back to their beds, promising she would wake them the minute the master returned. They were as worn out as the men and didn't argue. Someone had to keep watch for him, keep the fire in and the blankets warming and she had put herself in charge, which was only natural, they supposed, and so it was up to her to wait for the last survivor.

Clare stood by the kitchen window, staring out into the whirling white darkness until her eyes ached and her mouth, which she found she was holding in a grim line of what she knew was fear, became set and rigid, clamped to her teeth in order to stop them chattering. Her mind was a blank and yet in it, like a children's merry-go-round, her thoughts moved in shattered fragments. Not cohesive thoughts, nothing that could be sorted out and considered, but little chippings, images of what she had seen tonight, images of what her mind conjured up of the happenings beyond the window: the sheep . . . had they been found? where? how many? that had been a bad gash on George's chin . . . Adah weeping over young Job . . . the bloody cat which got under everyone's feet . . . the pattern of snowflakes sliding down the window looked like a fern . . . her feet were cold . . . and all these thoughts were the only thing that stood between her and the horror of where Martin was. Why had he not come in with the others? How dare he stay out so long since he knew she would be frantic. Quick, quick, have a cup of tea . . . the kettle . . . why had Gracie not wiped up the melted slush?

With a sigh of despair that whispered from her throat in what could only be described as a moan she fell to her knees, resting her forehead aginst the edge of the windowsill. She had not prayed, nor followed any tenet of the religion in which she had been raised since her daddy had died. How could she believe in the compassion and goodness and mercy of the holy Mother, of her sainted Son after what she had seen in Ireland? What she had seen happen to her own family, the suffering, the fear, the sorrow, the degradation of a people brought to the edge of madness by the madness of others. That was what it had been, madness, a mad nightmare in which, one by one, her mammy first, since every scrap of nourishment which Clare and Daddy salvaged was put in her children's mouths, they had all slipped quietly away. Daddy had died too on the day Mammy did, though his body was still alive, but he had not lasted long and neither had her brothers and sisters, the last the baby, Declan. She and Declan had made it to the fever hospital in some town or other – even now she couldn't recall its name – and then there was only her, and on that day she had cursed the Church and all its teachings. Now, dear sweet Mother in heaven, she wanted to pray again, to ask the Mother of God to send her love safely home, to grant her this one gift after denying her so many. Let him come home to me. Let him live. Don't take him from me as you took the others . . . please, please . . . if you are there listen to my prayer. Hail Mary, full of grace . . .

She roamed the house, going from room to room, peering from windows, the study, the dining-room, the drawing-room in the hope of seeing a let-up of the blinding whiteness that was hurtling against the glass and it was not until an hour later, when Lavender found her crouched by Martin Heywood's chair in the study, cold and dazed, and led her back to the warmth of the kitchen, that she came out of the shock which her brain had forced on her.

"Come, my lass; come wi' Lavender. I knew tha'd be grievin' on tha' own. See, sit by't fire an' warm thissen an' I'll mekk us a cup of tea."

"Where is he, Lavender?" she moaned, caution and sense thrown to the wind. "Why's he not come home with the rest?"

"Nay, lass, I don't know but it'll be light soon an' then they'll go out an' look fer 'im."

"Lavender, I can't stand it." And if Lavender was astonished by Clare's frantic grief she showed no signs of it.

When morning came they crept down the stairs in dribs and drabs, Belle first followed by Thirza who was mortified that the two scullery-maids were still in their beds when she, head parlour-maid, was up and about.

"Leave them, Thirza," Clare said wearily.

"Leave them! They should have had this floor scrubbed by now, the lazy little—"

"*Leave it,* Thirza. Let them sleep, all of them, at least until it stops snowing. The men will have to go out and look for the master."

Thirza put her hand to her mouth. "Dear God, don't tell me the master's not come in."

"No, he hasn't and as soon as—"

"It's stopped, Clare, it's stopped snowing," Lavender shouted from the window where she had been stationed ever since Thirza and Belle entered the kitchen. She flung open the door and was instantly engulfed in a cascade of snow which fell into the kitchen. Clare leaped from her chair and with Thirza and Belle at her back they all four fell silent as they looked on the white world beyond the door. The snow was halfway up the stable walls and the gate that led into the lane was completely hidden. The barn and the stable buildings hid the view of the moor, so with a cry Clare flew from the kitchen and up the stairs to the bedroom floor, throwing open the door of the first bedroom and flinging herself across the rich carpet. The three maids followed her.

They were silent as they looked out at the white world beyond the window. The only sound was the cry of the ravens on the crags and faintly, the distressed lowing of a cow. Great, smooth drifts of snow lay across the valleys, concealing walls, tracks and hedges, with nothing to show where one field began and another ended, the only landmarks the denuded outline of a tree, and edging the garden the thick-leafed spread of conifers, their branches weighed down with diamond-scattered snow. The sun shone, illuminating the rolling moorland, throwing into purple shadows the gullies where its rays did not reach. The sky was an incredible blue, as rich as the blue of Martin Heywood's eyes.

"Right, that's it," Clare declared firmly, energy bursting from her in gladdened relief. She turned on her heel and raced across the room on to the landing.

"What dost tha' mean, our Clare?" Lavender faltered, and Thirza frowned, ready to give the girl a piece of her mind, but Clare was shouting instructions over her shoulder as she raced towards her own room.

"Get the men up . . . yes, all of them, and the girls. I want a big pan of porridge made, Belle, and you, Thirza, go into the master's bedroom and get out all his warm trousers and coats; scarves, gloves."

"What!"

"You heard. Those men have got to be warmly wrapped and their own things are still wet through. They'll have to make do with their own boots which shouldn't be too bad, and Belle, you'd best get bacon on and fried bread; plenty of tea and tell Sammy he can start clearing a path to the stable and the cow byre right away. Those animals will need seeing to. When one of the men's dressed send him to the labourers' cottages, that's if he can manage it. Tell him to dig his way ... and fetch the ditchers and wallers and anybody else who can help to form a search party. I want every able-bodied man there is to look for Mar ... for Mr Heywood. Is that clear?"

The men were stoked up as though they were to be off to the north pole without a bit of sustenance in between here and there. There was some stifled laughter as they stuffed themselves into the master's good things, frock coats with woollen jerkins underneath and a fly-fronted chesterfield over the lot. Riding breeches, a raglan cape, an old-fashioned riding coat with a high collar fetched from the attic where Thirza remembered a trunkful of old Mr Heywood's garments had been stored for years, with pantaloons of white moleskin and trousers made from the finest merino. They were swathed in long woollen scarves, mittens knitted by Mrs Starling and found stuffed in the master's dressing-table drawer.

But it was not until Miss Hanrahan herself strode into the kitchen in a pair of the master's breeches held up by a stout belt, two jerseys on top of which was a knee-length overcoat, a shawl tied about her head, and her old, much-mended black boots brought from Ireland on her feet, that a strange and awkward silence fell on the company. The men shuffled their feet, their expressions saying that this was not women's business and the maids were slack-jawed with astonishment, all except Lavender who remembered the state

Miss Hanrahan had been in during the night while the others slept.

"Sure an' 'tis no good you men looking like that, for no matter what you say I'm going with you. The more people searching, the quicker the master'll be found. The sun's shining and the snow's frozen hard. I know, I've just been out and tested it so we should be able to walk across it."

"Don't be soft, lass," Eppy said flatly. "Minnit tha' walks on't crust it'll give way on tha'. 'Tis not thick enough ter 'old the weight of any man."

"I'm not a man, Eppy, and I'll be careful. I know the area pretty well by now and I've a good eye for direction."

"Nay, lass, I'll not allow it. None on us will. Besides, Laddie's not come 'ome which means 'e's still wi' t'maister. 'E'd not leave 'im. Dog'll be guardin' 'im so all us 'as ter do is find my Laddie. 'E'll be barkin' 'is bloody 'ead off – pardon the language – an' in this quiet us'll 'ave no trouble 'earin' 'im."

The men murmured among themselves, agreeing with Eppy, who was the oldest and wisest among them. He knew these moorlands better than any man living. He had seen which way the master had headed last night and with the help of his dogs, all their dogs, they'd have him dug out of whatever hole he had found for himself within the hour.

"What you say may be true but you have no jurisdiction over me, Eppy, and I shall do as I please. The master ..." She gulped as her throat closed up with desperate fear but managed to continue, though her voice was unsteady and the maids exchanged startled glances. "The master has been out on those moors for over sixteen hours and ..."

Eppy had no idea what "jurisdiction" meant but he could guess and it made no difference, choose how.

"Aye, lass, us knows that but tha'd only 'old us up an' if we 'ave ter keep botherin' about thi' ..."

"Please yourself, old man, but I'm going and I'm going now before any more time is wasted."

She struck out away from the rest of the men who were heading in pairs north towards Broadhead Noddle, west towards Friars Mere, and east towards Mill Stone Edge, all lying on the periphery of Martin Heywood's land. They watched her for an exasperated moment as she floundered up the slope that would lead her to Thorstone Ridge, telling one another sourly that they'd be off searching for her by the day's end and what the hell did she think she was up to, daft faggot. Her bright red shawl would be easy enough to spot as long as she didn't fall down some gully and break her silly neck and if she did then she'd nobody else to blame but herself.

She had expected that the invisible and flexible bond that exists between lovers, that stretch of magical connecting power known only to those who love, would guide her to him. She was so sure that her own instincts, her senses, the ties that bound her heart to his, would take her at once to where he lay, but she had not bargained for the depth of the snow and the many objects, rocks and dry-stone walls, patches of waist-high scrub hidden beneath the snow that got in her way. Taking heed of what Eppy had said about his dog, she stopped frequently to listen for the sound of barking and for the shouts of the men, for in this frozen, silent waste a voice would carry for miles, but there was nothing but the hoarse rasp of ravens and the cry of a dog fox which, knowing that sheep were trapped in the snow, was out on the hunt. She stopped frequently to get her breath, for the going was hard. Like Martin before her, though she was not aware of it, she was forced to lift her own legs out of the deep, crusted snow which gave way, as Eppy had said it would, beneath her weight. The sun shone across the brilliant landscape, sparkling and glittering as though some magnanimous hand had scattered diamonds freely and carelessly on the high moorland, and soon her eyes began to ache and blur. She tried to shade them with the edge of her shawl but within an hour her head was thudding and she felt sick.

She stopped for the umpteenth time, tempted to sit down

on the top of a dry-stone wall that she had just walked into. The cam stones that lay along its top were just visible but she had not seen them through her slitted eyelids. If she could just rest for a moment she would feel better, she knew she would, but hearing Eppy's warning voice in her head she gritted her teeth and floundered on. Her breath rasped in her throat, hurting her, and it was perhaps this, the harshness of her breathing that prevented her from hearing the sound which came from over on her right towards Diggle Brow. She pushed on, shading her eyes as best she could with her hand, then, beginning to tremble with exhaustion, she flopped down full-length in a snowdrift and lay there thankfully. Just for a moment, she promised herself, no more and it was then she heard the sound, the sound of a dog barking!

Holy Mother ... dear sweet Jesus who is our Saviour ... it was a dog barking, faint and sounding as weary as she felt but it was Laddie, it must be; she knew it was Laddie and with the dog would be Martin. She didn't know why he was still out here when all the rest had come home but by God she'd give him what for when she found him.

Hauling herself to her feet she turned in the direction from which she had first heard the dog's voice, but for some reason it had gone quiet. It didn't matter, she had heard it and she would make her way towards it.

She began to shout, to scream the dog's name.

"Laddie ... Laddie, where are you? Let me hear your voice, Laddie. Don't stop barking, for God's sake, don't give up now, Laddie. I'm coming ... Martin, I'm coming." And as though it had heard her shouts the dog began to howl as though it were in agony. Its voice rose high into the blue bowl of the sky and Eppy's second dog, who was sniffing at a snowdrift under which several sheep were buried, turned and looked towards the south-east. It lifted its paw, then turned to Eppy, its nose quivering, its eyes bright.

"Wha' is it, lad?" Eppy said and George, who was paired

with him, turned to stare at the shepherd and the dog. The dog whined, waiting for permission to move off and when Eppy gave the command, began to leap through the deep snow, turning back to make sure Eppy was following.

"Right, lad, away," and the dog needed no second bidding. Following as best they could, Eppy and George began to wallow through the deep snow after the animal.

The dog led them across a mile or more of undulating, exhausting snowland, great sweeps of moor which in ordinary circumstances they would have covered in half an hour. They could hear Laddie's barking the nearer they got, the sound that Eppy's second collie had picked up and it led them directly to him. Laddie was barking hoarsely, prancing and leaping in his ecstasy at seeing his master despite the solid mass of snow that clung to his fur. There was a great heap of disturbed snow about what appeared to be a hastily dug hole and about the hole were the tracks of where the dog had paced in his vigilant watch over the man.

Lying at the bottom of the hole, which was no more than four feet deep, was the master, and wrapped about him, her shawl round his head, her greatcoat draped across him, was his housekeeper. They both appeared to be smiling.

Chapter Nineteen

They carried Martin Heywood home on a farm gate dug out of the snow but first they had to release his ankle which had become trapped between two rocks and was the reason why he could not extricate himself from the snowdrift in the first place. Miss Hanrahan was everywhere, darting round them as they carefully released him from the drift in which he had lain for almost twenty-four hours, getting in their way and giving orders which they didn't need.

"Jesus, Mary an' Joseph, will you be careful with him. Mind his leg, George, it might be broken and the less it's handled the better."

"I know that, miss, an' I'm doin' the best I can so will tha' just stand aside . . ."

"No, I will not just stand aside. See, Eppy, can you not wrap my coat more tightly about him. He's quite blue with the cold."

"Dost tha' want ter perish thissen, lass? 'Tis cold enough ter freeze a brass . . . well, put tha' coat on or it'll be thee what's carried 'ome on't gate," Eppy protested irritably and uselessly. What was wrong with the lass and her usually so sensible? Plaguing them to death with her daft instructions just as though they had never rescued a chap from the snow before. Mind, she liked her own way, so the girls in the kitchen had told him, and he'd seen it for himself only this morning when she'd tramped off in search of the master.

"Now stand aside, my lass. 'E'll not 'arm. By Gow, poor wight's bin under't snow all this time an' if 'e survived that 'e'll survive owt."

"Do as you're told, Eppy," she snapped at him and him old enough to be her grandad. "See, put this shawl round him."

"Clare," a weak voice from the improvised stretcher murmured, discretion forgotten as he spoke her name. "Will you ... will you ... let them get on with it or we'll ... damn well be here ... another twenty-four hours. I'm all right, my lass. Let ... let Eppy and George ... fetch me down while you run on ... and tell them to get me a hot bath ready and a bowl of that good soup of yours." The words were spoken in a thready whisper but they were coherent and had a ring of command in them which said he would be obeyed.

"I will not run on ahead, Martin Heywood," Clare hissed in a scandalised voice, "if such a thing was possible which it's not in this snow. Anyway, I daren't let you out of my sight for what you'll get up to next," the astonished men heard her add. "And will you stand out of my way, Eppy Waring," for all she wanted to do was cling to Martin's hand, to the amazement of the two men, to pat his face and draw the shawl and his old greatcoat, which she had been wearing, more closely about his shoulders. She was like a mother fussing round a small child when it sets off to school, Eppy told the rest of them later, which was perhaps when the first suspicions of the true nature of the relationship between the master and his housekeeper trickled into one or two minds.

They got him down, but it had been hard going with only the two men to carry him in the deep snow and the lass constantly getting in their way as she begged them to be careful. Winging on the clear, thin air at last their shouts alerted the other men who came from as far away as Moor Croft and Harrop Edge, where they had been searching, floundering about in snowdrifts six feet deep, to give a hand. If it hadn't been for the dogs and the fact that the master had made them go in pairs it would have been more than Martin Heywood who was lost, for there was greater safety in numbers!

The kitchen was once again in turmoil, filled with exhausted, snow-encrusted men, excited maidservants and several dogs who, though they were not usually allowed in the house, anybody's house, had slunk over the doorstep looking for something to eat. Belle and Thirza, warned by Hammy who, though he was barely out of boyhood but who had been allowed to join the search, had soup bubbling on the stove in readiness for the stampede. Hammy was big and strong with hands on him like a man, and he had run . . . well, struggled more than run, down from the high moorland to let them know that the master had been found, that the men were on their way, that hot food and drinks would be needed and that somehow one of them was to fetch the doctor since it looked as though the master had broken his ankle.

"The doctor! In this? How in heaven's name are any of us to get to the doctor's and if we did how would we get him back here?" Thirza had exclaimed.

"I'll go," Lavender told them, reaching for a couple of shawls that hung at the back of the door and which were used when one of the maids had to cross the yard. She had a pair of boots, women's boots she had found in the cupboard at the back of the hall and which fitted her and with Clare's permission had been wearing them all winter. "Sammy can come wi' me an' we'll use that there sledge what's in the tack room."

"What sledge?"

"George reckoned it belonged ter't master when 'e were a lad. Come on, Sammy, are thi' game?"

Sammy was more than game. Sammy hadn't enjoyed himself so much since he'd come to work here for Mr Heywood. Polishing boots and brasses and cleaning lamps, good food, aye, and a warm bed at night, which was more than could be said for many a lad, especially those who worked in the mills of Crossfold, but the last twenty-four hours had been magical, especially now that it was known that every last man, including the master, were all safe.

Martin Heywood, the euphoria of being found wearing off as his leg was jolted to a blinding agony, was like a bear with a sore head, snarling at everyone who spoke a word to him, cursing when some well-intentioned servant joggled him, ferocious in his determination that he shouldn't suffer the fate of the rest of the men and be stripped naked of his snow-encrusted clothes, placed before the fire and rubbed raw with a bloody towel.

"Take no notice of him, Thirza," Clare was unwise enough to remark as the men, grinning every last one of them, lifted him gently on to a camp bed which had been brought down and placed in front of the fire. "Hand me those blankets."

Martin Heywood did not care to hear his servants told that they were to take no notice of him, even by the woman he loved, who loved him and wanted only what was best for him. He made his own decisions, she should know that by now.

"Get off me, woman. If you think you're going to strip me naked in front of all these gawking women then you can think again."

"Really, and if not me, then who, or are you to lie in those wet clothes until you die of pneumonia?"

His vast annoyance gave him strength. "The men can do it. See, Eppy, give me a hand, and George, and the rest of you, all of you can bugger off until I'm decent. And there's no need to think you're going to sit about on your arses and drink hot tea and soup all day. You men can clear the yard and paths to the stables and byre. Bloody hell, I can hear that cow bawling from here, and then when that's done you can start on the track to Edgeclough, for that's the way the doctor will come. Bloody Nora, that girl – what's her name? – aye, Lavender, she's got more gumption than the rest of you put together," which was unfair since they had all risked their lives to save his.

Clare was forced to "bugger off" with the rest of them while Eppy and George stripped their master, rubbed him down with the rough towels that had been placed to hand, then, when he was the nice pink colour she needed him to be, dressed him in his warmed nightshirt and wrapped him in blankets, just like a bloody baby, he bellowed, then placed him gently on the bed in front of the roaring fire, since it was evident that he was in great pain. All this was done accompanied by shouted instructions from Miss Hanrahan from beyond the kitchen door and the moment he was decent she was there beside him, feeling his forehead for signs of fever, kneeling to peer into his face, which was flushed now, holding his hands in both of hers until the servants gaped in astonishment. They swore they heard her whisper his name, his *christian* name and really, did she know what she was doing she was acting so strangely. Mind, she had been the same with Job; well, not exactly the same but kind and efficient. There was something definitely different about this though, but as yet they couldn't put their collective finger on it.

The snow had blown across the moor in such a way that the track to Edgeclough, though it had drifted deeply at one side, had no more than six to eight inches of snow down its centre and the doctor arrived two hours later. The two youngsters, Lavender and Sammy, were flushed and bright-eyed with excitement, having had great fun on the way down, both clinging precariously to the toboggan, so much fun in fact they had almost forgotten the purpose of their mission. The doctor had walked back with them, or, where it was suitable, clambered on to the toboggan and joined in the fun on the short down slopes.

Martin was in his own bed, his leg set, drowsing under the effect of the sleeping draught the doctor had given him, and it was then that it was noticed that Miss Hanrahan was missing. She had been bustling about the kitchen, seeing that the men were dry and stuffed to the gills with the good food she had prepared for them before they made their way to their own quarters across the cleared yard. They had brought down a good number of Martin Heywood's sheep and would be off again at first light, providing it didn't snow again, to search with their dogs and long shepherd's crooks for those still missing. The yard had been cleared and a path dug to the byre, the animals seen to, which was a great relief to George and Percy and a decent start had been made on the track to Edgeclough. The kitchen floor had been scrubbed, a pan of good shin beef and vegetable broth was bubbling on the range in readiness for the master when he awakened, and there was a casserole, easy to prepare and so left for Belle to see to, in the oven for the servants. The milk had been brought in and set in the pantry and Miss Hanrahan was seen to glance round her, checking that everything that had to be done, had been done. Then she was gone.

He smiled at her from his pillow as she kneeled by his bed and his smile closed like a fist around her heart, since she had been afraid she might never see it again. He raised a gentle hand and cupped her chin. She turned her mouth into the palm of his hand and rested her lips there, then she began to weep.

"I thought I'd lost you . . . I thought I'd lost you."

"Don't, my darling, don't cry; it'd take more than a bloody snowstorm to get rid of me." His hand rose to her cheek, his thumb brushing away the tears which ran unchecked across them, then lifted to her eyebrow, tracing its delicate arch. It travelled to her hair, pushing back the slipping glossy mass which had escaped the careless ribbon she had tied about it. His eyes wandered across her face, dreaming, as though he had not expected to see her again either, then he sighed, for sleep was creeping over him.

"Clare, my darling . . . you saved my life."

"No, the men would have found you."

"Why did you come that way?"

"I don't know. Dear God, what would I have done if I hadn't found you? I love you."

"I know ... I know."

"It was the dog."

"Aye, Laddie's a good dog. Confound it, this bloody leg." He gritted his teeth and a spasm of pain crossed his face. He closed his eyes and his hand fell to the coverlet but even as he drifted away from her into the sleep he needed she knew she could not leave him. Someone must stay with him and though it would cause talk who else was there but her? Thirza? One of the men? Hardly, since none of them would know what to do for him if he woke in pain. The doctor had given her clear instructions. He should not be moved. If he needed the ... well, to relieve his ... Miss Hanrahan would know what he meant, he must be tended in his bed, and anticipating his patient's incapacity he had brought this ... this bottle; well ... perhaps one of the men ...

"I shall see to it, doctor," she said firmly as she walked with him to the gate and the track that led up to Edgeclough. "I ... I nursed my family in Ireland, my brothers and father and ... well, I know what to do."

The doctor saw the bleak expression move in her eyes and, knowing she was Irish and the devastation that had come on that sad land, he understood.

He held her hand for a moment. "I'll be back first thing if the blasted snow doesn't start again. Now keep him warm, warm drinks ... well, you don't need me to tell you so I'll bid you good-afternoon, Miss Hanrahan." He went away, certain that his patient was in good and competent hands.

It was an hour later, dark as the inside of a parson's hat, and the maidservants were all just thinking they might get to their beds, wondering among themselves where Miss Hanrahan had got to, for surely she couldn't be with the master all this time, when she came in to the kitchen, her hair all over the place, and what looked like dried tears on her face.

"Help me to carry that bed upstairs, Sammy," she said quietly to the startled boy who was just about to sit down to a bowl of broth to sustain him until morning. He'd worked hard today and needed a bit of something to stoke up the energy he'd used. Belle said so.

The maids exchanged glances as the bed was folded and, between them, carried out of the room by the housekeeper and the boot-boy.

"Where's it goin', Miss Hanrahan?" they heard the boy say and were stunned by her answer which came clearly to them through the open kitchen door.

"The master's room."

"Right," the lad said, and being a lad and no more than twelve did not consider the implications. The others did.

"She's not goin' ter sleep in't master's room, surely!" Belle whispered to Thirza while the head parlour-maid shook her head in disbelief.

"Nay, never."

"Then wha' . . . ?"

They stared at one another in growing wonder while the two scullery-maids watched them in bewilderment.

"I don't know but, by God, I'll find out." And with a twitch of her apron and a grim line to her mouth Thirza strode across the kitchen and made for the stairs.

The master was asleep when she entered his bedroom. She was just in time to see Sammy and the housekeeper setting the narrow bed beside the master's. Quietly they put it up, the lad throwing nervous glances at the sleeping form of his master, then scurrying past Thirza as Miss Hanrahan began to make the bed up with clean sheets and blankets.

"An' what d'you think you're doing?" Thirza challenged in a stage whisper.

"What does it look like? Mr Heywood might need something in the night and someone must be here to see to him."

"Oh, an' you're the one, are you? What about one of the men? It would be more . . . well, proper."

"Proper! And what is meant by that?"

"You know what I mean. An unmarried couple in the same room together."

"So I'm to leave him completely unattended to satisfy your idea of the niceties of convention, is that it?"

"One of the men—" Thirza began stubbornly.

"All the men are exhausted and besides which they wouldn't know what to do. They would have to fetch me so I might as well—"

"Now you listen to me, madam. I don't know what you hope to gain by . . . by wheedling your way into the master's good graces."

"Wheedling! Don't be so damn stupid, Thirza. You're just making a fool of yourself."

"And what are *you* making of yourself, tell me that? You'll be the talk of—"

"You mean you'll make sure I'm the talk of the community, don't you, Thirza? Well, you must please yourself. I'm responsible for the man in that bed. There's nobody else able to look after him, unless you're offering to sit with him yourself."

"Sit with him, yes, but not lie in a bed next to his."

"Holy Mother, what's the difference! We must all try and get as much rest as we can, Thirza, and so, if you don't mind, I mean to do just that. Bank the fire up in the kitchen and make sure the kettle's full. The master might need a warm drink in the night. Now I'll say goodnight."

The kitchen was in a state of pandemonium. Sammy sat by the fire wondering what the hell all the fuss was about, spooning Miss Hanrahan's good broth into his mouth, toying with the idea that perhaps they might let him sleep here again tonight.

"She's sleeping with the master." Thirza crossed her arms over her flat bosom and grimaced, not with disapproval, which she knew she should feel, but with a certain air of satisfaction.

Belle's mouth fell open. "Yer what!"

Thirza explained sharply. "Well, not in the same bed," glancing meaningfully at Sammy and the two young maids, "but she says he might need something, the master I mean, in the night and so she's . . ." She grimaced again. "She's made the bed up."

"Lord! Does she mean ter . . . well, yer know, tekk 'er clothes off?"

Sammy's and the two maids' open-mouthed glances moved from Thirza to Belle and back again.

"Nay, don't ask me. But it's a disgrace, that's what it is. She should be settin' a good example to these two lasses here, not giving them ideas."

"Eeh, Thirza, what are we ter do?" Belle was obviously upset at what she saw as the feet of clay of the woman she had come to respect over the last year.

"Nay, it's nothin' to do wi' us, Belle. Let's just wait and see."

He was fretful the next morning, complaining that he had a headache and the light hurt his eyes. His damned leg was giving him gyp and he was bored. He wasn't used to lying about in bed and if she thought she could keep him here she was mistaken. He wanted to see Eppy about those missing sheep; had she heard anything? No, well would she kindly go downstairs and find out and if she tried to feed him any more of that slop he'd throw it at her.

He was sorry then, begging her to lie beside him and put her head on his shoulder, his eyes gleaming momentarily with sardonic humour as he wondered how long it would be before they could resume their loving. Why didn't she slip out of that bloody dress and let him put his hands on . . . dammit, he wasn't an invalid and if she loved him she'd see that it wouldn't hurt his wretched leg, not if they were careful.

She did her best to humour him, soothing him with promises and kisses that seemed to make him even worse-tempered. He had never been ill in his life, he told her petulantly, as though it were *her* fault. She begged him to be patient, telling him that the doctor would be here soon and perhaps he would allow him out of bed. He had slept all night without a murmur, and so had she, the sleep of total exhaustion, and she had thought he would be feeling a lot better; instead he was impatient, frustrated, bad-tempered, complaining that every movement jarred his leg, accusing her of keeping him here as though she did it just to annoy him.

The doctor was obviously concerned by his patient's irritable condition. "You must be patient, Mr Heywood. You are doing yourself no good insisting on getting up. In fact, I absolutely forbid you to get up. Just lie still and enjoy the ministrations of your . . . your housekeeper." For even the doctor had noticed the strange intimacy that seemed to exist between his patient and his patient's servant.

"I have business matters which need attending to, and half my flock is still buried under the snow. I cannot just lie here and let them perish."

"Are you suggesting that you should go out and search for them yourself? Have a bit of sense, man."

"No, of course not." Martin gritted his teeth in an attempt to hold on to his slipping temper. "But I want to see my head shepherd."

"That's as may be, sir, but you cannot put weight on that leg of yours. Dear Lord, it's only twenty-four hours, Mr Heywood. Perhaps tomorrow I will allow your farm manager to come up and see you."

"I have no farm manager. I run the place myself but my head shepherd—"

"Tomorrow, sir," the doctor said soothingly. "Perhaps tomorrow."

But by tomorrow Martin Heywood was running a high fever,

tossing on the bed and muttering, knocking away Clare's frantic hand when she placed it on his forehead, and from his restless body there began to come a fierce heat.

"Is he drinking much liquid?" the doctor asked when he came panting up the lane after being summoned for the second time that day by the distraught Miss Hanrahan.

"Sure an' I can't get more 'n a teaspoon past his lips."

"It's not enough, lass. He needs at least four or five cupfuls a day."

She felt the despair begin to catch her in its awful grip. She had sat beside his bed last night, the camp bed pushed roughly to one side, her elbows resting on the coverlet, her chin in her hands as she watched his face moving from side to side, listened to his mutterings and, when he woke for a moment and was lucid, his curses at his own weakness and the agony of his leg.

"And you look as though you could use some rest, Miss Hanrahan. Surely there's someone who could take your place for a few hours. That girl who came for me the other day seems very capable. Why don't you get her up here and you have a nap on that bed?"

She was ready to fall down in her exhaustion, to collapse on the bed beside Martin and sleep and sleep, but if he should wake and need her what good would she be to him, for she was at the limits of her endurance.

"Lavender."

"I beg your pardon?" the doctor asked.

"She's called Lavender and she can be trusted."

"Fetch her up here at once and let me talk to her. I'll soon tell whether she'll do. Mr Heywood is . . . I think there must be some infection, perhaps in the bone I set, and I need to know whether this lass is capable of watching him closely."

And so it was that between them Clare and Lavender nursed Martin Heywood and the tittle-tattle that had begun to spread round the farm about their master and his housekeeper died down a little, for if there was anything between them as was at first thought it wasn't happening with Lavender Bickerstaffe in the same room, was it. They took it in turns to watch over him, one of them always by his side, sleeping in shifts, alternately going down to the kitchen where Thirza was enjoying her spell of command, to eat, Lavender ravenously for she was not in love, Clare picking at her food, becoming rake thin, for she was! The doctor came every day, for some reason taking off the wrappings about the splint on Martin Heywood's leg and sniffing at it, his face relaxing in relief each time he did so.

"If . . . well . . . if you should smell something . . . well, nasty is the only word I can think of, send for me immediately. Bathe him in cool water several times a day," he told them, "and if he doesn't become more lucid I'll arrange for ice to be brought up. His heart's strong, which is a good sign, but I'd like that fever brought down."

If he had been conscious Clare knew Martin would have created a commotion of such proportions it would have been heard on the moorland where the snow was beginning to thaw. She and Lavender stripped him of his nightgown and bathed his wasting body with cold clear water, then, taking it in turns, fed him sips of water, drop by drop. They decided between them it was hardly worth the bother of putting him into a fresh nightshirt every couple of hours and the pair of them got used to the sight of his naked, defenceless body lying on the bed. The flesh had fallen from him and his ribcage stood proud leading down to his flat belly and the soft tumbled mass of his genitals hiding in the dark patch of hair between his legs, the long slenderness of his legs themselves, one of which ended in the ugly casing of the splint. She and Lavender worked as one unit, their thoughts seeming to unite and speak without words and Clare got down on her knees whenever she had a moment and thanked the holy Mother for sending Lavender to her, for she was convinced that without the girl's strength and hope and positive belief that between them they would restore him to full health, Clare alone could not have saved the life of Martin Heywood.

She sat by his bed in her usual position when she was "mindin'" him, as Lavender called it, her elbows on the coverlet, her chin propped in her hands, her eyes studying his face feature by feature. His lips were cracked and slightly parted. His closed eyes lay deep in their bony sockets and his cheekbones stood out sharply beneath. The doctor said that now he had begun to sweat lightly, which was a good sign, he had every hope that Mr Heywood would make a full recovery. It would take many weeks, of course, which would not be easy with a man like him, but with good food and plenty of rest, and a couple of nurses like Miss Hanrahan and Lavender, who he had learned was a housemaid, he should be up and about by spring.

"Tha' love 'im, don't tha'?" a quiet voice said to her from the bed which had been moved to the far side of the room to give them more space by Martin's bedside.

Clare lifted her head sharply to find Lavender's pale-blue eyes on her. There was kindness in them, and understanding, for though Lavender was barely seventeen she knew about love. Her mam and pa, Billy and Betty Bickerstaffe, married for twenty years and the parents of seven living children, desperately poor, were as much in love today as they had been over twenty years ago when young Billy Bickerstaffe, nineteen years old and as handsome and strutting as a farmyard cock, had caught sight of seventeen-year-old Annie Ashworth, who was as bonny as a wild hedge rose, or so he had thought. He still thought so today, though by now Annie was worn down with hard work and childbearing. They were both employed at Will Hopkinson's cotton mill, labouring to earn a few bob to feed their children and pay the rent of their cottage, which belonged to the man Lavender was helping to nurse. But Lavender had often gone to sleep in that tiny cottage where everyone slept almost on top of one another to the sound of her parents' tender loving.

"Don't worry, lass, I'll tell no one but if there's owt I can 'elp thi' with tha've only ter say."

"Lavender, dear Lavender, what am I to do? What *am* I to do? Yes, I love him" – there was no point in denying it— "and he loves me, I'm sure."

"So tha'll be married?" Lavender's voice became anxious. "Won't tha'?"

Clare sighed. "I wish I knew."

Chapter Twenty

The knock at the door startled them and for a second they froze. Martin's hand, which had just dipped inside the unbuttoned bodice of his housekeeper's gown, stopped its delightful exploring of her engorged nipple, then, with a smothered oath, he hastily withdrew his smoothing fingers.

"Bloody hell, is a man not to get a bit of peace in his own study?" he muttered, doing his best to help her put herself decently together again, and himself for that matter, since the bulge in his breeches was hardly invisible. Clare stood up and moved to the window, keeping her back to the door, trembling so violently she was forced to grip the thick curtains to steady herself as Martin shouted to whoever was on the other side of the door to enter.

Thirza sidled inside, not exactly smirking but with a look on her face and a gleam in her eyes that said she, even if some of the others were sceptical, believed the worst when it came to her master and the housekeeper. Well, you had to be blind, and deaf, and daft not to see what was going on under their very noses, hadn't you? Ever since Thirza had become suspicious on the evening the trundle bed was placed beside the master's when he was brought down injured from the snow-covered moors, and Miss Hanrahan had informed them that she meant to spend the night on it, Thirza had been distrustful of what Clare Hanrahan did her best to pass off as perfectly normal. It was *not* normal for a woman to sleep side by side with a man who was not her husband, even if he was injured. The presence of Lavender did little to allay her doubts, for Lavender Bickerstaffe was Clare Hanrahan's accomplice; that had been made perfectly obvious when it came to sharing the nursing of the master. She, Thirza, should have been Miss Hanrahan's first choice, not a slip of a lass who until recently had worked as a spinner in Will Hopkinson's cotton mill. What did she, or the housekeeper for that matter, know about looking after a sick man when she, Thirza, had helped to nurse old Mrs Heywood? But nevertheless, that's what the two of them made out they were doing and Thirza had to admit, reluctantly, he had survived!

Never, as long as she lived, would Thirza regret anything as much as she regretted refusing the master's offer of the job of housekeeper. She'd been a fool. The trouble was the sudden death of Mrs Case had thrown her into a panic and in that panic she had convinced herself that she could never take Mrs Case's place, the woman who had guided her for so many years. It had seemed an impertinence to step into the shoes of such a superior being, but had she known that Mr Heywood would give the post to "the new girl" instead of employing an experienced housekeeper, which Thirza had envisaged he would, she would have grabbed his offer with both hands. It still rankled, for she, Thirza, could have done the job just as well as Clare Hanrahan; better, in fact, for at least she had had many years' tuition under Mrs Case.

Her voice was smooth and her face expressionless as she stood just inside the door watching the Irish biddy doing her best to look as though gazing out of the master's study window was nothing out of the ordinary. If they had been conferring on . . . well, some aspect of the domestic running of the house, say a dinner party or some such thing, she would have been seated, or standing in front of his desk with him behind it but instead she was at the window and he was lounging on the leather chesterfield, his face like a turkeycock, his hands resting on his stick with which he looked as though he would like nothing better than to hit her.

"Yes, what is it?" he challenged, dipping his eyebrows in a frown.

"I'm sorry to disturb you, sir, but Mr Hopkinson is here to see you. Just a moment of your time, he said."

"Did he. Well, ask him to wait a minute. Miss Hanrahan and I were . . ."

"Yes, sir?" Thirza's voice was mild.

"Well, we've finished . . . we *have* finished, have we not, Miss Hanrahan?" turning towards the stiff back of his housekeeper.

Clare knew she could not stand there clutching the curtains and peering out into the front garden for much longer, not with Thirza's half-mocking gaze on her. She knew it would be mocking, just as she knew that Thirza was aware of the situation between her and Martin, and if Thirza knew she wouldn't keep it to herself. She would air her views to anyone who would listen, in the kitchen, the yard and, she supposed, wherever she went on her day off. There was nothing she, Clare, could do to stop it. There was nothing anyone, except Martin, could do to stop it, and how long this could go on she didn't know. It was March, four months since the big snowstorm that had given those who worked on the farm their first inkling of how things stood between her and Martin, and though some of them didn't believe it, or so Lavender loyally informed her, the rest were whispering behind her back, watching her, wondering what was to happen to her. There was one thing that was a certainty, at least to them, and that was that Martin Heywood would never marry his housekeeper, an Irish peasant who, until she crossed the Irish Sea, had never worn shoes.

She had not chosen to love him, for what woman in her right mind would choose to love a man who employed her as his housekeeper? She had not wanted to love him, nor wanted his love, but from the moment he had put his hands on her, had wrapped her about in arms that were strong, warm with masculine vigour, lifted her against him and laid his lips on hers, she had been lost in it, lost in him, wandering mindlessly forward in the belief that a love like theirs must come to its natural conclusion. Everywhere she went in the house she smelled the fragrance of him, the expensive cigars he smoked, the cologne he used, the brandy he drank, the very essence of Martin Heywood which was an irresistible magnet she could not deny. His lean, dark face with its curiously slanting smile enchanted her, and his vivid blue eyes, when they looked into hers, hypnotised, so that she felt she was under a spell and incapable of using her own intelligent mind to escape it.

But could they go on like this? Could *she* go on like this? For almost a year they had been lovers and for almost a year she had breathed a thankful sigh of relief when her monthly courses began. She wanted a child, how dearly she wanted a child, Martin's child, but she wanted that child, when it came, to be born to a loving mother and father who were married to one another. Dear Mother in heaven, blessed Virgin, what must I do? she had asked in the night, for she knew she committed a sin, but she loved him so hopelessly, so enduringly, so compulsively she knew she might as well beg the moon to help her, for she would listen to its voice as insensibly as she would listen to that of the Mother of God.

She turned and smiled brightly, the smile a servant exchanges with an employer.

"We have, sir. I'll be letting you have the menu as soon as . . . it's ready."

"Thank you, Miss Hanrahan. Now show Mr Hopkinson in, if you please, Thirza, and bring us a pot of coffee."

"Very well, sir."

Will Hopkinson was standing with his back to the hall fireplace, lifting his tails to allow the warmth of the flames to drift about his plump buttocks. He glanced appreciatively at the tall, slender woman in dark blue as she passed him on the way to the kitchen, admiring her in that coarse way gentlemen think they have a right to display with a woman of the lower orders. She was a looker all right and as he was ushered into Martin Heywood's study by the homely parlourmaid he wondered what the situation was there. He knew what he'd like to be doing to her if he was free enough to employ her as his housekeeper. Still, he mustn't let thoughts of such a nature interfere with what had brought him here. A favour he wanted of Martin Heywood, a favour between one gentleman and another and one that would be repaid, for that was how gentlemen did business.

It had been a difficult four months. Martin Heywood had been a difficult patient. From the moment he began to feel better he had the whole house, and not only the house but the stable yard and the moorland beyond where the shepherds guarded his sheep, in a turmoil of exasperation. A dozen times a day he summoned Eppy to the house for a full report on the state of his flock. Sheep, being perverse creatures, will not eat food to which they are unaccustomed, even if they are starving, so during the early winter months hay was fed to them so that when the snow came they would know what hay was, and eat it. Had they eaten it? How many of his ewes were in lamb? Those that were would need special foods in order to prevent lambing troubles. Was there plenty of grass on the lower pastures? And a hundred questions which, being unable to leave the house, Martin Heywood could not check for himself. Naturally, Eppy took no notice of his master's commands, for if he did, he told him, he'd be tramping up and down the bloody moor all day long.

It would be lambing time soon, the busiest time of the year for the sheep farmer. Hedges needed attention, for, again, sheep being what they were, they would push through to get to the grass in the next field. The dry-stone walls must be repaired and kept in good order if the pastures were to hold stock. Field gates to be mended, early potatoes to be planted, a dozen and one things that needed Martin Heywood's personal supervision otherwise they would never get done, or so he liked to believe, and if they were they wouldn't be done properly; and when he realised he could not give it, since it was impossible to walk the moors on sticks, his fury was laid about those who were nearest to him. The bloody doctor was a fool who absolutely refused his permission for him to get on a horse and had even had the temerity to have a word with his grooms so that all in all the atmosphere at Moorhouse was explosive, needing but a word to bring the roof down, or so it seemed to the cowering servants, and his roars of temper could be heard at the top of Friars Mere. He had never been incapacitated in his life and to be shut up, first in his bedroom and then in his study, was more than he could stand and he made the life of every living soul with whom he came into contact a living hell.

And the worst treated was, of course, Clare.

She could do nothing right. The food was too hot, or too cold and hadn't they had this damned chicken twice already this week and if she thought he was going to swallow that slop then she was mistaken. He had her heart banging and her stomach churning a dozen times a day when, changing course completely and with that certain look in his eyes, he demanded that she give him a kiss, lie down beside him, sit on his lap, spend the night with him, and not on the trundle bed which had been put away. He was quite capable of . . . well, if she came over here he would show her what he was quite capable of, he told her, his eyes gleaming with that magnetic blue she had grown to know so well.

"That damn doctor's a fool."

"Martin, your ankle is—"

"Damn my ankle. The part of my anatomy I'm thinking of is not damaged."

"But the doctor said you were to rest."

"Very well, I *will* rest. I will lie perfectly still on my back and you can do what's necessary and I promise I'll be as submissive as you want. I'll just lie here and let you do with me as you will. There, does that suit you?"

"Martin ..."

"Dear God in heaven, Clare, it's bloody weeks since we made love and my equipment is rusting away for lack of use. Now lie down here and do as you're told."

But the worst storms raged about the house on the days she walked over to Edgeclough. It had been three weeks before she felt he was able to be left alone for an hour or two while she visited Nelly and Lew and the rest of them, but she might have been going for a week's holiday in the Lake District the fuss he made.

"You can't mean to leave me here to the tender mercies of that frozen-faced harpy in the kitchen?" He was astounded and not only that, he was aggrieved. He had been allowed by the doctor to leave his bed for an hour and sit in a chair by the fire with his foot propped on a stool, and what a performance that had proved to be. Clare often wondered on the infantile behaviour of men, or at least some men, for her daddy had never been so, when they were incapacitated. Children were better patients than they were, she decided as she and Lavender carefully hoisted him from the bed to the chair and with great forbearance addressed his requests for a cushion at his back, the table pulled a little closer, his neck, which was stiff after so many weeks in bed, rubbed and his shoulders massaged. He thought he might like a cup of tea ... no, coffee and perhaps a sliver of toast, and really, must she pile the fire up so high. Did she want to return him to his feverish state ... and so on and so on until she and Lavender were forced to grit their teeth or she, at least, might have boxed his ears as one might a perverse child.

On the day she informed him she was going out for the first time she thought he might hit her.

"I haven't seen Nelly for weeks, Martin. I was due a day off the Sunday after your accident but I didn't go since sure an' wasn't I needed here but now you're recovering there is no need for me to—"

"No need for you to what?" he snarled. "Hang about in the bloody sick-room with a cripple. Is that it?"

"Don't be ridiculous. You're not a cripple. The doctor has every hope that—"

"Hope, is it? Well, lady, I'm not much good on hope at the moment. My farm's going to rack and ruin . . ."

"Rubbish! The men are taking care of everything in your absence and you are insulting them by inferring—"

"Never mind the men or the farm. What needs discussing is this liking you have for running off to those . . . friends of yours at every conceivable moment, every inconvenient—"

"Martin, you are making a fool of yourself."

"A fool, is it? You know I need . . . I need you here just at the moment and I would have thought that you could postpone your . . . your outings until I'm on my feet again." He was white with anger and resentment and she knew at that moment that unless she stood up for what was her right, which was a day off now and again to visit her old friends, he would have her fast in his power, reliant on him for any sort of company he chose to give her. It was what he wanted. He couldn't *order* her to stay at home, or, more to the point, keep away from Nelly and Lew – especially Lew, for she had seen his face harden when his name was mentioned – and it was making him wild. Especially now when he was fastened to his bed.

"Martin, I promise I won't be more than an hour but you must appreciate I have been shut up—"

"And I haven't?"

"Of course you have but I do my best to keep you . . . well, entertained, to keep your spirits up. I can't do more unless you want us talked about."

"Bugger it, Clare."

"I'm going, Martin. I need some air and a change."

"From me, you mean?" His frustrated jealousy was making

him nasty and she knew it would do no good to reason with him so she simply turned on her heel and marched from the room.

"Watch him, Lavender," she murmured as she threw her warm midnight-blue woollen cloak, the one Miss Hardacre had made her and which had a scarlet lining, about her shoulders. "He's in a foul mood because I'm going out."

"Give 'em all my love," Lavender said wistfully.

It was the same every time she walked over the moor to Edgeclough during the following weeks. Even as he progressed from bedroom to study, leaning heavily on her and Lavender as they negotiated the stairs, he was still narrow-eyed and resentful with what he liked to call her "neglect" of him and when she returned it took her days to charm him out of his black mood. The only way to restore him to his usual good humour, she found, was to slip from her bedroom when the others slept and tiptoe into his, kissing him awake to his great delight and, even if it was a mite awkward, as he put it, smiling now and eager, manage an approximation of their ardent lovemaking.

The following Sunday, again to his great displeasure, she left just after lunch to climb up to the top of Friars Mere and then on to Edgeclough. It was a mild spring day. The sky was a weak, pale blue, misted with a gauze of clouds through which the sun struggled to shine. The air was soft and fresh and the damp earth by the side of the path in the garden was pierced with the sharp green points of the spring bulbs Mr Starling and Hammy had planted.

As she strode up the track, dragging great lungfuls of the sweet air into her chest, she marvelled at the extremes of weather in this sometimes bleak part of Lancashire. A few weeks ago the elements had shrieked out of the east, bringing the bitter blizzard which had injured Martin and lost him several dozen of his ewes, and now would you look at it. As soft as the fleeces on the lambs that pranced beside their mothers in the lower pastures.

She stopped and rested for a moment on the great outcropping of rock where she and Martin had first spoken, looking out at the patterns of fields, criss-crossed by dry-stone walls, the winding river at the valley bottom glinting like silver as the fitful sun caught it. She was not tired, for she was young and strong but she was – what was the word – weary? She loved him so . . . Sweet Mother, she loved him despite his bad-tempered outbursts and what seemed to be his total refusal to see that what they had together could not go on and on as it had done for the past year. It must change. It must move on. They both wanted something else and the strange thing was it was the same thing but it seemed Martin was intent on hiding his head in the sand and hoping that somehow everything would work out to both their advantage. How? He was an intelligent man. He loved her, she knew that, for it seemed he could not bear her out of his sight so what then were they to do?

She sighed then rose and shook out her skirt. She was wearing what Lavender called her "best" dress, one Miss Hardacre had made up for her out of some fabric that had been left over from last year's fashions. It was the colour of poppies, exactly matching the lining of her cloak, a simple gown, for she was a simple servant girl, but it was beautifully made, elegantly fitted and suited her colouring. Martin had pulled a face when he saw it, though his eyes had been warm with admiration, but it seemed he could not bear another man to look at this woman who was his and the poppy-coloured dress would draw every man's eye to her.

"And where d'you think you're going in that?" he had asked her menacingly.

"It's my day off and I don't wear my housekeeper's dress on my day off."

"I see, so you're to flaunt yourself for Lew Earnshaw, are you?" he had shouted and downstairs those in the kitchen had cocked their heads to listen.

"You must stop this, Martin," she had answered him in some distress but she had still gone to Edgeclough in the poppy-coloured gown.

Despite the mildness of the day there was very little activity about the cottages, just one or two children digging in the dirt and Iggy Marsden carrying a pile of wood which he had evidently collected from somewhere.

"Morning, Iggy," she called out and was surprised by his less than cheerful answer. Without knocking she walked into Lew's cottage, as she always did, ready to smile and tell him to put the kettle on and was surprised again by the quiet, by the feeling of oppression that pervaded the usually cheerful kitchen. Nelly was there, rocking slowly and sadly on one side of the tiny fire and on the other Lew was perched on a low stool, his elbow on his knees, his head hanging, his eyes staring at the floor in what seemed to be utter dejection. Her heart slid down and then up again and began to jerk about in fright.

They both turned their heads and regarded her as though she were some stranger who had walked in uninvited and again her heart plummeted.

"What is it? Dear God, what's happened?"

Nelly lifted her iron-grey eyebrows and shrugged, but Lew did his best to smile as he stood up and held out his hands to her. She took them and was surprised when he put his arms about her, drawing her closely to him, for lately he had been somewhat stiff with her. Not unfriendly or unwelcoming, but slightly withdrawn, and she had wondered if Thirza's gossip had reached the ears of those in Edgeclough.

"A bit of a setback, lass, that's all, an' nowt ter worry about, so come in an' sit thissen down. Pour Clare a cup o' tea, Nelly."

"An' wheer's brass comin' from fer tea, Lew Earnshaw, tell me that if tha' can?"

"Bloody tea's already made, Nelly Bradbury, an' anyroad if I can't offer a cup o' tea ter me friends then 'tis a poor do."

"'Tis a poor do anyroad, tha' knows that."

"Will someone please tell me what's happened, for I know something has. What it it?"

"Lew's got 'is marchin' orders, that's what. Will 'Opkinson paid 'im off at th'end o' t' shift t'other night an' told 'im not ter come back."

"But why? He's worked there for years ... how many, Lew?"

"Twenty, man an' boy."

"And you were an overlooker."

"It medd no difference."

There was a long, strained silence. Lew looked apologetically at Clare as though he thought she might believe he was somehow to blame but Nelly's face assumed the patient look of someone speaking to the very simple.

"Why, lass? I'll answer tha' question. Because 'e's a troublemaker, that's why, or that's what maister ses."

"A troublemaker! Lew? There isn't a milder man in Lancashire."

"'E were a Chartist an' still is, I reckon, an' that's enough for some. There's bin no trouble, no strikes, no agitation at mill but Lew *speaks* 'is mind, dost see ..."

"An' I can speak fer missen now, Nelly, if tha' don't mind, an' it seems that's just what I shouldn't be doin'. Lass, tha'll 'ave 'eard o't 'Gagging Act', I reckon."

Clare shook her head helplessly.

"It's ter stop men like me from makin' what they call 'seditious speeches'. From stirrin' things up an' puttin' ideas in the minds o' men who lack the means, the will or education ter think fer theirselves an' so escape the exploitation o' men like Will Hopkinson. It's a crime I've bin guilty of many an' many a time but nobody's said owt, until now, but it seems I'm ter be singled out although there's thousands 'oo think like me, an' speak up about it. 'E don't want no trouble, Will 'Opkinson told me, an' so I were ter pick up me money and 'op it."

"Sit down, lass, afore tha' falls down," Nelly said sharply to Clare, who had both hands flat on the table as though for support, "an' drink tha' tea. It'll fetch tha' round."

"But what will you do, Lew? Can you . . . will you get another job? Oh, I'm sure you will, there are dozens who would employ you, a good worker like you."

"I'm known as a troublemaker," he said simply, then seeing the forlorn expression on her face he smiled and shook his head at her. "But tha've not ter worry. I'll soon find summat else. A well-thought-of chap like me." And his smile deepened into an impish grin.

"Of course you will, won't he, Nelly?"

"That remains ter be seen," Nelly said mysteriously and they both turned to look at her in surprise.

"What d'you mean, Nelly?" Clare's voice was anxious.

Nelly gave herself a little shake as though she were pulling herself together.

"Nay, tekk no notice o' me. I'm just a daft old woman." She sighed and placed her gnarled old hands on the arms of the chair, studying them as though she could not quite bear to meet Clare's eyes.

"Have you . . . I hate to ask this, Lew, but have you any money because—"

"Now, my girl, that's nowt ter do wi' you."

"Course 'e 'asn't," Nelly snorted. "'E give it all to that damn cause of 'is."

"I just wondered if . . . well, have you enough to tide you over until you find another job?" She lifted her head defiantly. He might say it was nothing to do with her but that wasn't true. These people were her friends, all of them in the row of cottages, and though she had barely any savings herself what she had was Lew's for the asking. Dear God in heaven, if it wasn't for him she wouldn't be alive today. She owed him so much and if she starved herself she wouldn't allow him to.

She had to leave, conscious at the back of her worried mind that Martin would be giving them all the rounds of the kitchen until she got back, but before she left she made Lew swear that if there was anything he needed, *anything,* he had only to send

Frankie Marsden or Charlie Cartwright to the kitchen door at Moorhouse and she would make it her business to make sure he had it. She even wondered out loud whether Mr Heywood might find something for him and was alarmed at Lew's sudden threatening gesture which, for a moment, looked as though he were going to take her by the throat and strangle her.

"Tha'll do no such thing, lass." His eyes glittered in his flushed face then he relented, doing his best to put a smile on his face. "Now, be on tha' way an' promise me tha'll not worry."

How could she not worry? she told herself a hundred times during the next week. It was the not knowing that got her down and she waited eagerly the following Sunday, which was Lavender's day off, for her return and the hoped-for news that Lew had found work. He was a man who could have run a cotton mill single-handed, she was sure of it, knowing all the processes of spinning and weaving from start to finish, and surely any cotton manufacturer would be glad to snap him up. But there was also his history of involvement in the Ten Hours Movement, or simply the "Act" as it had been called. His following of Richard Oastler behind whom he had tramped ninety miles with a few thousand others to York to get justice for factory children. Oastler was sent to prison, not for treason, but for debt since he had put all his money into the Short Term Movement. And factory owners remembered these things and the men who had been involved with them and would they take on Lew Earnshaw though it had happened years ago?

She knew something was wrong the moment Lavender threw herself across the threshold of the kitchen with such a clatter she fell against the table, banging her hip with considerable force. She did not even wince. Her eyes were wide and frightened, her face the colour of a winding sheet and she seemed unable to speak, her mouth opening and closing wordlessly. She was looking directly at Clare.

Clare put down the wooden spoon with which she was about to beat some eggs to make batter for Yorkshire pudding. She laid it carefully on the table, then moved slowly round it towards Lavender. The room was totally silent, even Sammy ceasing his tuneless whistle, as they waited to hear what appalling news young Lavender had brought back for Clare Hanrahan.

"What . . . ?" Clare quavered, wrapping her hands in her apron to still their trembling.

Lavender began to cry, great fat tears which rolled unchecked down her cheeks, just like a child who is heartbroken over some smashed toy.

"Dear God . . . what?" Clare whispered, her voice diminishing as her terror grew.

"Oh, Clare . . . Clare, what are we to do? How are we to manage?"

"Manage what? Manage what?"

"It's Lew."

"Lew?"

"Yes, he's leaving."

"Leaving?"

"He's going away. He's been turned out of his cottage and he's going away."

Chapter Twenty-one

Martin Heywood was just about to raise a pre-dinner brandy to his lips when the door to his study was flung open without so much as a by your leave and, as Lavender had done minutes earlier, Clare hurtled across the threshold, almost landing in his lap.

"God almighty," he spluttered, dabbing at his shirt front where his brandy had splashed, "could you not knock, woman, or at least come in somewhat more quietly? You know I'm always glad to see you but really, this is . . ."

His voice died away in bewilderment at the sight of the expression on her face and he turned to place the brandy glass carefully on the table at his side.

Clare knew she looked strange, odd; how could she help it? She *felt* strange, tongue-tied somehow, though the words she wanted to speak, *shriek* were fermenting like the yeast in the bread she made, bubbling and boiling just at the back of her throat in an effort to get out, to get at him, to tear him to pieces in her fury.

"What have you done?" she managed to shriek, so that all those in the kitchen who had watched her, goggle-eyed, race into the hall, heard her quite distinctly even though the door had swung shut behind her.

Martin's face showed his astonishment. "*Me!* What can you

mean, my pet? I've done nothing but sit here, since I am incapable of doing anything else. But having said that I think with your arm to steady me I might venture out into—"

"Stop it, Martin, stop it. Don't pretend you don't know what I mean."

"Sweetheart, believe me, I have been sitting here all afternoon which, if you'd come in to see me more often you would know. Mischief, which you seem to imply, is beyond me at the moment but as soon as—"

"If you don't stop babbling and tell me the truth I swear I'll hit you," she hissed, looming over him so that with an involuntary movement he flinched away from her.

He was getting irritable and it showed in the narrowing of his eyes and his frown which promised to be ferocious. Martin Heywood was not used to being brought to task about anything, at least not since his mother and father had died and though he loved this woman and knew he always would, he was not about to let her fling her weight about like a shrew in an ale-house. He didn't know what had awoken her temper, which he had not witnessed before, but something had and it seemed it was aimed at him. He couldn't think what could have incensed her since he had last seen her, for as far as he knew she had not been out of the house. He was not a particularly tolerant man, he knew that, but he loved her so he was willing to be patient. He had tried a bit of humour but it seemed she did not care for it and his own temper, which was none too reliable at the moment, began to erupt.

"It's you who are babbling, Clare," he said coldly, "and unless you tell me what all this is about I cannot answer your . . . well, what seem to be your accusations over something I know nothing about. Something you don't appear to like so—"

"What have you done to Lew?"

He had the grace to look slightly abashed but it did not last long, for Martin Heywood was not the sort of man to be abashed at anything.

"Lew!" His face assumed a mixture of amazement and a certain tendency to smile though the latter did not materialise, since the look on her face told him he was swimming in turbulent waters. "Lew Earnshaw, I presume you mean," he went on, "though why what he does is any concern of yours, or mine for that matter, I cannot imagine." His lean face darkened ominously as though daring her to question this statement.

"It matters to me, damn you. Now, I have one question for you, Martin." Her face was as white as the snow that had blasted the moorland in the winter but on each cheekbone was a vivid splash of scarlet. Her eyes glittered, green and menacing, slitted like those of a big cat about to lash out at an attacker. Her hands, which seemed to be unable to find a resting place, were clenched into tight fists, and now and again curved into claws, and Martin Heywood began to feel the first stirrings of alarm, and not just alarm but a madness as explosive as her own.

"Have you indeed? Well, if it's anything to do with that lout up at Edgeclough, which it seems it is, then let's have it. You seem to be annoyed by—"

"*Annoyed!* Jesus, Mary and, Joseph, annoyed doesn't half describe what I'm feeling right now, you bastard."

His eyes narrowed even more but a close observer might have noticed a certain wariness about him. A tendency to shift in his seat as though he were a trifle uncomfortable but her words had infuriated him. He was not accustomed to being called names, of any sort, and his mouth thinned into an ugly line.

"Dear God!"

"Aye, dear God it is, but you haven't answered my question."

"Which is?" His voice was icy.

"Do you own the cottages at Edgeclough? The ones where Lew and Nelly live and the rest of the men and women who are my friends. Don't try to deny it because I happen to know it's true but—"

"Then if you know it's true why bother to ask me?"

"Because I can't believe that ... I don't want to believe that you have done what you have done. It is mean-spirited and despicable. What have you against him?"

"He. Goddammit, the man is nothing to me."

"Then why have you turned him out of his cottage?"

"Good God above, woman," he roared, "I haven't been out of this bloody house for weeks, as you well know, and anyway, I have a man who looks after my properties, rents and suchlike and if he has given Lew Earnshaw notice to quit it's for a good reason."

"Yes, and we know what that is, don't we? He's been sacked from Hopkinson's."

"Jesus, am I to be blamed for that as well? Will Hopkinson—"

"Was here the other day. He was a troublemaker, they said, Lew, I mean, and so he was sacked and no more than a few days later you have him turned out of one of your cottages. Do you seriously expect me to believe that is a coincidence?"

"If the man had no job and, one supposes, no means to pay his rent then naturally my chap would evict him. I don't run a bloody charity. I expect a return from the properties I own."

"You bastard ... you bastard, Martin Heywood. I did at least think you were an honest man, not a liar and a cheat. It's got nothing to do with rents or wages, it's simply that Lew is my friend and you didn't like it. This is your way of getting rid of him. Getting him out of my life in case he should interfere with yours. Well, you have succeeded. He is leaving. I don't know where to but wherever it is, I'm going with him."

She had reached him now, touched him in a place he didn't often acknowledge which, had he been a romantic man, he would have called his heart. This woman had it. She had diverted him from his plans to marry the suitable young woman he had intended. She had caused him no end of problems, one way or another, but she had given him something he had received from no one, and though he had told himself time and time again that he could not possibly marry his own housekeeper he had known he was whistling in the wind. Nevertheless he was not going to be forced into something he was not quite sure he was ready for and she must be made to realise it.

"Don't be so bloody soft, woman," he sneered. "All this over a man who—"

"He's my friend and he loves me. He always has but I was too blinded by you to appreciate it. He wanted to marry me – did you know that? – but I wouldn't have him because all I could see was you and now . . ."

With a wild cry which grated somehow in his mouth as though it had dried up with his rage, he sprang to his feet, wincing as his weight fell on his injured leg. He reached for her, catching her wrists, holding them with one hand while the other dragged ruthlessly at her hair so that her head fell back and she was forced to look up at him.

"You're going nowhere, madam, and certainly not with that . . . that low-life who'll never be anything but a common factory hand. He'll drag you down to his level and keep you on your knees."

"And what can you offer me, tell me that? Certainly nothing that could be called decent. Your whore, that's what I am."

He winced at her choice of words and out in the kitchen every one of the servants, even Thirza, were frozen to the well-scrubbed flags. Lavender still wept, gulping in great sobs, and Adah and Gracie huddled together for comfort.

"Is that so?" His eyes were a gleaming brilliance of hot blue, his face the colour of suet and his mouth was stretched over his white teeth, giving the impression of fangs like that of a wolf. "Whore, is it, and what d'you think Lew Earnshaw will give you? Probably a true whore's life, earning coppers in back alleys."

She wrenched herself free. Her eyes glared at him through the tangle of her dark curls and again her hands formed themselves into claws. She reached for his face, but despite his ankle he darted away, laughing . . . laughing, for he knew that if he didn't laugh he would fall to his knees and beg her to stay. He would personally see that Lew Earnshaw had his job back and set him up in his cottage again if only she would not leave him, for how . . . Dear God, how was he to live without her? But he was Martin Heywood who had never begged for anything in his life. Cut off his nose to spite his own face, his mother used to say to him, in his obstinacy, and that was just what he was doing.

His hands shot out and gripped her upper arms with such force she knew she would have ten bruises the next day, five to each arm. His voice cracked, shrill with outrage and ugly with menace. "I'm beginning to see it now. You've been sharing your favours with him, haven't you? You bitch, you filthy slut. Going up to Edgeclough and lying down for him on his kitchen floor, I've no doubt. Well, go then, go to your hobbledehoy and good riddance, and yes, I did have the man turned out. Gentlemen have these arrangements with one another, you know, and when Will Hopkinson asked a favour of me, I obliged. He wanted rid of the man and, as it happened, so did I. Now, get out because I can't stand the sight of you a moment longer."

He let go of her so abruptly she fell against the door. Nevertheless she lifted her head imperiously, throwing back her gloriously tangled hair and Martin Heywood felt the blood run warm in his veins and the heat of it move to his belly with wanting her. Her little chin squared up to him and her eyes were a clear and transparent green, warning him that he had no authority over her, and, what was worse, that he had just seriously injured whatever it was that had been between them, an injury that might never heal. He felt her contempt shrivel him then watched as blindly she turned, feeling for the opening of the door, stumbling on the hem of her full skirt as she blundered into the hall. Slowly he felt for the arm of the chesterfield and, like an old, old man who is almost at the end of his days, lowered himself painfully to the seat.

She was surprised when her hand was taken as she walked

stiffly into the hall, for she had not noticed the small figure who stood there waiting for her and when Lavender began to lead her towards the staircase she went with her.

"Come, lass . . . come, sweetheart; there, don't cry," Lavender kept repeating, though it was Lavender who was crying, not Clare. "We'll get us things an' be off. Tha're best out of it, an' so am I. Come, lass. Come wi' Lavender."

"Lavender . . . oh dear God. Lavender, did you hear him?"

"Aye, we all did but tha' must put it behind thi'."

"I can't stay here, Lavender. Not now . . . not . . ."

"Then us'll go right away."

"Why has he done this? . . . why?"

"Because he loves thi' an' 'e's jealous o'—"

"Jealous of Lew?" Her voice was wild and it broke on his name and all the time she clung to Lavender as Lavender almost carried her up the flight of stairs to her room.

"Don't think on it, lass. Forget 'im."

"If only I could."

"Tha've friends, tha' knows that an' we'll 'elp thi'. See, 'old on ter me." And as she did so, clinging as though to a lifeline attached to a small boat, she felt her life, which had slipped madly in the last hour, right itself for a moment in the vastness, the emptiness of her heart which had held her love for Martin.

She went in her poppy-red dress, her warm woollen cloak lined with scarlet and the black boots that had travelled with her from Ireland. She and Lavender, their heads held high and their bundles containing their clothes under their arms, walked through the silent kitchen, watched by the maidservants. Even the cat by the fire lifted her head and gave them a frosty glare. Adah and Gracie still huddled together, their faces wet with tears, for how were they to manage without Miss Hanrahan? There was Thirza, of course, but she was not as fair nor as warm-hearted as Miss

Hanrahan and they had both suffered under her icy commands. Sammy stood with his mouth open, knowing something terrible was taking place but not actually sure what it was or how it would affect him, and Belle, always one to seize an opportunity, wondered if Miss Hanrahan had left Mrs Case's recipe books. There might be a good chance she could become cook to Mr Heywood if she prepared him a decent meal tonight.

"So are the mighty fallen," Thirza sniffed triumphantly, her eyes blazing with joy, for hadn't she been proved right in her disapproval, nay, downright loathing of "the new girl". The master had had his hand up her skirt all this time and the others saying they didn't believe it; well, they'd believe it now. Whore was right and good riddance to bad rubbish was all she could say.

She said it out loud, exultantly. "Good riddance to bad rubbish," but barely had she got the last word out when Lavender, who was nearest to her, turned like a vixen cornered by the hounds and lifting her free arm struck her forcibly across the face, snapping her head to one side with a crack which they all heard.

"I bin wantin' ter do that ever since I come," Lavender said quietly.

"Strewth!" said Sammy admiringly, and then they were out in the yard where the stable lads were grooming the horses. The men stopped for a moment to stare in wonder at the woman who had been keeping the master's bed warm.

"Good luck, lass," George called, for he'd always admired the durability of the girl who had, it was said, suffered so much in the land from which she came.

Then they were out of the gate and on the track that led away from Moorhouse Farm and up on to the moor. They held hands though Clare was barely aware of it. She only knew she felt a degree of comfort in the touch of another human being and it was not until they reached Friars Mere that she suddenly stopped in her tracks and turned, horrified, to Lavender.

"Jesus, Mary and Joseph, what are you doing? What are you doing here with me? What am I after thinking of? This is not your problem. You shouldn't be here with me. You'll lose your job, acushla. Run back, please run back."

"Don't be daft, our Clare, it's too late fer that. Didn't tha' see way I whacked that bloody Thirza? She'll not forget that in a 'urry. Anyroad, I can't work there wi'out thi'. I'll find summat, same as tha' will."

"Oh, Lavender, what have I done?"

"Tha've done nowt. Now put tha' best foot forward an' let's get 'ome. I'm dyin' fer a cup o' tea."

Nelly was in her back yard feeding her hens, wondering whether it might be time to wring the neck of the little russet hen with the comb and wattles of pure scarlet. It had proved a poor layer but it was a nice little thing and came running to greet her cackling with ecstasy every time she stepped out of her kitchen door. She had been doing her own, her lad's – by which she meant her husband – and Lew Earnshaw's laundry and had come out into the yard to escape the steam and the odour of drying shirts. She'd get the flat-iron out when she'd had a breath of fresh air and get Lew's shirts looking decent, for if there was one thing she could do for the lad it was send him off in a proper way. There was a pan of broth bubbling on the fire, for he would need a bit of decent grub inside him before he set off, but a moment out here with her hens, of whom she was strangely fond, would perhaps make her feel more herself. She'd never felt so wretched in her life, she admitted to herself, not even when she'd lost one of her children, for wasn't Lew Earnshaw like a son to her? She wouldn't have dreamed of telling him so, of course, but how was she to manage without him. Her "lad" whose name she used so seldom she quite forgot it at times, was a good lad but he was quiet with barely a word for the cat whereas Lew had made her laugh, or what passed for laughter in Nelly Bradbury.

She'd scrubbed all morning, the flagged floor, the plain kitchen table, the stairs that led up to the bedroom, the bedroom floor itself and when the hens were fed she meant to start on the windows.

She saw them coming up the track where it dipped before rising again to the beginning of the moor. For a moment she wasn't sure who it could be, for they weren't expecting anyone, then the cloak on the tall woman flapped open and its scarlet lining was revealed and she knew who it was. And what in heaven's name was Lavender Bickerstaffe doing back here? She'd only just gone, or so it seemed, after spending her day off with her mam and pa.

"It's our Lavender," a puzzled voice said beside her. Billy Bickerstaffe had been carefully weeding his little plot of ground in preparation for the potatoes he meant to put in and he shaded his eyes with a dirt-encrusted hand.

"She's told Clare," Nelly said flatly. "She's told Clare about our Lew."

"Well, we reckoned she would but that's no reason fer the pair of 'em ter come home. Sweet Jesus, 'er mam'll go mad if she loses this job."

"There's no need fer that, Billy Bickerstaffe," Nelly snapped absent-mindedly but her own heart was thumping under the bib of her pinny and she put out a hand to the wall to steady herself. She'd worked damned hard today, and her not as young as once she'd been but it had always been her maxim that hard work took your mind off things and only the good Lord knew how much she needed her mind taken off things just now.

"An' what're you two doin' 'ome?" she called ungraciously as they approached, but it didn't take Lavender's mouthings and nodding head to see there was something seriously wrong with their Clare.

"Come in, come in the pair o' thi' an' mind that floor, Lavender Bickerstaffe. I've just done it. Blasted dog fetched in enough dirt ter fill a 'tater field," scowling at Fred who lay humbly on the mat in front of her fire. At the bottom of the stairs that led up to the first floor was a neatly tied bundle, fastened to which were a pair of polished black boots.

"Now then, me lass, what's ter do wi' thi'?" she began, then in one of her unexpected demonstrations of the great and bursting love she had in her heart, she dragged Clare into her arms and held her. She had to stand on her toes to do it. Nothing was said, by her or Clare but the shudders which had afflicted Clare ever since she had walked out of Martin Heywood's study began to subside. She rested her forehead on Nelly's shoulder then, as footsteps sounded at the door, she turned and looked into Lew's incredulous eyes.

"Eeh, lass," he whispered in wonder. "Only thing I wanted was ter see thi' afore I went an' 'ere tha' are. I can't believe it."

"Lew, I'm sorry."

"Sorry! What the 'ell for? It's not your fault."

"Yes, it is, it is."

"I don't know 'ow tha' work that out, an' lass, I don't want ter know. Understand?"

He was telling her that he knew about her and Martin Heywood. That they all did, for Thirza's lines of communication, which stretched from Moorhouse to Edgeclough and beyond, had made sure of that. That he did not blame her or love her the less but he didn't want to hear a word about it. His face was strained, pale, his usual colour drained away and yet he did his best to smile, even to grin.

"But what's brought thi'?" He hovered in the doorway, wearing a shirt that was obviously not his, for Nelly had taken the only two shirts he had and treated them to a pulverising wash in her dolly tub. Thrusting one of "her lad's" in his hand she'd told him brusquely to get that on him and who was he to argue with Nelly Bradbury.

"You."

"Me?" He stared at her in bewilderment.

"Lew, do you think I could let you go, just say to Lavender, who brought me the news, 'Oh, what a shame,' and go on as if it were of no importance? I was horrified when you lost your job, but this ... to turn you out of your cottage. Lew ... oh, Lew."

"Nay, lass ..." But before he could continue she flew across the kitchen and flung herself into his arms. They closed hungrily about her and he buried his face in the curve of her shoulder. Nelly turned away jerkily, moving to the fire where she picked up the poker and gave the coals a good thrashing. Fred was alarmed and leaped a foot in the air, then sidled over to Lew, looking up at him with the same bewilderment Lew had shown a few moments ago. What the devil as going on? he seemed to be saying. He was comfortable at Nelly's fireside but why couldn't they go back to their own?

"Where are you to go, Lew?" Clare asked him as she stepped back. It was very evident that he was reluctant to let go of her so she reached for his hands and held them between her two, just beneath her chin. "What will you do?"

"Now tha've no need to worrit about me, Clare. Things'll turn out fer't best."

"I'm to blame."

"No ... no, stop it, lass. If I'd stayed at 'ome an' read me newspaper instead o't walking hills openin' me mouth an' tellin' folk what they should do ter mekk their lives better then I'd be as right as rain. I followed Richard Oastler years ago an' they'd not forgotten. What they say about me's true an' I'm proud of it. I *am* a troublemaker."

"But where will you go?"

"Manchester."

"*Manchester!* But what's in Manchester? It's so far ..."

"Theer's work there, lass, an' I've ter go where't work is. I've a friend, 'e were a Chartist, like me, an' 'e always said ... Well, 'e runs a newspaper an' I reckon I could write a few things that might mekk folk sit up an' tekk notice."

"In other words you're to get into the same sort of trouble as here?"

He grinned. "Aye, tha' could say that. I can't just sit on me be'ind an' watch the rest bein' ground down. We may not get t' vote soon enough ter suit me or soon enough ter do me any good but we'll get it, Clare, one day. All on us. Even you, lass. At least if I've owt ter do wi' it."

He was the best man she had ever known or was likely to know. She cared for him, she trusted him and what was there here for her now? She needed work as badly as he did and surely in that big city in which cotton was king and industry thrived there would be something for her.

"When are you going, Lew?"

"In't mornin', first thing. Nelly's give me a bed on her kitchen floor but first thing tomorrow I'll be off. It's a fair walk ter Manchester and I want ter be there before dark."

He smiled down into her face. He released the hands she was still holding and cupped them about her face. Silently Nelly and Lavender watched, mesmerised by the simple truth of this man's love for this woman. It asked nothing of her, it just *gave*. So it had always been ever since that first day when she had fallen into his care and he had brought her back to life. Between them he and Nelly had nursed her. He had bathed her naked body and sat beside her while she slept. He had spoon-fed her with the life-giving sustenance Nelly had prepared, watched over her night after night and then the next morning walked to Crossfold to the mill from which he had just been sacked.

Putting her hands on his where they held her face she smiled, suddenly as radiant as the golden sunlight which was just about to leave the sky, as radiant as the sky itself, a silvery blue fading to gold and lemon and apricot.

"I'm coming with you, Lew." Her face was serenely untroubled and yet there was a hint of fierceness in it which said she would have no argument.

For a moment his face lit up with the wonder of it, then it

darkened and he stepped back from her, from the temptation of her. Nelly sat down heavily in the chair by the fire and, putting her chin in her hand, stared into the flames as though she could bear no more of this drama. The dog sidled up to her and so distracted was she, she actually put out a hand and fondled his head.

"Lass . . . lass," Lew said at last. "Tha' know theer's nowt in this world I'd like better than to—"

"Then that's settled," she said briskly, ready to turn away, but he caught her hands and studied her face as though trying to see what was really inside her head. Was she running away from Martin Heywood or was she running towards Lew Earnshaw?

Lew Earnshaw was strong and yet vulnerable, a potent combination. He was not handsome but his pleasant face was good-humoured, his mouth wide and compassionate and his manners engaging. There had been more than a few women at the mill who had made it quite clear to him that he had only to look in their direction and they'd make it worth his while, but for the past two and a half years he had looked at no one but Clare Hanrahan.

"No, lass, it's not settled," he said quietly, rubbing his thumbs across the backs of her hands. "It's not settled at all. I don't know wheer the 'ell I'll finish up."

"Neither did I when I left Ireland, Lew, but it didn't stop me. I've nothing here, nothing" – throwing a swift smile which encompassed both Lavender and Nelly – "except these two, but they know I must work. I want a fresh start and so do you so why cannot we do it together? Take me with you to Manchester, Lew, or must I go alone? I mean to leave here and it would be so much easier if I had you with me."

Her face was soft and lovely and before he realised what she was about she reached up and laid her mouth on his. A gentle kiss but warm with promise and Lew Earnshaw was but a man, a man in love with the woman who had just kissed him.

Chapter Twenty-two

Nelly said she would keep the damned cat because she was no trouble and could be fed on scraps, besides which the thing didn't traipse muck on to her clean floor but they must take Fred with them or find another home for him. The dratted thing was always under her feet anyway and with them muddy paws brought in more mess than "her lad" and she'd be glad to be shut of it. They knew she didn't mean a word she said about poor Fred but was just grumbling to cover the devastation she felt at their going, so they set out as soon as it was light, she and Lew with Fred trotting at their heels. It was ten miles as the crow flies from Edgeclough to the outskirts of Manchester but, as Lew said, his smile lopsided, they weren't bloody crows and must tramp it. They could have caught the train from Oldham but neither of them had spare cash to jingle in their pocket and besides, they would need every penny they had until they began to earn a wage.

There were no tears, not even from Lavender. They had said their goodbyes the night before to most of the residents of the row of cottages, since all the men and most of the women and the older children had to be up before cock-crow if they were to be at the mill gates by six. Wordlessly Clare folded Lavender in her arms, then smiled down into her face and kissed her cheek. Turning to Nelly she attempted to do the same but Nelly was too upset and her distress would not allow her to show her true feelings.

"Get on wi' thi'," she declared testily, doing her best to shrug off Clare's enfolding arms. "An' thi' an' all, Lew Earnshaw," struggling to escape his determined embrace, then, at the last moment, laying her face on his chest. Her voice was muffled as she spoke. "Tekk care o' this lass, dost 'ear, or tha'll feel the back o' me 'and, so think on," knowing that she might see neither of them again.

Clare wore the plain grey homespun skirt, well mended, and the bodice in which she had travelled from Ireland. Mrs Case had told her to burn them but her thrifty nature had forbidden it. She had put on weight since then and the bodice clung tightly to her high, rounded breasts, the nipples clearly outlined beneath the worn material.

"Lap tha' shawl about thi' wilta, our Clare?" Nelly had begged her anxiously, for what might would-be employers think of this fine-looking woman with a proud lift to her head, with a bosom and a straight back on her like a young queen, and who was about to stride off down the track and out of Nelly's life. "It's nippy out," she added, her face flinty in her effort not to weep, or even show sign that this parting was pulling her to ribbons.

Clare had on her clogs. Her boots, her scarlet-lined cloak and poppy-red dress were wrapped up in her bundle with a change of underclothing and a pair of stockings. Her bonnet, the one Miss Hardacre had fashioned for her, had been left behind. Fighting for composure, she had told Nelly to keep it safe for her and she'd pick it up the next time they met, wondering desperately when that would be. She was a working woman, or at least she hoped to be, and the bonnet would have been no use to her where she was going, wherever that might be. Neither would the dress and cloak, but somehow they were a symbol of her success since she left Ireland and she could not bear to discard them.

She and Lew turned a dozen times as they moved down

the track in the direction of Crossfold, waving to Nelly and Lavender and the group of neighbours, mostly young children who watched them go until they dropped down the slope that led on to the road. She wanted to weep noisily as Marie Bretherton's three-year-old Maidie had done at the last moment. Maidie had hidden her face in Lavender's skirt as though she couldn't bear to watch them go and for a moment or two she longed to turn back, run into Nelly's arms and tell them all that she wasn't going, that she would find work round here, in the mill or indeed anything that would bring her in a few bob a week. But Lew took her hand and drew her gently on and she knew it was right, for how could she continue to live in Edgeclough, even if there had been somewhere to lay her head, with Martin only a stone's throw away? Martin who, now that she was out of the way, would undoubtedly marry that banker's daughter, the one that the kitchen-maids had gossiped about last year. The very thought of it devastated her and the sooner she was away the better. Dear Mother of God, she had not known there could be such pain, not twice in one lifetime, but Lew's arm steadied her and she straightened her already straight back and squared her shoulders.

Lew was filled with wellbeing, a physical wellbeing and one that was ready to burst his heart with joy. Now that Clare was really going with him, now that she had put that bastard up at Moorhouse firmly from her life, Lew had great hopes that . . . well, that something wonderful would happen, by which he meant that Clare would finally marry him and they would start their new life together. Properly together. He knew, as they had all known, that she had been more to Martin Heywood than his housekeeper – he could not bear to put it into any other words, shying away from *mistress* or *lover* – but that was over and, loving her so deeply, so compassionately, so enduringly all this time, his forgiveness was without condemnation.

"Don't look back, lass," he murmured gently, then, letting

her hand go, he put his arm about her shoulders, leading her towards their future.

They passed through sun-filtered woods, down into deep sheltered valleys, digging their heels into the springy turf to gain purchase, then up again, bending their backs as they climbed, breathing deeply as they crossed the vastness of the moorlands of the South Pennine heartland. It was March and the wind still had a bitter edge to it but the sun floated behind a ribbon of velvet cloud and at least it wasn't raining, Lew said. They stopped to rest a time or two and drink from the clear waters of a tumbling stream and eat the delicious meat and potato pies – more potato than meat – that Nelly had made for them last night. They were quiet as they bit into them, both busy with their own thoughts. Most of Clare's pie went to Fred who sat politely begging by her side. She was composed and none of the anguish she was suffering showed in her face, or even in her answers to Lew's idle observations, in itself an indication of her detachment from the reality of the present.

It had all happened so quickly. The shock of Lavender's news that Lew was leaving Edgeclough. The appalling realisation that it was Martin's doing. That Martin had – as a favour to a business acquaintance – deliberately turned Lew from his cottage. The terrible blankness in his eyes as she attacked him, defending Lew, his vicious words, his attack on her friendship with Lew, his spitting jealousy, which had darted her in agony, and her own contemptuous response which had finished whatever there had been between them. Twenty-four hours ago she had been Miss Hanrahan, poring over Mrs Case's recipe books wondering what to cook for Martin's evening meal. Now she was tramping to a new life with Lew beside her and wondering, not what to cook for dinner but what lay ahead of her. In her chest, where her heart was, she supposed, was a leaden weight and yet at the same time she felt a great emptiness, hollow and dragging her down. There was stealthily hiding inside her what she knew was a foolish refusal to believe what was happening because it was too awful to contemplate. Too awful to consider that she would never see Martin again. She would never see him again. He had fallen out of her life, ripping a jagged hole in the fabric of it and it was as though he were dead. He might as well be dead, and though she walked steadfastly beside Lew, smiling at times, and nodding when he pointed something of interest out to her, she knew she would never recover from the loss of him, from the breaking up of her world, for Martin had been that. She was glad in a way of her own detachment, her sense of disorientation as though she were watching another woman's agony, pitiful but nothing to do with her. The pain inside her was another woman's pain but when her frozen state thawed she knew the pain was going to get worse with every bitter moment of accepting that he was gone.

They didn't speak much as they strode forth, both strong and vigorous with a determined look about them, two young people with a purpose in life, or so it would seem to the casual observer. Though he sensed Clare's suffering and withdrawal, Lew could not help being elated as they neared Manchester, for he had no conception of her true feelings. He was a kind man, good-hearted and loving, but like many people, especially men, he was of the opinion that given time and a decent attempt to start afresh, Clare would forget Martin Heywood, and though he was not fool enough to believe she would instantly fall in love with him, he felt he had enough love in him to make up for any lack in her. He was aware that they were reserved with one another, that Martin Heywood stood between them, like an eavesdropper to their every word, but this would disappear, as the memory of Martin Heywood would disappear given time. It was as though they must both be careful in what they said for the moment, for neither wished to distress the other.

To keep her mind from today's parting and for something to say that did not stray into dangerous territory, he had told her of the day a young Joss Greenwood, one of the first radical parliamentary candidates for Oldham, Royton,

Crompton and Chadderton and who had been returned as a member of parliament in 1832, had marched this very route with thousands of others over thirty years ago. They had gone, singing and laughing, ready for a good day out and to listen to the words of the great orator and radical leader, Henry Hunt, fetching up at St Peter's Fields in the middle of Manchester on a hot, sunny day in August, sixty thousand of them. At the end of the day fifteen of them were dead and almost five hundred dreadfully wounded. Peterloo, they had called it, the Peterloo Massacre, and it was on tales such as these that he had been brought up, tales of great suffering, of exploitation and humiliation, of starving children with deformed limbs and men who hanged themselves rather than watch their families dragged into the mills, tales told to him by his father, Jack Earnshaw, as avid a radical and Chartist as Joss Greenwood. And would she believe him if he told her that young Joss, the one who had become a member of parliament, had once lived in the very cottage from which Lew had just been evicted.

She did her best to show interest and in normal circumstances would have been fascinated, but the best she could manage was a polite murmur, so Lew took her hand and became quiet as they walked through the outskirts of Manchester.

Clare had come through Liverpool three years ago, clawing her way along the heaving docklands and into the equally heaving streets but she had been half stupefied by her own desolation, by her overwhelming grief and loss, not to mention her lack of anything that might be called strength, or health. Half starved and barely recovered from the cholera which had wiped out not only her entire family – helped by starvation – but thousands upon thousands of her fellow countrymen, she had stumbled through the streets of Liverpool on her way to she did not know where and had scarcely noticed if those streets had been thriving, a great whirling vortex of industry as she had heard it would be, or as peaceful as her own rural village in the county of Clare. The only memory that seemed to cling in her mind was that of trying to cross a busy road, and succeeding!

The streets of Manchester were like a labyrinth in which beehives had been turned over and the bees allowed to buzz in a frenzy of madness, ready to turn and sting anyone who got in their way. Fred pressed close to Lew's heels, his ears pricked, his head warily turning from side to side, his nose twitching at the scents he had, being a country dog, never smelled before. Now and again he growled threateningly, for it seemed to him there was much to threaten his master in this new hostile world.

Lew seemed to know his way towards what he told her was the central business district of Manchester where this fellow he knew had a small newspaper. The streets were like deep, noisy chasms which the sunlight scarcely reached, dominated by looming warehouses, superbly façaded banks, grand hotels with fancy names like the Albion, the Victoria, the Imperial, railways stations and a great many splendid shops and, halfway along Oldham Street, down a narrow side street, and up a set of dark and dirty stairs, the offices of the *Hopwood Review*.

On the ground floor there were what she later discovered to be printing presses, none of them at work at that precise moment. A spare, wiry little man in a cloth cap and a filthy apron was busy tinkering with something or other, whistling through his broken teeth but throwing them a cheerful sort of a grin as they passed him and climbed the stairs. On this floor were a couple of offices, divided by a thin partition and in each was a vast quantity of paper, documents, odds and ends, all floundering on top of two ancient desks, spilling from half-open drawers and spreading in an avalanche all over the floor so that it was difficult to know where to put your feet. There hung about the rooms an air of comfortable confusion, a smell of beer and cigar smoke and a man's sweat.

The man was bending over a table in the far corner of the room, very much "at work" so that his frown of annoyance at the disturbance gave his face a distinct lack of humour.

He was thin, loosely put together and in a definite state of disarray.

"Who the hell let you up here?" he began, but as he recognised Lew his face lit up and he threw up his arms with the obvious intention of clasping him to his thin chest.

"Bloody hell, man ... bloody hell, where did you spring from? It's bloody years – what? how many? – bloody years and now you just turn up on my doorstep as though it were bloody yesterday."

He and Lew proceeded to pound one another on the back in the way that men do with one another to demonstrate their joy, thumping and punching so that Clare was convinced they must be hurting one another. They seemed to have totally forgotten her so she sat down patiently in the nearest chair and Fred pressed against her skirt. She fondled his head as she glanced about her at the place where Lew hoped to get a job. The *Hopwood Review* the newspaper was called, so Lew had told her as they strode out together that morning, and the man who owned it and ran it single-handed apart, one supposed, from the cheerful little man at the printing presses, was called Henry Hopwood. He and Lew had met many years ago on one of the eternal marches, or at one of the eternal meetings that were carried out in the north of England on behalf of the cause and had become friends. He was an educated man, a man from a middle-class family but with a concern for flesh-and-blood humanity which had led him to believe that if he was to be of any help to the people, the common, working classes, then he must learn to understand them. And the only way he could do that was to live among them, which was precisely what he did. Lew had admired and respected him from the beginning and so their friendship had grown. He lived precariously in a room above a decrepit inn just off Oldham Road on the fifty pounds a year left him by his mother and the few bob a week he made from his newspaper.

"So, you've come to look me over, have you?" he clamoured,

for, as Clare was to learn, Henry Hopwood was a man who delighted in noise. "I wondered how long it would take you to give up on that miserable bloody job you had at the mill. With your mind and learning you're worth better than that, my lad, and you bloody well know it."

They both suddenly became aware of Clare at the same time and Henry Hopwood, for it must be he, clapped his hand to his forehead and closed his eyes in what seemed to be complete embarrassment.

"God almighty, Lew, why didn't you stop me from . . . this must be your good lady and here have I been making free with my language. You must forgive me, Mrs Earnshaw, my manners are simply appalling but I was so surprised and pleased to see Lew I quite forgot myself. Please say you accept my apologies."

He bowed over her hand but his eyes twinkled a clear pale blue as though to say she could not help but forgive him since he was such a hell of a nice fellow and meant no harm.

Lew leaped forward as though he knew she was weary and heartsore. Tenderly he lifted her gently to her feet. Henry Hopwood still held her hand and she smiled, for his impish charm and certainty that she would like him immediately lightened her sore heart.

"Nay, Henry lad," Lew was protesting, "Clare isn't me wife, though 'tis not fer want o' tryin' on my part."

"And I can see why, Lew, my good fellow, but perhaps you'd best introduce us," still smiling and holding her hand.

"'Tis Miss Clare Hanrahan, Henry, and this, lass, is Henry Hopwood, proprietor of this newspaper."

"Miss Hanrahan."

"Mr Hopwood."

"Now then, sit yourself down, Miss Hanrahan and I'll get my chap to make you a cup of tea though I can't vouch for it not tasting like engine oil. Albert's a grand lad and a great help to me but he's not exactly domesticated."

"That would be lovely, Mr Hopwood, and very welcome."

She inclined her head in the gracious way she had picked up from somewhere or other, or perhaps she had been born with it, then sat down again, tiredly, her face falling again into the pale suffering he had noticed as he bent his head over her hand. He wondered what it was but this was not the time for enquiring nor for delving into what her relationship was to Lew Earnshaw. Neither was it the time to ask what she was doing here with him, but she was very lovely, despite the strained look about her, and very intriguing.

She lay back in the squashed leather armchair, resting her head against the plump cushion that was attached to it, receiving the cup of tea the man called Albert put in her hand and then let the rest of the conversation begin to lap around her as she sipped it. If it tasted of engine oil she did not notice it. Lew and Mr Hopwood were talking ten to the dozen, Lew animated as she had never before seen him, discussing what she supposed were the conditions and state of health of the inhabitants of the squat, two-roomed houses which abounded in the slums of Manchester, through some of which she and Lew had walked today and which, it seemed, Mr Hopwood was doing his best to highlight in his weekly newspaper. It appeared that Lew would be a godsend to him since he was run off his feet and he had been about to advertise for a man to give him a hand. Albert was a stalwart but only in the realm of the mechanics of the printing presses, which, he said, he could take apart and put together again with the ease with which another man might hoe a row of potatoes. He could set the print and work the machines but ask him to string two words together, on paper that is, and he was flummoxed.

"I've never done journalistic work, Henry, tha' knows that but if tha' could find me a job, any sort of a job, I'd be that thankful. Me an' Clare've tramped over't moors from Edgeclough. I were sacked last week fer what they said were seditious behaviour, then ter top it all me landlord evicted me from—"

He stopped speaking abruptly and gave a sidelong look at Clare who, thankfully, did not appear to be listening and Henry caught the look though he said nothing.

"Lew, lad, you're just the man I want." Again he looked at Clare as though to say where did she fit into the equation but Lew shook his head slightly and the conversation went on to more general matters and when Clare woke from what she supposed was a light doze she had fallen into, they were discussing where she and Lew were to spend the night.

"I'd gladly share my place with you, old man, you know, but it isn't big enough to swing the proverbial cat. One room with a bed in it, a chair and table, more books than I know what to do with, which is all I need since I spend all my time here but . . ."

"Wharrabout them rooms up top?" A laconic voice drifted up the open stairs from the ground floor. "Them's not in bad condition considerin'. Roof's sound enough burrit'll need a damn good cleaning afore a body could live in 'em."

Henry turned from Lew to Clare and back again, shrugging his shoulders and raising his eyebrows and it was then that Clare noticed a set of rickety stairs leading out of the corner of the room and up into what appeared to be an attic. Henry plucked at his lip, still turning to look first at Lew and then back to Clare. It was obvious that, as a gentleman, he didn't want to offend anyone's susceptibilities and since he knew nothing of the relationship between these two surprising visitors he thought it best to let one of them speak first.

"Us could soon clear out rubbish you gorrup there, Mr Hopwood," the disembodied voice continued; then, before anyone could answer, the presses sprang into action and conversation was rendered impossible.

Nothing was said for several moments then Lew spoke hesitantly. "What dost say, lass? It'll be dark before long and I don't fancy trampin' the streets lookin' fer *two* rooms," making it at once clear to Henry the situation between himself and Clare.

"Even if it's only fer one night it'd give us a breathin' space, that's if Henry don't mind."

Henry sprang into enthusiastic life. "Mind! I'd be delighted if you and Miss Hanrahan could make use of the rooms. I did consider doing them up for myself but I'm a lazy sod . . . sorry, Miss Hanrahan, and besides it suits me to live over the Dog and Duck. It's cheerful and I like a bit of company at the end of the day so go ahead and make what use of it you can. Albert will tell you what to throw out and what we might need down here."

The presses, as though by magic, fell silent again and the voice from downstairs informed anyone who cared to listen that there was a bed up there that'd suit the lady and then tomorrow they could set to and . . . The presses again roared into life and the rest of Albert's words were drowned out.

The rooms, which were indeed filthy, gave Clare something to occupy her mind during the next few days. Somewhere to direct it whenever the face of Martin Heywood crowded her senses. The familiar task of scrubbing, mindless and exhausting, was just what she needed as, hour after hour, she scoured the two rooms, the small windows set in the roof, the stairs that led down to the offices and, had she been let, the offices themselves, though Henry, as she had been told to call him, drew the line at that.

"They would only get dirty again, my dear Clare. You might just as well scrub the printing presses."

"Sure an' I will if you like."

"She would an' all, Henry," Lew told him, smiling that sweet and loving smile he kept exclusively for Clare.

"That she won't, Lew," Henry declared stoutly, turning to Lew who had now taken a cautious place at the desk in the room beyond the partition. He didn't know what Henry wanted him to do yet though there had been talk of articles and if he could spare the time, just as though he were already rushed off his feet, he was to go out into the alleyways of Newtown, Angel Meadow and the Ancoats district where the great mass of the "mill hands" lived and investigate their living conditions. Henry would publish Lew's survey in weekly instalments in the *Hopwood Review* if he was interested. It was a job worth doing though he had to admit he couldn't pay much in the way of wages.

"In other words, tha're exploitin' me." Lew grinned.

"Lad, I'll never be rich and neither will you but my readership has extended from a few radical hot-heads like you and me to a wider circle of the working class and I mean to spread it even further. There are some who can read now, thanks to the Mechanics Institute, and those who can read to those who can't. I mean to show up many of the evils of this bloody city so best get used to it."

Clare listened to these lively exchanges between Lew and Henry, keeping her mind busy and her heart from breaking further by the simple expedient of wearing herself into an exhausted state tramping the second-hand shops to look for the means of putting together a home for her and Lew in the tall attic rooms at the top of the building that housed the *Hopwood Review*. While Lew and Henry busied themselves with the poor and downtrodden of the city's teeming thousands, she searched shops and the markets, of which there were several in the city, purchasing threadbare blankets and bed linen, two chairs and an old table, a set of drawers, a pan which would be used for all their cooking needs, two cups and plates and forks, with one knife between them. They had little money to spare and, as she said, they might not be living in luxury but they were clean and had a roof over their heads and if, with Lew wrapped in blankets on the floor in the second room, and herself in the narrow bed in what was the kitchen-cum-living-room, she wept in the night for Martin Heywood, no one heard her.

They had been in Manchester for two weeks when she knew she was pregnant.

Chapter Twenty-three

It was again as though she were some sympathetic spectator to another woman's dilemma, if you could describe the wretchedness she was trapped in with the bland word, *dilemma*. She was choosing, or her stunned senses were choosing for her at that moment, to put to the back of her mind the fact that she was carrying Martin's child, which would have been predicament enough had she still been with him, but now, in this daze of misery and uncertainty she had blundered into, was quite devastating. That is if she allowed herself to dwell on it, so, she told herself, she would consider it later when . . . well, when she felt more able to cope with it. In the meantime she must find work of some sort despite what Lew said.

"Theer's no need fer thi' ter tramp streets lookin' fer work, lass," he reproved her sternly. "Tha' knows I'll look after thi'. I realise what Henry's offerin's not much but we're livin' rent-free and me wage covers what we need in't way o' grub. Especially wi' thi' so thrifty, shoppin' in't markets an' such. Tha' remind me o' Nelly." He smiled affectionately, for they both missed the sharp tongue and big heart of Nelly Bradbury. "But I'll tell thi' summat, I'll not 'ave thi' tekkin' some scrubbin' job or workin' be'ind a bar fer a few bob a week. Not while I'm 'ere ter see ter thi', so think on."

"What d'you propose I should do then, Lew Earnshaw?

Knock on the door of one of the mills about here and beg to be put on a machine?"

"Good God, no, lass," Lew cried, clearly horrified by the very idea. "I've seen too many lasses worked inter't ground ter't point where they could 'ardly drag theirselves 'ome at th'end o't day. I'll not 'ave that for thi', Clare, not if I've ter rob a bank." His voice softened. "Nay, bide a while. 'Ave a rest fer a month or two then, if tha's set on workin' us'll find summat ... well, summat suitable. I dunno ..."

For who, after several weeks of what the inhabitants called "poking his nose in", was more familiar with the conditions in which women in Swan Street, Marshall Street and Addington Street lived and raised their families than Lew Earnshaw. Northern folk were, on the whole, an enduring breed of men and women and even where there was not much money, hard work and good management kept them out of the workhouse. They were shrewd, down-to-earth, philosophical about their station in life. Husband and wife kept the family united – and limited! – facing insurmountable hurdles and, more often then not, surmounting them. But they were the exception to the rule. The rest lived in a squalor that ravaged him and he was quick to realise, and be ashamed of it since he was a man with a man's desires, that one of the causes of it was the fumbling, often drunken attentions, for what other pleasures did they have in their drab lives, that husbands forced on their wives, attentions that resulted in a child every year. In their one-up, one-down, back-to-back hovels which often housed a shifting population of perhaps fifteen to twenty people, they slept a dozen to a bed, if they had a bed, or sprawled on the rotting floorboards, girls and boys together, until the lads drifted off to a life of petty crime and the lasses to one of prostitution. Incredibly, they took in lodgers and kept a pig in the back yard, again if they had a back yard, and somehow or other held body and soul together. They were hard-handed and foul-mouthed – they had to be to keep their children out of trouble – and most of them, working in the mills, were "chesty". If they could get themselves from Monday morning to Friday night without coming a cropper, then that was all they asked.

But Lew Earnshaw, who was ready to marry Clare Hanrahan the moment she gave him the word, did not want this for her and would fight tooth and nail to prevent it. He saw them in a small cottage, similar to the one from which he had been evicted, with children about them, a bit of a garden in which he could grow vegetables to supplement his earnings, with Clare waiting at the end of each day to welcome him home. He had loved her for so long and sometimes felt his heart would break at the thought of what had been done to her, by life and by a man he detested. Though he was a self-educated man and had read many books on many subjects he could not, to his own satisfaction, express himself to her in the way he would have liked. Clare Hanrahan was a part of him, like his good strong arm or his eyes, and he longed to offer her all he possessed but that, apart from himself, was little enough. He was a peace-loving man, but he was fast losing his peace of mind over the complexities of loving Clare Hanrahan. He delighted shyly at the notion of them lying snug and warm together in the bed he would make for her, but at the same time he could make no sense of his need to keep away from her. His love was as honest as himself and the idea of marriage to Clare filled him with joy but he still fretted on how he was to keep her safe and comfortable on the meagre wage Henry Hopwood paid him.

So, until then they would live under the same roof of the tall and teetering building that housed the *Hopwood Review,* live like brother and sister, or the good friends they already were and hang the conventions. When he was securely on his feet, when they were more settled, which, being the careful, responsible man he was, would hopefully be this side of Christmas, he would broach again the subject of marriage.

She had made the top floor of what had once been a middle-class terraced family house in a row of middle-class houses into a cosy home for them, adding to the bare essentials with which they had started out with bargains she had reaped from the second-hand stalls in the market. Lew was not to know and would have been appalled had she told him, for he knew what they meant to her, that she had sold her poppy-red gown and warm winter cloak to a pleasant-faced woman who ran one of the stalls on the market. The woman had hummed and hawed, saying there was really no call for this sort of stuff, not on this market, which was used by working women as poor as Clare, but she recognised quality when she saw it and when Clare picked up her bundle and made to move on she finally made an offer Clare was satisfied with. She wanted to weep for the loss of the symbol of her success but she merely squared her shoulders and moved on to the next stall which sold garments more suited to this new life of hers.

Well, she told herself bravely, determined to stand no nonsense from that foolishly unmanageable heart of hers, when would she ever wear a poppy-coloured dress in her circumstances? It was much more sensible to clothe herself in the drab but hardwearing skirt and long-sleeved bodice, the large warm shawl that was the uniform of every other working-class woman who frequented the market. She did notice that many of them wore some sort of a battered hat, or bonnet but, remembering the pretty straw hat she had left with Nelly and which seemed to her to hold a promise that one day she would return to retrieve it, she found she hadn't the heart to purchase another. Instead she bought a bunch of scarlet ribbons with which she tied back her dark, glossy hair in a bouncing bunch of loose curls at the crown of her head. It won her an appreciative glance from Henry Hopwood who was still undecided on the status of the relationship between her and Lew, but if she noticed it, it meant little or nothing to her.

Just as most things meant nothing to her at the moment as she struggled to get through each day without Martin.

The proceeds from the sale of her dress and cloak enabled

her to buy a rug for the floor of the attic, a couple of threadbare cushions for the chairs, several dishes and pans and even an ancient clock which, the stall holder confessed, did not work, but when Lew took it to pieces, oiled it and put it together again, ticked companionably on the mantelshelf.

That had been another pleasant surprise. When the rubbish on the top floor had been picked over by the cheerful Albert, a small, blackleaded fireplace had been discovered, directly above the one in Henry's office. It was a great find, for it not only solved Clare's cooking problems but how they were to heat the place which, Henry said cheerfully, clearly expecting their stay to be a long one, would be bloody cold in winter. She began to cook cheap nourishing meals, those that could be managed over an open fire, mutton stew, soups, boiled skate, boiled fillets of mackerel which she and Lew shared, and sometimes Henry who did not seem to consider the drain feeding a third person was on their slender resources.

And the "rubbish" itself, which, Henry said, had cluttered the attics for years, had been found to include several items that could be made use of. A bucket with a hole in it which Lew plugged, and proved invaluable for carrying up clean water from the standpipe in the back lane. A great pile of tattered books all lined neatly on shelves which had been covered up with what had once been curtains and were totally hidden from view. There were three watercolours of some rural landscape which astonished Henry who said he had not the vaguest idea how all this lumber came to be here in the first place. There was a set of fire-irons, a coal scuttle and a small pair of kitchen scales, buried under which was a large pie dish and a set of baking trays. They could only assume, they told one another in wonderment, that the former occupants of the place, when it had been a house and not commercial premises, had stored these unwanted objects up there and when they had left they had been forgotten.

She moved through the days and weeks like some actor

playing a part that she had been given, the lines of which she had learned but which she did not really understand, nor even fit into. She knew she must tell Lew about the child soon, for already she was putting on weight and it would be obvious, not only to him but to Henry and Albert. She couldn't seem to think ahead, to look into the future and see anything there for her, or Martin's child. It was like drifting through a fog, a clinging mist which, in time, would clear, for mists always do, but to walk on placing one foot in front of the other without knowing what lay ahead was confusing. Not frightening, for nothing frightened her these days. When the worst has happened what is there to be afraid of? She could rely on Lew no matter what came, she knew that, but something in her told her that Lew would be quite devastated by the knowledge that she was carrying Martin Heywood's child. When he felt it was right he would press her to marry him, she was sure of that, and perhaps it might be for the best but he must be told the truth in order to make his decision.

She had taken to walking down to Philips Park which was the only public park within the boundary of Manchester. It was the closest she could get to the wide and rolling moors, the countryside in which she had spent the past three years. Before that she and her family had lived and worked in what her daddy had called "God's green land" – until it was shrivelled by blight – wandering country lanes massed with wild flowers and the heady scents they exuded. There had been fields awash with buttercups and poppies and clover and she and her brothers and sisters had played beneath the hedgerows, gathering blackberries in season, or perhaps just a simple posy for the mammy. She had been born to it, and though the high moorland of the South Pennine heartland was vastly different to the lush green fields of her home, it had been open and fresh with the scent of tumbling water, of heather and bilberry and the sharp winds that ruffled the bracken.

Here, in this place to which she and Lew had been exiled,

there was nothing to please the eye, the ear or the nose. Packed and bustling pavements, the clatter of steel-tipped clogs, the rattle of waggons and drays, the clop of horses' hooves, the stink of horse droppings, the stench of the factory chimneys, the shrill pierce of the factory hooters, and even in the place she was to call home, the roar of the machinery that printed Henry's newspaper.

She was accompanied by Fred, Fred tied to her wrist by a length of string, for he found the clamour as disturbing as she did and was wont to dart off nervously at the raucous noises which were so strange to him. Like her he had known nothing but the gentle sounds of the countryside, the cackle of hens, a pig snuffling in a cottager's back yard, sheep mewing on the hills, cows calling anxiously to their calves, the rush of water over rough stones, the song of children at play.

But in Philips Park she and he found a modicum of peace, particularly during a weekday when those who used the park were at their desks or looms or spinning frames. There was a bandstand though she had yet to hear a band play. It was April now and the glowing colours of tulip, scilla, hyacinth, aconite and narcissus delighted the eye, their brilliant beauty a soporific to Clare's wounded heart. She took a few sandwiches with her, though the bread was quite appalling to her taste after her own baking. She would have liked to make bread, pies, all the delicacies, or which would seem to be delicacies to her now though once she had taken them for granted. But nevertheless she and Fred would chew their way through the rough texture and strange-tasting slabs, sitting beside the lake until the dusk began to fall when they would both stand up reluctantly and make for the ornate wrought-iron gate. She would let Fred have a run on the grass, making sure first that the park-keeper was not about, and then head off back to what she supposed she should call home.

She was idly watching Albert setting up a type-mould which ensured that the type was exactly the same thickness and height in the printing process. Each character had to be accurately reproduced so that Albert might have enough e's and a's and h's and all the other letters he used in printing the paper. He was taking no notice of her presence and she was just about to go back upstairs, telling herself that she could no longer drift about like she had been doing for several weeks and must go out and look for work, despite her pregnancy, when Albert moved away from his machine and opened a door behind it.

He was gone for several minutes, disappearing like a rabbit down a hole and she was just about to follow him to see where he had gone when he reappeared, carrying some object which he attached to the side of the press.

"Where does that door go to, Albert?" she asked him idly, one foot on the bottom step ready to make her way up to the attic.

"Only to't store-room, lass."

"The store-room? I didn't even know there was another room down here."

"Oh aye." His voice was vague as he adjusted something on his machine.

"What sort of room is it?"

"Nay, don't ask me, lass. But it's got a right big range in it so I reckon it must've bin a kitchen."

She didn't speak or move for several moments as she digested this astonishing bit of information. She still had one foot on the bottom stair, her hand on the banister, her eyes wide and wondering as she stared in disbelief at Albert.

He looked up and was distracted by the expression on her face.

"What?" he asked truculently. Women were queer creatures as far as Albert Grimes was concerned. You never knew where the hell you were with them, which was why Albert had never married. He had a room further along the street in which he could do as he damn well liked without having to consider the whims and vagaries of the female sex, and though this one was quiet enough, making no demands on his male sensibilities she looked as though she were just about to do something Albert knew he wouldn't like.

"What?" he said again, then stepped hastily to one side as she pushed past him and opened the door to the room that he considered his own private province. He kept all his "stuff" in there, all the bits and pieces to do with the printing of the *Hopwood Review* and he didn't like them being messed about with. He knew it was in a clutter but then there was only him came in here and he knew just where to lay his hands on anything that might be needed.

"'Ere," he snorted testily. "Yer can't go in there . . ." But she was in, shoving to one side the boxes in which he kept his characters, stepping over rolls of printing paper and the debris of the ten years he had worked with Mr Hopwood on the newspaper.

"Jesus, Mary and Joseph," she whispered, shocking Albert badly, for he had been brought up by a strict Wesleyan father.

"Will yer look at that?" she went on, her Irish lilt coming back to her voice in her excitement.

"Now listen 'ere . . ." he began, but she had whirled away from what she had been looking at, an ancient kitchen range, turning on her heel to peer into every dark corner, at shelves and dressers and a great wooden table standing on its end against the far wall. There was a door at the back of the room which, when she creaked it open, revealed a scullery with a shallow sink, more shelves with rubbish piled a foot high and beyond that another door which when she hauled it open let in the last rays of the bit of sunshine that lay across a cobbled alleyway.

"This is it," she was saying, a lovely wash of colour in her face that he had never seen before and a gleam in her vivid green eyes that he knew was going to spell trouble.

"This is what?" he began but she slammed the back door so violently dust and plaster sifted into the air about her head and laid itself across her snug grey bodice.

"What yer up to?" he asked her suspiciously from the door between the kitchen and the scullery. "An' I'd be obliged if yer'd leave me store-room."

"This is a kitchen, you fool, a kitchen where I can make bread and cakes and pies and biscuits. Things I can't make on an open fire. All this stuff that's cluttering up the place can be stored elsewhere."

"'Ere, what yer talking about, yer daft faggot?" Albert didn't care to be called a fool, and in his own workroom as well, which is what he considered the old kitchen to be. The scullery had been a bit of a surprise to him as well as Clare, since he had ventured no further than what he called his store-room. But he wasn't having it. The sooner this trollop, oh aye, that was what she was, for her and that new chap weren't married, living over the brush in the attic room which he had obligingly cleared out for them, but the sooner she realised that she couldn't just come barging into other folk's places and take charge of them, the better. Talk about gratitude. A snug little place upstairs with no rent to pay and here she was gloating all over the place at the sight of the rusted kitchen range which was nowt, *nowt* to do with her.

"Holy Mary, Mother of God, will yer look at it?" she breathed reverently. "This is it, Albert, can't you see? This is what I've been looking for though to be sure I didn't know it. All these weeks with Lew telling me I was to have a rest and me wondering what sort of a job I could do when all the time this was here under my very nose. It's all I can do, Albert. I'm a cook, a good cook. I've got all Mrs Case's recipe books with me. I don't know what made me pack them because they were damned heavy to carry. Lew doesn't know, of course, but something made me bring them and here it it. This" – indicating with a wide sweep of her hand the room where Albert was readying the presses to roar into life— "this must have been the parlour, don't you see, leading into the kitchen and scullery."

"What you on about, lady?" Albert interrupted her, but

already he was beginning to crumble beneath the sheer magnetism of her, by the dash and fire he had not believed could be in her. She had been so quiet, so pale, so wilting, almost as though life had given her a few hard knocks and here she was prancing about like a bloody kid. Her enthusiasm began to infect him and his tone altered.

"But what d'yer mean ter do?" he ventured hesitantly, scratching his greasy locks with an equally greasy finger.

"We should have known really that this was once a parlour. This was a dwelling house before Mr Hopwood took it over for his newspaper; the fireplaces should have told us. And now this . . ."

"Aye, true, but what I want ter know is what yer think yer gonner do wi' it. This is a ruddy newspaper an' Mr Hopwood won't—"

"Oh, I wouldn't interfere with you, Albert, or the life of the newspaper. There's a back door into the lane where stuff can be delivered."

"Stuff?"

"And where I can take out my produce."

"Produce?"

"I shall need a handcart, a decent one, mind . . ."

"A handcart?"

"I'll start with the inns . . . what was the name of the one where Henry has a room?"

"The Dog an' Duck."

"That's it. And there must be dozens who would be glad of the chance to sell decent meals to their customers."

"God in 'eaven, are yer ter tell me what yer gonner do or are we ter stand 'ere babblin' bloody nonsense fer't rest o't day?"

"Do? What am I going to do? Sure an' I'm to start me own business, Albert, that's what I'm going to do. Now, I shall need a hand with this stuff and a word with Henry as to where it's going to be put, though by the look of it most of it could be thrown out."

"'Ere, don't you start throwing owt away. There's all sorts I might use an' Mr 'Opwood's bound ter want a say in't matter so yer'd best ..."

She whirled to face him, her full skirt disturbing the dust of years. It puffed up around her in little waves, clinging to her skirt but she didn't seem to care. She had her hands to her face which was suffused with a bright pink now as her excitement mounted and he was struck again by what a bonny lass she was. He'd thought her pale and skinny when she first came but now she was glowing with colour and getting as plump as a little bantam hen. For a moment he guessed Clare's secret then it slipped from his mind as she took his hands and began a sort of little dance so that he himself was capering like a bloody fool.

"'Ere, give over, what'll folk think," he stuttered, but her jubilation infected him so that when Mr Hopwood and the new chap came down to see what all the fuss was about, he and the lass were jigging about like a couple of kids.

"What the devil's happening here?" Mr Hopwood asked in astonishment, then, seeing the open door on the other side of the presses, brushed past them and peered inside.

"Well, I'm damned," he said, turning to look at the others, "where did this come from? Did you know about it, Albert?"

"Oh, aye, it's me store-room but this 'ere lass wants ter—"

"Oh, Mr Hopwood ... Henry ... Lew ... this is it, don't you see? This is what I'm going to be doing ..."

It poured from her in a flow of words that were jumbled and incoherent at times but gradually they began to understand what it was she wanted, what she not only wanted but what she meant to do and they exchanged bewildered glances.

They thought on principle it was a good idea, they said hesitantly, but really, was it practical? This was a noisy, dirty workplace and folk would think it very strange to be purchasing food from the back of a building in which a newspaper was printed. Housewives wouldn't care to walk up the alley at the back, which, after all, was not as clean as it might be, to buy her pies and cakes and biscuits, or even bread which, granted, would all be fresh baked. The handcart would be useful for her deliveries to the public houses and inns where she meant to find trade but how was she to push a heavily laden cart about the congested streets? She couldn't manage it on her own and for a moment she knew they were right, for her condition would soon be obvious but it didn't matter, she would get over that hurdle as she had got over all the others that had been erected in her path.

They went on and on and on and on but she had an answer for every obstacle they threw across the route she meant to take. It was as though she had been planning this new endeavour for weeks and weeks instead of minutes, for everything slotted into place, every question they asked she had the answer to, an answer that tripped off her tongue, delighting her with its rightness, its simplicity, its perfection. She had wanted work, employment of some sort, since she and Lew couldn't live for ever on the pittance which was all Henry could afford to pay him and this was a way to earn her own living, doing what Mrs Case had taught her to do with such efficiency. And where might it lead? Where might she find herself if she became known for freshly baked food, value for money, punctuality in deliveries, all the merits that were hard to find in this area of mills and factories where decent food was so rare. She remembered the bread she had eaten in the park, tough and as tasty as an old mat, the flour, she was pretty certain, mixed with chalk to increase its bulk and give it the appearance of being whiter than it would naturally be. She had heard of it from Mrs Case who abhorred such practices: brick dust in cocoa, sand in sugar, water added to cow's milk.

She would have none of that in her business. She would sell decent, home-baked food, cheap and nourishing and good value, she told them, her lovely colour fascinating the three men who watched her, and when she went upstairs to fetch her bucket with the clear intention of starting her scrubbing and scouring right away, they stared at one another speechlessly, even Henry with nothing to say on the matter of the change there was to be in *his* premises.

Her voice floated down from the top floor, lively as Lew had not heard it for many a week.

"I will, naturally, pay rent for the rooms, Henry, if we can agree on what is fair. Now, where . . ."

The rest was lost as she began on the first stage of what she was determined would be her new career.

Chapter Twenty-four

They were sitting one on either side of the small, glowing fire, Fred twitching in his sleep at their feet, when she told him.

She was sewing, something Betty Bickerstaffe, Lavender's mother, had taught her in the days before Clare went to work at Moorhouse Farm. She had been looking for something to do, refusing to watch Nelly scour her little cottage while she sat idly by and did nothing, she had told Nelly and if she didn't find something to occupy her she'd go mad. She had still been weak from her journey across Lancashire, and from her illness and when Nelly, exasperated beyond measure by her determination at least to give the windows a polish, or peel the 'taters, saying she wasn't up to it, had shouted for Betty, she had been startled.

"See, Betty," Nelly had screeched, "wilta give this lass summat ter do or she'll drive me barmy, road she's goin'. Let 'er try 'er 'and at a plain seam on that there little shirt tha's mekkin' fer tha Joe. Betty gets bits o' cotton stuff from't mill an's a dab 'and at a bit o' plain sewin'," Nelly explained to Clare. "Go on, Betty, show 'er fer God's sake an' give 'er summat what she can do sittin' down."

And so, on and off during the three months of her recuperation she had sat in front of Nelly's or Lew's kitchen fire and sewed on the little garments Betty made up to earn herself an extra bob or two to go into her family's financial pocket. The scraps of cotton she got for next to nothing from the mill and, as her own mother had taught her, Betty passed on what she knew to Clare. She was right glad of the help, she said, for Marie Bretherton was expecting and had a fancy for a little nightshirt for the new baby and if Clare was interested she might even show her how to do what her mam, who had been apprenticed to a seamstress, had called a French knot, another called a chain stitch and a third a coral stitch. Simple things but which, when applied to the yoke, lifted a plain garment into something a bit special. They cost nothing, a bit of silk thread, of which Betty had yards, for she had been left her mam's workbox when she died. She had the needles and the patterns, the scissors and everything that was needed to make a child's garment and her five daughters and two sons had been the best-dressed children in the row. The sewing box was her most treasured possession, an unusual one for a woman who lived from one week to the next wondering if she could scrape together the money for the rent, but she and her Billy had pulled through and though it had come close a time or two she had managed to hang on to her mam's sewing box which, along with one or two other items, might have fetched up in the pawn shop.

Betty had taught Clare how to mend and darn, for not everyone in the row could afford to buy new, not even Betty for the most part, and Clare's mending, and the neat way she darned Lew's socks so that the darn was barely visible, was much admired.

Clare had picked over every scrap of fabric that was for sale on the market stalls of Smithfield and along St George's Road where there were small shops selling second-hand or even third-hand clothing. A blouse or a white lawn petticoat, gleaned from God knows where, and bought for a few pence, could be unpicked and remade into a small garment, the material often very fine and yet serviceable and it was on one of these that she was working that evening.

Lew was perched on the edge of the chair and on the floor about his feet were spread sheets of paper on which he had written the notes from his latest sortie into Angel Meadow, Ancoats and the worst of the slums on the east side of Manchester. When he had them arranged to his liking they would be prepared ready for printing in the *Hopwood Review* at the end of the week when the newspaper was published. Clare watched him, her sewing in her lap, her hands idle, brooding on what was to happen, for she knew she could no longer put off telling him about Martin's child. How would he take it? What would he think? She didn't know what she herself thought; she had been so busy during the last week she had had no time to dwell on anything but the setting up of her kitchen on the ground floor.

She didn't think she would have managed without Mrs Case's books. Not only had the cook written down every recipe for every dish she had ever prepared but, going back to the days when she had been a scullery-maid, then kitchen-maid when her duties had been cleaning not cooking, she had meticulously recorded all the things she had been taught on how to clean different things in the home and, more importantly, what to use to clean them. For instance there was a paragraph on how to remove rust on a grate, how to make the blackleading, the polish for the black grate, or kitchen range in Clare's case, how to clean marble, though Clare had none of that, decanters and gilt frames and, when she had removed the rust from the range, how to make a strong paste of fresh lime and water which when smeared on the surface would preserve it from becoming rusty again.

It had taken her the best part of a week to return the range to its original shining condition. But before she could tackle the range all that she called "junk" but what Albert considered to be a vital part of his work as a printer, had to be shifted and a home found for what he insisted upon keeping. If she heard it once over the next week or two, she heard it a hundred times.

"'Ere, where yer goin' with that?" he would protest, tearing some unidentifiable object from her hands which she had been just about to tip into the lane ready to be carried away on the handcart, which was the first thing she had bought.

"It looks totally useless, Albert, but if you can prove to me that it is a necessity to your job then we will put it in the attic space with the rest. Do you need it?"

"Well, I might do one day." Albert glowered at her.

"What is it?" Her voice was cool and Albert wondered what he had done to deserve the upheaval this beautiful woman had brought to his simple life.

"It's summat to do with ..." He scratched his head because quite simply he couldn't remember, just like he couldn't remember the purpose of half the items she was so carelessly chucking away.

"What? Prove to me that you need this ... whatever it is" – turning it over in her hands, the expression on her face distasteful – "and you shall keep it."

He couldn't, and it was the same with everything except the rolls of paper, his boxes of characters, his tools of the trade and the brushes he used to clean the presses. He grumbled about everything from morning until night, asking them how he was expected to keep running up and down them bloody stairs every time he needed something from the bloody attic when all he had had to do before *she* came was open his store-room door and reach inside for whatever he wanted.

Nevertheless, though he tried to hide it under a show of indignation, he took a great interest in everything Clare did, inclined to admire her, for, by God, she knew how to put in a hard day's work. The kitchen had been in an appalling state; filth into which their feet literally sank lay across the floor as though no feet had disturbed it for many years except for the square yard or so where Albert had trodden just inside the door. Cobwebs were draped like lace from floor to ceiling and from one end of the room to another, floating across the kitchen and into the scullery, clinging in loathsome wisps about their heads, but, give her her due, the lass didn't scream like many would, but carefully removed them before she began her scrubbing. The unoiled hinges of the doors shrieked and Albert found, to his own surprise, he was helping her out with oil cans and spanners and such in many of the jobs that needed doing. She was up to her elbows in pails of hot water for days on end, moving steadily from one end of the kitchen to the other, then on into the scullery before she tackled the range.

And when it was all done, when the windows winked in the pale spring sunshine, when the floor had come up a treat, its flags of every shade of red and pink and terracotta glowing like jewels, when the deal table which the men had lifted from its vertical position and placed in the centre of the room had been scoured and was as white as the driven snow, when the sinks and draining boards had been endlessly scrubbed, it was all so breathtakingly splendid, even they, who thought the whole scheme was mad, could not but admit that she'd done a bloody good job.

But it was the range that was the showpiece of the room. It stood proudly against the wall, as black and gleaming as wet coal, its brass handles shining spectacularly so that you could see your own face in them, small and a funny shape, true, but as bright as a mirror, Albert said, awed almost to speechlessness. He had done his part by printing for her dozens of small notifications, which she had tacked on walls and doors in the immediate vicinity of the newspaper offices, advertising that the Bakery, as she had decided to call her small business, was open for the sale of meat pies, meat and potato pies, custard tarts, pork pies, even pickled eggs which were included in Mrs Case's book of wonders. Clare knew that many of the denizens of the area could not read but, showing great ingenuity, Henry had helped her to *draw* pictures of her wares with arrows and pictured instructions on the whereabouts of her business.

And tomorrow she was to start. She was to be up at four

o'clock to start her baking, for she meant to produce the cheapest, freshest, most nourishing food that money could buy, bearing in mind that those who would be her customers had to make a farthing do the work of two.

She was waiting for Lew to go to bed. Her own bed was standing against the wall and before she got into it she would pull it up close to the fire, for the day had been cold and wet and the fire was welcome. Fred, with the usual instincts of animals who know which side their bread is buttered, would remain with her, curled up against the fender, or snuggled into her back on the bed. She and Fred had become close since she came to Manchester, for they had been thrown into one another's company while Lew was working. It was strange but even now after all these weeks and with her ambition about to be realised she still had that feeling of desolation, still suffered the pain of losing Martin. She still had that feeling of being outside the problems of others, and even herself, watching as a disinterested stranger might watch, knowing that their hopes and fears could not touch her any more. She was no longer involved and in a strange way she took melancholy pleasure from the fact.

She sighed deeply and Lew glanced up as though suddenly conscious of her gaze upon him. He smiled and bent to pick up the papers strewn about the floor, shuffling them together in a neat pile.

"Art ready fer tha' bed, lass? I'll be outer tha' way in a minute. I bin trackin' down what they say is a brothel at th'end o' Elizabeth Street. I met a doctor t'other day, nice chap, an' 'e were tellin' me 'e's bin mendin' little lasses of eight or nine who've bin sold inter't trade. Eeh, Clare, there's some things need puttin' right in this world."

"And you're just the man to do it, Lew. If anybody can, you can."

"I'll do me bloody best but even I, wi' all the stuff I read, 'ad no idea what went on in . . . Nay, I musn't keep thi', lass. Tha've a big day on termorrer an' tha'll need a good night's sleep."

He stood up, taking her hand to lift her, noticing the bit of sewing in her hand and smiling down into her face, his eyes narrowed and ready, she thought, to tell her something. Almost idly he asked, "What yer mekkin, my lass?"

Though she felt a wave of sickness wash over her she knew that the time for the truth which *must* come, had arrived.

"It's a baby's nightgown, Lew." She looked steadily into his face.

"Oh aye, an' 'oo's that for?"

"It's for the child I am to have in September. Martin Heywood's child." It was a bald statement but was there any other way to tell him?

He began to smile. It was a ghastly smile, a sort of a mixture between appalled disbelief, foolish, almost hysterical amusement, fear and hatred, the latter directed at her who had broken his heart so many times but never like this.

He continued to cling to her hand just as though, should he let go, he might fall over. Every scrap of colour drained from his face, leaving it ashen, and before her eyes, his own seemed to sink into great black pools of despair.

Carefully she detached her hand from his and then, like someone assisting an elderly relative to a chair, sat him in the one from which he had just risen. She knelt at his feet and took hold of his hands again, tenderly stroking them, then bending her head to rest her cheek on them for a moment. He was in such a state of shock he let her, sitting obediently, his eyes never moving from her face.

"I'm sorry, Lew. I should have told you more gently but the moment came . . ."

"*Gently!*" His voice came out as a croak and he tried to clear his throat, then as movement returned to him he pushed her away from him so violently she fell back on the floor. He strode across the small room to the door that led to his, crashing his hip against the table and almost knocking it over. Fred leaped to his feet, his ears twitching nervously, in two minds whether to bark or not, then moved to hide behind Clare. She got slowly to her feet, then bent to pick him up, fondling his ears before putting him down again. She was not really aware of what she was doing, her distress was so great, and when Lew strode back towards her she cowered away from him.

"Nay, lass, I'll not 'it thi'," he told her bitterly, "but by Gow I'd like ter 'ave that bastard 'ere fer I swear I'd break every bone in 'is body. Ter leave a woman in . . . in your condition can only be the work of a total brute . . . a monster."

"No, Lew, no! He didn't know about . . . about me. Sure an' I didn't meself. Not until . . . well, it doesn't matter. He doesn't know so you can't blame him."

"Sweet Jesus, will tha' listen ter thissen protectin' 'im." He threw himself backwards, again striking the table, crashing his fist into the palm of his hand, then lifting it to strike the frame of the door. "I can't bear ter 'ear thi' standin' up fer 'im. The sod wants a bloody good 'idin' an' I swear if we was still in Edgeclough I'd be off after 'im right now. Dear God, Clare . . . Dear sweet God. 'Ow could thi'? 'Ow could thi' get thissen in such a bloody pickle which is a daft question, for any woman what lies wi' a man runs t'risk o' gettin' 'ersen in't family way. An' it's common knowledge tha've bin Martin bloody Heywood's whore."

"Don't . . . please, Lew."

"That's what tha' should've said, Clare. That's what tha' should've said to 'im: *Don't*! 'E didn't want ter wed thi', did 'e? But *I* did, Clare, an' yer said no ter me an' then went an' lifted tha' skirts fer that bugger. I tried ter understand an' forgive, an' I did but this . . . this . . ."

"Don't, Lew. It's no good . . . it does no good. It's too late for recriminations. I deserve everything you say but it's over and . . . I must make preparations for the child."

"*His bloody child!*" He groaned, then making his way back to his chair slumped down into it, covering his face with his hand and bending his head in agony. "I don't think I can stand it, Clare."

"No." She turned to the fireplace and putting both hands on the mantelshelf leaned over it, in as great a suffering as he was. "I'll go in the morning . . . if . . . I'll go . . ." Her mind wandered desolately to the shining kitchen downstairs, to the fresh meat, the peeled potatoes standing in a bucket of water, to the crocks of good flour, the clear dripping, the suet ready for the rich crust to go on her suet puddings. All the ingredients that were waiting for her own clever hands to turn into the mouth-watering pies and puddings she meant to sell. Tomorrow, later on, she was to walk down to the Dog and Duck with her basket, bought at the market, in which she would wrap a selection of her baking and show it to a Mrs Kitty Mullaney, the landlady, who, having been warned by Henry, had promised to have a look and a taste, with the idea, if they were good enough, of course, of putting a few out on her bar. It was all there waiting for her, for her and Lew, but if Lew was unable to stomach the idea of her bearing Martin's child then it would all disappear like mist in sunlight.

"Don't talk so daft, girl." His voice was muffled in his hand but the words were clear enough. "'E might abandon yer but I'd not." And she did not contradict him again, since it seemed to help him to believe that Martin had left her in the lurch. "Tha' mun stay 'ere. We's must mekk a life fer oursenns, and fer't . . . fer't babby. I'll mekk arrangements in't mornin'."

She turned and looked at him wonderingly but he did not meet her gaze. His elbows were on his knees, his shoulders were slumped and his head hung down, his thick, untidy brown hair falling over his brow. He pushed a hand through it then lifted his head and looked up at her. His eyes were a steady, flinty grey, almost colourless and certainly expressionless but in their depth was a gleam which said Lew Earnshaw might be a man of good humour, of good heart, easy-going and ready to do anyone a good turn, but he was also single-minded and not easy to lead by the nose. He had regained some of his colour.

"What . . . what arrangements, Lew?" she faltered.

"For us ter be wed. That babby'll need a father an' it's not much hope o' claimin' Martin Heywood, 'as it?"

"Lew, I can't. I can't marry you." She sat down heavily in her chair and Fred crept up to her skirts. She put out a hand to his head, not to comfort him but to steady herself. Contact with another living being at this moment of stress was badly needed.

"Can't bear another chap ter touch thi', is that it? Not after bein' Martin Heywood's whore."

"No . . . don't, Lew, don't."

"Well, tha've no need ter fash thissen fer I've no fancy fer *'is* leavin's an' I'll not touch thi'. No," he lied, "I'm doin' it fer't babby. Poor little bugger's got a 'ard enough row ter hoe wi'out bein' a bastard an' all. So, what's it ter be?"

He stood up and towered over her, his face implacable, his eyes blank, a grey blankness which told her how much he was suffering. He had wanted to marry her for nearly three years now, she knew that, but he had let her be, had even ignored the gossip about her and Martin, probably to save himself pain, perhaps not even believing it, and while there was no visible proof of what she and Martin had been to each other, he had found it easy to keep up that belief. If he had been astonished that she had come with him to Manchester, leaving her lover behind, he had not questioned it, waiting, she believed, for the right moment when, his eager heart had hoped, she would turn to him.

But not like this. She was to bear the child of the man who had used her, yes, she admitted it to herself, used her for his own convenience, and Lew was almost destroyed by it but, as he believed Martin had done, he would not desert her. So, for the sake of her child, was she to marry him? He was waiting for an answer and she knew from the rigid inflexibility of his expression that he would have her answer now. Not tomorrow, or when she had had time to think about it, to mull it over, but now, this minute, or the offer would be withdrawn.

And was there any other way? A woman alone with an

illegitimate child was prey to the pitilessness of a society that believed that the sin was all the woman's, that she was to blame for being in the condition she had brought on herself and that her child, as well as herself, must be shunned lest it contaminate them. If she married Lew – dear God, he deserved better – then she, and her child, would be safe. She could continue in the work she had planned for herself, perhaps even help Lew in his own future hopes. He was enjoying the work he was doing, using his clever brain, revealing to the apathetic world through his weekly column in the *Hopwood Review* the wrongs of society and, at the same time, working for those who had his heart and his pity. The poor, the downtrodden, the exploited, the thousands of his fellow men whose miserable existence he longed to improve. If she worked beside him, not on the newspaper, but doing the job for which Mrs Case had so superbly trained her and of which she meant to make a success, perhaps she might help him redress the ills of the people who had put their faith in the six points of the People's Charter and who had been sold out as the divide grew and the rich got richer and the poor got poorer.

"Lew, can we not talk of this . . . perhaps . . ."

He whirled away from her and with one pace stood with his face to the wall, his forehead resting on the cracking plaster which she had scrubbed for the third time only that day. He was going to whitewash it, he had told her enthusiastically, and then, later, they might manage to get together one or two bits of furniture, an armchair apiece, a cupboard, ornaments, little things to make it more homely and less bare. He meant to buy a couple of decent beds – they would only need one if she took him for a husband – for they would probably have to spend some time here until the day they had enough to rent a cottage somewhere on the outskirts of the city. Perhaps towards Broughton or Cheetham where there were new houses being built. He had been filled with hope and vigour in the certainty that one day, if he was patient, he would obtain what his true and steadfast heart had always longed for.

Now it had all been swept away on the crest of his desolation.

"Well?" he asked her harshly, his face still to the wall.

"Lew . . ." Her voice trembled and she gripped her hands together in her lap. Fred nosed at them in sympathy, or looking for comfort, and she knew, as she reached to fondle his ears, that she really had no choice. Lew would have nothing but marriage. Her lovely new kitchen downstairs could go to the devil for all he cared and, knowing what she had to do she bent her head, wanting to weep, not sure over what.

They were married three weeks later in the small church of St George which lay just off St George's Road on the edge of the city. Henry and Albert didn't seem unduly surprised when Lew told them brusquely what was to happen, though Albert got his head bitten off when he was unwise enough to remark – and it was only a joke, he was to say later to Mr Hopwood and he'd meant no disrespect – that it was about time, too. He had known all along that there was more to their relationship than a casual friendship and with the baby coming, obvious now as Miss Hanrahan, or should he begin to call her Mrs Earnshaw, began to grow plump and bonny, it was time they were wed.

He and Henry were the only guests, Henry quite unrecognisable in his smart frock coat and top hat and looking as though he had strayed into the wrong ceremony next to Albert and Lew. They were both spruced up, shaved and wearing a clean shirt but their plain buff breeches and corduroy jackets, their neckerchiefs and caps and sturdy boots advised them to be of the working class. Clare wore what she put on every day, freshly washed and pressed, though she had foraged on a stall at the market and found a cheap straw bonnet on which she had sewn a bunch of green satin ribbons which exactly matched her eyes. She carried a small posy of anemones.

If Henry and Albert were disconcerted by the bride and groom's coolness with one another, apart from exchanging surprised glances, they had little to say, at least not until later. It was nothing to do with them, was it, if the bride and groom had had a falling out. Henry produced a bottle of wine and Clare had baked a few things – not knowing what else to do to make the occasion a bit festive – a rabbit pie, a custard tart and what Mrs Case's book called a pavini cake which had currants and sweet almonds and raisins in it and was declared to be delicious by an awkward Henry who looked as though he would be glad when the wedding breakfast was over and he could get back to his desk. It seemed that they, meaning the newly married Mr and Mrs Earnshaw, had no intention of taking off any more time than was necessary but he was surprised, and so was Albert, when Lew, after changing into his working clothes, came clattering down the stairs with every intention of getting on with editing the column he had written for next week's edition.

"Come on, old fellow," Henry was unwise enough to venture, "this is your wedding day. You should be taking the bride on an outing, not hanging about—"

"Shurrup, wilta," Lew snarled and Henry reared back in alarm. "What me an' . . . an' me wife do is our own business so tha' can keep tha' smart chat ter thissen."

Chapter Twenty-five

The customers were slow to discover that Mrs Earnshaw's bread and cakes and pies were not only the best they'd ever tasted but the best value for money, and they'd little enough of that to spare. First off, they told her, standing in the open doorway of her scullery, they hadn't known she was here, not in this back alley. The notices pinned to the walls in the vicinity? Well, not being able to read they had not even glanced at them and if she wanted to know what had fetched them here, it was the smell. Many of them had to walk through Stevenson Square, Newton Street and Dale Street on their way to the gates of the many mills, factories, sweat shops and shirt makers in the centre of the city where they laboured. On the corner of Dale Street and Lever Street stood the building that housed the *Hopwood Review* and the tantalising smell of fresh-baked bread, of succulent meat pies and all the other delicious food Mrs Earnshaw baked in her shining kitchen had drifted over the rooftops on the air, assailing their nostrils every morning and had driven them mad until they had discovered the source of it. They had not expected to find a bakery down such an unappetising back alley, they told her, but even to them who were not overly concerned with soap and water, it was obvious that not only did Mrs Earnshaw keep her premises scrupulously clean, but every morning she swept and scoured the cobbles that led from the corner of Dale Street and Lever Street up to her bakery. And her in the family way an' all!

For three weeks she and Lew, Henry and Albert had eaten nothing but meat and potato pies, steak and kidney pies, small raised pork pies, fish pie made from cod or haddock, which was cheap, rabbit pie and cheese and onion pie which was also cheap and, with the fish pie, was cut into quarters and sold separately. Albert was heard to remark morosely that he never wanted to see a bloody pie again but he supposed some bugger had to eat up what she had made and hadn't sold, for you couldn't waste it, could you? Not that it wasn't good, it was, bloody good, but a daily ration of pies and more pies began to get a bit much after three weeks.

Clare had decided not to make cakes or biscuits until she had gauged her market, for the people she was to sell to did not want fancy stuff, which they couldn't afford anyway, but good, nourishing filling meals. Every day she made fresh bread which, when cut into slices and spread with her good dripping made from the meats she cooked, would make a grand "noon-piece" for a hungry worker. But day after day she stood at the little portable counter at her back door and waited in vain for the men and women whose trade she was after. Behind her in an attractive display set out on shelves was stacked what she had baked that morning, but though she even went as far as trailing down to the end of the alley to look for customers in those first few days she met with none, for by eight o'clock they were all in their loom gates, at their spinning-machines or bent over their sewing-machines. She had one customer. Mrs Mullaney of the Dog and Duck, after tasting her wares, had ordered a dozen or so pies each day, and had promised to sample her pickled onions and pickled eggs when they were ready. The pies had apparently gone down well with Mrs Mullaney's customers and she thought she might be able to order a few more if Mrs Earnshaw could supply her.

Suddenly it all changed. It was a Tuesday and though she

had plenty of leftovers from Monday – despite the meal they had all eaten the night before – and which, Henry told her, could easily be sold as fresh-baked that morning, she had been in her kitchen since four that morning, kneading her dough, sifting her flour, testing her lard on a knife for sweetness, chopping her suet and her meats, and measuring her clarified dripping which had to be used sparingly.

It was a grand morning, mild and sunny, just the sort of day to put a glow of gladness in the heart and a bit of a spring in the step and when, from the open scullery door a woman's voice called, "Anyone there?" Clare nearly dropped the bowl of pure, golden dripping she was carrying from the kitchen to the counter.

"Yes, I'm here," she answered, moving into the patch of sunlight by the door, her smile ready, her heart beating furiously beneath the bib of her snow-white apron, for this, surely, was her first customer.

"Yer well 'idden," the woman said accusingly. It was seven thirty and the woman was dressed in the drab uniform of a mill worker. A sleeveless blouse covered by her well-worn shawl, a short skirt that just skimmed her ankle bone, and clogs. She was thin, careworn, as were all the women who worked in the mills and factories of Manchester. Her grey hair hung in greasy hanks about her face but she was smiling and sniffing, and smiling with all the signs of deeply pleasurable surprise.

"What can I do for you?" Clare invited the woman to tell her. "The bread's just come out of the oven and there's pies, meat, fish, rabbit, or perhaps a dripping butty?" She smiled again, for the Lancashire folk did love their butties. A vagrant thought passed through her mind that perhaps *bacon* butties might go down well.

"Eh, I never saw such grand pies," the woman told her, quite bemused, "but 'ow much?" Her voice was slightly wistful.

"A halfpenny each or three for a penny."

"An' fresh baked?" Just as though she would eat nothing else.

"Of course."

Just then the woman turned to look towards the end of the alley and catching sight of two or three shawl-wrapped women and a couple of children passing the entrance, called out to them.

"'Ere, Minnie, come an' tekk a look. If yer've got nowt fer tha' dinner this 'ere's the place."

They came hesitantly, their noses wrinkling in pleasure, their pale faces showing not only surprise but their mouths filling with saliva. They had tramped along smoky brown streets beneath skies which, though a clear blue this early in the morning, would soon be as smoky brown as the streets. Tall chimneys already belched throat-catching filth from the hellish workshops in which these women laboured and already the noise and clatter of ponderous waggons, heavily laden with casks and bales, filled the narrow streets, going to the same destination: the long piles of warehouses, many of them with pillared and stately fronts, the great grimy mills with their smoke-pouring shafts. The principal thoroughfares were as busy and swarming as any great city and would be crowded in several hours by the carriages and phaetons of men of wealth and commerce. There would be clerks and travellers and agents bustling from counting house to counting house and bank to bank. But the women who were beginning to crowd round her bakery, many of them only having a "scen", for that was all they could afford, were not of these. They came from the class who were mechanics and artisans, factory operatives, undersized, sallow, stunted and pale. Beyond the far outskirts of the city lay handsome houses and squares and between these and the dull stacks of warehouses and ugly mills lay the great mass of smoky, dingy, sweltering and toiling Manchester, a network of mean and miserable streets which housed the women who stood at the back door of Clare Earnshaw's bakery.

"By gum," said one of them. "We wondered where't good smell were comin' from, didn't we, Ida? All this week I've said to 'er, where's that smell comin' from, 'aven't I, Ida?"

Ida confirmed that she had. Ida was probably about thirty but looked closer to fifty, her body sagging and swollen with the everlasting childbearing that was forced on her annually. But her expression was cheerful, her eyes bright in the folds of her grimy face. Her hair, its colour not easily discernible, was tucked back behind her grimy ears and when she smiled the teeth she had left were like tombstones in the cavern of her mouth. Her shawl was held about her shoulders and from its fold a small child peeped, still half asleep but ready to "piece" or "scavenge" for its mother for the next twelve hours or so. The Ten Hour Bill was not taken a great deal of notice of in Manchester, or indeed in any part of Lancashire, where the factory inspectors whose job it was to enforce it were hard pressed to visit a mill once in twelve months, if that.

The children pressed their noses up to the counter, their filthy fingers clutching its well-scrubbed edge and without thinking Clare pressed a pork pie into each hand.

"Well," the women said, slightly put out, for were they not as hungry and hard up as the bairns, but Clare knew what to do. "And one for each of you seeing that you're my first customers."

"Eh . . ." They were delighted, cramming the flaky pastry into their mouths, grinning at one another with their blackened teeth, wiping their fingers on their greasy skirts while their eyes roamed over the good things that were on display. Could they afford them, their eyes asked one another and it was Ida who chirped up.

"Halfpenny each or three fer a penny. Shall us 'ave a pennyworth atween us, Minnie?"

"Aye, go on."

"An' 'ow about a drippin' butty fer't bairns?"

"'Ow much?"

"A halfpenny each." When the women saw the size and thickness of the butties they exchanged glances, for there was enough in one to do two bairns.

She even wrapped up their purchases in a bit of clean, white paper, treating them, they told one another as they set off at a run up the alley since the whistle would be going in a minute, as if they were quality and wait till they told Etty an' Mary an' the others.

The next day Clare could hardly keep up with the queue that formed at her back door, for Minnie and Ida and the others had spread the word that there was good food to be had at the Bakery and at prices that even they could afford. Aye, they said, preening a little as though it were all their doing, that's what it was called, the Bakery, and the woman who ran it was as pleasant as could be but if they didn't believe it, they must try it for themselves. Which they did and in vast numbers, spreading the word among not only the spinners and weavers alongside whom they worked but others who were in the same trade and circumstances as they themselves.

Several weeks later, when the growing child inside her began to slow her down and her bulk became so big as to make it awkward for her to inch her way about the slip of a scullery, she knew that she couldn't manage this fast-growing business on her own. The small handcart with which she delivered her goods was difficult to handle and the load so heavy that she was afraid she might damage the child. Mrs Mullaney was becoming restive, demanding more and more pies and was quite put out when Clare had to tell her that there was none to spare at the moment. After all, Mrs Mullaney reminded her, she had been Mrs Earnshaw's first customer, but she promised the landlady, who was herself spreading the news of the Bakery to other public houses providing it didn't interfere with *her* supply, that she was to take on more staff and Mrs Mullaney would be top of her list of customers.

She tackled Lew about her need to have help that evening.

They had been married for two months and though they were perfectly polite with one another they might have been two strangers lodging beneath the same roof.

From the moment he had been told about the child Lew's attitude had become one of cool self-possession. He had retreated into himself and she was fast becoming aware that if she didn't take the initiative, in what way she wasn't sure, he would lose that lovely, endearing quality which drew others to him and which had been sadly lacking since he was told of her pregnancy. He hated. He hated Martin Heywood for taking what Lew cherished and throwing it carelessly away, and he hated her who had been thrown away. He wanted nothing to do with her, his attitude said, beyond the bounds of the necessity of sharing a roof, for though they were man and wife in the sight of the law he made it clear it was for the sake of the child only. It was not his child and he would have no part in its upbringing. He had loved her. He had longed to marry her but now they were man and wife and he could do with her as he willed, his will was against it. The child in her belly drew them together and it held them apart, for how could he take a woman who carried Martin Heywood's bastard? Though the thought of it was abhorrent to her, loving Martin as she still did, Clare sometimes wondered whether it would have been better if, on their wedding night, he had taken her to his bed, indeed had half expected it, but he had done what he always did every night, inclined his head politely in her direction and murmured his goodnight. He spent all his time in his own slip of a room, as soon as they had eaten going in there and closing the door behind him. Some evenings he would go down to the office, sitting at his desk and putting together the articles he wrote for the newspaper and when he did, though she stayed awake for a long time, he did not come back upstairs which would have necessitated him creeping through her room to get to his own.

It tore her to tatters, as Nelly would have said, for during the past years she had come to rely on Lew's steadfast friendship, his loving companionship, his enduring support, and this cool civility, this stranger who had come to live in Lew's skin was unknown to her and hard to bear. His steel-hard determination, his rigid resolution to treat her as no more than a passing acquaintance baffled her, for though she knew he had been crucified by what she had done and what had been done to her, the result of which was the child she carried, she had not thought him capable of turning from her so cruelly. He who had been so open-hearted, so generous with his emotions had become an enigma, an unknown quantity, and rather than beat her head and heart against it she had let it run on. Perhaps when the child came, he who had loved and been loved by the children of Edgeclough would turn to it, and then to her, for they must make some sort of a life, not like this, apart and cool, but as a man and wife.

Had it not been for her tiny, budding business and the pleasure she took in it, and in the timid friendship of the women who came to her back door every day, she would have been borne down by the wretchedness of it. She loved Lew. She had loved him for nearly three years and it was like having a beloved brother, a treasured friend, turn his face from her, his smile from her, his hand from her just when she most needed the steadiness of him. When he did look at her, which was seldom, his eyes were glazed, unreadable and her heart was wrenched for him and for herself.

"May I talk to you, Lew," she asked him that night just as he was about to go down the stairs again after their evening meal. They had eaten the delicious casserole she had put in her oven first thing this morning, along with her first batch of pork pies. She had served it with fresh vegetables which she had tramped to Smithfield Market to fetch, a journey that became increasingly hard as her swollen body slowed her down.

He paused politely, not looking at her. Fred strolled over to him and sniffed his leg, then sat down and scratched his ear vigorously and for a moment a faint smile lit Lew's face as he bent down to put a hand to the dog's head.

"Yes?" No more. Just an indication that he was prepared to listen providing she was quick about it.

"It's about Lavender."

This time he turned and looked at her, surprise on his lean face.

"Lavender?"

"I . . . I'm finding it hard to . . . get about as . . ."

An expression of distaste crossed his face and he swivelled away from her, almost with violence as though he couldn't find it in him to look at her.

"I . . . I would like to get a message to her. I need help, not only with the baking but with the deliveries. Sure an' I find I can't be handlin' the . . . the handcart as easily as I did. I'm sorry, I know it . . . I know you don't care to be reminded but . . . well, the business is doing well and I know Lavender would . . . We are both fond of her and she would be of enormous help."

"I see, an' wheer's lass ter live? Theer's 'ardly room fer two on us, never mind three, an' four soon." His face spasmed and he seemed to twitch as though doing his best to rid himself of something nasty.

"There's room to put a trundle bed in the kitchen. It could be pushed under the table during the day."

"'Appen Henry wouldna care fer another lodger, 'ave tha' thought on that? It were good of 'im ter tekk us in an' give us somewhere ter lay our 'eads an' now tha're askin' 'im ter give room ter another."

"You know Lavender wouldn't be in Henry's way. I'll ask him myself if you like. I really am finding it difficult to manage at the moment and it's—"

"Tha' should o' thought on that afore tha' let that bugger interfere wi' thi'." His voice was bitter and it was clear that forgiveness was far from his heart.

"Lew, don't . . . don't talk like that. If you object to Lavender living here with us then she and I will get rooms somewhere else. I'm sure Henry would still let us rent his kitchen and scullery."

"That'd look a right joke, wouldn't it. 'Usband an' wife livin' under separate roofs. We'd be talk o't neighbourhood."

"Do you care, Lew? You don't seem to care about anything at all except the people you write about in the newspaper."

"Decent folk who've 'ad a hard life through no fault of their own."

"I'm not going to quarrel with you, Lew. I thought when we married we would both make a decent effort to be husband and wife, in the true sense, but it seems . . ."

"Aah, tha're offerin' ter drop tha' drawers fer me now, are thi'?" he sneered, turning a contorted face to her and she was appalled at the agony he displayed there.

"I'll be wife to you, Lew, if that's what you want," she said quietly, "when . . . when the baby's born, but in the meantime will you consider sending a message to Lavender. I would be grateful. Will I be after writing a note?"

He flung himself about, almost falling down the stairs in his need to get away from her and the suffering she had caused him, *was* causing him.

"Nay, I'll do it. Theer's a chap I know. 'E's ter go ter Oldham in a few days. 'E'll tekk a message."

"Thank you, Lew."

"Nay, don't thank me. An' *I'll* sleep in't kitchen on't trundle bed. I'd rather . . ." Telling her it would be a relief for him to get away from her and their closeness at the top of the house.

She was coming back from the Dog and Duck after delivering two dozen pies, meat and potato, and meat and gravy, to Mrs Mullaney. Mrs Mullaney had drawn her to one side and questioned her on the possibility of her baking even more, for, she confided, she was pretty certain Mrs Earnshaw's delicacies were beginning to fetch more customers in. A man liked a bit of something decent with his pint of ale. Of course

Mrs Mullaney had always served the customary cheese and hunks of bread, pease pudding and faggots, but the pies were a big draw and if she could fetch those pickled onions and eggs she'd promised Mrs Mullaney would be most appreciative. Mrs Mullaney was very popular with her customers, despite her husband's grim face at the back of her, for she was cheerful and brazen and good-looking in a coarse sort of way. She swung her hips as she walked and tossed her long black hair and her place at the back of the bar was always packed with workmen who liked a joke.

"I'll do my best, Mrs Mullaney, but just at the moment" – grimacing down at her distended belly— "you can see the way of it. I'm not as agile as I was but I've hopes of a friend coming to give me a hand so as soon as she gets here I'm sure I'll be able to accommodate you."

"Right, lass, and when yer time comes see that someone lets me know, will yer?"

"Oh, I won't let you down, Mrs Mullaney."

"I don't mean that, Mrs Earnshaw. I'd like ter know, that's all."

If Clare was surprised by what Mrs Mullaney had said she had no time to dwell on it, for as she pushed her now empty handcart towards Lever Street she was considerably startled to hear her name called out, not her new married name but her christian name, and by a woman.

She turned, twisting the handcart so that an enormous horse pulling a dray piled with casks of beer was forced to come to a frantic stop as his reins were yanked on by his irate driver.

"Yer wanna watch wheer yer goin', yer daft cow," the drayman shouted, then looked rather ashamed to be caught calling names at a woman who was so obviously with child.

Trembling somewhat with shock, Clare pulled into the gutter, leaning on the cart, and when her arm was taken and a piercing shriek sounded in her ear, as she said later, she nearly gave birth on the spot.

"Clare ... Clare, it's me, lass. It's me."

She turned jerkily and was drawn into Lavender's frantic embrace. Lavender was weeping, great fat tears running across her still childishly rounded face. She wore a bonnet, comically large and old-fashioned, but her skirt was decently clean and mended and so was her shawl. She wore her clogs and a pair of black woollen stockings.

"I come as soon as tha' message said. I'd started in't mill again but I were glad ter get shut ... Oh Clare, we've missed thi' an' Nelly ses ter tell thi' ter drink plenty o' milk ... Well, we'd no idea you an' Lew were wed an' then ... will tha' look at yer" – holding wide Clare's arms – "wi' a babby on't way already ..."

Her voice faltered as her eyes ran up and down Clare's swollen figure. Lavender had grown from babyhood in the row of cottages at Edgeclough and had seen getting on for twenty babies born to the women who lived beside her. Though she hadn't been told, or even consciously imbibed the knowledge, she knew as much about childbirth and the process leading up to it as anyone and it was plain that this baby had not been conceived in wedlock. The man who had delivered the message had told them as much as he knew about Mr and Mrs Earnshaw but it had not included details of when they were married or how far along Mrs Earnshaw was with her baby, only the bare facts that Mrs Earnshaw needed her help and was offering her a job. What sort of job it was and how Clare had got herself into the position of being able to offer employment to her had not been made awfully clear.

Clare drew breath and began to laugh. "Lavender ... dear Lavender, will you let me get a word in edgeways? Jesus and all his angels, am I glad to see you. You're an answer to a prayer, so you are and if you knew how I've ... but what the devil are we doing standing here like a couple of eejits. Let's get home at once, for I know Lew'll be glad to see you and I'll be glad to get the weight off my feet. Put your bundle on the handcart and let's try and get through this traffic."

"It's a bugger, ain't it? I'm sorry I shouted and nearly got tha' run over but I were that surprised an' pleased ter see thi'. I were that excited an' all what with the train."

"You've come on a train! Lavender, how brave of you. I've never been on a train in my life. How?"

"Oh, Lew sent the fare fer me to come from Oldham. By Gow, it were that frightenin'."

"Lew sent your fare?" For a moment the dear face of Lew Earnshaw as he used to be crossed her bemused mind and she realised that really he hadn't changed, not one scrap. Under the hurt and the betrayal he felt the old Lew still lurked, for not only had he agreed to send for Lavender to help her in this birth of another man's child, he had sent the money to Edgeclough so that Lavender could get here as soon as possible. It gladdened her heart, for it gave her a glimmer of hope that with time she would be able to ease the old Lew Earnshaw to the surface again. To be as once he had been, to love and be loved and have the pain taken away from him in her arms. She would be his wife, bear his children . . . Jesus, Mary and Joseph, would you listen to her running on about the future and the child not even born yet. But there was hope and Lavender had brought it with her.

"See, let me push the cart," Lavender was saying. "Tha' must be near tha' time an' what Lew's thinkin' on, lettin' tha' push the thing about in this traffic I don't know. Now, is it far?"

"No, just across the street and down that back alley."

They were smiling with the delight of seeing one another after all these months, five was it, they begged to know, and how were Nelly and all the others and there was so much to catch up on and when was the babby due and what was this wonderful job Lavender was to do, not that it mattered, she was just so pleased to be with Clare again and did she remember old Thirza and perhaps if things worked out and with Lavender to stand in for her Clare might go on that fantastic train journey to see Nelly, for Nelly missed her and on and on and on, so overjoyed to be together again neither of them was aware of what was going on about them in the busy street as they trundled the handcart round the corner to the door above which a neat sign had been pinned proclaiming it to be *The Bakery*.

Lavender stopped and stared in reverence.

"Eeh," was all she could manage to say.

Chapter Twenty-six

Rory Patrick Earnshaw was born on a warm night in September. When he was put into her arms, dark and lusty and shouting his vast displeasure at being thrust into a world he did not care for, his mother loved him as passionately as she loved his father. Lavender had held him first, for it was she who had helped Clare bring him forth. Lavender knew what to do for hadn't she been at her mam's side for the birth of her six brothers and sisters, even Poppy who was but two years younger than she was. When you lived in close proximity in a tiny moorland cottage there was not much you didn't know about life in it. Lavender had expertly cut the angry purple cord and then lifted the boy from between Clare's thighs but Clare's arms had reached for him hungrily, almost angrily as though she begrudged him even a moment of Lavender's attention. He was still unwashed with the milky white and blood-red detritus of his passage about him but neither woman cared as they hung over him, adoring him as they were both to do in the years to come.

In the office on the first floor where he had gone when Clare's waters broke, Lew Earnshaw crossed his arms on the rough wooden table, put his head on them and cried with relief and pain, for it was another man's child who was voicing infant rage in the room above and it was another man's woman who had given the child life. He wept for the anguish of it for perhaps five minutes, emptying the grief he had held inside him for so many months, then, wiping his eyes on the arm of his shirt, he stood up and wandered over to the office window, looking out into the darkness of Dale Street. He had never felt so lonely in his life. He had never felt so wretched in his life and the difficulty was he didn't know how to go about getting rid of it. He was, or had been, a man who liked a laugh and making others laugh with him, and sometimes *at* him, since he was not one of those who are conscious of their own importance. He liked people and they liked him. They responded to his amiability, he supposed you would call it and he found he could draw them out and get them to talk, which had been a great advantage since he had become what Henry called a "reporter" for the *Hopwood Review*.

He had loved the same woman for almost three years, hopefully, patiently, but she had loved another man and the result was the wailing cry of the baby just born and how was he to fit into their lives? He wanted to run up the stairs, push the child aside and pull *her* into his arms. He wanted to beg her to love him, to give him another chance, but he had made it quite clear to her over the past months that she, and her coming child, were abhorrent to him. He had found it impossible to forgive her but he had married her hoping for God only knew what, but he was honest enough to admit that the failure of their new relationship had been his fault. So now what?

He stared out into the street, watching without interest as several men wandered by going towards the inn that stood further down towards Piccadilly. A cab, pulled by an ancient, swaybacked nag, ambled in their wake. The window was open and Lew could hear the men's voices and the slow clip of the horse's hooves on the setts. He sighed, leaning his shoulder on the window frame. He could hear small noises from above as the child quietened. A soft laugh, the clink of a bowl against something as the trauma of birth was cleaned up and then the cheerful sound of footsteps clattering down the stairs.

He moved away from the window and sat down hastily at

his desk, hating himself for the small deceit of pretending to be unconcerned about the occurrence upstairs, and when Lavender thrust the door open with her hip and poked her head inside he lifted his head enquiringly as though he had been engrossed with his task and had not noticed.

"'Tis a lad, Lew. A bonny lad an' the image of 'is mam," which was not strictly true for his eyes promised to be as blue as his father's. "Dost tha' not want ter go an' see 'im?" she added, almost as though Lew himself was the proud father.

"Nay, lass, I'm that busy . . ."

"Don't talk rubbish, Lew Earnshaw. Theer's a lovely little lad upstairs 'oo's done nowt ter harm thi', not ter mention 'is mam, 'oo's wantin' ter see thi'." Her voice softened and she looked at him with a compassion far beyond her years. Lavender knew, none better, of Lew's feelings for Clare. The row of cottages in Edgeclough were crammed with families, each of whom knew exactly what went on in the one next door. The Bickerstaffes, the Brethertons, the Cartwrights, the Marsdens and Nelly Bradbury, the matriarch of them all, just as though they were one big family, which they were in a way, had hoped, with Lew, that Clare would eventually wed him. She'd a grand job, true, up at Moorhouse Farm and was still young, only seventeen when she came to them nearly three years ago, so there was plenty of time. But the disaster that had engulfed them, for they were all as stricken as Lew over Clare's affair with Martin Heywood, had seemed to crush any hopes they might have had of a happy ending. When word had come that Lew and Clare were married and there was a babby on the way there had been wild excitement. Lavender was needed, bugger her job at the mill, and so she had to go, Nelly decided and would she do her best to get word to them when the babby was born.

But the situation in the tall house on the corner of Dale Street where both Lew and Clare worked was a terrible shock to young Lavender Bickerstaffe and it had taken her a long time to get used to the idea that though they were married they were not husband and wife, for the child Clare carried belonged to Martin Heywood. She had been appalled when she discovered that Lew was to sleep on a trundle bed in the kitchen, that she was to have Lew's bed at the top of the house and Clare was to sleep in the old iron bedstead where, apparently, she had spent each night, alone, since she and Lew had come to Manchester.

Lavender walked slowly into the office and put the bowl that contained the warm water and stained cloths that had been used to wash Clare and her baby on a side table. Her apron was bloodied and her fair, almost white hair fell in disarray about her pale cheeks, and for a moment Lew felt a spasm of revulsion shiver through him and Lavender saw it.

"Tha' mustn't tekk against this bairn, Lew. 'E's a grand little lad an' Clare's a grand lass, tha' know that. She medd a mistake when she . . . well, we'll say no more about that, but give 'er a chance, lad. She wants ter see thi'. She said ter ask thi' ter come up. Please, Lew. I've known thi' all me life an' tha've never turned their back on anyone. Tha've never bin owt but good-'earted an' generous. I've seen thi' nurse one o't bairns when theer's bin sickness an' I know tha'd put tha' last crust inter a child's mouth. All them childer in the places tha' goes to. Aye, I've read the things tha've wrote about them. Well, this 'un deserves tha' compassion an' all."

She leaned on the desk and her face turned pink with her emotional appeal. Her blue eyes bored into his and they held no judgement, only a great pleading. There was so much at stake. A baby, a good woman, for Clare *was* a good woman despite her fall from grace, and a man who loved her. They had a chance of happiness, couldn't he see that? her expression asked him.

"Go up an' see them, Lew. Tha' don't 'ave ter say owt, neither on yer. Just . . . well, just go up an' see 'em."

"I didn't know tha' read my articles, lass," he said musingly, his eyes looking somewhere into the distance and she wondered if he had heard one word she had said to him. "I didn't know tha' could read?"

She was impatient with him. "Tha' taught me," she said tartly, "an' so did Clare, but don't try ter change subject, Lew Earnshaw. Are thi' ter go up or not?"

He stood up and squared his shoulders, lifting his chin as though he were about to go into a prize-fighting ring and for a moment Lavender had the impression he was going to raise his clenched fists. His face was strained, pale, desperate, but he nodded brusquely.

She was lying in her bed next to the fire which Lavender had heaped up and which crackled cheerfully, spitting out sparks and flinging red and gold shadows across the walls and sloping ceiling. There was a smell, the smell of birth, he supposed, and yet there was also a fragrance that he knew was Clare's, for he had smelled it as she moved about the place. The child lay beside her in the crook of her arm and he felt a sudden surge of relief that she was not suckling him. He did not think he could bear the sight of her breasts which had known the touch of that sod up at Moorhouse.

He stood awkwardly at the top of the stairs, one hand on the banister, waiting, since he did not know what was expected of him. He had come. He had given her the opportunity, and himself, he realised that, to try and mend the yawning rift that stood between them and so what was to come next?

She turned her head from her contemplation of her child and his heart moved crazily in his chest, for he thought he had never seen her look so beautiful. She was tired, he could see that, though it had been a quick and easy birth, with dark circles beneath her eyes. She was pale as though the child had drained her blood with his arrival but she was beautiful, like a madonna, he thought, which he supposed was sacrilegious. It was difficult to imagine her with her body entwined with that of another man, the man who had sired this child and so, with the strength and vigour that he brought to his cause, his fight on behalf of his fellow man, he cast it from his mind. She and the bairn deserved no less.

"Lew," she murmured hesitantly, then held out her hand to him, the desperate appeal in her face melting the doubts and uncertainty, the hatred and jealousy which had sunk their poisonous fangs into his heart and almost destroyed him. Almost destroyed the man he had been and which, God willing, he would become again. His spirit had been badly bruised by the events of the past few months but she seemed to be telling him that if they both were willing to make the effort towards friendship and perhaps more, his wounds would be healed and the scars would fade.

Slowly he walked over to the bed and looked down into her face. His hand reached out and took hers gently, then was tucked between both his. Hers, which was roughened with the hard work she had done all her life, was small and long-fingered and disappeared inside his, which were strong, brown but very gentle. He could not as yet speak, for his throat was clogged with a hundred words that he wanted to say but couldn't. He smiled, then knelt at the bed and, still holding her hand with one of his, turned his gaze on Martin Heywood's son. He touched a tentative forefinger to the child's rosy cheek then to the dark, curling fluff on his head. The baby snuffled as though not quite used to the necessary act of breathing, his nose a soft and shapeless blob above his small, pouting mouth. A starfish hand escaped from the woollen shawl he was wrapped in and waved languidly in the air and without thought Lew put a finger to it and gasped as it was gripped tightly in a fierce fist. He grinned delightedly, the end of the grin washing over Clare as he turned his face to her.

They still did not speak. The child was the bond between them, the link from one to the other and the link was frail. The child held Lew to the side of the bed. It was because of the child that he was here and though he could not yet admit to the hope that he and Clare were to be the man and wife he had yearned for, he knew it was a beginning.

She was up and about within three days though Lew and Lavender swore they would tie her to the bloody bed if she tried to get out of it.

"Don't talk daft, Lavender," she said shortly when Lew went downstairs. She swung her legs out of the bed. "I've a business to run and can't be lolling about like some lady of leisure. Yes, sweetheart, I know you've done wonders during the past few weeks and all our customers have been very loyal but . . . well, I mean to expand. To see if I can't sell to some of the smarter shops along Deansgate and Market Street, even to the stall holders in Smithfield Market and I mean to have a walk over to St Ann's Square to see if there are any provision merchants that are in need of high-class foodstuffs."

"Foodstuffs?" Lavender questioned blankly, as she did her best to lever Clare back into bed.

"Yes, the kind of things we make. I still have Mrs Case's recipe books and with that kitchen range downstairs I think I could make any of the dishes she writes about. Certainly those made with pastry. And then there's bread. Those high-class places who sell unadulterated tea and coffee and flour will require their goods to be—"

"Unadulterated?" Lavender's voice was wary, for she did not know what the word meant but the tone was also strong with her determination to stuff Clare under the bed covers for at least another week.

"Yes, with nothing added like the chalk and brick dust they put in some things to make them weigh heavier, and will you, by all that's holy, stop trying to keep me in this bloody bed, for I mean to get up the minute your back's turned, or do you intend sitting beside me all day in which case my customers will go elsewhere."

"Stuff an' nonsense, there's not one of 'em 'oo doesn't ask after thi' an' that Mrs Mullaney tha' knows, from 't Dog an' Duck, she ses to call the minute tha' can. Oh, an' I forgot, she asked me ter give thi' this."

"This" turned out to be a tiny frilled bonnet, tucked and adorned with a multitude of embroidered motifs, so dainty and exquisite it seemed a shame to use it.

"She never made it?" Clare said with awe, for Kitty Mullaney was the last person she would have expected to be so handy with a needle.

"Nay, don't ask me but it's right pretty, innit?"

"It's the loveliest thing I've ever seen. Sure an' doesn't it put to shame the bits o' things I made meself."

Giving up the battle and deciding that if she couldn't keep Clare in her bed she'd best be at her side to give her a hand in whatever she meant to do, Lavender sighed resignedly and passed her the skirt and bodice Clare indicated, the woollen stockings Clare herself had knitted and the sturdy clogs that kept her feet off the cold stone flags of the kitchen.

It was a Sunday and the presses were silent. Henry and Albert were about their own weekend business, whatever that might be, but from downstairs there came the sound of hammering. It seemed to be quite a distance away, hollow and echoing up the staircase as though it were taking place in a confined space.

"What's going on downstairs?"

Lavender moved across the room, bending her head to avoid the sloping ceiling. She peered down into the large cardboard box that was the baby's cradle, her face taking on that infatuated look of adoration which infects women when they look on a newborn infant as she gazed at the tiny, sleeping face of Rory Earnshaw. He wasn't her baby but he was so handsome and not a scrap of trouble to her or his mam, sleeping peacefully and when he was not sleeping taking sustenance from his mam's overflowing breast. Lavender had doted on him from the moment he had come yelling from his mother's womb.

"It's Lew."

"Lew? What's he making all that row for?"

"He's down in't cellar wi' a—"

"Cellar? What cellar?" Clare looked up in astonishment in the act of pulling on her stockings.

"Well, Mr 'Opwood's cellar, I suppose."

"Mr 'Opwood's cellar." Clare shook her head as though to clear the befuddlement that seemed to have lodged there. "I didn't know Mr Hopwood *had* a cellar."

"Neither did I. Neither did anybody, not even that Albert. Lew was lookin' fer somewhere ter do a bit o' woodwork and Mr 'Opwood said, casual-like, why didn't Lew use t'cellar seeing as there were nowt but junk in it."

"Holy Mary Mother of God, what next? First the kitchen, now a bloody cellar. This house is like . . . well, sure an' I don't know what it's like, rooms appearing in every nook an' cranny and round every corner. Where was it hidden, for heaven's sake?"

"Behind that big cupboard in't th'allway. Theer's a door an' steps leadin' down."

"Into a cellar! And all this time I've been looking for somewhere to store my stuff, flour and suchlike. I could buy in bulk if I had somewhere to put it. What the devil is Lew making down there? I didn't know he was handy with a hammer and nails."

"Oh aye," Lavender said placidly. "'E often used ter mekk things for't folk in't row. Cupboards an' shelves an' such. I've sin 'im put together a grand chair an' once—"

"Watch the baby," Clare called to her from halfway down the stairs, holding her skirt high and making an enormous clatter on the bare treads with her clogs.

"'Ere, tha' shouldn't be dashin' about like that," Lavender remonstrated, but she might as well have addressed her remark to the sleeping infant in the cardboard box for all the notice that was taken of her.

The cupboard in question had been moved further up the hallway, almost blocking the door that led into Albert's sanctum and Clare had time to wonder what Albert would think about that. Poor chap was already working in half the space he once had. She supposed he'd known nothing about it or he would have put what he called his "equipment" down there instead of traipsing up and down two flights of stairs to the bit of the attic space he had been allowed. Honestly, Henry really was a scatterbrain, totally impractical and thoughtless except when it came to his newspaper and what was written in it. He cared as passionately as Lew about the redress of social ills, clean water, universal franchise, the six points of the People's Charter, education for all, and, like Feargus O'Connor, was a champion of "the unshorn chins, the blistered hands and the fustian jackets" of the working man. But he came from a cushioned background and had never shared the suffering of those he fought for, as Lew had, and though all this was nothing to do with his feather-headed forgetfulness regarding the cellar, it was an indication of his drifting approach to life in general.

Cautiously she moved down the cellar steps, met by a mixture of smells. There was damp, for the cellar was below ground. There was the hot whiff of an oil lamp, there was an aroma of pipe tobacco and there was the fragrance of what smelled like new wood.

Lew had his back to her, leaning over something on a sturdy table and for a moment she was again plagued by the wonderment of how such an enormous piece of furniture had been got down the narrow stairs. Lew was smoothing something with short gentle strokes and when, hearing her on the bottom step, he turned abruptly she saw it was a simple cradle. A cradle of plain pine, practical and sturdy. It had two rockers, one at each end and on the small headboard was carved a bird standing on a twig.

He wanted to smile and show his pleasure at her appearance. He wanted to take her hand and lead her forward to see what he had made for her son, but it was too early for that in the fragile mending of their life together and so he frowned and shook his head in exasperation.

"Now then, what the devil are tha' doin' outa tha' bed, woman? 'Tis but three days since the lad were born an' 'ere tha' are gallopin' about like a bairn." He glared at her, standing in front of his handiwork in an attempt to hide it, the sandpaper with which he had been smoothing the wood held in his big, workman's hand. "Now, get thi' gone an' don't let me see tha' downstairs fer a fortnight. Lavender can see ter all that's necessary. Go an' see to't babby."

"The babby has been seen to, Lew, and is sleeping."

"An' so should tha' be, an' all. Tha' needs ter get tha' strength back afore tha' comes racin' up an' down them bloody stairs. See, if tha' won't do as tha're told, sit thi' down an' rest," indicating a frayed and faded old armchair which she would have given her right arm for while she was pregnant.

"Lew, stop it. I'm quite recovered and feel as fit as a butcher's dog so won't you show me what you're doing?"

He moved clumsily, still awkward with her and she knew it would be a long time before their old ease and friendship with one another returned. Stepping away from the table he let her see what it was that he was making, making for her and for her son.

"'Tis fer't little lad," he said shyly, his lean face colouring up, his eyes soft with some deep emotion. "'Appen tha' could line it wi' summat so 'e don't knock his little 'ands against wood. Mind, I've smoothed it down an' then buffed it so there'll be no splinters ter bother 'im. Feel it, lass."

He watched as she ran her hands over the honey-coloured wood.

"It's like silk, Lew," she whispered, her eyes beginning to film with tears. "It's beautiful . . ."

"Nay," he protested, "'tis plain an'—"

"It's beautiful," she insisted, and the tears ran across her cheeks and splashed on to the clean cotton of her bodice, leaving round stains the size of a penny. This was the most important moment of her life, she acknowledged it, for it was from this moment her future would be decided. This man was her husband. He was a good man, the kindest she had ever known and would be a fine father for her child. He would make no move until she had shown him it was welcome. It must be she who took the next step.

"Nay," he was saying, "it's nowt ter skrike over, lass, just a bit of a thing ter put lad in of a night. See, dry tha' eyes an' I'll tell thi' what I'm ter mekk next."

"Next?"

"Oh aye, I've allus bin 'andy wi' a bit o' wood."

"Lavender said," she sniffed.

"Theer's a timber merchant up along an' 'e said I could 'ave bits an' pieces what 'e couldn't use. Fer a price, like, so . . ."

"How big are these bits and pieces, Lew?"

He looked perplexed, bending to peer into her wet face, still embarrassed but doing his best to be easy with her.

"Nay, lass, was there summat tha' wanted then? 'Appen a chair or . . ."

"A bed, Lew. A big bed. The sort of bed husband and wife sleep in."

She bent her head and stared at the floor on which shavings of wood were scattered, stirring them with her toe, then looked up abruptly and was shattered by the look of joy on his face. It was followed by disbelief and a kind of haunted suffering as though he really could not stand this if it turned out not to be the truth. It was unbelievable that she would be teasing, pulling his leg, he knew that, but he just could not believe in what she *seemed* to be telling him.

"A . . . bed?" he stammered and it was perhaps this, his boyish awkwardness, his hope and incredulity as though some great boon had been granted him, something he had hankered after as a boy and as a man, that gave her the courage to lift her arms and put them round his trembling shoulders. He stood for so long, his arms hanging by his side, that she began to believe that she had been mistaken, that he wanted nothing from her but the friendship they had known in the past, then his arms lifted and with a great shout he put them round her, gripping her so fiercely she shut her eyes in pain. He lifted her from her feet and in his exultation she thought he might swing her round like he would a child but she was no child and Lew Earnshaw was no boy.

Gently he set her down, then, his hands on her shoulders as though she still might escape him, he bent his head and brushed her lips with his. It was a soft, butterfly kiss, barely flattening her lips, then, when she responded just as gently but with warmth, the kiss deepened. His lips folded about hers, and he moved his head as his tongue gently probed, then entered her mouth.

For a dreadful moment she felt her flesh, which still loved and longed for Martin Heywood, shrivel and begin to recoil from this stranger's body, then she sank against him, for only in complete submission could she convince him that she loved him. She *did* love him and surely it would be no hardship to allow her husband the complete freedom of her body.

"Christ Jesus," he murmured, bending his tall frame and sliding his lips along the line of her jaw. "Clare … Clare, is this what you want? Can it be true?"

"Yes, acushla," using her mother's endearment.

"Acushla …" He strained her body closer to his and she felt the swelling in his breeches press against her, then she began to laugh softly.

At once he drew back, for Lew Earnshaw was still unsure about this woman's feelings for him.

"I'm sorry, Lew," she murmured, her eyes shining up into his face so that he was in no doubt of her meaning. "I was just thinking you'd best get over to that timber merchant's as soon as you can since it seems we are in sore need of a bed!"

Chapter Twenty-seven

It was just before Christmas when she and Lavender were running round like demented souls with the devil on their tails trying to complete every order; when every room, even the one in which she and Lew slept, was bursting at the seams with provisions for the festive season; when the baby was howling his protests at being kept waiting for his dinner, then his tea and then his supper, that Clare made her decision. It would be a gamble, for though she was run off her feet, she and Lavender baking, or so it seemed, for every family in Manchester and its environs, and the profits were growing nicely in her brand-new bank account, was she ready after such a short period of time to expand her business? The problem was that the house in which, let's face it, two businesses were vying with one another for space was just not big enough for five adults and a demanding baby and it would not be long before she would need to employ another girl to help in the kitchen.

It was when the sign was tacked into the window of the shop on the opposite corner to the newspaper, stating that it was for rent, that she knew she must grit her teeth and take the chance. The shop, exactly like the one in which Henry ran his newspaper, was in a choice position, only halfway down Dale Street on the corner of Lever Street not far from the main thoroughfare of Oldham Street, and had the advantage that her customers, growing every day, had only to cross the street to find her. She would have a shop window in which to display her wares, an enormous kitchen behind the shop area, a scullery and her own tiny back yard in which to store the handcart at night. There would be a parlour and dining-room on the first floor and above that three bedrooms and an airy attic and beneath the shop a cellar for Lew's own tiny business venture.

Lew was still involved with his mission in Church Row and Dyche Street. Children still went to work in the mills for thirteen hours a day, deprived of anything that might be called an education, exercise, fresh air or sleep. They were stunted and had deformities caused by malnutrition and the dreadful conditions in which they existed, the filthy atmosphere of the streets, their homes and the mills themselves, and Lew would still go on writing about it in the *Hopwood Review* in the hope that his words might be the instrument to change their lives. No, he wouldn't give up his work on the newspaper, for his ties to its radical beliefs were strong and unbreakable, but the little oddments of furniture he "knocked up", his words, when Clare was busy of an evening, gave him great satisfaction.

It had begun with Kitty Mullaney. To Clare's great surprise, about two weeks after the birth of Rory, Albert had shouted up the stairs that there was someone to see her and was it all right if she came up.

Clare was just settling Rory into his new cradle which she had lined with pale blue flannelette padded with felt, all bought for next to nothing on the market. Lew had been aghast when she stated her intention of just taking a stroll down to Smithfield which, after all, was a fair step when it was no more than ten days since she had had a child, or so he told her and if she'd write down what she wanted he'd go for her. Or better yet, why didn't she send Lavender?

"In the name o' God, Lew, can you not see Lavender's

run off her feet keeping the bakery going an' hasn't time to be running errands for me. Anyway, I fancy a bit of fresh air, or what passes for fresh air in this benighted town so I'm to wrap Rory Patrick in me shawl, like the mammy used to do and walk with him down to the market."

They argued for five minutes or more but Lew was beginning to realise that his wife had a mind of her own and when she made it up to do something nothing would stop her. He'd known that before he married her, of course, but in his heart, where wisdom over a loved one was not known to thrive, once they had begun to share a bed he had hoped that she would become as obedient and docile as a husband would like a wife to be. He didn't know why, really, for it was her vitality, her spirit, her dash and fire he loved and if she had begun to say "yes, Lew" and "no, Lew" he supposed he would have been bewildered by it. But he did think she was not yet strong enough to walk the length of Oldham Street and along Swann Street to the market, especially carrying the boy who was thriving and plump.

She went, leaving him standing on the doorstep exhorting her to have a rest at the other end if she could find a handy seat and to take it steady and why didn't she let him call her a cab, but she only laughed over her shoulder.

"Get on with ye, Lew Earnshaw, I'm not in me dotage yet and if I can't walk a few steps up the street then it's in a wheelchair I should be. Now go inside and get on with that article or you'll have Henry on your tail, so you will."

She enjoyed herself, showing off her son to all the stall holders who knew her, proud as punch and so happy, or perhaps content would be a better description, after the months of tribulation and misery, that she barely noticed the child's weight or her own growing desire to have a sit down, which she did the minute she got home.

Her visitor was Kitty Mullaney. She came puffing up the stairs, barely recognisable in her "walking out" clothes: a bonnet of straw trailing with feathers and ribbons and on top of which a dejected bird lolled, a wide skirt of purple satin held out by a vast crinoline – which could barely be got up the narrow stairs – a bodice to match which was so tight it seemed her bosom was struggling to get out, a mantle of violent emerald-green velvet and boots with a fringed top. Evidently her corset was laced so tightly she was ready to faint and she had to stand at the top of the stairs, her hand to her heaving bosom, doing her best to get her breath.

"These bloody corsets'll be the death o' me one o' these days, but yer've ter put up wi' it if yer want ter be fashionable, isn't that so, chuck? Good job I don't have ter wear the things in the bar or I'd get nowt done."

She was like a peacock in her glory, even Rory seeming to turn his vague gaze in her direction.

"Mrs Mullaney, how lovely to see you," Clare stammered in the best manner of Elizabeth Bennet in *Pride and Prejudice*. "Won't you come in and ... well, do sit down. Can I offer you a cup of tea?"

"Yer can that, lass, an' 'appen yer've got one of them cakes yer were telling me about a while back. That's if yer've returned ter yer kitchen after yer lyin'in."

"Of course, I'll run down and fetch a selection for you to choose from. I made them last night while Rory—"

"Nay, I 'aven't even had a look at ... what's 'is name, Rory? Irish, is he?"

Mrs Mullaney pursed her lips but though she knew Mrs Earnshaw had been married only three or four months who was she to pass judgement?

"Not really, but I was born in Ireland as you can possibly tell."

"Aye, that I can but hubby's not from there, is he?"

"Oh, no, he's ..."

"Aye, Lancashire, just like me an' none the worse fer it, lass. It's Mullaney who comes from the 'owd country', as he calls it. Now, get babby outer that cradle an' put 'im on me knee while I get a look at 'im."

Rory allowed himself to be handled with great good humour, seeming to be aware of the honour that was being bestowed on him, for Kitty Mullaney, having none of her own, and wanting none, was not particularly fond of children. She looked him up and down, even turning him over a time or two but he bore it equably and when Clare laid him back in his cradle he at once fell asleep as though the experience had exhausted him.

Kitty, as she begged Clare to call her, said she was glad she'd liked the little cap but she couldn't claim credit for it. Her sister was a seamstress and did the loveliest embroidery but many thanks for the note Clare'd sent which she'd passed on to their Beatrice. She'd got one of the chaps in the bar parlour to read it to her so she could tell her the gist of it since neither she nor Beatrice could read. She drank her tea with her little finger crooked in what she evidently thought was the height of gentility and complimented Clare on her cakes which, when Clare was back on her feet, she might try a few of on a daily basis. Not that men liked a cake with their ale, she explained, but she herself was very partial to a coconut macaroon which her mam used to make and Mr Mullaney was the same.

"Now then," she said, abruptly cutting short Clare's appreciative thanks and assurances that she'd certainly do her best, "what about that there cradle?"

Clare turned to stare at it in bewilderment, the change from confectionery to woodwork quite taking her breath away.

"The cradle?"

"Aye, where did yer get it?"

"My husband made it, Mrs ... Kitty. It seems, though I wasn't aware of it myself, he is quite adept with saws and hammers and such."

"Good with 'is hands, yer mean?" Kitty Mullaney liked to call a spade a spade.

"Well, yes."

"Would he mekk me one?" She began to laugh, tickled by the expression of astonishment on Clare's face. "Nay, lass, it's not fer me. I'm past such things, even if I was interested, which I'm not. My Alfie knows that. No, it's our Beatrice's lass. She's expectin' her first at Christmas and I thought that'd mekk a nice present for 'er. Special like seein' as it's the first grandchild in't family. Would hubby be interested? I'd pay 'im, of course."

That was how it began, Lew's own small venture. If you put a picture in front of him he seemed to have a knack for copying pieces of furniture. Simple things at first, a kitchen chair of beech; a firescreen of walnut in which the lady who had ordered it, a friend of Henry's, had the flowers she had embroidered on canvas, framed. A small wall cabinet with a bit of carving on the door, a side table with barley-sugar legs, and a padded stool which Clare was to put her feet on when she rested.

"Rest," she said later to Lavender. "The only rest I get is in me bed. But I suppose I'd better let him see me with me feet on the thing or he'll be upset."

They had shared the same bed for a month before Lew, at her invitation, first became a husband to her. She had thought during that month that perhaps it had been a mistake for them to sleep together until she was healed from her birth wounds and she was right, for she could sense each night the strained prescence, the tense rigidity of her husband next to her in the bed he had made for them. He kissed her gently and, when they were not in their bed, held her in his arms, or even laughingly sat her on his knee, but she knew the strain on him was enormous. She had known only one man before him. Martin Heywood had been a passionate man, taking the initiative with vigour, taking her whenever he could get his hands on her, but Lew Earnshaw was a man of great inner quietness totally unlike the arrogance of Martin despite his merry sense of humour. He had a warmth and a gentleness about him that cushioned her from hurt but also created a diffidence in him, particularly in the circumstances of their marriage.

He waited each night until she was under the covers before coming up the stairs and slipping beside her into the bed he had made.

"Go to sleep, lass," he would say. "Tha'll be tired." He would take her face between his hands and kiss the corners of her mouth lightly before turning his back to her and falling asleep himself. She was thankful and grateful, for though she was healing quickly from the birth of Rory Patrick she was still afraid that at the last moment, when the time came for her body to accept Lew's, she might shrink from it. In her mind she did not feel repelled by the thought of another man being to her what Martin had once been, but her heart, which still mourned the loss of the man she loved, might rebel and cause her to give offence.

She woke far into the night, aware, in the confused moment of waking that something was wrong, that the warmth she had become used to was missing. That the space beside her was empty.

"Lew," she called, sitting up and peering into the shadows about the room, thinking perhaps he had gone to the cradle to check the baby, which he did now and again.

"Lew," she repeated.

"I'm 'ere, sweet'eart."

He was sitting on one of the straight-backed chairs which had been one of the first things they had bought for their small home. His upright posture, outlined by the flickering flames of the fire, was rigid with some dreadful burden he carried and with that part of her that Martin Heywood had brought to life she knew exactly what it was.

"Come to me, Lew," she said in a low voice.

She did not expect pleasure from this first encounter and was not surprised when she found none. Lew groaned in what seemed to be despair but his hands were gentle on her body and when she removed her nightgown and allowed him to gaze at her wonderingly she thought he might weep, which was ridiculous for there was no stronger man than Lew Earnshaw. His stroking, enquiring fingertips, ready to withdraw at her slightest protest, released in her none of the feline languour, the great stretching and purring that she had known with Martin, but there was no disgust as he penetrated her, taking final possession of her with a long shuddering cry of triumph that she was sure Lavender must have heard.

When it was done he got up abruptly and walked naked across the room and she saw for the first time the lean strength of his body, the deep chest, the flat belly, the perfectly proportioned legs, the dark mat of hair on his chest which ran down his stomach to the soft bulge of his genitals. He was a fine man, not handsome, but pleasing to any woman and she knew she must let him know it, and at once. She was not sure what was in his mind. Had she pleased *him*, or had her submissiveness given him the impression that she was merely being the obedient wife?

"Turn round, Lew, and come back to bed. I love you and want you with me. We are ... please, Lew, come to me again."

He made love to her three times that night, doing his best to handle her gently, for she was only just recovered from childbirth but she would not let him leave her this time and when it was over she held him to her, his cheek resting on her full breast, kissing him lovingly, not desiring him but wanting him to desire her and requiring most urgently to fulfil his every need.

"I love thi', Clare."

"I know you do, acushla, and I'm glad of it."

And so their marriage began. Every night he made love to her in the deep and comfortable feather bed which she and Lavender had made themselves and which lay on the frame Lew had fashioned. It was sweet-smelling, for they had sewn lavender into it. Every day he made numerous excuses to come down to the bakery to snatch a kiss when no one was looking, to caress her breasts and hold her close to him as though he had to put his mark on her time and time again to convince himself that this woman was, at last, his. He couldn't get enough of her. He was besotted with her, rapturous in his happiness, doting on the child because it was hers, Martin Heywood completely wiped from his mind, or so he would have her think.

"This lad gets more like thi' every day, my lass," he would say, which was true except for the colour of his eyes which were the deep penetrating blue of his father. They were the blue of hyacinths in spring, harebells in May, the sky over Badgers Edge on a hot summer day and yet in some light they were the colour of the heather that spread across the moorland beyond Edgeclough. Lew would sit in the armchair they had found in the cellar, bend his leg, the ankle resting on the other knee and hold the boy in the safe nest it made. They would study one another with great intent, then Rory would smile with a wobbly movement of his head as though the smile had made him unsteady and Lew would lean to place a soft kiss on his cheek. It was as though as he did with her, he was putting his mark, his impression on the mind of Martin Heywood's child, making him his.

There was a feeling of great content in the house on Dale Street that winter so that even Henry, who had been horrified when it was revealed that Clare was pregnant, whistled about his desk and even condescended to peep into the cradle when he thought no one was looking. Albert would often sneak up to the attic, leaving his machines, which were grinding out handbills and posters, and the lumbering great flatbed on which the *Hopwood Review* was printed each Friday. Still wearing the indescribably filthy apron in which he worked he was often to be found with Rory Patrick in his arms, pretending he had been crying and needed a bit of a "hold", and was most distressed when he was informed that the babby, who was by then five months old, was moving out of the establishment of the *Hopwood Review* to take up residence elsewhere.

"Yer what?" He was appalled, ready to argue and perhaps burst into tears, for what was the little lad to do without Albert to comfort him. He said so with great indignation just as though the poor little lad would fade away and die without Albert to watch over his upbringing.

"Albert, we's only goin' across road. Clare needs more space fer 'er pies an' what-not an' I'll be glad o't cellar ter messen. I'm pulled out wi' orders fer cradles an' such. I'm beginning ter think every lass in Manchester's 'avin' a bairn. Anyroad, we've tekken th'ouse on't next corner so tha'll only 'ave a step or two ter come an' see our Rory."

"It won't be't same," Albert said petulantly, in high dudgeon over the plan to move "our Rory" to a new home. He was fond of Clare and Lavender who were both grand lasses and good workers, which meant a lot in Albert's eyes, for like most northeners he did admire lasses who could "fettle", but their intended removal, even if it would give them a step up in the world, meant little to him. The fact that he was to have his store-room back was a bit of good news but it could not make up for the move across the street and the loss of Rory Patrick.

"Dammit, tha'd think we was goin' ter Timbuctoo, wherever that is, the way 'e carries on." Lew smiled as he pulled his wife down in the bed next to him and began to stroke her thigh under her nightgown. Obligingly she took it off and pushed the bed clothes down, offering the whole of her body to his eyes since she knew it pleased him and Clare Earnshaw's chief role in life was to please this good man who was her husband.

"Our Rory's made a lot of difference to Albert, you should be able to see that, acushla. He's never had children or even a woman as far as I can make out and his life must have been pretty empty. He loves the boy."

"I know, my queen, we all do."

"I'm not so sure about Henry. He was glad enough to see you last year when you turned up but I think I was a bit of a facer. He's another chap who—"

"Give over, my lass. What the 'ell do I care fer Henry or anyone come to that when I've me wife in me arms which brings me ter this . . ." And with the confidence that had grown in him over the months he took possession of her and seemed quite satisfied with her warmth and eager responsiveness, unaware that her body was as unawakened as that of a woman who had never known the touch of a man. He knew she loved him. He had her here in his bed, didn't he, and he knew his Clare well enough by now to know that she would never lie with a man whom she did not love. He questioned no further than that and deep inside him, where no one, even himself, could hear, or refused to hear, that part of him that whispered of his wife's past, of the man in it and the boy in the cradle who was the result of it, lay sleeping.

The house across the street was scrubbed and whitewashed – three coats! – from its attics to its cellars. Its kitchen range, the exact same design as the one in the kitchen in the house on the opposite corner of the street, was given the same dramatic treatment with the rust remover, the paste of fresh lime and water and a thorough going over with the blacklead until it gleamed like ebony. But the greatest marvel was when she discovered, as the agent showed her round what was to be her new premises, that there was piped water into the house, installed by the previous owner, which came out of a tap, her very own tap, in to the scullery sink.

"The water comes from Glossop, madam," the agent had

told her proudly as though he himself had laid the pipes that brought it.

She bought remnants of material from the market and made curtains and a counterpane for their bed. Lavender's room was given as much attention as the rest of the house with even a bit of carpet for her to put her feet on when she rose from her bed. They bought two ewers and basins for the bedrooms, slightly chipped but pretty with birds and flowers painted on them and as the new year took hold they moved in, running across the street with this or that, or dragging what couldn't be carried. Albert, much against his will, for wasn't the move to take "their Rory" from under Albert's roof, helped with bits and pieces, even offering to mind the lad while they were busy.

Lew ran down to the Dog and Duck and came back with a foaming jug of ale and, from Kitty, a small bottle of port for the ladies. After they were settled into the big, sparklingly clean kitchen, sitting about the new work table, for the old one could not be moved owing to its size, they drank health to their new home and those who were to live in it, eating the delicious meat and potato pies that Clare had hurriedly baked in her new oven, along with the deep custard tart that was Lavender's contribution. Albert began to mellow, especially as the missis insisted that he was to come round any time he wanted, for Rory was bound to miss him and he wouldn't want him upset, would he? Though he wouldn't have said so for the world, Albert was as pleased as punch by her words, wending his way back to his spartan rooms which, before the missis and her family had come into his life, had seemed perfectly adequate.

Her customers, those who worked in the mills and factories, came somewhat diffidently at first, since her shop was so much grander than her back scullery door. There was even a sign painted on the window in a curlicued and stylish arc which said: *Earnshaw's Bakery*. Her pies and tarts, her pickles and jams and marmalades, her fresh bread made daily, her scones, her brawn, her pickled tongues, cheap and nourishing, her biscuits and cakes, her pickled eggs, all the wonderful recipes in Mrs Case's books, were arranged in attractive display on fancy doilies on the graduated shelves Lew had made for her. They soon became accustomed to standing in line inside the shop, which was a great deal warmer than hanging about in the cold morning air of the back alley. They couldn't get over her success, they told one another, but then she was a working lass just like themselves and didn't she deserve it, the way she worked. She'd certainly made a difference to their lives. And that babby of hers was a charmer, lying in his little cradle against the counter, smiling at everyone who peeped in on him, and later, when he could sit up, strapped in the grand chair his pa made for him and, in his baby fashion, talking to them all as though they were his greatest friends. They were a gradely couple and if they wondered at times where the boy got his vivid blue eyes since hers were green and his were grey they made no mention of it. Well, she had been five months pregnant when they were wed so who knew what her past contained but it was nothing to do with them, for they had been brought up to mind their own business. Aye, a grand lass with no side to her and so was Lavender, as she begged them to call her, and when a young lass of no more than twelve was taken on, scrubbing and polishing as though her life depended on it, it was felt that Mrs Earnshaw was well on the way to competing with the Manchester Co-operative Society who had, it was said, nineteen branches in the area!

And although Clare was starting to branch out into more ornate dishes, for now she had the shop she was catering to a better class of customer, the lower-middle-class housewife who was thrifty but could afford to pay a few more pence for her family's food, she never forgot her first customers. Every morning at just gone seven o'clock there would be Minnie and Ida, Etty and Mary and the others with their stunted children about them, buying her dripping butties, her three for a penny pies, her fresh bread spread with butter and sometimes the jam she had made from Mrs Case's recipes. She had bought fruit at the back-end of the year, not exactly on the turn, but getting a bit soft for most customers' taste, which was sold at a fraction of its normal price since the stall holders were glad to be shut of it. Strawberries, raspberries, blackcurrants, damson and plum, all boiled up in a big pan on her kitchen range then put into pots, covered with oiled paper and then tissue-paper brushed on both sides with the white of an egg. It was cheap and added the sweet taste the children craved on their butties.

She was content. Though she was married to Lew and was now pretty certain she was carrying his child, she still retained that feeling of separateness, that sense of being apart from others that she had known when she became housekeeper to Martin Heywood. She supposed it was because she had never forgotten her family in Ireland and what she and they had experienced. She could still see in her mind's eye her mother's dead face as she lay, arms outstretched, doing her tragic best to protect her young family in a ditch on the road to Dublin and memories such as these were bound to shape the way her life had gone. Only her passionate love for Martin had sheltered her from these horrors and she was aware, sadly, that she would love him until the day she died. He had her heart. Her affection for Lew was boundless, but she did not have that bond with him she had known with Martin. He was a good man, a simple man who was completely satisfied in his life with her and would be ecstatic when she told him of the coming child but she did not feel that he really *knew* her, despite living side by side with her for so long.

Nevertheless, life was good. She had her work, her son, Martin's son, her friendship with Lavender who was as her younger sister, and her growing fondness for Kitty Mullaney. If she had any regrets about their move to Manchester it was that she missed Nelly but, when her baby was born and she could leave Lavender in charge of Earnshaw's Bakery, she meant to take her children and visit the woman who loved her as her own mammy had done.

Chapter Twenty-eight

Her second son was born in November that year. They called him Joss in memory of the man who had lived in Edgeclough and who had led the men of the north, just before Lew was born, in the cause for equality for all men which Lew held so dear. The radical cause was still being fought in newspapers like the *Hopwood Review*, the *Poor Man's Guardian*, with its banner *Knowledge is Power*, and the Chartist newspaper, the *Northern Star* owned by Feargus O'Connor, the leader of the great Chartist demonstration in London three years before.

Joss Earnshaw. He was a miniature replica of his father. Not as handsome as his older brother and without that rosy-cheeked, chubby look of the newborn, he was long in the leg and in the body and though it seemed a strange thing to say about a baby, almost lean, just like Lew. His hair was thick and brown with no curl in it and even from the first day always looked untidy no matter how many times his mother or Lavender brushed it. His eyes, when he opened them lazily as though not awfully sure he wanted to look at this new world into which he had been precipitated, were long and silvery grey. His mouth was wide and his chin pugnacious and Henry was heard to remark that Rory Patrick would have his work cut out dominating his little brother as he dominated everyone else in the household. Except him, of course, and perhaps Kitty Mullaney.

Within an hour of his birth Clare was sitting up, her hair brushed back and tied with a green ribbon, her face flushed with triumph, her green eyes snapping, tucking into the apricot flan Lavender had just taken from the oven. She was famished, she protested, and so would they be, meaning Lavender and Lew, if they had worked as hard as she had.

But for once she was not the centre around which Lew Earnshaw's world orbited. Lew Earnshaw had thought his world was complete when he and Clare became not only husband and wife, but lovers. Now, with his son in his arms he knew he had been wrong. Clare was the woman, the only woman he had ever loved, or would ever love. His life was her, his heart was her, for she was in the core of it, but this scrap of humanity was flesh of his flesh, a small part of him that had been reborn and he loved him as passionately as Clare had loved *her* son when he was born.

Neither Clare nor Lavender remembered, or if they did chose not to dwell on it, the way Clare had acted when Rory Patrick came yelling into the world. Her eagerness to get him in her arms and no one else's. Her reluctance to let him go even to be cleaned and her inclination to hang over his cradle when he was not actually in her arms. She was much more casual about this one.

"Well, acushla, will he do?" Clare demanded, quite spellbound by the way Lew cradled the boy, by the protective, defensive manner in which he cushioned him against his own strong chest, the way in which his hands trembled with some deep emotion that had been unlocked from within him, his marvelling look of wonder and joy. His eyes slowly looked away from his son to her as though they could not really bear to tear themselves away from the red and clamouring face of Joss Earnshaw even for her and his worship, of her and of the boy she had given him, was almost embarrassing in its exultation.

But Rory Patrick, just at the toddling stage and who had been denied access to his mother's room for several hours and had not liked it, was shouting to climb on her bed, to share her apricot flan which he thought a splendid idea to eat there instead of at the table. He began to leap about, demanding that they look at him and not at the strange noisy creature who had invaded what he had come to regard as his territory.

At once Lew handed the baby to Lavender and took Rory on to his lap and held him close, kissing his cheek and blowing into the creases of his chubby neck to make him squeal with laughter, and Clare felt tears come to her eyes for love of this good man who was showing such sensitivity for a boy who was not his son. Lew had treated him as such for fourteen months now, giving him the love he would have done to a boy of his own, but now he *had* a boy of his own in the bigness of his heart he was willing to pass the baby to Lavender while he made a fuss of Rory.

They exchanged glances over Rory's head and Lew was mesmerised by the warmth and depth of her love which showed in her eyes and in her smiling expression. She sat up and leaned towards him, taking his hand and with the boy between them, chortling with laughter and enormously pleased at being squeezed between his mother and father, she kissed him. She put a hand to his cheek and held it lovingly, looking into his eyes, and though she did not speak her love for him shone in hers.

Joss was three days old when she insisted on getting up.

"Clare, tha' can't mean ter get out o' tha' bed so soon,' the shocked Lavender said. "Lew'll 'ave a bloody fit. 'E told me most particular that I weren't ter tekk me eyes off thi' an' I'm . . ."

Clare sighed dramatically, handing Lavender the baby who had just been fed, then, Lavender having her hands full and temporarily unable to prevent it, threw back the covers and got out of bed.

"Lavender Bickerstaffe, did anyone ever tell you that you are fast becoming a dictator. I've heard the way you boss poor Tilly about but all I can say is it won't work with me. Heaven help us if I don't get back to work soon. It needs all of us to keep the deliveries going out and the supplies to make them coming in. You and Tilly have been wonderful but I can see how tired you are."

"Me! Tired? Never. An' as fer Tilly, she's a right little work'orse an'—"

"I know that and so I'm getting up. Even if I don't get down to the shop I shall at least sit at the table in the dining-room and take a look at the books. You shall shout up to me what provisions we have and—"

"Clare, Lew'll never speak ter me again."

"It's not up to Lew, nor you, my dear. You remember how I was with our Rory Patrick and sure I came to no harm."

"No, but tha' only 'ad the one bairn then an't shop were no bigger than a . . ."

The argument rumbled on but Lavender knew in her anxious heart that it did no good, for Clare Earnshaw was no longer the frail, shy and self-effacing young woman who had stumbled into their midst four years ago. Her experiences before she came, which had still not been vouchsafed to them though they could guess at them, as the Irish problem was well documented by now, and her painful love for Martin Heywood since; her success at Moorhouse Farm and her small but growing business here, had built her into a strong, self-confident, independent young woman who demanded her own way over all things to do with her venture. She would not dream of interfering with what Lew did in the cellar from where the most marvellous and handsome pieces of furniture came, nor in his column each week, she said hotly, and he must pay her the same privilege. Only Lew himself, gently but firmly, knew how to manage her, to persuade her – to talk some bloody sense into her, Lavender said privately to Albert – make her see reason, but that was mainly to do with her sons. *His* sons as he called them and when she wanted to keep them out of their beds at the end of the day so that she could play furious and exciting games with them, particularly

Rory, making him shriek with hysterical laughter, having been deprived of it during the day, she complained, Lew was the one who took over. He would get out the bath and place it on the rug in front of the kitchen fire, putting first one small wriggling body in the warm water and then the other, soaping them and kissing their wet cheeks before handing them one by one to Clare to be dried, to be kissed and cuddled and put in the small bed and the cradle which he himself had made.

He knew she felt guilty that so much of her time was taken up with the business, the baking which began at four o'clock each morning and serving her growing number of customers. She insisted on calling personally at the public houses and inns and even one or two shops in Market Street and King Street who sold her appetising pies and other goods. She wanted to make sure that they were satisfied with her service and quality, she said, but as the months moved on she knew she could no longer carry this heavy load alone but for Lavender and Tilly.

She hired a boy for the deliveries who pushed the handcart – even that no longer quite big enough so that two trips had to be made – efficient and reliable and polite who answered to the name of Jack. She could do with another girl, she confessed to Lew, chewing her lips on the advisability of taking on more staff with the business so newly budding. A young lass to serve in the shop and someone steady and reliable to keep an eye on the boys when Clare was absent. Rory Patrick, who had no *one* steady, ever-present person in his life to discipline him, was becoming unruly. When Lew was there he was noisy but obedient, though his face would turn mutinous. He was a handsome child, always ready to rush here and there on his tumble of sturdy toddler's legs. He had tousled ebony curls, bold blue eyes and could be destructive with toys belonging to his brother, of whom he was enormously jealous, but beneath it all he had a sunny nature and a good heart, though he firmly believed he was the most important person in the world and that everyone loved him the best. Clare did!

Joss was six months old when her world fell apart.

Lew was down in the cellar. He had come across an illustration of a perambulator said to be very popular with the young Queen Victoria who was adding almost yearly to her own large family. Lew was determined that Clare should have one so that they could take their sons to Philips Park on a fine Sunday. At the moment when they had a day out Clare wrapped Joss in her shawl and Lew carried Rory, but how lovely it would be, Clare said, if she could put the pair of them in one of these new contraptions and push them to the park. It was the only bit of green in Manchester, built just five years ago when the Public Walks, Parks and Playgrounds Committee decided that the city, so progressive in other respects, was sadly lacking in open spaces where its people might enjoy their leisure, what they had of it, in pleasant surroundings. At the instigation of the Manchester member of parliament, Mark Philips, but paid for out of local rates, the splendid park was laid out. It was described as bold and romantic in character, with high knolls, gardens and walks and a pretty little amphitheatre sloping down to the River Medlock which was dammed to provide two lakes. There was a gymnasium, an archery ground, playgrounds for boys and girls, a skittle alley, quoits grounds and a refreshment house. Clare loved it, declaring that you could spend a whole day there and not see everything and it was ideal for Rory whose enthusiasm for running like the wind, no matter how many times you called out to him, could be allowed free rein.

But it was a fair tramp up there and the perambulator Lew had set his heart on, copied from a picture in *The Illustrated News*, would be so constructed that Clare would be able to put both babies in it, Rory firmly strapped in, and push the pair of them up Oldham Street, turning into Hulme Hall Lane to the park. There was a set of strict rules at the park gates, regarding intoxication, gambling and improper language. The refreshment house was closed during Divine Service on a Sunday morning. It was severely frowned upon and as severely dealt with if a male person intruded upon the playground of the females and there were several constables who were instructed to preserve order, to enforce the regulations and to see that all was decent.

"Can't you leave that for a few hours and come with us, acushla?" Clare fretted, reaching out to Rory who was just about to attack an unfinished cabinet his father was fashioning for a customer. He had a chisel in his hand and on his face the same determined expression with which Clare had once been familiar on Martin Heywood, but had not seen for over two years except on the boy. She often wondered if it distressed Lew, the likeness of Rory Patrick to his natural father. The same fearless blue eyes the colour of harebells, the same arrogantly jutting chin and, though still that of a baby, a firm mouth that could thin with temper if he was opposed. He needed a firm hand – a good smack bottom, Lavender was heard to say – and he was not getting it, for Lew was too indulgent, too fond, too content with his boys and the life he led with them and his beloved wife.

"Sweetheart, I've to get that cabinet our Rory's bent on destroyin' finished by ternight an' I've not yet done copy fer't paper. Can we not go next Sunday?"

"But it's such a lovely day. We could take a picnic and let Rory wear himself out on the grass. And Fred loves a walk up there and I can't manage him and the two boys."

"Lass, if tha'll be patient I'll 'ave this baby carriage ready by next Sunday an' then we's can all go." Lew ran a distracted hand through his hair, leaving a scattering of sawdust there. He lunged frantically at Rory Patrick who, having had the chisel taken from him, was reaching for the hacksaw, bent, it seemed, on "helping" his father in the construction of the baby carriage.

"Sweetheart, tha'll 'ave ter tekk our Rory upstairs or 'e'll do 'imself a mischief. No, lad, them wheels is fer't perambulator. Sweet Jesus, Clare, I've ter get on or . . ."

"Well, Rory and I will just have to go alone," she said haughtily. "If my own husband can't—"

"Be fair, lass. If tha' 'ad summat ter do wi' that bakery o' yourn you'd be doin' it, not mitherin' ter go ter't park."

"Very well, Lew Earnshaw, if that's your answer I shall take Rory and Fred and leave Joss with Lavender."

"Why don't tha' tekk Lavender with thi'? She'd like a day out in't park."

"No, I shall go alone."

"Tha' can't carry that great lump of a boy all the way ter Philips Park, lass," he remonstrated, which was exactly the kind of remark that was certain to make Clare Earnshaw, who was now her own woman and though she loved her husband had become accustomed to having her own way with him, do just what she pleased.

"Of course I can. I shall tie him in my shawl and carry him as I've carried many a baby when I was . . ."

For a second a brief spasm of memory crossed her face and she turned away abruptly but Lew was engrossed again in the construction of the perambulator, which would look exactly like the one that was used in royal circles!

Fortunately her son, who objected to being carried anywhere, after a bit of a struggle fell asleep in her arms and the walk to the park was fraught with nothing more than making sure Fred stayed close to her skirts on the length of string fastened to his collar.

It took her longer than she had thought, not because the route was long but because Hulme Hall Lane, once she had passed the Manchester Steel Works and crossed the bridge that spanned the canal, was a treasure of birdlife and a glory of wild flowers growing in the hedges. She didn't know the names of the birds that darted in and out of the trees bordering the lane, though several had a rich red-pink chest and a redder cap, and others, perched on a grassy bank, were a sleek grey with brown-black and a pure white rump. She stood and watched them for a while but the boy was growing heavy so she strode on, admiring the variety of richly coloured wild flowers on either side of the lane. Some she knew, wild hyacinths, violets and the bright blue of speedwell. The warmth was bringing out their lovely fragrance and she drew it deep into her lungs, savouring it after the heavy stink of Manchester mill chimneys.

"Change not a clout till May be out," so the saying went but if Clare had not had the burden of Rory in her shawl she would have removed it the day was so warm. She had on a new gown, a gown the colour of heather in a fine wool. It was plain but the skirt was fashionably held out, not with a crinoline but by several white, lace-edged petticoats. At her neck and wrists was a frill of cream lace taken from a blouse she had bought on the market, the rest of the garment in cream shantung made into a little dress for Joss. She had brushed her hair with the vigour she employed every morning but today, instead of twisting it up into the severe chignon she wore in the shop and when visiting her customers, she had left it to hang down her back, held only by a knot of cream satin ribbons. She looked about fifteen, though her figure was mature, full-bosomed, her waist still slender even after two children, her hips rounded and gracefully swaying.

She was glad when they reached the park. She had a small wicker basket with a couple of her cheese and onion pies in it, Rory's favourite, some almond biscuits and a small bottle of milk. Later, when he had run off some of his high spirits, she thought she might take Rory into the refreshment house and treat herself to a cup of tea, that's if Rory could be persuaded to behave himself.

The park was not as crowded as she had expected it to be. She set her son down just inside the gate where several boys were having great fun round the drinking fountain, fun which the constable would have put an immediate stop to if he had been about. They could not be everywhere at once, she supposed, but if one came along and caught these lads flinging caps full of water at one another, wetting not only each other but people harmlessly strolling by, there would be trouble.

Rory thought it was glorious. Before she could catch him

he was in among them, shrieking with laughter, darting between their legs, almost tripping them up, longing to join in their game and babbling his great command of the English language which nobody but his parents and Lavender could decipher.

"'Ere, get out of it, kid," one irritated lad told him and though he did not exactly push him, Rory was jostled and fell over on the gravel path, ready to howl his anger and pain, for the gravel had bitten into his knees, which began to bleed.

"Get away, you bullies," Clare screeched, tearing into the midst of them and reaching for her son, but before she could pick him up strong male arms lifted him high, a hard male hand clouted the boy who had jostled him across his ear and with a shock which tightened itself inexorably about her heart, nearly asphyxiating her, and fastened her feet to the ground as though they grew roots there, she looked into the face of Martin Heywood.

She knew by his expression that he was not as stunned as she was; in fact he was not stunned at all. He watched her calmly, all the while holding the incensed child firmly to his chest, saying nothing and doing nothing, not even to quieten the boy, and incredibly Rory seemed to understand that he'd best behave. Clare felt as though she had been struck, like Lot's wife, to a pillar of salt, unable to move, unable to breathe, certainly unable to form any sort of coherent thought. She was mindless, senseless, an inanimate object without the power to reason or wonder, and she thought she might have remained this way for ever with the curious crowd milling round them, with the boy who had had his ears boxed whingeing that he would tell his pa, with Rory Patrick Earnshaw leaning down to examine his grazed knees, then up again to stare with interest at the man who held him. Rory loved anything out of the ordinary in his commonplace child's life and this man promised to be something of that nature. In his twenty months of life he had been loved and cherished and indulged and had never known a moment that did not contain the utter belief that this would not go on for ever. He was a bright child, too bright, Lavender was inclined to think. He was self-willed and assertive, afraid of nothing and no one, but somehow this man who held him in his arms also held him quiet and he settled there amicably.

They stood quite still in those first moments, savouring them, their eyes seeking the truth, which was that what they had known, what they had felt for one another was still there.

"Jesus, you're beautiful," he said softly, his eyes brilliant with his love for her. Clare felt herself relax, every limb slowly settling into its everyday posture, her eyes still fastened to his, drifting on the enchantment of being in the same space as Martin, breathing the same air as Martin, of knowing that she had only to lift her hand and she could touch Martin. Although there was noise, laughter, shouting, children playing some game in the distance, the conversation of the people who used this park since they had no garden of their own, there was stillness and silence about them. She shivered slightly, though it was warm. The boy began to wriggle, peering into Martin's face with the greatest curiosity and blue eyes were so like blue eyes it was impossible to deny they were father and son.

Martin broke the spell again.

"He's mine, isn't he?" he asked her simply.

Could she deny it when two faces, two identical faces looked at her, their cheeks almost touching, even their expressions the same? Audacious, fearless, compelling and yet with a quirk of humour at the corner of each upturned mouth. Rory Patrick Earnshaw and his father Martin Heywood and how was she to manage this calamity, this yawning rift that had opened beneath her feet which had thought themselves at last on firm ground. It was a disaster, for who knew better than she that when Martin Heywood wanted something he went after it with every weapon at his command, his greatest being her love for him.

She found her voice at last. "He's my son."

"It takes two to make a child, Clare, and you and I made this one together."

"Please," she whispered, wanting to snatch her boy and run like the wind for home. For the strength and safety of Lew and Lavender and Joss, but at the same time her treacherous woman's body longed to take the boy from him, set him on the ground and fling herself into the space he left. Into Martin's arms.

"Please what?" he asked her softly. "Please go away and leave your son alone? Is that it?"

"Yes."

"Have I no rights where he is concerned?"

"No . . . no, he is not yours, not really."

He glanced about him, still holding the boy who was beginning to wriggle in his arms, for the attention span of a boy not yet two years old was short.

"Be quiet, lad, and keep still," his father told him and at once Rory quietened, though he was seen to look at his mother in some alarm. Interested he might be in this big stranger who held him but he was not too certain he cared to be spoken to in such firm tones. His pa didn't speak like that, nor Albert, nor his mother and Lavender. His bottom lip began to quiver and two fat tears tangled on his lower lashes.

"Give him to me, Martin. He is becoming afraid."

"Nonsense. A great lad like him. You're not afraid of me, are you, boy?" and with a gesture which was lovely to see he hugged his son to him and gently kissed his rosy cheeks. The boy, astoundingly, put both arms about his neck and hugged him back, then wriggled again and reluctantly Martin set him down on the walk. He knelt down beside him, pushing off the small dog who came nosing curiously at his boots and with great seriousness examined his son's "wounds" and asked him if perhaps an ice-cream might make them feel better, and when assured that it would turned to look up at Clare, grinning engagingly.

"Come on then, son, let's go and find the tea house," he said, and holding out his hand which the boy took, he moved off across the grass, even Fred prancing round him as though they were old friends and Clare had no option but to follow.

It was an hour later, an hour that she spent in a daze of emotions that consisted of bewilderment, joy, despair, hopelessness, terror, that he led her, like some half-witted creature without a sensible thought in her head, to an area of lawn which was virtually empty since it seemed the families who came here liked to use the playgrounds, the archery grounds – a vastly new experience for all of them – and sitting down in the shade of an enormous horse chestnut tree, brilliant with flowers, the boy spiralling round them in a game with Fred, he began to speak.

"You know, of course, that I still love you, Clare, and that—"

"Don't, Martin. I won't listen."

"You will listen, my darling, and you won't interrupt. I have known where you were almost from the first day. I don't know why I took it into my head to learn your whereabouts because for many months I *hated* you and Lew Earnshaw with a bitterness that corroded my life and was quite determined to put you out of it. I was resolute that I would marry Mayhew's lass and start my own family and that Clare Hanrahan would soon become nothing to me."

He smiled as though in disbelief at the very idea, shaking his head at his own foolishness.

"But, of course, I couldn't forget you. When I learned you had . . . had married Lew Earnshaw and had two sons, both his, I thought, then I began to despair. I was . . . I became something of a recluse, Clare, shunning people except through my business and I believe folk thought I was going off my head. I think I was; that is until, being in Manchester on business, I chanced to walk up Oldham Street and saw you." He bent his head as though in great pain. "I saw you with the boy and knew at once that . . . that he was mine."

"Don't, Martin." Her voice cracked with agony but he would not let her stop him.

"I made up my mind that I must see you, talk to you and the boy . . . of the future."

"We have no future, Martin. Lew is—"

"You are mine, Clare," he said with great gravity, "and so is Rory and I mean to have you, both of you. I've been watching you, every weekend, waiting for a chance to speak to you alone and today my chance came."

"Martin!" Her voice rose on a crescendo of appalled pain and their son turned to look at them, the stick he was holding and about to throw for Fred stilled for a moment.

"Mama . . . ?" he said questioningly and was quite beside himself with temper when his mama got to her feet, gathered him roughly in her arms, grabbed Fred's lead and began to run on flying feet for the open gates of the park.

Chapter Twenty-nine

Rory's garbled account of what had happened that afternoon in which the words "water", "boy", "man", and "smack" were the only ones to be distinguishable went unheeded by his audience. They listened in the way adults do to a child's prattle, nodding and smiling and putting in an appropriate word now and again, but they did not *hear* what he said, not really. Clare was eternally grateful that he wasn't a few months older and more articulate or his description of the man who had kissed him in the park might have met with some incredulity, and suspicion.

She often wondered during the next few days how she got through them, for her emotions were in turmoil and she was amazed that not one member of her household noticed it. Lew had asked her if she had enjoyed her outing, scolding her for rushing back – running like a hare he had described it – with the boy in her arms since he was a sturdy chap and really too heavy for her to carry. No wonder she looked so pale, he told her solicitously, but never mind, by this time next week she'd have the baby carriage. He had been somewhat surprised, but pleased nevertheless, by the warmth of her greeting as she flung herself into his arms when she got back; after all she had been gone no more than three hours but if this was to be the effect it had on her then she must go more often! He had kissed her lovingly and though she had burned to be taken upstairs and made love to, his body taming hers, submitting hers to whatever took his fancy and therefore erasing the memory of Martin Heywood, he had been preoccupied with the copy he must rewrite for the newspaper and had turned back to his notes.

The serenity she had acquired so painfully over the past year had gone, leaving her in mourning again, grieving for the man she loved. Oh, yes, she still loved him, there was no doubt about that. From the very instant in the park when their eyes had locked together over the head of their son, she had admitted that, her despair flooding back over her like a giant wave on a stormy beach. How fragile it all was, this world of hers, which had seemed so strong and safe with Lew, but an hour spent with Martin had shown her it was nothing but fantasy, shadows on a blank wall, an ephemeral dream, a bubble that had burst when Martin smiled at her. That's all it had taken. A smile. The happy family, the loving husband, her business which had so fulfilled her, had, in one afternoon, all been knocked down like a house of cards. Her mind since leaving Moorhouse Farm had been filled with angry recriminations, with contempt for Martin Heywood for what he had done not only to her but to Lew, but her flesh had not stopped loving his, hungering for his no matter how savagely she pushed the feelings away. Her woman's body was not concerned with matters that went on in her mind, only the physical need to be close to the one it longed for. The few hours in the park had shown her that!

While Lew was down in his workroom putting together the perambulator of which he was so proud, she sat by her fire, staring into the flames, her fingers clinging to receipts and invoices she was supposed to be studying. The children were in bed and Lavender, who had begun to take an interest in the lad who drove the delivery van for one of their suppliers, had been persuaded by him to go to the Music Hall on Oxford Street.

"No, we're *not* courtin'," she protested stormily when Lew teased her about it, but it had been noticed and remarked upon that she was taking a great deal of trouble with her appearance these days. Not that she hadn't always been neat and clean and well turned out, for she had learned it from Clare, but now she often had a knot of ribbons that bounced roguishly in her fair curls as she served her customers and bustled through to the back to receive the deliveries.

"Arthur's at the yard gate," Clare would shout, winking at Ida who was standing in the shop waiting for the hot meat and potato pies to come out of the oven. "Shall I go?" she would add; but Lavender was through the door that led from the shop into the kitchen and scullery like a terrier down a rabbit hole, as Ida said, and thence to the back yard to unlock the gate. Arthur was a homely lad, tall and lean but as strong as a horse, with a quick wit which appealed to Lavender and was as steady as he was strong. His employer, the wholesaler from where Clare purchased her supplies, thought very highly of him, Lavender told them, and he had good prospects, for he was one of the fortunates whose parents had made sure he was taught to read and write. They had "stepped out" very respectably several times now, a walk on a Sunday afternoon to the park, a visit to the art gallery and now, greatly daring for it was an *evening* engagement, a visit to the Music Hall.

The flickering flames seemed to hypnotise her, taking her back to last Sunday afternoon, to the park from where her thoughts had barely wandered ever since. She could still see him in her mind's eye leading his chattering son by the hand into the Refreshment House with herself following blindly behind. With his usual confidence which implied he had a perfect right to do whatever he wanted with *his* son, he had sat her and Rory down at one of the round wrought-iron tables. He lifted a peremptory hand, beckoning to a waitress who immediately left the couple from whom she had been about to take an order, her cap bobbing in her eagerness to be of service to a gentleman, for not many of these were seen in this park of the people.

"Might I trouble you for a bowl of warm water?" he had asked her, smiling so charmingly that Clare, even in the midst of chaos, felt an inclination to smile at the girl's simpering attention. "My son" – *My son!* – "has had a tumble and his knees are grazed." He had bent his head to smile into Rory's bewildered and somewhat apprehensive face, then reached for him and, lifting him from his chair, sat him on his lap. Clare had watched silently, quiet and afraid as a deer trapped in a forest glade by the huntsman, for with the instinct of an animal she knew there was great peril here. That she and Lew and their little family were in the gravest danger and the source of it sat smiling and unconcerned with her son on his lap.

The bowl of water had been brought across to them with not just the waitress but the manageress fussing round the charming gentleman and his tearful son, perhaps wondering what the heck was up with the boy's mother who sat like a bloody statue during the whole procedure.

"There, son, there . . . what a brave lad. No, it won't hurt in a minute, Rory. See, a hug and a kiss" – giving him both – "will soon make it better and now, as you've been the bravest boy in the world you shall have your ice-cream."

Sweet Mary, he'll be calling himself "Papa" in a minute, she remembered thinking dazedly, still frozen in that block of ice that Martin's appearance had encased her in. Rory, once his knees had been bathed, ate his way through two ice-creams, chattering non-stop and, being no more than a toddler with no knowledge of tension, took no account of the painful silence that settled between the man and his mother.

They had drunk the tea Martin insisted on buying and as he listened gravely to the babbling voice of his son, trying his best to make sense of it, she had had a chance to study him. He looked older, not just the two years that had gone past since she had seen him but in experience and what looked like pain. The lines about his mouth were deeper, turning down bleakly when he was not smiling at the boy. His face was still the face of a man in his prime, smooth and taut with good health but his eyes no longer had that careless good humour lurking in their blue depths. They were wary, again except when they studied his son. He looked immaculate in his dark-grey, swallow-tailed walking coat and narrow-legged grey and black check trousers, his white ruffled shirt front and grey cravat, and she wondered with that part of her mind that was not totally numb with shock whether Maddie still did his laundry. He carried the customary walking-stick with a gold top, his silk top hat under his arm, his dark curling hair, so like his son's, tumbled by the breeze and falling over his forehead.

"When can I see my son again?" he had asked her with the arrogance and certainty that said that it would do her no good to argue.

The answer stuck in her throat and she felt as though she had swallowed glass.

"It's not possible. Lew would—"

"Bugger Lew. This is my son, not his. Let him make do with his own."

Her hands had squirmed in torment in her lap though she did her best to hide them and, his eyes softening, when he reached out and took one, bringing it to his lips with the gallantry of a knight greeting his lady, the boy stopped slurping his ice-cream, his eyes round with wonderment, the spoon halfway to his mouth and at the next table a family of four watched with open-mouthed amazement.

"Clare." His voice was low. "Clare, it's no good fighting me, my darling, you should know that by now. He is my son and I will have him, one way or the other, and you too. I will come and see Lew Earnshaw and explain."

"He knows."

"Of course he does, since you would be pregnant when you left Edgeclough and being the perfect gentleman he took on another man's woman, and his son, making them both his. But not for long, my darling, not for long ..."

She remembered every word of the conversation in the Refreshment House and beneath the horse chestnut tree where he led her afterwards, for she had been over it again and again. She was tempted to unburden herself to Lavender, for she knew her to be a sensible, compassionate young woman, but didn't she know exactly what Lavender would say, so what was the point of begging her advice, or even her support. She felt even her movements had been stiff and slow over the last few days as though she had grown old with the wretchedness of it, the misery, the worry. It was as though Martin had taken with him the spring of life which Lew and his love had welled within her. The weight of her love for Martin Heywood, which she had successfully laid down since her marriage to Lew, was back a thousandfold, dragging her down and the weight of it was almost more than she could bear.

She worked during that first week like some clockwork doll that has been wound up and will go on automatically until it runs down. She even obliged her husband in their bed and though she did her best to put some warmth, some life, into the encounter, that was just what it was, an encounter, a duty.

"I'm sorry, Lew, you deserve more than my acquiescence but I seem to have a . . . headache."

"Tha're not breedin' again, are thi'?" he asked her hopefully, but she shook her head and wrapped him in her arms, kissing him as she might one of her sons when they needed her comfort.

"We's 'll 'ave another, won't we, my lass?" he asked her wistfully, one hand holding her breast where it usually lay as he fell asleep.

"I hope so, Lew," she whispered desperately into the darkness.

Though she knew it was quite ridiculous, for Martin had a farm to run and other business concerns to see to and could not afford to hang about the streets of Manchester on the chance of seeing her, or Rory, she had been reluctant to leave the house. There were customers she should visit, on missions of goodwill. Lavender and Tilly, once the baking was complete, were quite capable of managing in the shop without her. In fact she was beginning to realise that in their particular field, confectionery and pastry, Lavender was becoming as good a cook as she herself was.

When Arthur, who had just come from the Dog and Duck, passed on the message that Mrs Mullaney was beginning to wonder where she was, she knew she could not hide indoors any longer. Joss was asleep in the kitchen, his cradle set out of Rory's mischievous way and, with the back door open the boy played happily with his toys, in and out of the scullery and the back yard, the gate of which was securely padlocked.

"Well, me lass, I were beginning to wonder if me an' you 'ad 'ad a fallin' out. I've not seen yer fer a week or more. Is summat up? Yer look a bit peaked about the eyes. 'Ave yer not bin well?" Kitty leaned forward and peered solicitously into Clare's face. Though it was May it was cold and a damp mist drifted across the city. There was a good fire in the grate and the flames turned Kitty's good-natured face, always highly coloured, to a bright brick red. The room was just as Kitty was, cheerful, overstuffed with furniture in vivid colours, but comfortable, homely, a place of refuge to Clare.

"No, Kitty, I'm fine, really I am. Just a bit tired, that's all. We've been really busy in the shop and I've made up my mind I will have to take on another girl."

"Hmmm . . ." Kitty studied her face, suspiciously this time, and asked her the same question Lew had put to her in their bed.

"Another babby?" Kitty raised her eyebrows delicately.

"Oh, no." Clare tried to laugh. "Jesus, Mary and Joseph, Joss is only six months old."

"That wouldn't stop a lot o' men, chuck. But that Lew o' yours is a considerate sort o' chap an' would leave yer alone until . . ."

"Oh no, we . . . he . . ."

Clare buried her nose in the teacup and took a deep draught of the tea Kitty had poured for her, her face rosy with embarrassment.

"Right, lass, there's no need ter say owt more. Them bairns o' yourn are …"

What Kitty was about to say about Clare's bairns was never uttered, for after a light tap on the door to Kitty's private parlour, her barmaid, Flo, popped her head round the door, a somewhat excited expression on her face.

"Theer's a chap asking for yer," she hissed as though it were a secret. "In't bar parlour."

Kitty looked irritated, clattering her teacup into her saucer with a great show of annoyance. She had seen right away that there was something troubling this woman who sat opposite her and of whom she had become inordinately fond and the interruption was unwelcome. Clare was sipping her tea with an air of abstraction and it had seemed to Kitty Mullaney that she was just about to get to the root of it.

"'Oo is it? Can't yer say I'm busy, fer God's sake. Am I never ter get a minnit's peace?"

"Oh, it's not thi' 'e wants, Mrs Mullaney, it's Mrs Earnshaw."

"Mrs Earnshaw! 'Oo the devil …"

Clare could feel herself becoming enveloped in an icy mist. She could almost see it shrouding round her and because she didn't know what else to do she continued sipping her tea as though she hadn't heard a word of what Flo had said.

Kitty sat up straighter and though she had no reason to believe that this interruption was anything but some chap, a customer of Clare's, who had seen her come in perhaps, she felt a feather of unease run up her spine. Kitty Mullaney was not a fanciful woman, ask her Alfie, or indeed any of her customers who drank at her bar every day, but there was something very strange about Clare Earnshaw today. Right from the start, when she had been forced to send a message by the delivery lad, not that she needed anything from Clare but because she had become used to seeing her about the place, having a gossip over a cup of tea, a bit of a laugh over this and that, she had sensed that something was dreadfully wrong. She was not fanciful but she was astute, sharp-witted, again ask her Alfie.

"Did 'e give a name?" Her tone was abrupt and she kept her eyes on Clare.

"No, Mrs Mullaney, but 'e's a toff."

"A toff?"

Flo was evidently enjoying this break in her tedious day enormously. She preened, sidling a little further into the room as though to make sure she was included in whatever was going on.

"Oh aye, a real gentleman, an' a good looker an' all. I wish 'e were askin' fer me, I can tell—"

"Bugger off, Flo, an' tell the gentleman ... someone'll be out ter see 'im directly."

Crestfallen, Flo flung herself from the room, leaving an empty, hollow silence behind her. Clare continued to drink her tea, her eyes blind and hopeless and Kitty, for the first time in her adult life, was lost for words. She didn't know why, really, for there could be a perfectly innocent reason for Clare's strangeness, for the enquiry at Kitty's bar, but her shrewd instincts told her this was not so, so she waited for Clare to speak and when she didn't she leaned forward, took the cup and saucer from her hand and put it on a table by her side.

"What's up, chuck? Summat is, so don't try fobbin' me off wi' a load o' doodle-alley. What's 'appened since I saw yer an' 'oo is this chap askin' fer yer? An' why are yer ... well, it's obvious to a blind man on a gallopin' 'orse yer don't want ter see 'im so ..."

Clare's voice was harsh as she spoke. "If I don't see him he'll just keep on and on until I do or he'll go round to the shop and ... speak to Lew."

"About what, lass? What's 'e got on yer that 'e can mekk yer scared witless?"

"He's Rory Patrick's father." Her teeth had begun to chatter and she felt a great need to moan deep in the back of her throat. Her world was falling apart. For the second time in her life she was faced with the loss of everything she held most dear and there seemed nothing to be done about it. She knew Martin Heywood – for it was he – better than anyone in the world and if there was something he wanted he would just wait and wait, or go blundering right in if he thought that was the best tack, to get whatever it was. She loved him to distraction and she hated him bitterly. He had kept her by his side three years ago with the vague and foolish hope that he would marry her, that they were to share their lives in the bright sunshine of honesty and trust. He had betrayed her, but, as she had done when she left her home in Ireland, she had dragged herself to her feet and begun again. She had suffered but she had done it and now here he was prepared to knock it all down again and for his own selfish ends.

Kitty was still holding her hand with both her own, rubbing her thumbs on the back of it, doing her best to give comfort, to let Clare see she was not alone and it was perhaps this that brought her out of the echoing fog that surrounded her and gave her back a modicum of the strength she had gathered over the years.

"I'll get shut of 'im, if that's what yer want," Kitty said hesitantly.

"No, you wouldn't, Kitty. You don't know him. He's already seen Rory and knows he's his son. When you meet him you'll know too, for they're the spit of one another." She sighed, then smiled tiredly into Kitty's concerned face. "No, I'll have to see him though what I shall say I don't know."

"I know what *I'd* say to 'im," Kitty began belligerently, tossing her long dark hair over her shoulder.

Clare squeezed her hand and smiled a little. "I know, too, Kitty, but he still wouldn't go away."

She stood up and smoothed down her skirt. She lifted her head. "If it's all right with you, Kitty, I'll see him in here."

"Nay, lass, do as yer want. Shall I stay wi' yer?"

"No, but don't go far away. Stay within … within call."

"'E wouldn't 'urt yer?"

"No, not physically. Just break my heart all over again."

He seemed to fill the small, cluttered room with his large masculine presence and Clare felt the need to back away from him but there was nowhere to go except into the fireplace. Kitty had gone, nodding knowingly and grimly at Clare, glaring up at the tall man who seemed unaware of her, and in her own parlour, too. Anyroad, she'd not go far, just to the foot of the narrow stairs in the passage.

"Clare …" He cleared his throat and she knew he was profoundly moved.

"Yes?"

"I followed you here. I couldn't leave it as it was. Don't you see, you and the boy belong …" His face worked and for a horror-filled moment she felt herself drawn towards him, ready to put a hand out to him to comfort his pain. Dear sweet Mary, after all he had done to her, all she had suffered because of him, and probably would again, she was ready to drift over to him and … and what? She knew what she wanted to do, and she knew what he wanted to do and the battle within her to stand upright, to look aloof, to show contempt was breaking her up inside.

"Martin, you must see …" Her voice cracked and he took a step towards her, almost knocking over some heavily laden table that was, like the rest of her knick-knacks, Kitty's pride and joy.

"No, I don't see … I won't. I love you and I want you to be my wife."

Her mouth fell open and she began to laugh.

"Your wife! *Your wife!*

"I've always wanted it but I was too much of a fool to see it. I had . . . I was stubborn thinking it mattered that—"

"That I was a peasant without shoes and you were a gentleman?" Her voice was caustic and he winced.

"Yes, but I was wrong and so now—"

"Now you are too late, Martin. I am another man's wife. I have a son by him. I love him."

"No . . . no . . ."

"And I would not hurt him for you or anybody. He is the best man in the world and—"

"You cannot love him, Clare." His voice had strengthened. "You love me. That is the one thing of which I am completely sure. That and the boy. If I were to touch you now you . . ."

"Stay away from me, Martin. Kitty is within earshot."

"You're afraid of me, aren't you, my love?" His voice had a thread of triumph in it. "You're afraid that if I touched you, like this" – putting a gentle hand on her arm – "you would not be able to resist me. That's the truth of it, isn't it?"

How had he got so close to her and why hadn't she called out to Kitty? She could feel the warmth of him, the heat of his body almost touching hers and when he put his arms round her, since she was about to fall she had the sweet and awful sense of coming home, home at last where she belonged. His long, hard body was fused to hers, just as she remembered it, aroused and demanding and she was wrapped about in his magic, his love and the shuddering knowledge of his pain, the pain he was furious at feeling, but felt just the same. She gripped her hands together behind his back in case he should try to escape her. Her face was buried under his chin and his was in her hair and his hands moved to her head, pressing it further into the hollow of his throat, then moving down her back, forcing her body even closer to his.

They were both trembling violently.

"Christ Jesus! Christ Jesus?" she heard him cry over and over again and she thought he might be about to weep and for five minutes they stood in the circle of one another's arms and in the bar Clare heard Flo shouting to Alfie to bring up some more tankards.

He raised his head at last and with a tender hand lifted her chin. His eyes were like blue lanterns glowing in his brown face and then she could no longer see them as hers closed and his lips came down on hers. She felt herself sigh in total rapture. Her body was light, buoyant, but held securely by this man who loved her. Who had always loved her but had let the moment slip by him. What were they to do? She did not know, nor, at that precise moment, with his lips folding and caressing hers, did she care. She knew she would. She knew that this moment of complete love, of renewed love, would be shattered and her heart would be asked to make its choice but this and this and this, the curve of his mouth, the warmth of his eyes, the smoothness of his cheek, the hardness of his hands and body, were hers for this fraction of timelessness. Dear God, she loved him!

Chapter Thirty

She was bathing the children in readiness for bed when the letter came. It was addressed to her in an ill-formed hand, somewhat grubby, for it was delivered by a chap who said he had worked in the carding shed at Hopkinson's but, being young and single, had fancied a change and decided to try his luck in Manchester. It had been a long tramp and he hadn't had a chance to have a wash, he apologised. Young Daisy Bickerstaffe had put the note in his hand when she heard he was coming this way, he added. She had written it herself, for she was a sensible lass like her sister and was attending Sunday school, determined, also like Lavender, to get an education and make something of herself. Despite this it seemed that Daisy had no knowledge of the postal services which had been in general usage for over ten years – either that or she didn't trust them – where, by the simple expedient of sticking a stamp on an envelope that envelope would be delivered to any address in Britain.

He was a garrulous chap, obviously hoping to be asked in, for hadn't he done them a good turn, perhaps offered a cup of tea by the pretty lass who answered the door, but Lavender was so alarmed by the note and whatever might be in it she almost slammed the door in his face as she turned to gallop into the kitchen where the boys were shrieking their delight in the bathtub before the fire.

Clare wiped her face with her apron, as Rory didn't care where he aimed the soap suds. She turned fearfully to Lavender, her face pale and anxious. It didn't take a lot to make her anxious these days. Every time the door in the shop opened, or Arthur knocked at the back gate into the yard she jumped and she wanted to hide, to dither about at the window in an attempt to see who was there, to peer into the street on the lookout for a tall, well-dressed gentleman, her apprehension that Martin might take the bull by the horns as he was threatening to do and accost Lew wearing her to a shadow.

She knew she was beginning to worry both Lew and Lavender, for ever since Martin had walked into Kitty's parlour at the Dog and Duck and taken her in his arms she had lived in fear and in rapture. The two were inextricably mixed in her heart and she reeled hourly between intoxication and terror. Her joy at seeing him, being close to him, her body clamped to his, overwhelmed her, filled her with enchantment and yet at the same time frightened her to death. She could not let this happen, her cool mind kept telling her; and "Don't be daft", her heart answered, "this is Martin, *Martin,* and you can't lose him again."

That day he had held her in the close circle of his arms, soothing her trembling body as a mother might a sick child, reassuring her over and over again that he would do nothing to frighten her, that he would respect her wishes, at least for the time being, and stay away from her home and her family, and she had believed him because she wanted to. She wanted to believe that he would keep his distance, at least until she had had time to unthread the tangled weave of her emotions, but she should have known better. Martin's son belonged to Martin, and not Lew Earnshaw, he told her furiously, trying to shake her into acquiescence and submission whenever they met.

Her nerves were a jangled mass of discordant vibration. She lived each day looking over her shoulder, peeping round corners, holding her breath as she hurried up Dale Street. She dreaded seeing him but at the same time was delirious with joy when she did. She didn't know when or where he would spring out at her as she went about her day's business. From shop doorways in Deansgate, rising from a bench on the Esplanade in front of the Infirmary on Piccadilly, and on two occasions in Kitty Mullaney's bar parlour where he was eyed with suspicion and curiosity by the working men who drank there.

"I've taken a suite at the Albion Hotel," he told her abruptly, "a permanent suite so that we can have some privacy. You could bring the boy."

She had been horrified, her eyes wide and dark with terror, her hands against his chest pushing him away. Kitty had discreetly slipped out of her own private parlour, leaving them alone, though she didn't approve of Martin Heywood, not one little bit, she told Clare tartly, and if Clare would take her advice she'd get shut of him, for he'd bring her nothing but grief.

"Martin, in God's name, do you know what you're saying? I can't meet you in a hotel and I certainly can't bring Rory with me. Sure an' won't he be saying something soon? He speaks more clearly every day and how would it be if he was to—"

"D'you think I care? I want you to come away with me, you and the boy. We could live anywhere, start a new life, but in the meanwhile we must have somewhere we can meet."

"No, we must not. I won't have it. Go away, Martin, please. Leave me alone."

"I can't do that, Clare, you know that," he said impatiently, aggravated by her inability to comprehend the seriousness of this quagmire they floundered in, holding her by her upper arms and glaring into her face. The strain of the past weeks had stained his eyelids and engraved lines about his mouth that had not been there when Clare first knew him, He had aged, this strong, proud man who was not accustomed to begging, to going down on his knees to plead, especially for something that was rightfully his in the first place. He was doing his best to be patient but it was not in his nature to await the decision of others. His dark face had closed in a scowl, then he bent his head to kiss her clasped hands with a gentleness and a pain she could herself feel in her heart.

"Come to the hotel, my love. If not with the boy, then by yourself," he had entreated and she had wondered despairingly how long she could stand against him. He had only to put his mouth against hers and a bolt of lightning ripped through her and she knew that for the last seventeen or eighteen months her body had slept under Lew's gentle handling but was now vigorously awake.

But she would not go to his hotel room!

Taking the slippery, eel-like body of Joss Earnshaw in her arms and wrapping him in a towel, Lavender wordlessly handed the crumpled note to Clare. She knew it must be from someone in Edgeclough, for the chap had intimated as much. A lass at Hopkinson's could only be their Daisy, especially as she was the only one among them who could read and write, and who could it be who was in trouble but her mam or pa? But then why would Daisy write to Clare and not her own sister?

She watched as Clare opened the note and read it swiftly.

"Me … me mam?" she asked hesitantly.

Clare looked up swiftly, frowning, then she put out a comforting hand to Lavender.

"Oh, no, acushla. See, read it. It's Nelly."

"Nelly?" Lavender snatched the note from Clare, allowing the lively boy, who was crawling now, to make a naked dash for Fred, of whom he was inordinately fond, while Rory, still in the bath tub, stood up and began to jump up and down, washing the water over its side.

Somehow order was restored, the children settled down in the bedroom they shared and at last the three of them could give their attention to the note that Daisy had so laboriously spelled out. It seemed Nelly had been ailing for some time though none of them, not even her, could or would put a name to it. But she had mentioned several times that she had a longing to see Clare and Lew's lad. Not that she was asking for Clare to come or anything like that, for that was not Nelly's way, but it was thought that perhaps a sight of her and her bairns, a reassurance that at last Clare and Lew were settled and prospering might put the roses back in Nelly's cheeks. Daisy's letter did not say all this in so many words, for it was not within her vocabulary, but the implication was there and, as Lew said, the others must be worried about Nelly even to have considered the awe-inspiring and serious business of writing to Clare.

"Can you manage if I take a few days off?" she asked Lavender anxiously. "I mean in the shop, with the baking as well? I know we haven't had much time to train Betty" – who was their new scullery-maid – "but she seems a good lass and eager to learn the trade. She can help with the scrubbing and so on and will take some of the pressure off you and Tilly. But I must go, you do see that, don't you, and take the children. This note is very vague so I'm wondering . . ." She frowned and sighed worriedly. "Anyway, it might do her good to see them, besides which I'd like to see her for myself. I'll take the train to Oldham tomorrow and then a cab up to Edgeclough."

If her heart was fluttering at the prospect of being so close to Martin Heywood's farm, neither Lew nor Lavender noticed anything amiss with her. Lavender had known for a long time, even before the pair of them left Moorhouse, what Clare's feelings were for Martin. But so much time had elapsed and so many things had happened that, if she thought of it at all, which was unlikely, she thought it was ended, forgotten. Clare was happily married to Lew now and Martin Heywood was out of her life for good.

She clung to Lew that night, trying to wrap his goodness and strength around herself as he made love to her, doing her best to build a firm and insurmountable wall, like a fortification defending a castle, that Martin Heywood could never storm. And yet, even as Lew groaned himself to a climax, his face beaded with sweat as he fell against her, it was as though she were watching another woman going through the motions of being made love to. He had done his best, his hands at her face and neck and breasts, his lips exploring the outer curve of her ear, his tongue probing the softness inside it but none of it touched her, though she made sure he was not aware of it. The ice inside her, trickling along her veins, the frosted feather that ran down her spine were as cold and impenetrable as the drifts of snow she had encountered on the day Martin was lost on the moors. She loved Lew. Dear God, how many times had she told herself that, but the words would not melt the dread and the hopelessness of her love for Martin Heywood which was preventing her from responding as she longed to do to this good man who was her husband.

Rory was so excited as Lew lifted him into the compartment of the train it was as though his brain had become numbed with it all and he sat, for once speechless, his eyes wide and vividly bright, looking about him. His head swivelled constantly from side to side, determined not to miss one moment of this splendid and unexpected journey he and his mama were about to make. Joss was too young for such marvels as this, Rory's scornful expression seemed to say but *he* wasn't and though he didn't know where they were going, or why, he was enjoying every second of it.

"Now then, son, tha're ter be a good lad fer tha' mam and do as tha're told, so think on. Now, give me a kiss . . . eeh, I'll miss thi', an' little 'un." And while his pa kissed and hugged his mam, which was nothing new to Rory Patrick, he climbed up to kneel on the seat and gaze out of the window, watching travellers as they passed in and out of the steam that drifted about the station, listening to the shrieking whistles of the engines and the hoarse shouts of those saying goodbye to others, gazing in awe at the hurrying men in uniforms who hoisted this and that about the platform on trolleys. He longed to put his head out of the window so that he could see the length of the wonderful train but his mama's hand on his arm prevented him and though he tried to shake it off indignantly since he was, after all, a big boy now, she kept a firm grip on him.

It was the same at the other end of the journey which had been filled with sights so incredible he was still struck speechless. The train had rapidly left behind the marching rows of identical, back-to-back houses all pierced with identical chimneys with which he was familiar, the chimneys belching smoke into the pale-blue sky. They rushed past tiny cottages set in multicoloured gardens then came to mile after mile of fields patched with yellow flowers in which cows, their heads down, chewed at the grass. It was a marvel to the boy whose only introduction to flowers and grass was the occasional outing they took to Philips Park.

When they alighted from the train his mama allowed him no time to stand and stare and soon had them in a cab with their luggage, helped by a respectful porter. He had pulled on her determined hand, for he would have liked to look around him, to inspect all the marvellous things that filled the platform but she hurried him, protesting loudly, out of the station.

Soon he had other wondrous spectacles to goggle at as the cab they were in began to climb up and up, away from the houses, which were no novelty to Rory, and on to a great sweep of open space which seemed to go on for ever and ever and which his mama told him was called a "moorland". His little brother was fast asleep and saw none of it but he, Rory Patrick, did. The sheep clustered high above them on the hills, like tiny white clouds against the dark rocks that grew there, the cattle down below moving slowly across a field, the birds swooping overhead against the washed blue of the sky, and he wondered why it was he had never seen this before. He was almost two years old and had been born and bred in a city, but from the moment he first clapped eyes on it Rory Patrick Earnshaw loved the spacious, everlasting fold upon fold of the moors on which his ancestors had walked for centuries. It was perhaps then that he made up his unconscious mind that this was where he was meant to be!

It was a Saturday afternoon and they were all there, having come at noon from the mills in Crossfold. They were shy with her, hanging back from the cab, each waiting for the other to make the first move, for she looked a very different young woman to the one who had tramped off with Lew Earnshaw over two years ago. That Clare had left in a worn skirt and bodice, clogs and a shawl, carrying all she owned in a bundle. This elegant lady who climbed down from the cab, unceremoniously handing her sleeping baby to Betty Marsden as though they had parted only yesterday, wore a sprigged cotton gown in a pretty shade of rose, a slipping shawl in which swirls of rose and honey and ivory were mixed together, a straw bonnet with silk roses beneath the brim and a pair of brown, ankle-length boots. The cab driver, though he had been somewhat alarmed by the climb up to Edgeclough, called her "ma'am" respectfully, wondering as he looked about him at the poor folk clustered to greet her what the devil a lady such as she was doing up here. He hauled down what seemed to be a tremendous amount of luggage, and tipped his hat to her before turning the horse and cab and heading off back to Oldham.

It was, of course, Rory Patrick who broke the ice and for a dreadful moment Clare was convinced they would at once see whose son he was. Certainly not Lew's! He had allowed Davy Bretherton to lift him down from the cab but would not be held in his arms. Struggling vigorously he escaped, then stood, several feet away, his hands on his hips, his face defiant, his scowl telling them all that he was a special sort of boy and they had best recognise it.

"I've got a dog called Fred," he announced importantly, though it didn't quite come out of his mouth in such an articulate manner. They watched him, quite mesmerised, then four-year-old Joe Bretherton began to laugh and nudge his friend, Ernie Marsden, who was a year younger.

"What dost think 'e said, Ernie?"

"Nay, don't ask me," Ernie answered and before anyone could stop him Rory launched himself at the two boys, his fists flying, his face as bright as a ripe tomato, his boots ready to kick at any bit of flesh that was handy. Rory Patrick Earnshaw had never been in the company of other children in his short life, except that of his little brother, and in that short life he had been petted and pampered, especially by Albert, who, now he had taken over the rooms above the printing presses where Clare and Lew once lived, took him over there as often as he could and spoiled him shamelessly. The boy could wind Albert, and Lavender, round his little finger, and frequently did so, and Lew, who was a gentle man and could not abide striking a child, had failed to give him the punishment he often deserved. Rory had grown to believe that he was all-important. Whatever he said was considered to be a wonder and these two boys, who were very obviously laughing at *him*, had to be taught a lesson.

The women began to laugh at his antics, for it was evident that Lew had been overly indulgent with his son. If he had been theirs he would have had a good leathering. It seemed that Lew Earnshaw was an indulgent father; soft, they would have called it, but it was nothing to do with them, was it? The thought was illuminated on their faces and in their inclination to be a bit shocked and at the same time amused, but suddenly their laugher faltered as each one, who had seen Martin Heywood go past a hundred times, recognised who his father, his *real* father was.

But it brought them back to how they had once been with Clare as the men sorted out the scrapping boys, Rory Patrick Earnshaw getting a cuff on the ear along with the other two. For a moment he was astounded, then, as Joe and Ernie, undaunted, grinned amiably at him, he grinned back and before you could say "if anyone needs a good hiding this one does", he was in the dirt playing with them.

Clare watched him for a moment then turned, somewhat abashed, to the group of women, and one by one they approached her, Betty and Marie, Maggie and Annie, toddlers about their feet, the older children clustering shyly at their mothers' backs. She was hugged and wondered over, their hands smoothing her shawl, their "eeh, will tha' look at our Clare," murmured affectionately in her ears, for that was what she was. Their Clare. One of them. They might have reservations about her association with him up at Moorhouse Farm which had resulted in the lad who was rolling on the doorstep with young Joe and Ernie, but the little lad, meaning Joss, who slept peacefully in Betty's arms, was the spit of their Lew. They didn't know how to take to her elder lad but this one, this one who was so obviously Lew Earnshaw's bairn, was loved from the moment they first set eyes on him.

But Clare hadn't come to gossip, though that would take place later, naturally, for there was a lot to catch up on, but to see Nelly, who must have heard the commotion outside and would be demanding what the dickens was going on before long. She hadn't the strength to shout as once she had but Marie had lent her the brass handbell her own mam had prized and left to her when she died and it was ringing demandingly now.

"Tha'd best get in there, lass," Betty said, handing her the baby, "or there'll be 'ell ter pay. I should leave little lad," turning to stare curiously at Martin Heywood's son who was by now as filthy dirty as his two companions. "'E'd be too much fer 'er just now."

Clare had a quiet word with Will who sat in front of the fire in the chair where he had sat for twenty years, his expression lost and forlorn like a child whose mother has left him to fend for himself.

"Will."

"Clare, lass, 'tis grand ter see thi'," he said, giving her a wan smile then turning once more to stare into the empty grate. Will

Bradbury didn't know what he would do without his Nelly to tell him.

Nelly was lying in the bed she had shared with Will Bradbury for twenty years. Nelly had married Will when she was twenty-five, though none but Will knew it. It had seemed to them all that Nelly was well into middle age and always had been, though she was, in fact, only forty-five. Her eldest, Arthur, was seventeen and off trapping rabbits on the moorland which was his usual weekend activity, for a rabbit stew was very acceptable to these people who had to make a penny do the work of two. Her girls, Mildred and Dorcas, sixteen and fifteen, had both been fortunate in finding employment away from the mills and were in service over at the Hall.

She was forty-five and looked sixty and though Clare knew she could not possibly be as old as that she was badly shocked, not only by Will's fearful lethargy, but by the changes the years had wrought in Nelly. Her hands, frail and thin, plucked at the snow-white coverlet that crossed her thin chest and for a terrible moment Clare's heart almost stopped beating. Nelly was pale, but not just pale, for her skin was dead-looking, the colour of the ash in her fireplace which, had she been up to it, would have caused someone to get the rounds of the kitchen for not clearing it away. Her eyes had fallen into deep, plum-coloured sockets and her nose stood out from her sunken flesh like the beak of a small bird. There seemed to be a hint of blue to her lips and Clare felt a sudden rush of terror, for she knew she was looking at a dying woman.

Her voice was thready but still as peremptory. "Well, don't just stand there lak a great lump, Clare Earnshaw. Come over 'ere where I can get a good look at thi'."

It was evident that, despite being ill, she was just as sharp, just as aggravated with folk who would insist on being awkward with her and what she knew was best for them, but there was little strength in her voice. Her eyes were almost colourless and for a moment Clare had great difficulty in remembering what colour they had once been. She was shrivelled, as tiny as a child beneath the covers and her hair, which had been a mixture of grey and brown, was now snow white.

Putting the sleeping baby on the rug before the dead fire where he at once slipped into that relaxed posture that only children can achieve when they sleep, Clare hurried across the room to kneel at Nelly's bedside and taking her cold, thin hands – why were her hands so cold on such a mild day? – between her own strong, warm ones, she chafed them lovingly, then bent her head to kiss them. Nelly, in that way Clare remembered so well, tugged them away weakly, on her face an expression of exasperation.

"Nay, give over, lass. Theer's no need ter tekk on so. An' I'll 'ave a word wi' that Daisy soon as mebbe. She said she were goin' ter write ter thi' an' though I said 'nay' it seems she did. Daft 'apporth. I'll be up an' about as soon as I've 'ad me a bit of a rest, so there were no need fer tha' ter come traipsin' all this way. Them damned fools downstairs will keep fussin' and frettin' but if they think I'm stayin' 'ere, then they can think again. Mind, I'll not say it isn't grand ter see tha', an't bairn. Lew's bairn," she added as though Clare had only the one. "Give over mitherin', will tha'. I'm as right as ninepence."

Her words were sharp but there was a glimmer of a smile about her lips as though her own wit amused her.

"You don't look right as ninepence to me, Nelly. You look as though a few days in bed will do you the world of good and I'm here to make sure you get it."

"When I want tha' opinion I'll ask fer it, my lass," Nelly snapped. "Any road what dost tha' know about it?" She slapped Clare's hands away impatiently, then tried to lift herself to a sitting position, her eyes going to the child on the floor who was making noises in his throat indicating that he was about to awaken.

"Give us a 'and, lass," she demanded testily, as though she resented being forced to ask for assistance. She was the one who helped others. She was the one who nursed the sick, and mixed infusions for a poorly child. She was the one who scrubbed floors in the ferocious fight she warred on dirt which she abhorred. She was the one who told others what to do. She was the one who decided who should be in their bed and, when they were better, told them they could get up. She had worked herself to a standstill in the service of others. They had only to knock on her door at any time of the day or night and she'd be there helping with a difficult labour or a feverish bairn and was it any wonder, Clare agonised, that she looked so ill? Mind you, she'd perked up a bit since Clare had knelt by her bed, even though, when Clare had lifted her to a sitting position and propped her up with several pillows, she still gave the impression that it was only her own iron will that was keeping her there.

"Fetch babby, Clare," she said softly. "Let's get a look at Lew's son."

Clare lifted the baby, Lew's son, who had inherited his father's good humour, and immediately at the sight of her he began to chuckle and lift his arms to be picked up and when she settled him gently by the old woman's side, he turned to study her with great interest and with what seemed to be great courtesy. His smile broadened and he put out a finger and delicately touched her cheek and when, surprisingly, Nelly let a tear or two roll down her cheek he turned to his mother, his baby mouth pursed in a circle of amazement. Again he leaned forward and again he put out a baby finger, this time catching one of Nelly's tears on the end of it.

"Eh, my lad . . ." Nelly managed to utter. "Eh, my dear lad." On her face was an expression of unutterable joy. "I remember 'is pa at same age. This little lad's just like 'im. By 'eck, our Clare. Tha's done me't world o' good fetchin' 'im ter see me."

"I've another downstairs, Nelly," Clare said gently, taking the baby on her lap where she sat on the edge of Nelly's bed.

At once Nelly turned her head away fretfully.

"I'm tired now, lass, so if tha'll just pull me pillows down I'll close me eyes fer a minnit."

With these words Nelly dismissed Martin Heywood's son and Clare's association with the boy's father. Nelly, like Lew, had forgiven her but she had not forgotten. Nelly loved Clare as though she were her own daughter, her own flesh and blood, but until the end of her days, which by the look of her would not be long, she would never understand.

Chapter Thirty-one

Clare remained in Edgeclough for seven weeks, the time it took Nelly to die. Though Daisy had not used the postal service Clare did, sending loving notes to Lew, explaining that Nelly needed her, but, more importantly, needed the joy that Lew's son gave her in these last days of her life, Lew's son whom she had loved from the first moment his finger had touched her cheek and whom, in a strange way, she had come to regard as her grandchild. She would never see another, she knew that, and so did Clare.

Betty and Maggie, Marie and Annie were plainly relieved to have Clare taking Nelly into her care. Betty, Maggie and Annie were spinners at Hopkinson's Mill but when Nelly took to her bed Marie, who had also worked as a spinner and whose children were the youngest, was forced to stay at home and mind them, and the others who had been in Nelly's care. There were six children still considered to be too young – by their mothers at least – to go as scavengers or little piecers in the spinning-room, and so Marie had taken over Nelly's role and was paid the few pence a week once given to Nelly. Besides which, she was pregnant again with her fourth. But Marie was near her time and the burden of looking out for six children, three of them boys who wandered off as boys will, and at the same time seeing to Nelly, was becoming too much for her. Her relief was written on her face as she lowered herself heavily into Nelly's chair opposite Clare and gratefully took the cup of tea Clare offered her. Clare had sent Daisy into Crossfold on the day after she arrived to purchase groceries, especially tea which was a real pick-me-up in times of trouble, and other comestibles that were needed, since she could not expect Nelly and Will to feed herself and two growing children on what Will earned. She had made bread that morning and a batch of scones plus a large meat and potato pie, and the aroma in the kitchen was mouthwatering.

Clare passed Marie a hot buttered scone. She could remember how Marie had been when Clare had first come to Edgeclough, a young mother with one child, bright and cheerful and optimistic about the future, for weren't she and her Davy to confine their family to no more than two, which was enough for any man to support. But here she was, nearly five years later, with three, one still a toddler and another in her belly dragging her down. She was twenty-two and looked ten years older, as they all did in the hard life that was thrust upon them. No wonder Lew was such an agitator for the rights of man – and woman – Clare thought, since it was these women and their oppressed children he fought for. Given a decent wage their husbands could be the sole breadwinners and the mothers remain at their own hearth, as mothers should, to bring up their children in a decent home.

"How long to your time, Marie?" she asked her compassionately.

"Two weeks, I reckon, p'raps less." She did her best to smile. "But us'll manage. Tha' dids't right thing leavin', Clare, fer theer's nowt but 'ard work an' worry 'ere, lass."

Clare smiled. "I work hard, Marie, harder than I've ever worked in my life, so I do."

"Aye, tha' were never a shirker but tha've done well on it. You an' Lew."

"Yes, we've been lucky. Now, I'd best go and see what that

naughty lad of mine is doing. I think I'll have to tie him to the table leg or he'll be off up the track on to the moor."

"Gets it from his pa, I reckon. He allus loved t'moorland, right from bein' a nipper, I were told." And Clare was left with the feeling that Marie did not mean Lew Earnshaw.

What she had dreaded ever since she had made up her mind to come to Edgeclough had not happened. She was not naïve enough to believe that Martin was unaware of her presence so close to Moorhouse Farm, nor that she had her son, *his* son with her. She had expected him to come galloping up on that black mare of his demanding, if not to see the boy, at least making some lame excuse as to why he was in Nelly and Will Bradbury's cottage – *his* cottage – which he rented to them. She had not been out of the place since she had arrived, for Nelly needed all her attention, and Rory and Joss demanded a great deal of her time. She had watched for him as she sat beside the sleeping form of Nelly, rocking in the rocking-chair which had been brought up from the kitchen. The window of the bedroom was low, only about a foot from the floor and looked out on the lane that passed the cottage but not once had she seen him go by. She was relieved but at the same time astonished, for the lane led down to the main road to Crossfold which Martin visited regularly so perhaps he was going the long way round, as she had done once when she drove the little gig he had given her. But why? she asked herself, for Martin was the last man to avoid a confrontation and since it involved his own son, who he would surely want to see, she was doubly confused.

Nelly's slow deterioration was not the only difficulty she had to deal with, for Rory was a bright and intelligent child and knew exactly how to get what he wanted. At the rear of the shop in Manchester he could be allowed to play in the yard with the growing number of toys Lew carved or hammered together for him. He was safe there, fastened in by high walls and a sturdy gate and knowing nothing else had been content with it but here all he had to do was open the front door of the

Bradbury cottage, which he did by dragging Nelly's stool across the flagged floor, lift the latch, climb down the steps and run like the wind wherever he liked. Joe and Ernie, having parents who had disciplined their children to the strict obedience that was vital in their world, not to mention Nelly, who would have their hide if they stepped out of line, could be trusted to wander no more than a few yards from their own front doors. They had been brought up on the edge of the moorland which they had been taught from an early age was dangerous, but Rory Patrick had no such fears and could think of nothing more splendid than escaping into it.

He had been brought back a dozen times by folk on the tramp up to Old Delph or down to Dobens, by shepherds who were irascible at the waste of their time and who declared the lad needed a clip roun't lug. Joe or Ernie had become his warders, young as they were, running to tell her that Rory was off up the track to Friars Mere, with that self-satisfied smugness about them that was the mark of the *good* boy. When he saw her coming up behind him he would break into laughter and run like the wind rustling through the gorse and heather which grew as high as his head and though he nearly drove her demented she could not help but love him, feeling the swell of it inside her, as she felt it for his father. He was naughty, disobedient and afraid of nothing, but his charm, his chuckling laughter caught at her heart and she could not bear to "leather" him as the rest of the folk at Edgeclough advised her to do before it was too late. They would roll over and over on the tufted, springy grass, she and her son, shrieking with laughter, their arms about one another and though she knew she should scold him she found she couldn't, for there was something special, something that only this boy, and this boy's father, awoke in her.

Marie's baby was born during the second week of Clare's return, another girl who she called Emmy, and within a few days Marie declared herself able to take over the children, which included Rory Patrick and baby Joss, for by this time Nelly needed Clare's constant attention. Her mind was beginning to roam and she often spoke of Bertha and Jeannie beside whom she imagined she was minding a spinning frame, of Will who, in her mind's dip back into the past was a young man who had tried, and failed, to take liberties with his bride-to-be. When she was lucid she did her best to pass on to Clare some of the healing remedies her mam had passed on to her and which, now, she needed for herself. An infusion of meadowsweet to make her sleep, and something else, a liquid that was kept in a bottle on the top shelf at the back of her kitchen dresser but whose name she would not divulge to Clare. She was often in pain and begged Clare to reach it down and mix a certain amount with water.

"It's nowt ter 'urt me, lass, at least not now, but it fair tekks pain away. Nay, don't mither me fer't name of it fer I'll not tell thi'. It's all in me 'ead, what me mam told me an' theer's enough ter see me out."

"Will you stop talking like that, Nelly. While I'm here to see to you—"

"Give over, lass," Nelly said scornfully, "it's no good pretendin'. Now see, why don't tha' fetch that little lad?"

"Will you let me fetch the doctor, Nelly? I'm sure he could prescribe something."

"Lass, lass, I don't want no doctors. Theer's nowt a doctor can do that a sight o' Lew's lad wouldn't cure. Fetch 'im up, theer's a good lass."

As the weeks drew on Nelly began to be troubled with bedsores and again at Nelly's direction Clare made up a mixture which, with the help of the other women, was applied daily to each weeping spot with a feather, but Nelly's suffering grew worse so that when Maggie or Betty came reluctantly up the stairs, Nelly awaited their ministrations with dread, Clare despaired and began to long for her beloved friend to die and escape the torture they put her through. Clare slept downstairs on a palliasse before the kitchen fire, her sons curled up like puppies beside her, with either Betty, Annie, Maggie or

Marie taking a turn at sitting beside the bed with Nelly, whose gasps and moans could be heard downstairs.

Clare was with her when she died. She had lain quietly and free from pain due to the enormous amount of the liquid that Clare had mixed in a little brandy and, one by one, knowing the end was near, they slipped in to see her, her daughters who had been sent for and her son, and all the women whose burdens she had taken so willingly on her own narrow shoulders. She smiled at each one as they came in, kissed her cheek and went out silently, holding back their tears until they were out of her sight.

At the last minute she called out weakly for her Will, who was the only one to break down in her presence and it was she who comforted him while Clare stood at the top of the stairs and tried not to listen to what husband and wife said to one another. When Will blundered past her, his face spasming in grief, Clare moved sadly back to Nelly's bedside and took her hand.

"E's a good lad, that 'un," Nelly said, allowing her hand to be held, then she seemed to doze. Her breathing became laboured, a pause, a gasp, two longer pauses, then, opening her eyes and seeing Clare she said tenderly, "Eeh, I do like thi'."

They were the last words she spoke.

The moorland about the tiny church above Old Delph was so crowded those who came late were forced to stand at the back of the ever-growing press of people. There were hundreds of them, women, and some men, who owed their lives to Nelly Bradbury and her purges, her infusions, her plain good sense and no-nonsense approach to their problems which had got most of them through the adversities that were the scourge of their class. As they stood quietly on the hillside those on the crowd's edge could see nothing except the back of the person in front of them but they had come to pay homage to the woman who was being laid to rest and though they might not hear the service, or even witness her coffin being put in the ground, they were there to honour her.

Inside the church the service was simple and short, attended by those who had lived beside her, who had suffered under her sharp tongue, who had flourished under her benevolent rule and who had all loved Nelly Bradbury though they had perhaps not known it at the time. The only one missing was Lew which had been a great blow, not just to him who had looked on Nelly as he might his own mother, but to Clare who needed his patient strength and sound good sense to get her through. It seemed that Henry had been struck down with a strange fever and had been ordered to his bed by his doctor and who else was there to get out the *Hopwood Review* at the end of the week. Clare knew that Lew would be torn between his need to say goodbye to Nelly and his duty to the men whose cause he upheld and wrote about in the newspaper. His duty won, as it always would.

She was gathering her things ready for her journey home the next day when, perhaps sensing that he was to leave this magical place where his mother had brought him and where he was determined in his child's mind to remain, Rory was discovered to be missing.

Clare was doing her best to comfort Will and at the same time coax him out of the misery Nelly's death had caused in him. He would be all right, he told her, doing his best to smile, for was he not a Lancashire lad and everyone knew what strong stuff *they* were made of, but he would keep listening for his lass's tart-voiced commands, he said, and it was going to take a bit of doing having to think for himself. He knew the others would rally round. Betty had told him she'd cook a bit of something each day with her own for him and Arthur, and he could manage the odds and ends of washing and such. He and Arthur would have to keep the place spotless, he smiled sadly, or Nelly up in that heaven where she was sure to have gone would give them what for, but it was just that ... well, Clare wasn't to worry about him. He'd go back to work tomorrow and with a bit of company he'd do right enough.

"Anyroad, wheer's that rascal o' thine got to? Cottage is quiet enough wi'out our Nelly never mind 'is endless chatter."

He wasn't in the lane, nor in any of the cottages where he thought himself to be enormously welcome and neither of his special friends, or at least he considered them to be, Joe and Ernie, had seen him for ages. Ages to them might mean ten minutes or an hour, since time means nothing to a child.

Clare sighed wearily. Really, Rory was getting to be beyond her control and the sooner they got back to Manchester the better. At least he couldn't escape from the back yard and she could get on with her work without feeling she daren't take her eyes off him. He was a little devil and needed a strong hand to rule him and she wondered despairingly if Lew was up to it, or even cared enough. Rory was not his son and though he loved him and showed no difference in his treatment between Rory and Joss, would it not be understandable if he was inclined to favour his own lad and leave Martin Heywood's son to her. He was a fair man, scrupulous in his dealings with others but a father's love for his own flesh and blood would be bound to dominate.

"I'd best go an' look for him, Will, or God knows where he could get to. Trouble is we don't know how long he's been gone. I blame myself. I should have watched him more closely but . . ."

"I know, lass. Tha've 'ad a lot on tha' mind an' what we'd a' done wi'out thi' I don't know—"

"I thought he was with Marie," she interrupted distractedly. She was dressed in the plain grey skirt and bodice she wore at home when she was cooking or serving in the shop, simple and practical. She had even brought her old clogs which had seen such service in those first days after her arrival at Edgeclough and during her time as scullery-maid at Moorhouse. It was the beginning of August and a clear, warm, sunny day and so, not needing her shawl and with her hair tied carelessly back with a scrap of ribbon, the ends of it curling vigorously into the small of her back, she began to climb the track towards Friars Mere.

It was as though she had known even as she had run from house to house looking for Rory exactly where he would be and with whom. Martin was dressed as casually as she, breeches and riding boots, and a shirt open at the neck with the sleeves rolled up. He was sitting on the tufted grass, his back against the same rock she and he had once leaned on, and between his knees, held in loving and proprietory arms, was their son. The boy was drowsing, perfectly at ease with this man who, as a child will, he remembered vaguely as the one who had bought him ice-cream.

"I wondered how long you'd be," Martin said casually, just as though she were expected and was late. "I've been up here at some part of every day since you arrived. I was sorry to hear about Mrs Bradbury. I know how fond you were of her. I didn't call because ... well ..." He became somewhat embarrassed at being caught out in thoughts of a good deed.

It was many weeks since she had seen him in Manchester, but somehow, up here where their love had started and where, possibly, their son had been conceived, she was as relaxed as the boy.

"I've only just missed him, the little tinker. He's always doing this, running off the minute my back's turned. He loves the moor and the open spaces."

"Naturally he would. He's a Heywood. One day he'll live up here, run the farm when I've gone. He's not a city child, my darling. It's in his blood to run free, as I did as a lad, to escape the restrictions put on him by a life in the city. You must see that, Clare, and come home."

Come home! What a man this was who held his son as though he had every right to do so. What a man for seeing only one side. His! He believed that he had only to point out to her how things should be, how he thought they should be, and she would, in the end, quietly give in. It was so *right* to him. There was no grey, only black and white and it amazed him that she didn't seem to realise it. She was *his* woman even though she might be married to another man. This was *his* son and he could see no reason why they should not live together at Moorhouse Farm. Bugger the scandal, he would say. As long as he had her and Rory and his farm what did the chitter-chatter of neighbours matter? His business concerns would continue to thrive, for the men he was involved with were businessmen themselves and did not care about things that might appal their wives as long as a profit was to come from it. They would be received nowhere. They would live a life isolated from the people he now entertained and was entertained by, but now, because of his son, she suspected, though she knew he loved her to the depth of his soul, he was prepared to give it all up.

She stared out across the valley that lay beneath them, her face sad and brooding, for she knew he spoke the truth. About Rory. The boy was at home, not just here up on the high moorland but in the arms of the man who was his father. Lew had been nothing but kindness itself to the lad, but perhaps there was some bond between a natural father and son that the boy, young as he was, sensed and found he liked.

How lovely it all was up here. The sky was a high, placid blue and the sun fell in a warm haze on her head and shoulders. The slight breeze was fresh and soaked in the fragrance of heather and gorse. A curlew took flight, alarmed by the wickering of Martin's mare which was tethered at the side of the outcropping of rock, the bird's song rippling through the clear air. There was a thick pall of smoke rising from the direction of Crossfold, sour and yellow, where the mill chimneys spewed it upwards, but before them was a great sweep of wildly rolling moorland, serene and beautiful on this soft summer day. It was rough and uneven, patched with bracken, gorse and heather, brown and yellow and purple which, in a few weeks' time, would begin to fade as autumn approached. Far down in the valley the fields were green, lush with the grass at which the tiny figures of the cows pulled and grew fat on as they moved slowly from place to place. She had not realised until now how much she had missed this quiet, often bleak and sombre beauty that was spread at her feet, and for a moment her heart quailed at the thought that she was to leave it, perhaps for ever, and return to the stinking mills and factories of Manchester.

The boy slept and Martin laid him gently on a patch of cushioning clover. He gazed down at him for a moment, reaching out a finger to brush his flushed, rounded cheek, then turned, squatting down beside her, his arm placed in what seemed to be no more than companionable comfort across her shoulder.

"You love it as much as I do, don't you?" he said quietly. "You always have."

"Yes." She could say no more, for what was there to add?

"Don't go back, my love. Pack your things and I'll send the gig over to fetch you. You shall be mistress of Moorhouse."

"And mistress to you, as you've always wanted."

"I would marry you if I could, you must know that. I want the boy to have my name, to be a Heywood but I want *you* just as much, Clare. I didn't know how much until I lost you. I want you in my life always, you and the boy."

"I have another son, Martin. Lew's son, but he's my child as much as Rory is."

He rested his head against hers and his voice was so low she could barely hear it.

"I know, and I cannot imagine what . . . what we are to do about it." He was telling her that though he wanted her and Rory he had no room for Lew Earnshaw's son in his life.

"There is nothing to be done. I cannot leave him and I cannot take him from his father who loves him as much as you love Rory. Even if I could, he wouldn't let me."

"So, what are we to do? I cannot allow you or Rory to go out of my life."

"Allow! It has nothing to do with you, Martin. You are not

the one who says whether we go or stay. This is my life, my sons' lives, Lew's life and you don't even come into the equation."

She felt him stiffen against her, then, before she could resist, that is if she had wanted to, he pulled her down flat on the grass, held her hands above her head in one of his and began to kiss her, slowly, lingeringly, his lips folding about hers as they parted, his tongue finding hers while with his other hand he began to caress her breast, seeking her nipple beneath the thin cotton fabric of her bodice. He found it but, not satisfied, he began to undo the buttons one by one, turning back the fabric, untying the drawstring and pulling down the cotton of her white chemise until both her breasts were exposed, not just to the teasing breeze, the warmth of the sun, but to his hand, to his lips, his gaze, his searching tongue. She began to moan, her senses, her *sense* gone, for did not her son lie sleeping only a yard or two away, but her body cared nought for that, only the feel of Martin's hand, his flesh on hers, her flesh which had lusted for his for over two years.

Stifling the sounds she was making with his mouth, his hand moved down to the hem of her skirt and without gentleness or compassion or indeed any of the delicacy a man shows the woman he loves, dragged it up about her waist. Her drawers were discarded, as were his breeches and there, with the sun beating down, the sound of sheep bleating from higher up the moor and the soft deep breathing of their sleeping child in their ears, he took her. Like a man paying for a sixpenny tart he took her, penetrating her so deeply she gasped and almost choked against his rapacious mouth. He was a knife fitting to a scabbard, quickly, expertly bringing her again and again to the peaks of sensation and as she moved with him she didn't care what he did to her or even who saw him doing it. It was glorious, lusty, with no love in it only need, wanting, two starving bodies falling on a feast and gorging themselves, for who knew when they would eat again.

He was gentle with her later, helping her with her clothing, wiping away the tears which, unaccountably, ran down her face, kissing her with a passion of love and holding her in arms that warned her that though they might be tender, gentle, would never let her go.

He said so. "You're mine again, Clare Hanrahan. Mine and no other man's. D'you understand? You know about desire now and what you and Lew Earnshaw have has nothing to do with it. Don't tell me again that you love him, for you do not. You may be *fond* of him, I dare say but it's me you love and you'll not forget it, or me, not ever. So get back to Edgeclough and pack your things. I'll be over in an hour to pick you up. D'you hear?"

"Yes, I hear, Martin."

"I'll wake the boy and carry him to the top of the village. You can manage the rest. Now, tell me you love me quickly. Dear God . . ." as her mouth rose instinctively seeking his. "Dear God in heaven, I could start all over again."

She lay as one drugged in his arms and would have let him, her face soft, her eyes unfocused and he laughed triumphantly, crushing her to him, a man victorious, believing that he had won the day, and not only the day but her and their son. She was submissive now, still cast in the aftermath of loving, her limbs inclined to be flaccid and he laughed softly as he helped her to her feet.

His son chuckled in delight as Martin Heywood woke him and tossed him in the air, then began the walk back to Edgeclough with Rory Patrick's mother, bemused, drifting behind them.

He kissed her again with all the possessive pride of a man who has taken his woman to the edge of enchantment, and will do so again at the earliest opportunity, then watched her go, their son in her arms, down the track towards Edgeclough.

"An hour," he called after her confidently, but when that hour had passed and he drew up smartly in the little gig to take his woman and his son back to their rightful place beside him, they had gone.

Chapter Thirty-two

She knew, of course, that he would come after them but at least in her own home with her husband beside her she was better equipped to protect herself against Martin and his preposterous demands. Against his pleas to give everything up and come and live with him, against his tortured longing for her and their son, against the strength and sweetness and passion of their love, the fierceness of it which had shown itself on Friars Mere, and against her own weakness which yearned to give in to him.

The speed with which she had packed had astonished the residents of the row of cottages but, knowing her past and the fact that she had just come down from Friars Mere looking as though a violent storm had buffeted her and at the same time in a sort of trance, they guessed it was something to do with Martin Heywood who was known to be single-minded in his pursuit of what he wanted. Presumably this time it was not only her but her elder son.

"Is there a carter about here who would take me and the children to the station?" she had asked breathlessly, stuffing her own and the children's clothes any old how into the wicker baskets she had brought with her from Manchester, and when they said there was she had begged Frankie Marsden to run down and fetch him. Before an hour had gone by she and her children, with their luggage, were in the back of the cart, she still in her plain grey servant's gown, the baby grizzling and bewildered by his mother's sharpness and the boy, that Rory, shouting that he wasn't going anywhere and demanding to be taken back to "the man". "The man!" And who else could that be but Martin Heywood?

When, half an hour later, Martin Heywood had thundered down the track in the gig and come to a frantic stop in front of Nelly's cottage, the women had run for cover and the men, though standing shoulder to shoulder in defence of the woman who had come from nowhere and become one of their own, looked uneasy.

"Where is she?" he had roared, knowing at once that she had gone and though he had the look of a man who would kill should he be crossed there was also a desolation about him that, rough working men that they were, touched their hearts. He had whipped the poor beast that pulled the gig into a frantic gallop, moving so fast he was in danger of tipping the vehicle on its side, making for the railway station in Oldham they suspected, praying that Clare was already on a train and beyond his reach. The way he had looked as he leaped into the gig they would not have been surprised to hear that he had dragged her and his son out of the compartment and taken them to Moorhouse by force.

They had looked at her askance at the railway station in Oldham when she paid for her ticket to Manchester, for it was not often a servant girl, which was what they supposed her to be, perhaps the children's nursemaid, and in clogs and a shawl, travelled about on a train. Nevertheless she had a somewhat grand manner about her as though she were used to receiving respect and service, and the porter who put her and her children in the railway compartment was surprised and gratified by the size of the tip she gave him.

The same porter was distinctly startled half an hour later when a gentleman, leaving his heaving pony and the trap it pulled on the forecourt of the station where it blocked the incoming and outgoing traffic, causing pandemonium, dragged him by the lapels and demanded if he had seen a lady with two children getting on the train to Manchester.

"A lady, sir . . . well, depends what tha' mean by a lady."

"Surely to God you know a female from a male," the man had snarled, shaking him fiercely. "A female with two children."

"Oh, aye, but train's gone 'alf an 'our since an'—"

"When's the next one?" the man snapped, giving him another shake for good measure.

"To Manchester, sir?"

"Of course to bloody Manchester, you fool."

"Well, I reckon tha'll 'ave a long wait. Best ask station-master . . ." And he was vastly relieved when the man dropped him and stalked off.

She had had no time to let Lew or Lavender know that she was coming home and was compelled to find a cab at Victoria Station and get herself and her entourage to Dale Street, where she was greeted with a rapture that went some way to alleviate the dragging pain in her breast. There was nothing inside her now except a patient waiting for the hurt to go. To have the weeks and months and years pass so that the pain of losing Martin all over again would lessen, the pain that was overwhelming her but which must be hidden not only from Lew but from Lavender. She felt lost and frightened, though why that should be with Lew's arms warmly about her she didn't know. She could feel something thump and shake inside her, as if her poor aching heart had come loose and was surprised that Lew did not remark on it when he dragged her into his arms. She could feel the dread of the future settle like a heavy armour about her body, as heavy as the arms that held her and which weren't Martin's.

"Sweetheart, sweetheart, we weren't expectin' thi', were we, Lavender? Not that we're not glad ter see thi', lass," kissing her heartily, not caring who was watching. "Why didn't tha' let us know tha' were comin'?" he kept repeating, eventually letting her go, reaching for his son and cradling him to his chest, exclaiming on how he had grown, asking about Nelly and wondering sadly how they were to manage without her, his voice going on and on as he told her of his own doings, innocently expecting her to be vastly interested in everything that had happened since she left.

Lavender was the same, rattling on about profits and the success of the small shop which was packed out every day and what a find Betty had turned out to be and Kitty, Mrs Mullaney, was always asking after her. At the same time Lavender did her best to get a turn at holding young Joss whom Lew seemed reluctant to part with, and trying to hug the mutinous Rory who told them all coldly that he didn't like this place and wanted to go back to "the man". He was almost two years old and speaking more clearly and Clare watched as Lew turned his head, looking at Rory with a puzzled expression which said that he *almost* knew who the boy was talking about. It was there on the edge of his perception but Rory began to babble about Joe and Ernie and to describe his adventures on the moors where Frankie, who was a big boy, caught rabbits and that one day soon, when they went back on the train to the place, he, Rory Patrick, would catch rabbits too. They were to grow accustomed to *the place* and Rory's constant reference to it. Will and Davy were mentioned and Clare saw Lew begin to smile, the look of puzzlement melting away as the boy spoke of men that Lew knew.

Lew made love to her that night and though her heart jibbed and panicked at it, remembering that only hours ago it had been enchanted by the encounter with Martin Heywood, her body was submissive, for this man who loved her so gently was her husband and for the rest of their lives, or a good part of it, would be doing this to her. Though she shed no tears, she wept inside for her love, lying beside her husband when he slept. He was satisfied, for she had folded him in her arms and kissed him lovingly but late into the night she lay awake, her soul bruised, for what sort of a woman allows two men to take her body within hours of one another and the answer was not pleasant. Dear sweet Mother in heaven, how was she to go on with this charade? But then it had not been a charade before Martin came back into her life. She had been content, satisfied with her life with Lew, with her children, her work, her friends and had believed that it would go on for ever. And she could not pretend to herself that this struggle with Martin was ended. That Martin would casually give up on her and their child and calmly walk away. That from now on, dragging herself from the pit of despair she was in, she would resume that life, that gladness would return and if she herself was not happy, then she would make sure that Lew was. It was not over by a long chalk. She, who knew Martin Heywood better than any living soul, was certain of that.

Martin Heywood strode into her shop the next day, arrogant, stiff-necked, commanding and the women who were gossiping at her counter fell silent, making way for him as he moved towards her where she was wrapping up two meat pies for a customer, clearly expecting them to do so.

"Mrs Earnshaw," he said politely enough, "may I have a private word with you."

Though she had known he would waylay her somewhere she had not expected it to be in her own home. Perhaps the park, or at Kitty's or indeed any of the shops or in any of the streets she moved along, but she might have known, really she might. He had done all that in the weeks before she went to Edgeclough and it had not worked. He had waited patiently, catching her here and there outside her home, so now, knowing she would be wary, he had trapped her where she could not escape him. He meant to challenge Lew, demand his rights, stake his claim for she was *his woman* and Rory was *his* son and Lew Earnshaw must accept it.

Her expression became haunted, her eyes deep pools of horror, almost black and when she opened her mouth to speak nothing came out except perhaps a whispered moan. Her customers gazed at her, as open-mouthed as she, then turned to look at the well-dressed gentleman. It was only just gone seven o'clock and they themselves were off to their machines in the mill, but what the hell was this toff doing here so early in the morning, and all dressed up like a dog's dinner into the bargain? Lavender, whose own face was as white as a sheet, moved protectively towards her and Tilly stared in astonishment from one to the other. Clare could hear Lew whistling down in his cellar, putting some finishing touches to something or other he was making, before crossing the road to the offices of the *Hopwood Review*. Henry was still somewhat weak after his bout of fever and Lew and Albert were hard pressed without him, but so far they had managed. From the back yard came the sound of Rory scolding Betty as she refused to open the back gate, since he was determined to go to the train, he was telling her, and Joss was howling, probably for some toy Rory, as big brothers do, had snatched from him.

Suddenly her brain cleared and her heart stopped its frantic clanging about in her chest and with a bright smile, as false as the one on his face, she beckoned to him to come behind the counter, lifting the flap to allow him to pass the two slack-jawed assistants.

"Come into the kitchen, sir," she invited him, then, turning to her customers and to Lavender and Tilly, her appalling smile widened.

"I won't be long," she told them. "I just have some business to transact with this gentleman."

She and the gentleman disappeared into the kitchen. Closing the door behind her and praying that Lew would stay down in the cellar where he was still whistling tunelessly, and that Betty would keep Rory out of sight, she turned like a tigress and would have had his eyes out if he had not seen what she was about and caught her wrists, holding her at bay with an amused smile on his face. He seemed to be enjoying himself.

"How dare you," she hissed, struggling to get herself free. "How dare you come into my home . . ."

"Let me remind you I came into your *shop* which, I presume, is open to members of the public."

"You know what I mean, damn you. You are not here to buy a bloody meat pie."

"No, I am come for my son, madam, and if you should care to come as well I . . . I . . ." He hesitated for a second, not being a man who cared to beg. "If you will come too, I should be enormously glad, Clare."

"Stop it, stop it! Are you mad? Haven't I made it plain enough? I am married to Lew and can go nowhere."

"You were not concerned with Lew yesterday on Friars Mere, my pet, as I recall. In fact, he was furthest from your mind as you—"

"Stop it. Will you leave me in peace? I cannot leave Lew and Joss. I take it you don't want Joss?" Her eyes had turned the yellow-green of a leopard's, slitted with rage.

His face hardened and his mouth twisted in a cruel snarl. "Then I will take my boy and you can go to the devil."

"No. No, you cannot take Rory, you know you cannot. Jesus, Mary and Joseph, he is . . . I love him and he is mine . . . mine."

"And mine."

"Please, Martin, please, won't you . . . ?" Her rage had drained away to be replaced by hopelessness.

"What? Just go away and leave you alone? Never. You will never be rid of me, you must know that. I am here to see your . . . Lew Earnshaw. I mean to tell him that I wish my son to be with me, and my son's mother as well but I dare say you don't want me to do that, do you?"

"No. Dear God in heaven, please. I swear if you continue to hector me I shall go away and take my sons with me. Somewhere you'll never find us. I shall convince Lew, somehow, that we must leave. I'll tell him you are threatening me."

"And I shall tell him that you and I are lovers again. That we have lain together on Friars Mere, which he will believe since that is where it happened in the past and he will be well aware of it. They all know one another's business over there and I dare say mine is of a more interesting nature than most. That already you may be carrying another of my children. I fight dirty, my love, to get what I want and you know what that is."

All this was carried out in a stage whisper, Martin keeping his voice as low as hers, as though even yet he had hopes that she would simply slip upstairs, pack a bag and, putting their son on her hip, come away with him without disturbing the unsuspecting man whose whistle floated up to them.

Perhaps it was her despair, her pathetic attempt at bravado, or just the deep and enduring love he felt for her, but a change came over his face and it softened fractionally.

"I'm sorry. Hell and damnation, do you think I like doing this to you? I'm desperate, don't you see? If it comes to hurting Lew Earnshaw or denying myself what is rightfully mine, then Lew Earnshaw can go to the devil. He has a son. I want mine!"

She bent her head in a gesture of utter despair, her sweep of dark hair, which had come from its fastening in their struggle, falling across her blanched face.

"Martin ..." she moaned and at once he moved forward and lifting her chin placed his lips gently on hers.

"I'm sorry, my darling. It is my love for you and the boy that drives me to blackmail. I'll go now but I shall be at the Albion. Come to me today and we will talk sensibly." Meaning, of course, that he would have his way, which was, after all, the only sensible way there was.

When she turned blindly, her face wet with tears and her hair in a tangle, he had gone. Leaving the shop to manage without her – after all Lavender was as capable as she was at running it – she fled up to the bedroom she shared with Lew and lying down carefully on their bed as though she might break into a thousand pieces if she should be rough or hurried, she stared up at the ceiling, her face expressionless, her mind blank and empty of all but the thought of Martin, alone in a nameless room waiting for her. A room where no one came who was not invited. A room that was empty of anything other than her and Martin, and a bed!

He was waiting for her in the foyer, standing up when she entered so that she had no need to enquire at the reception desk. No one took any notice of the well-dressed lady and gentleman who sauntered up the wide staircase, itself busy with dozens of visitors hurrying or strolling like themselves up and down its curving length. His suite looked out on to the busy thoroughfare of Piccadilly from which the buzz of the traffic drifted up to them. He locked the door, then, with the infinite patience of a true lover he undressed her slowly, sighing over every inch of exposed flesh, the length of her long, slender neck, the white curve of a shoulder, the soft swell of her breasts and the engorged and rosy red of her nipples, the small of her back, the white satin of her belly, the dark triangle between her thighs, the back of her knees and the arched instep of her foot. She sighed and stretched and moaned, moving herself this way and that at his command, allowing him to see her in every sensual position that might delight him, and did. Somehow, she was too engrossed to notice when he had discarded his own garments and when he lay beside her on the bed, stretching his body the length of hers, his flesh merging with her though he had not yet entered her she began to plead with him, to moan her need, her limbs quivering with joy, her whole body throbbing with it. Still he would not oblige. Easing himself away and casting his eyes down the length of her body he put his mouth delicately against her ankle and let it travel upwards, inch by lingering inch until it reached her mouth before he thrust himself inside her, moving gently at first and then fiercer and fiercer which she met with a fierceness of her own. She clung to him as wave after wave of sensual rejoicing swept through her and she cried out loud with the ecstasy of it.

"I love you, Martin," she wept.

"I know you do, my darling. That is why you are here."

As long as she allowed him to see his boy and consented to come to him at the Albion, it seemed he was prepared to allow her more time. To do what she didn't know. Choose between him and Lew, perhaps. To get used to the idea that he would, in the end, take her back to Moorhouse, her and their son. To give her time to ready herself for her parting, not just with Lew but with Joss, whom he made clear was not to go with them. She was playing for time, she knew that and she spent hours agonising over what she was to do, for whatever it was it would break her heart. There was no answer. There was no way out. She could not part with either of her children, what mother could? She could not simply choose which one she was to keep with her. So she continued to play for time, praying for some miracle – of what sort, her breaking heart asked? – to settle this thing once and for all.

They were together at the Albion as often as he could get over to Manchester which was as often as his many business concerns and his farm would allow, but she was well aware that it would not last long, this acceptance on his part that this was all he could have. He would come to the park, Philips Park, almost every weekend, and there he would spend some time with his son, ignoring her fears that the child would speak of him to Lew. Very often Lew was with her, pushing the perambulator that he himself had made, his own son seated at one end, Martin's at the other. Rory would state indignantly that he was a big boy now and demand to walk, or run, or jump, or hop or do any of the lively things a two-year-old will do and as Lew's son almost reached his first birthday and began to toddle, he set up a caterwauling to do the same. Furtively she would look about her for Martin, praying that he was either not here, or, if he was, would do as she begged him and remain hidden. A hard thing for a man of Martin Heywood's proud nature.

But Lew could not always get away, since Henry was slow to recover from his illness and then she would go alone, pushing the perambulator with both boys fastened in securely with the strap Lew had fashioned, otherwise Rory would be over the side and away, with Joss doing his best to follow. To Rory's delight "the man" would be there, strolling towards him across the grass, holding out his arms to catch him, laughing and throwing him up in the air, playing games with a ball which they took in turns to throw for Fred. She was very careful never to call Martin by his name and the child did not ask. For the moment he was happy with "the man".

Sometimes "the man" would take the boy out on the lake, holding him between his knees as he rowed steadily from side to side, ignoring his son's imperious demands to go faster, or even to have a turn with the oars. He was delighted by his son's fearlessness and though privately he believed the boy needed some discipline, that would come when he took up residence in his real home at Moorhouse Farm. The child was only two years old, young enough yet to be taught to show some respect for those who had him in their charge, himself eventually, of course, and in the meanwhile he would be patient. Not for ever, naturally, for the sooner he had Rory and Rory's mother back where they belonged, the better.

He found, to his consternation, that he had become somewhat attached to Lew Earnshaw's boy who had a streak of obstinacy in him, a determination to do exactly what his older brother did, that pleased Martin. Joss would crow with delight when he too was thrown up in the air and Clare was astonished by the gentleness with which Martin treated him, picking him up and putting him on his shoulders, or tumbling over and over with the pair of them on the grass. Passers-by would stop and smile at the lovely family picture, the proud and handsome father, the pretty smiling mother, the two excited boys, and it was then that Clare's heart would plunge with guilt and shame. But her body was too enthralled with Martin's even to dream of giving this up and she knew this was the only way she could keep Martin from challenging Lew for the right to steal his family from him.

It was Kitty Mullaney who first became aware of the change in Clare but she said nothing initially, since it might have something to do with that husband of hers and Kitty was not a woman to interfere in another woman's marriage. Perhaps she was breeding, something she had heard could alter a woman's character though she knew nothing about it personally. Clare, who had once called purely on business, taking samples of a new dish she though might do well at the bar counter, perhaps a different pie or tart, called now just for a cup of tea, a chat, for they had become good friends in the two years they had known one another. As she said to her Alfie, she was right fond of the lass and though she didn't like doing it, if the lass was in trouble, which Kitty had begun to feel might be the case since that chap had appeared on the scene, what sort of a friend would she be if she didn't do something to help her.

It was October and was turning cold and the fire in Kitty's grate was roaring halfway up the chimney. She liked a good fire, did Kitty, sitting before it with her skirts up to her knees, her shins criss-crossed with the marks that came from sitting too close to an open fire. Her mam had had them and so did their Beattie, for the area round the fire was the only warm spot in a room and the women congregated in it.

She and Clare were sipping tea. Clare had been quiet, barely listening to Kitty's monologue about the fun and games that had gone on last night in the snug when a prostitute, no more than twelve, Kitty said, had slipped in and tried to importune her customers. Kitty had thought she was the daughter of one of the men drinking there at first, come to fetch him home, and had not bothered overmuch but when her true purpose was revealed Kitty had given her the rounds of the kitchen before chucking her out. Well, Kitty might be easy-going but she'd have none of their sort in her place, she said indignantly and, moving smoothly on without a pause to what she really had in her mind, if Clare felt she could, she, Kitty, would be glad if Clare would tell her what the hell was wrong with her! Mind her own business she would, if Clare told her to, but if there was anything she could do, Clare had only to say.

Clare put her cup carefully on the small table beside her, frozen with astonishment and confusion, for she had been barely aware of Kitty's voice as she drifted through the mists in which she increasingly found herself.

"What?" she quavered.

"You 'eard, my lass. There's summat up wi' yer. 'As bin since yer come back from over yonder. 'Alf time yer don't listen to owt I say ter yer. You an' me used ter 'ave a bit of a laugh an' a gossip but now yer seem ter be off somewhere an' . . ."

To her astonishment and vast dismay Kitty watched as Clare bent her head until her chin rested on her chest and began to weep with all the abandonment of a broken-hearted child.

"Nay, lass, nay. I didn't mean ter upset yer. Yer know I'm right fond o' yer and wouldn't . . . eeh, come 'ere." And without giving Clare time to object Kitty dragged her into her arms, patting her shoulder, clucking and saying "There, there," just as though Clare were a child.

Clare began to talk then, wild talk, half of which Kitty didn't understand, on and on and on, like a river that has been dammed by a clutter of logs and branches and broken undergrowth and is suddenly free, the murky waters thundering out in mad escape, swirling round and round and gathering speed until at last all is free and the waters settle again to calm.

"I know what I should do, Kitty. It's as plain as day what I should do."

"Tell Lew." Kitty came straight to the truth of it, honest and simple.

"Yes."

"But yer afraid if yer do there'd be trouble between Lew an' this chap? Lass, I didn't know 'e were still botherin' yer."

"Oh yes. There would be violence. Martin won't be satisfied until he has Rory with him. He wants me too but if I refuse to leave Lew I'm afraid he might kidnap Rory. And blessed Mother, I don't know what to do."

"Yer love this Martin, don't yer?" Kitty said sadly.

"More than life. If there was only me to consider I wouldn't hesitate."

"Lass, I don't believe in givin' advice. You mun choose what's best fer the two bairns."

"Three! I'm pregnant and so help me God I don't know who the father is!"

Chapter Thirty-three

"'Oo's this 'ere chap our Rory keeps on about?" Lew asked her one Monday dinner-time as November drew on. She had taken the boys to the park the day before, without Lew, since the doctor had warned Henry that he was to take it easy as the fever he had suffered earlier in the year had weakened his heart. He was up and about and doing what he always did, editing the newspaper, writing articles and setting out the advertisements that helped to pay for its upkeep, but Lew had been forced to take on some of Henry's work, which meant he couldn't always accompany his wife and sons on a Sunday outing. So the day before, Clare had taken the boys to the park alone where Rory had flown like a homing pigeon into "the man's" arms, twining his own with great affection round his father's neck.

As it had done then, Clare's heart, in a constant state of stress these days, missed a beat now, and she turned hastily to the table where she was siding the dinner things, doing her best to hide her expression which surely would give her away.

"What man's that?" she managed to ask casually, piling the plates one on top of the other and moving with them into the scullery.

Lew reached for his pipe before he answered, filling it with tobacco then lighting it with slow deliberation. He drew on it, blowing a drift of smoke towards the ceiling.

"I don't know, sweetheart. I was 'oping tha' could tell me. He's for ever on about this chap what throws t' ball for him and sticks for Fred. 'E seems ter 'ave great fun wi' 'im, whoever he is. 'E even mentioned a boat."

Her brain made an enormous effort to conquer her fear and produce an answer that Lew could accept, but in those first few seconds it just froze in her skull, as heavy as a cannon ball out of which no good reason could possibly escape.

It was Lew himself who gave her the answer. "When I asked 'im, he just said the man was *always* there so I presumed it was one o't park-keepers or summat."

Lew was not suspicious, just curious and somewhat confused. All these months, ever since Martin had come back into their lives, hers and Rory's, and with Rory still in that stage where no coherent speech, understandable speech that is, ruled his tongue, there had been no need of explanations to cover up "the man's" presence in the park, but as the boy grew and his vocabulary improved it was becoming increasingly difficult to prevent her son from describing all the fun he and his father had in the park. He was full of it when they got home, longing to tell anyone who would listen about the fine adventures he and "the man" had had and Lavender, who knew all about Martin and his reappearance in Clare's life, was beginning to look alarmed as Lew did his best to decipher what the lad was saying. Surely, before long, when the boy had a full command of language, Lew would begin to realise there was something strange in his excited description of what they had done, he and "the man", in the park that day.

Why in the name of Jesus, Mary and Joseph, Clare agonised, hadn't she foreseen this dilemma, this possibility that Rory's prattle would excite Lew's interest, and even concern. Why hadn't she prepared some excuse, something plausible to explain to Lew what the boy was chattering on about? Blessed Mother, help me, help me not to hurt this good man with the truth. I know if I go on this way, with Martin, it's bound to come out sooner or later and as Rory grows it is fast becoming sooner. All these months and still I have no answer to this appalling situation I have made for myself. I must choose. Oh sweet Lord, how am I to choose?

"There is a chap, I think he's a park attendant who seems to have taken a fancy to Rory, and Rory to him. I do wish you could come more often to the park with us, acushla. The boys do love a bit of rough and tumble."

"And the park attendant gives it them?" Lew asked incredulously. "An' on a Sunday an' all when tha'd think he'd be that busy wi' folk 'e wouldn't have time fer owt except his duties."

"Oh, 'tis only fer a minute, so it is. Rory makes more of it than it is."

"And the boat?"

"Sure an' doesn't he love the boats on the lake and is always begging me to take him on but with Joss . . ."

"We'll go next Sunday, lass, and we'll all go on the lake. That's a promise an' I'll tell the lad this minute."

"I wouldn't, Lew. If anything should happen to prevent it he'd be so disappointed. Wait until Sunday," which would give her time to warn Martin that Lew would be with them next Sunday.

She waited until they had made deep and satisfying love in the bedroom of the Albion, when she knew he would be receptive and therefore take it more reasonably, to tell him, *ask* him to stay away from Philips Park next Sunday, which was the first of December. She was just entering her fourth month of pregnancy and neither of the men in her life, one of whom was the father, had yet noticed the slight amount of weight she was putting on. Her capacious apron hid it when she was at home, and her nightgown which was loose. Her full and fashionable gown she wore when she was with Martin was at this stage of her pregnancy very concealing. When she was naked she was lying down and the small bulge to her belly was barely noticeable. It soon would be though, to both men, and that would be another Herculean task to overcome. She felt as though she were in a maze, like the one she had read about at Hampton Court and though she went round and round every corner, blundering about lost and terrified of what she might come across, she could not find the way out, and never would. There was no one to help her, even Kitty who begged her to give Martin up, to tell Lew the truth and beg his forgiveness. He loved her and though it would crucify him, he was a man who recognised the faults and weaknesses of others, as he did his own, and because of it, and for the sake of their son, would not turn from her. Start again, in other words, and hope to God he was big enough to show her mercy.

"Rightio, lass," Lew said now, putting his arms about her and nuzzling in the back of her neck under her hair. "You know best but tha'll not let this chap, 'ooever 'e is, tekk our Rory outer tha' sight, will tha'?"

She was aghast, turning in his arms and twisting away from him. "Lew Earnshaw, as if I would. He's not that sort of a man."

"'Ow dost know, Clare? There's all sorts 'angin' about in them sorta places."

"Lew, stop it. This man's perfectly respectable and if he's around next Sunday I'll introduce you to him."

Martin, though his face was as grim as a stone slab and his eyes as flinty as the stone it had been cut from, had agreed reluctantly, but she knew it would not be long now before he had reached the end of his patience. Especially when he heard about the coming child. She herself believed it was his, for in the months since Joss was born Lew had not impregnated her but the moment she had lain with Martin it had happened. Then again, Martin had been her lover for many months before he got her with child so perhaps Lew was the father. She would know, of course, the moment she saw it, and so would Lew! Mary, Mother of God, how was she to get herself from this ... She didn't even know what to call it since it was far beyond being described as a problem. She knew she was drifting along in the hope that something – *what,* for Christ's sake? – something would happen to resolve it and she knew, deep in her heart where she preferred not to look, that the answer lay in persuading Lew that they must move away from this place where they had found a life and start a new one elsewhere. Somewhere Martin Heywood could not find them. He would never give her up. He would never give up his son and there would be violence done if he and Lew had a confrontation. They must be kept apart ... Lord, she was tired. If only, if only; her life was made up of *if only's* and sometimes, though she knew it was a sin, she wished she had died with the rest of her family in the bad times.

"Anyroad, I've ter go up ter't stationer's an' see what's 'oldin' up that paper," Lew was saying. "'Ave I ter tekk our Rory with us? It'll get 'im out from under tha' feet for an hour. Betty ses 'e's that frachetty at not bein' able ter play out in't yard 'e's drivin' 'er mad. I'll not tekk buggy. If he gets tired wi' walkin' I'll put 'im up on me shoulders. Tha' go an' get 'im ready, sweetheart. Wrap 'im up warm, fer it's bloody perishin' out there. Just gone two o'clock an' already it's beginning to freeze again and this mornin's frost not melted yet. Tha' don't expect this in November. Right pretty it looks but it's a bit tricky underfoot."

She and Lavender took advantage of the peace and quiet while Joss had an afternoon nap to bake up a batch of scones, several dozen loaves and a big tray of cheese and onion pies, for they had found that if they kept the shop open until after the mill hooter went at six o'clock many of the women bought their families' tea on their way home. Everything was fresh from the oven at Earnshaw's, and cheap and delicious too, better than they could make themselves, which meant that when they got home all they need do was put the kettle on, throw off their clogs and settle down in front of their fires until bedtime.

The boy never stopped chattering, his small hand held tightly in Lew's for safety's sake since he was an extremely active child, his short legs going ten to the dozen; though Lew did his best to shorten his own long stride, Rory was impatient with anything that was slow or careful and was always half a step ahead of him. The questions poured from him at a rate that made it difficult for the man to keep up with what he was saying, particularly as his pronunciation was not yet as clear as it might be.

"Look, Papa, look at the boy with the brush. What's he doing, Papa?"

"'E's clearin' up 'orse droppin's, lad. It's a mucky job."

"Why, Papa?"

"Well, it wouldn't do ter leave it lyin' about. It gives off a rare stink."

"What's stink, Papa?"

"Smell, Rory." But by this time something else had caught the child's eye and the matter of the sweeping boy was cast aside.

"Look, Papa, what's that man doing?"

"'E's sellin' fruit, lad."

"And look at those boys. They've no shoes, Papa. Why have they no shoes?"

"Because their mothers and fathers have no money to buy them, Rory."

"Why not, Papa?"

Lew was casting about in his mind how to explain to a child only just two years old the complexities of poverty when, thankfully, Rory's attention was captured by the sight and sound of a band of street musicians and, beside them, ready to vie with them for the pennies the passers-by chucked in their caps, was an organ-grinder with a scarlet-jacketed monkey perched on his shoulder. The monkey chattered and grinned and lifted its tiny pillbox hat as the organ-grinder lethargically turned the handle of the machine, then at a word from its master the monkey ran down his arm, hopped on the top of the organ and began a parody of a dance. Rory was enchanted and Lew sighed, for he was well aware that the lad was about to make a scene – have one of his bloody tantrums, as Lew had heard Lavender mutter – if he was dragged away.

He did, protesting loudly and angrily as Lew picked him up, but at the next street corner was a further diversion in the sight of a small crowd being entertained by a dancing bear. A man, smiling falsely, prodded the bear with a stick which encouraged it to "dance" more energetically and again Rory was entranced, seeing not the cruelty but the novelty which appealed to his child's mind.

Having walked the length of Piccadilly with frequent halts to look in shop windows, to watch the horses that pulled the cabs, to stare with interest at a uniformed policeman and to pull faces at another boy who was walking by with *his* papa, they were at the corner of London Road and Granby Row where the stationer's was situated and again Lew had to use a great deal of persuasion to drag the child away.

"Rory, wills't do as tha's told an' 'old me hand. Tha've seen t'bear an't monkey; besides, it's too cold ter 'ang about." The hoar frost, despite the number of feet that tramped across it, was a thick white carpet across the pavement, slippery and a threat to those who did not walk with care. "Now get 'old o' Papa's 'and an' if tha're a good boy I'll buy thi' a . . ."

It was never vouchsafed what Lew Earnshaw was to buy for the boy he had accepted as his son, for just at that moment Rory Patrick spotted something on the other side of the busy street, something so exciting, so inviting his rosy face lit up with an expression that said, with the forthright determination that was his, he absolutely must get to it. Lew's heart dipped frantically in his chest as the child eluded his restraining hand as quick as an eel and just as slippery, bringing those about him to a horrified standstill. Lew's mouth opened on an appalled shout as, without a thought for danger, Rory darted out into the road. Lew thought he heard his piping voice say something about a man, but there was nothing in his mind but the frantic necessity of grabbing the boy before he was crushed beneath the wheels of an enormous brewer's dray, so enormous it needed two gigantic Shire horses to pull it. The crowd about him stood frozen to the pavement, watching in horror, women with their hands to their mouths, men ready to dash with Lew into the road to save the tiny, laughing figure of Rory Earnshaw who was running, not even darting, just running in a straight line towards his father who stood, fixed like a white-faced marble statue to the pavement on the opposite side of the road.

Lew did not see Martin Heywood. His whole attention was on the boy. He was afraid to shout, afraid to distract the lad's attention, for if he did might he not stop in confusion and go under the great iron-shod wheels of the dray. The man who was driving it was white-faced with shock, doing his best to draw his giant horses to a standstill and when the man followed the child, grabbing him and throwing him as one might a parcel on to the pavement he distinctly heard the crack as one of the horses, rearing in alarm, struck the man's head with his hoof which was the size of a dinner plate. Women had begun to scream and men to shout and the man on the pavement who had picked up the babbling, excited boy sank to his knees and buried his face in the child's neck.

She took Lew home to Edgeclough, closing the shop and, as was the custom, or so Lavender told her gently since she was in a state of extreme shock, hanging black drapes at the windows. Not that she cared about black drapes or any of the other customs that went with death, and it was Lavender again who arranged the dyeing of her rose-coloured gown to black and put her in it, saying it was only right to pay the greatest respect for such a great man. He had given his life to save that of her son and Lavender was of the opinion that no man could do more than that.

She didn't know what she would have done without Lavender, though Kitty Mullaney barely left her side on that first dreadful day. She wondered idly as she sat at her kitchen table with her elder son tight in her arms how Kitty had known, for no sooner had Martin left than Kitty was there, her face distorted with grief for her. They had all been, in that first hour, in a dreadful state of near hysteria, the two maids weeping noisily, Rory, not understanding why his mother held him so fiercely, and protesting over it, the baby grizzling for his tea and Lavender standing like one turned to stone between them. Kitty had pulled them all together.

"See, you, what's your name, Tilly; then, Tilly, put kettle on and brew up an' you – what, Betty – well, Betty, yer'd best give this baby summat ter eat an' 'appen it'd be a good idea if yer took the lad."

But Clare was having none of that. She had lost her husband, a man she had loved and respected above any man, and she could not bear to have her son, whom she also had almost lost, taken from her arms, even though he struggled impatiently. He didn't know what all the fuss was about, his attitude said, and why had "the man" gone away and where was Papa and did Mama know he and Papa had seen a bear that danced and a monkey ...

"Let him go, love," Kitty said compassionately. "He doesn't understand an' best he doesn't. Not yet. Let this lass tekk 'im and't babby and give 'em their tea. See, put 'im down and drink this," thrusting a cup of tea into Clare's flaccid hand. Kitty thought it would be a great help if Clare could have a damn good cry but she just sat there, white and as still as the death that had come to claim Lew Earnshaw.

At last, with everyone in the household occupied with some task or other; with all the women, Clare's customers, who had knocked timidly on the door to see if there was owt they could do to help the widow, sent kindly on their way; with Albert and Henry, sadly shaking their heads, gone back to their own quarters, Lavender and Kitty sat with Clare and the body of her husband which had been brought home to lie in the parlour, which, again according to Lavender, and Kitty agreed, was another custom. Lew had been pronounced dead at the Infirmary where he had been taken and where his body was claimed by a gentleman whose intention it was to take him to his home, he had said. He was a friend of the family and would take full responsibility. He had a small boy with him who, it seemed, he could not bear out of his arms, let alone his sight. He arranged for a decent, horse-drawn conveyance to carry the body to his home and family, following behind with the child in a cab. The doctor had thought it somewhat strange but the man seemed genuinely filled with grief and had given the widow's name and address should it need to be checked.

Tilly and Betty were given a fortnight's wages and told to go home to their families until Lavender got in touch with them. They crept about the place getting their things together, afraid to speak to the frozen-faced, dead-eyed woman who employed them, overcome with awe and sadness, for Mr Earnshaw had been a lovely man with a joke and a wink for them both. When Kitty had gone, reluctantly, Lavender was the one who took charge, even writing the notice that was posted in the shop window informing their customers that, owing to a bereavement, the shop would be closed until further notice.

Lew was taken home by train from Manchester to Oldham, his coffin treated with the respect accorded to royalty as it was placed reverently in the guard's van, the staff standing to attention along the platform, male passengers removing their hats just as though they knew they were seeing the passing of a great and good man. Women wiped a surreptitious tear as the tall and lovely widow followed behind, a small, chattering boy at her side, for even in the presence of death, though he was not aware of it, Rory Patrick was irrepressible, a woman following behind, also in the deepest black, holding a baby in her arms. Such a young family to be struck down, the thought was written on every face. Nobody noticed the tall, grey-faced gentleman who stepped into a compartment further up the train and if they had would not have connected him to the bereaved family.

It was at Oldham that the frozen calm that had enveloped Clare Earnshaw since the hour they had brought Lew home to her finally cracked and broke open. It was as though the whole of Crossfold where Lew had worked in Hopkinson's Mill had come to see him go by, even though it was a working day and bugger Will Hopkinson. But it was not just those from Crossfold who lined up to pay their final respects to the man who had tried all his life to make their lives better, but every man, woman and child from Edgeclough, for whom he had done the same service. They had walked the wearying miles, some carrying small children, and would walk them back behind the coffin which was placed with great reverence on the flat cart pulled by a sturdy pony which Clare did not recognise as the one that had once pulled her gig. There was a cab which carried Lavender and the children who were too young to walk, while Clare, with her friends about her, fell in behind. The procession stretched for miles, the station yard crowded as those who were at the rear waited their turn to join it. Clare wept beneath her short widow's veil, though her head was high and her back straight, for she had never been so proud in her life, proud of the man who had generated this lovely human spirit and whom she had been honoured to know. She had wronged him many times, but right up to the end he had not known of it and though she knew she did not deserve it she thanked the Lord of heaven who had granted her this boon.

And the man who was also suffering for his part in it, for Lew Earnshaw had died saving *his* son, waited discreetly out of sight, ready to walk behind the stragglers.

It was the same at his funeral where, in the cold December sunshine with the birds singing their own paeon of praise for the good man who had died, hundreds of folk gathered, including men who still carried the flag for the radical cause, including Henry and Albert and others who cherished the People's Charter and, if they did not see his coffin laid in the ground next to Nelly Bradbury's, waited patiently for their turn to stand for a moment at his grave.

Clare moved through the next few days in a daze, which in a way was quite painless since she felt nothing. She was staying with Will Bradbury who had insisted she sleep in the bed, her children beside her, that he had shared with his Nelly for so many years. He and Arthur would be quite comfy on the palliasse by the fire, he told her, and she was to stay as long as she wanted. It was a rare treat to have someone to cook him a hot meal each night, when he got back from the mill, though Betty had been very kind to him and Arthur since Nelly went, and besides, a bit of fresh air would do her good. There were folk hereabouts who wanted to come and see her, if she was up to it, for Lew had been their hero and they would be glad of a word with his widow.

It was a week later when Lavender, who had squashed in with her mam and pa and six siblings, knocked on Will's door.

They sat and drank the inevitable cup of tea, saying nothing much, for Clare knew Lavender had come with some purpose in mind. She had not lived with Lavender all these years without coming to know when she had something on her mind but when it was disclosed to her she was taken by surprise.

"What about shop, our Clare?" Lavender asked abruptly. "Tha're not givin' it up, are thi'?"

"Acushla, Lew's only been gone a few days and ..."

"I know, lass, an' I think tha' should stay 'ere fer a while. Just until tha' knows what tha' wants ter do."

"To do?"

"Tha' knows what I mean, Clare. Tha've more than one choice open ter tha'." Lavender looked stern, as though explaining something to an obtuse child.

Clare's face closed up and she lifted her head angrily as though to say how dare Lavender interfere in Clare's private life but Lavender leaned forward and took her hand.

"Listen to me. It's nowt ter do wi' me what ... what tha' decide ter do about ... about 'im up theer." She nodded her head in the vague direction of Moorhouse Farm. "But that business o' thine in Manchester is thrivin' but if it's left fer long it'll go under. Besides, Tilly an' Betty need their jobs. Now if I go back" — she drew a deep breath, like a swimmer about to dive into unknown waters — "I could keep it goin' until ... well, until tha' decides what tha're ter do. Anyroad ..."

"Anyroad what?"

"Theer's Arthur."

Clare smiled and squeezed the hand that held hers.

"Of course there's Arthur."

"We'm ter be wed, me an' Arthur. As soon as ... well, we need ter know ..."

"If I'm to go back to Earnshaw's, is that it?"

"Aye. Me an' Arthur mean to gerron. 'E don't want ter be at someone else's beck an' call all his life. 'E wants his own place an' so do I." Her voice was defiant just as though she were expecting Clare to tell her not to be so presumptuous.

"Of course you do. Haven't you always been a girl who goes after what she wants."

"Thanks ter thi'."

"Well, I don't know about that but, Lavender, if you know what you want I'm not sure I do. Not yet. You must be patient with me. I'm still ... in limbo. D'you know what that means?"

"Aye, I reckon so, an' don't think I'm tryin' ter push thi'. I just want tha' ter know what's in me mind."

"Lavender, you're my dearest friend. You've got me through some bad times and I might have gone under but for you."

"Nay ..." Lavender was deeply embarrassed.

"It's true."

"Well, I'm glad. Anyroad ..." She stood up briskly. "I'll be off termorrer then an' tha've not ter worry about shop. Me an' Tilly an' Betty'll keep it goin' until ... well, whatever tha' decide."

"I know you will."

He waited a month, four whole weeks which she knew must have cost him dear, for he was never a patient man. He drove up in the small gig drawn by the pony that had pulled the cart on which Lew's coffin had rested. He carried flowers.